CANAAN

CANAAN

A NOVEL

Donald McCaig

W. W. NORTON & COMPANY

New York London

Copyright © 2007 by Donald McCaig

For information about permission to reproduce selections from this
book, write to Permissions, W. W. Norton & Company, Inc.,
500 Fifth Avenue, New York, NY 10110

Manufacturing by Courier Westford
Book design by Barbara M. Bachman
Production manager: Anna Oler

LIBRARY OF CONGRESS CATALOGING-IN-PUBLICATION DATA

McCaig, Donald.
Canaan : a novel / Donald McCaig.—1st ed.
p. cm.
ISBN-13: 978-0-393-06246-5
ISBN-10: 0-393-06246-5
1. Indian women—Fiction. 2. Santee Indians—Fiction. 3. Freedmen—
Fiction. 4. Reconstruction (U.S. history, 1865–1877)—Fiction.
5. Indians of North America—Government relations—1869–1934—
Fiction. 6. Little Bighorn, Battle of the, Mont., 1876—Fiction.
7. United States—History—1865–1898—Fiction. I. Title.
PS3563.A2555C36 2007
813'.54—dc22

2006034218

W. W. Norton & Company, Inc.
500 Fifth Avenue, New York, N.Y. 10110
www.wwnorton.com

W. W. Norton & Company Ltd.
Castle House, 75/76 Wells Street, London W1T 3QT

1 2 3 4 5 6 7 8 9 0

For CAROL MAE BUTLER

who counted white horses from Butte to the Falls

For the LORD thy God bringeth thee into a good land,
a land of brooks of water, of fountains and depths
that spring out of valleys and hills;
A land of wheat, and barley, and vines, and fig trees,
and pomegranates; a land of oil olive, and honey;
A land wherein ye shall eat bread without scarceness,
thou shalt not lack any *thing* in it; a land whose
stones *are* iron, and out of whose hills thou
mayest dig brass.
When thou hast eaten and art full, then thou shalt bless
the LORD thy God for the good land which he
hast given thee.

−DEUTERONOMY 8:7–10

CONTENTS

PART ONE: THE GREAT DAY OF HIS WRATH

PART TWO: THE ATLANTIC, MISSISSIPPI & OHIO RAILROAD

PART THREE: IN THE VALLEY OF THE GREASY GRASS

THE GREAT DAY OF HIS WRATH

HOW A MAN IS MADE

Before he was hanged, my father gave me his Low Dog cape and his dreaming.

We Lakota honor dreamers; dreamers show us the way. But Red Leaf's dreaming was too big, covering the people like a blackhorn robe over a newborn. His dreaming was as vast, beautiful, and bleak as the moon when the boughs break with snow.

Low Dog—coyote—is the unluckiest medicine animal a Santee Lakota can have. Low Dog took Red Leaf's dreaming wherever Low Dog wished to go, to see whatever Low Dog wished to see. Low Dog is curious about everything.

My father was hanged in Mankato, Minnesota, the day after Christmas, the Washitu year "1862." It was the second year of the Washitu's Southern war, before the Lakota pushed the Crows out of the Powder River basin, before the Washitu found gold in Montana and Red Cloud became a great chief fighting them. On the last day I was with my father I had sixteen summers and knew much I don't know now.

My father sat cross-legged, daubing vermilion from his cheekbone to the corner of his mouth. He dipped a forefinger in the paint pot and lined his other cheek. "Daughter, I had a dream . . ."

"Anyone can dream," I replied.

Although it was ten below zero, the stone building's small windows were open against the fug of cheap tobacco and the sweat of men soon to die.

My father raised an eyebrow. "Doesn't JesuChrist come to you in dreams?"

When I shook my head my starched collar scratched my neck. The sore on my father's right ankle was broader than his shackle. "JesuChrist speaks in his book," I said.

"And you can read his book? Daughter, how clever you are. What a Santee you would have been."

The Christian converts prayed aloud and beseeched one another with glances. They sang "Nearer My God to Thee."

> *Mita wani kiya,*
> *I ma cu ye*
> *te hi a wa ki pa*
> *Esa na kun*
> *kici ciun wacin*
> *mita wani kiya*
> *I ma cu ye.*

The Old Way Santee sat apart, seemingly indifferent. Chaska packed his pipe; Tazoo prayed to his medicine animal. Cut Nose unrolled the brown muslin hood down over his face so his inhalation sucked the cloth back against his mouth and cheeks. When he rolled it up, he smiled at his joke.

The Santee prisoners had refused to wear their hoods until Father Ravoux showed them how to roll them like french voyageurs' caps.

Red Leaf painted a green stripe above the vermilion. "Low Dog came to me in my dream. Low Dog promised he would guide me across the Shadowland." At an unbidden thought, the mockery left my father's eyes. "Daughter, you will care for my body?"

Old Way Santee lay their dead on platforms so nothing can impede the spirit's escape and its journey across the Shadowland. A warrior's bow, his knife, some food are laid beside the body, and sometimes a favorite dog is killed to guide the wanderer; but the Santee had eaten their dogs last winter when the Washitu's promised annuities did not come.

"Mary"—I was "She Goes Before" to the Santee and my father had never before used my Christian name—"that is your father's wish."

My hands were scrubbed red, but they were clean. "JesuChrist was killed and three days later he came back from the Shadowland and ascended into heaven and when we Christians die we go to be with him. Father, please accept JesuChrist as your savior."

Thirty-eight condemned warriors were shackled to the wooden floor. The two hundred and seventy others Father Lincoln had pardoned were kept in a pole stockade. Others had escaped with Inkpaduta. My half-brother, White Bull, had fled with his family to the Dakotas.

I was an accomplished convert. I could read a little, write a little. I could sew, card, spin, and weave. I knew how to iron the Reverend Riggs's shirtfront and starched collars and I had learned to cook oatmeal porridge. After several failures I understood the mysteries of the soft-boiled egg as Mrs. Reverend Riggs understood them.

Four years ago, missionaries came to Little Crow's band on Spirit Lake. Many Santee spurned their preaching, but I was moved by the promises of their powerful God. A year later, when they came again, I followed them to the mission at Yellow Medicine, where Reverend Riggs baptized me "Mary."

Santee grandfathers said life had been better before the Washitu came. Blackhorns—buffalo—had been plentiful and no Santee went hungry. Old Way Santee like my father prayed the blackhorns would forgive the offense of the Washitu presence and come back to us again.

These prayers made me angry. The Old Way was gone forever. "Father, how many years has it been since you last saw a Real Dog [wolf] or heard him howling in the night? The seed corn the Washitu gives us—that seed sprouts into corn when we tend it as we have been taught. The blackhorns have fled west with our Brulé and Oglala cousins. Your blackhorns are dream blackhorns. Can we eat dreams? Perhaps Washitu annuities are not as much as the White Father promised and perhaps they are slow to come, but they are better than ghost blackhorns or Real Dogs you only meet in dreams."

My father asked me why I was so angry.

"You aren't guilty. You didn't kill Myrick."

Reverend Riggs had translated the New Testament into Lakota. Because Riggs had lived with the Santee, he knew which man lied and who told the truth. The Reverend Riggs had interrogated the Santee at their trial and through him many were condemned that might otherwise have gone free.

"Has your father accepted his Savior, Mary?"

"Red Leaf is proud."

"Pride has kept many worthy souls from salvation."

Red Leaf smiled. "When the people came to the Agency for their annuities, trader Myrick sent them away saying, 'If they are hungry let them eat grass.' When we Santee returned to our lodges our children asked when would they eat and where were the annuities our White Father had promised us. So we Santee returned to the Agency with our weapons and after I killed trader Myrick, we stuffed his mouth with all the grass he could eat."

"And the innocent women and children you murdered? When did they harm your people?"

"It takes many moons for children to starve. Their faces change as the hunger eats them and they become their bones. When they ask their father for food he has nothing to give them. The Washitu children were fat as puppies when they died."

Reverend Riggs was tall and spindle-shanked; my father was built like a bear. Reverend Riggs's thin hair was slicked back over his skull. My father's hair dangled beneath the hangman's rolled hood in thick braids. Riggs wore a black suit, a gray waistcoat, a black foulard; Red Leaf, leggings, breechclout, moccasins. He sat cross-legged on his folded Low Dog cape.

"Red Leaf, when the Great Spirit looks down on his Santee children and sees what they did to his white children, he is very angry!"

"I do not believe it. In your Southern war, Washitu are fighting Washitu. You are killing more people than Red Leaf could count all the days of his life. Does your JesuChrist look down and say, 'Good Washitu. He has my book! Washitu go to heaven when he die. Santee does not have JesuChrist's book and kills a few Washitu. This makes the Great Spirit angry? I do not believe it."

"Mary, time is short."

"My father did not harm the trader Myrick. Red Leaf lied."

"I'm sure Red Leaf is entirely innocent." Riggs encompassed the prisoners with his gesture. "So many unjustly condemned! How can such injustice be?"

Red Leaf smiled. "Inkpaduta killed seventeen Washitu. I am ashamed I killed only one."

"Father! You didn't kill anyone!"

"Red Leaf, you are condemned from your own mouth."

"It was a whiskey boast. Dear Reverend Riggs, do you think the real murderers waited for soldiers to come and arrest them? Little Crow and Shakopee and Inkpaduta have fled to the Grandmother's land."

"Each man has been properly tried and condemned; and had matters been left to General Pope, every one would have been executed. Two hundred seventy murderers pardoned—President Lincoln is apparently loath to sign a death sentence."

Red Leaf chuckled. "Father Lincoln overcame his loathing thirty-eight times. I pray to meet Father Lincoln in the Shadowland."

"Red Leaf, would you spend eternity in hell?"

"I pray we will meet the traders who starved our children. Cut Nose and I will make them cry."

Reverend Riggs closed his eyes to intone, "Repentance, though it be with the last breath of life, is pleasing in the eyes of the Lord."

When Red Leaf rolled the hood down over his face he became a mute, faceless statue.

Reverend Riggs said, "Mary, there are other souls," and left us.

Red Leaf's chest rose and fell with his breathing. He rolled his hood back up. "Why do the Washitu want us to die blind? Are they afraid to look in the eyes of men they kill?"

"Father, we can be together one day in Paradise!"

"Raven came to me in my dream. Raven flies everywhere and sees everything. Raven had something to show me, so I climbed on his back and we flew away."

"Those are foolish stories, my father."

He raised one eyebrow. "Daughter? You reprove your father?"

The converted indians were singing again and I had to lean close to hear my father's words.

"Raven and I flew many days and nights. We were flying over the Shadowland. It was green like the Moon of Ripening Blackberries and the waters ran fast and so clear I could see fish swimming. There were blackhorns in the forest and I heard Real Dog calling his songs.

"We came to a black lake. The shore was dark with trees and between big rocks upright on the shore was the entrance to the Washitu's heaven. Blanket indians waited there—I did not know them and since they wore Washitu clothing I did not know their tribe. They were shivering and downcast because they were indians and had been turned away from Washitu heaven. Since they had given up their medicine animals to JesuChrist, no medicine animal would guide them across the Shadowland. They were forever lost, not of one people nor of the other. They would wander forever. Daughter, I wept to see them." My father continued, "Daughter, JesuChrist has powerful medicine and has made the Washitu mighty. He has given them our land and our lakes. He has told them to kill the Real Dogs and drive the blackhorns from our land. He has given them guns which kill farther than Santee arrows. JesuChrist has given them all these things. But I am Santee and when I go to the Shadowland I will find your mother, my father and mother, and all my brothers too.

"Do you wish to spend forever with the Washitu? You dress like Washitu, you have learned Washitu talk and taken his ways." He sniffed. "You even smell Washitu!"

I remember that I blushed.

"But to the Washitu you will always be Santee and if the Washitu cannot mistake you for one of their own, how can their JesuChrist mistake you? My daughter, you will spend forever with the blanket indians who can never cross the Shadowland and cannot enter Washitu heaven."

"Your words hurt me, Father," I said.

He looked at me for a long time. "Daughter, today I will die. Is that not a good time to say what a man is made of? Until the day they die these Washitu will see Santee warriors in their dreams."

"But you killed nobody."

He sighed. "Daughter, I would be proud if I had killed Myrick. If I had taken as many scalps as Cut Nose or Inkpaduta, I should be singing today. But my medicine was weak, so I counted no coups and took no scalps.

"When we found the whiskey and drank it, I was filled with unhappiness. While the others danced around the fire, I boasted. Last winter when I sold my pelts, trader Myrick cheated me and I ate my shame. So now I boasted of killing Myrick and as soon as I boasted falsely, every Santee turned his back, for they knew Shakopee had killed Myrick and stuffed grass in his mouth. Daughter, when the Washitu condemned me, they restored my honor."

The door was flung open and blue-coated Seizers rushed in.

As Reverend Riggs raised his arms in blessing, Seizers broke leg chains with hammer and anvil. After they could move freely again, the Santee began visiting with one other.

"Tazoo, your wife. Is she well?"

"Your daughter, Many Ponies, has she birthed her child?"

A Seizer officer said, "Mustn't keep the hangman waiting. Corporal, bring 'em out singly; we'll chain 'em together outside."

"Goodbye, Father."

My father gave me his Low Dog cape and, though I did not know it, his dreaming. "Let this keep you from cold," he said. He began to sing the triumphant notes of the death song and other Santee took it up.

"Stop that racket! Stop it, I say!"

All the indians sang. Even the converts sang. The death song sheltered them.

Reverend Riggs clamped his hands to his ears. Father Ravoux was smiling and weeping.

The Seizer officer cupped his hands to his mouth. "Stop that!" he bellowed, and the Santee fell silent.

As the prisoners stepped outdoors, each was chained again and his hood jerked over his eyes.

Their scaffold was Mankato's largest structure. A tall pole thrust through the center of the hanging platform with thirty-eight ropes spread out like cords from the Sun Dance pole.

Armed Seizers surrounded this scaffold and many Washitu had come to watch. The Reverend Riggs stood beside me shivering. I was warm inside my Low Dog cape.

A Seizer drummer thumped, but the chained and hooded Santee couldn't march to his cadence. The condemned men bumped into each other and stumbled. Each had to be helped up the stairs and guided to his proper trap.

The Santee began singing and stamping their feet and their medicine was very strong, so the Seizers cried for them to stop. They stopped stamping but continued singing.

In his deep voice, Cut Nose sang his kill song:

> *At New Ulm, a body will be found.*
> *A Dead Washitu at New Ulm.*
> *Why, see it has no head!*
> *Washitu's head is where his prick used to be.*
> *Cut Nose did this deed!*
> *It was I, Cut Nose!*

Cut Nose hoisted his loincloth at the Washitu, to show his disdain. Others Santee sang their names, and the names of those they loved. These softer tunes prevailed over Cut Nose's defiance and hooded men groped for the hands of the men nearest them. One old man stretched out his hands as far as he could reach but failed to touch anyone.

The Seizer drum rolled angrily as the hangman set each man's noose.

A Washitu whose wife and children had been killed stepped forward with a long knife. He sawed through a rope until all the traps banged open and the Santee were hanged.

The Washitu made a noise like wind sighing over the lake.

Some Santee hung like stones, some spun. One rope broke and the dead Santee was lifted onto the scaffold and hanged again.

I thought that the Washitu killed to make order, that Mrs. Reverend Riggs would have killed rather than eat an improperly boiled egg.

After the Santee had hung long enough, the Washitu cut them down and stacked them in wagons and drove them to the riverbank for burial.

Reverend Riggs asked me for Red Leaf's Low Dog cape for his cabinet of indian curiosities.

"No," I said. Had I known that Red Leaf's dreaming came with the cape, Riggs could have had it.

That night I walked to the riverbank to find my father and take him to a burial platform. I had stolen a butcher knife from the Mission to lay beside his body. It was the only weapon I could find.

But when I came where the Santee had been buried, Washitu medicine men were digging them up by lantern light. When they unearthed a body, they threw it into a wagon or tied it across a packhorse and took it away.

Some of these medicine men had come to the mission and drunk coffee with Reverend Riggs and Mrs. Reverend Riggs.

I did not know what the Washitu medicine men wanted with the dead Santee until Low Dog made me dream of Washitu medicine men boiling the Santee in great iron hog kettles until flesh floated off their bones.

I prayed to JesuChrist that I might never dream again, but JesuChrist did not answer. I have come to believe that despite His mighty powers, JesuChrist cannot quench Low Dog's desire to know what he does not need to know.

Later, when I was living with my brother White Bull on the Tongue River near the Montana Road, the whiskey trader Pommerlau told me the Washitu medicine men had wired the boiled Santee bones together into skeletons to show their apprentices how a man is made.

CHAPTER 1

TWO TAN EGGS

THE ONE-ARMED CONFEDERATE MAJOR THREADED HIS RIB-SPRUNG
horse through the ruins of Petersburg, Virginia. Shell holes pocked once-
handsome brick houses. A Union cavalry squadron trotted past, casting
early-morning shadows on the rubble piles. The major turned into an
alleyway to a familiar garden gate. Deftly, he flipped the reins over gateposts
worn from similar use. As he came down the path, two small Leghorns fluttered and squawked chicken alarms, the back door opened, and a young
woman stepped into the sunlight.

She shook her head from side to side as if doubting her eyes.

"Well, Sallie . . ."

Though the major was young, his wounds had etched years into his
face and his eyes flickered with weariness and pain.

"Oh, Duncan . . ." she gasped as if long-held breath could, at last, safely
be released. "I feared . . ."

"Thomas Byrd, he got through without a scratch. That boy is heading
home at the double-quick." He removed his gray slouch hat and dropped
it beside the path and pressed her against his chest and buried his face
in her hair. "It was a near thing," he muttered. "God Damn, if it wasn't a
near thing."

She pushed him to arm's length and searched his countenance. Her
lively face suddenly fragmented.

"Don't weep, dear heart. You needn't weep ever again."

Sallie sniffled and rubbed her eyes and announced that she had no handkerchief. Nor, alas, did he, which occasioned more tears—laughing tears—as she wiped her face on her apron.

Sallie Gatewood was short, dark-haired, and possessed an independent turn of mind. Her husband Duncan's easy grace had been sobered by four years of war.

"I've some yankee coffee." Duncan Gatewood smiled. "One day we were trying to kill 'em, next day we were eating their rations."

Their rooms were the kitchen and back bedroom of a house whose front half had been made uninhabitable by shells during the nine-month siege of Petersburg. The northwest corner of the house was in the rubble pile across the street.

Every morning during the final weeks of that siege, Major Gatewood had left this nest for General Mahone's staff while his bride took a train into Richmond, the beleaguered Confederate capital, to work with the wounded.

Mrs. Duncan Gatewood's kitchen contained a wooden table, a bench, an iron cookstove, and shelves supported by loose bricks upon which rested several chipped bowls, plates, and two blue willow cups of different manufacture. The wooden box that served as pantry had once contained "1000 Balls, 58 Calibre, U.S." A translucent white bowl with a hairline crack from rim to foot was the deal table's centerpiece. It held two smallish tan eggs. The mullioned window faced the garden where the eggs' providers scratched for insects.

After four years' intimate acquaintance with Death, Death was banished from their company and the couple were lighthearted as children. Duncan held an egg to the light. "I believe I have never before truly considered the egg. It is entirely smooth without slipperiness. What a shapely creation!"

"They are hard-boiled, dear husband. If you sit, I will remove the shell and you may feast upon them."

"I am feasting upon you," Duncan said. Which not-quite-innocent remark produced her blushes. While eggs and coffee waited, the two repaired to their bedroom for an intimacy that seemed novel each time they embarked upon it.

Afterward, she traced the burn scar his sparse beard partially concealed. "Dear Duncan," she said. "My dearest, dearest . . ." Under her touch his smile trembled. "I am so grateful you weren't taken prisoner. The Federals who captured our Winder Hospital took all our poor boys prisoner. Surgeon Chambliss and Lane too. For a moment I feared Cousin Molly Semple and I would be captured."

"No telling when those poor bastards will be coming home."

"But the War is over."

"It's over when the Federals say it's over. Jeff Davis is still on the run."

"But General Lee has surrendered."

"Yes, ma'am. He has."

"And my Darling Husband is paroled, never to fight anymore."

Tenderly, he touched the slope of her breast. "We are free to go where we will."

"Must we go? Cannot we remain here and"—Sallie smiled—"feast upon one another?"

SALLIE AND DUNCAN HAD KNOWN each other since childhood. Sallie's schoolmaster father, Uther Botkin, had taught Sallie and Duncan and, though it was illegal under Virginia law, he had taught the negro Jesse Burns too.

When the slave girl, Maggie, bore fifteen-year-old Duncan's child, Duncan's father, Samuel, had sold mother and child south. Even now, five years later, neither Duncan nor Samuel mentioned the affair. The hurt was too fresh.

Sallie had married, but her husband disappeared in the war.

When the badly wounded Duncan was brought to Winder Hospital, the childhood friends were reunited. It was not too much to say—certainly Duncan believed—that Sallie's nursing saved his life. They married.

Restored to duty, Sallie's husband followed General Lee on that final, forlorn Confederate retreat while Sallie waited in this sunny kitchen, which she contrived to make agreeable with strands of herbs hanging over the table, bay leaves curling as they gave up their fragrance on the woodstove, and three tulips, two yellow, one scarlet, sprouting from the mouth of a wooden canteen beside the door.

Now the smug cackles of the Leghorns accompanied the music from the bedroom as Duncan and Sallie took pleasure behind these ruined walls from which war was banished; in which generosity prevailed and anger and disgrace lay abandoned outside the door.

LATER, AS HER HUSBAND SLEPT, Sally snipped the insignia from his gray military collar and replaced every CSA button with a button of plain bone.

STILL LATER EACH ATE an egg and drank a cup of yankee coffee. They spent the afternoon in speech and touch and silence.

Sometime after midnight they were wakened by shouts, galloping horses, and torches in the street. President Lincoln had been shot.

CHAPTER 2

—

LETTER FROM SAMUEL GATEWOOD TO
SERGEANT JESSE BURNS, 23RD INFANTRY,
UNITED STATES COLORED TROOPS

STRATFORD PLANTATION,
SUNRISE, VIRGINIA
MAY 24, 1865

Dear Jesse,

I was gratified to receive your communication of May 6th. Franky and Jack, your old driver, send warm regards. Sallie, the child who studied her McGuffey's under your first master, Uther Botkin—little Sallie has wed my son Duncan. Though frightfully wounded in the recent conflict, Duncan has come home. My son-in-law, Catesby Byrd, died at Spotsylvania and not long afterwards my dear, dear daughter Leona joined her husband in Paradise. My grandson, Thomas, is reading for the law in Staunton with Mr. Alexander Stuart, Secretary of the Interior under President Fillmore and a devoted Union man, Stuart opposed secession and seeks to heal the wounds of this dreadful war.

It was bitter to find our trusted servants in the Federal armies arrayed against us. Tell me, Jesse, was I such an unkind master?

Last winter, Aunt Opal and my houseman Pompey took up

residence in Uther Botkin's former home. I tried to dissuade them but they were heedless. More runaway Coloreds took refuge there and the establishment fell into disrepute. Its occupants were blamed for numerous petty thefts. These Coloreds showed none of the respect they had once so freely rendered. Consequently, one night, vigilantes descended upon them. When Pompey defied them with a shotgun he was shot dead. After they torched Uther Botkin's home, Aunt Opal returned to Stratford.

The hand of God's Providence lies heavily upon the South. Most of our servants are gone and Stratford is impoverished. I fear that God has judged us for our stewardship and found us wanting; I, not least among my fellows. Our neglect of morality and the integrity of negro families has delivered us into the hands of our enemies.

You wrote to ask particularly of your wife Maggie's whereabouts and it grieves me to confess I do not know. Your wife Maggie and infant son, Jacob, were given over to Silas Omohundru, the slave speculator, and how Omohundru disposed of them, I never asked. Omohundru was killed in the final days of the war.

Though I would gladly help you reclaim what you have lost, I cannot. There is much these days I would reclaim, little I can.

Your Old Master,
Samuel Gatewood

CHAPTER 3

LOW DOG DREAMING

I asked Low Dog, "Have you no others to dream for you?"

I dreamed of Lakota villages burning, dreamed of blue soldiers falling from the sky. My dreams tumbled over one another like a mountain stream. I woke wearier than when I closed my eyes.

When the surviving Santee started moving west, I walked with them, ate what there was to eat, hungered when there was nothing. I walked many miles to outrun Low Dog, but every night when I closed my eyes he was there, grinning. "Ah," he said, "so there you are."

I dreamed of the Seizers warring among themselves, of cities burning and so many corpses they carpeted the ground.

The Washitu are merciless. Even to their own.

I passed through country that had belonged to the Ree before the Lakota took it. I passed through the Powder River, which had been Crow country.

On the Tongue River my brother White Bull and his wives, Rattling Blanket Woman and Fox Head, welcomed me. When I closed my eyes that night in their lodge, I did not dream.

But the next night, Low Dog took me far away to a great Seizer village where they were celebrating the Northern Seizers' victory over the Southern Seizers.

Dream Seizers paraded before me like blackhorns on the plains; so *many, they took two days to pass. I could not count their horses and iron cannons.*

Down a broad road between white marble dwellings they marched, and their bands played Seizer music and Seizer drums said "rat-a-tat-tat."

I woke in my brother's lodge weeping. White Bull was a great warrior and feared by our enemies. But White Bull could not save me from Low Dog dreaming.

White Bull's sits-beside-wife, Rattling Blanket Woman, was stirring the fire. Rattling Blanket Woman made beautiful moccasins and I loved her as a sister. Her deft hands could not stay my Low Dog dreams.

I told my brother I must go somewhere else. I must find someplace where Low Dog could not find me. I said I would die from my dreaming and could not stay with the Lakota anymore.

CHAPTER 4

A BIG PLUM

THE GRAND ARMY OF THE POTOMAC HAD PARADED YESTERDAY: spit and polish, one-two, one-two; ten in the morning until five at night; a hundred forty thousand men saluted the reviewing stand: General Grant and General Meade and President Johnson and the Honorable Thaddeus Stevens and top Republican congressmen. The only lively moment came when General Custer lost control of his stallion—trust Custer to ride a stallion in a parade—and he galloped down Pennsylvania Avenue with his yellow hair streaming behind him. He saluted the reviewing stand as he passed.

Today was the Army of Tennessee's turn.

General William Sherman (Uncle Billy) didn't order his soldiers to spruce up nor polish their boots, and those that didn't have shoes, why, they weren't issued any. And the colored gals who'd followed them through Georgia and the Carolinas were following 'em today. There were hundreds of bird dogs—some of the best bird dogs in the South—running loose and squabbling. There were thoroughbred horses with their previous Confederate owners' names painted on their flanks. There were fine purebred cattle and sheep and even two Cape buffalo liberated from the rebel General Wade Hampton's private park. How the brave boys cheered! How they sang! "As we go marching through Georgia!"

Reclining on the Capitol Mall, picnic basket beside him, Eben Barnwell had enjoyed every patriotic aspect of Sherman's victorious, yet so *human* army, and when pretty schoolgirls started pelting the veterans with flowers, Eben Barnwell began to weep. Those carefree children primed his melancholy. From weeping, Eban began to gasp and dropped his face into his hands. No! He was not that frightened boy! He was not him anymore!

After he recovered, Eben wiped his face with his handkerchief and invited several soldiers to "have a drink with a grateful citizen. You, sir"—indicating a dour civilian beside a soldier—"if you've befriended these fine boys, you've befriended me."

Shortly afterward in Ebbett's Saloon, Eben Barnwell hoisted his glass. "I give you the Union, gentlemen! One and indivisible!" Flushed from the sun, Eben's countenance was wreathed in smiles. What a grand parade! In this glorious, optimistic America, what parade could compare? "To patriots!" he added.

"Damn all rebels!" Mr. Charles Chepstow amended. A small-chested man with large buttocks, Mr. Chepstow's expression was as low as his center of gravity. Chepstow was Private Hayward's kinsman.

"I am so very very happy!" Eben beamed.

The small party perched behind the mezzanine railing above a turbulent sea of blue backs, blue trousers, and blue forage caps. This dominant scheme was speckled with gray and brown civilians like toast crumbs floating on the blue ocean. Eben's raised finger secured a harried waiter's attention.

Sergeant Wilson's tobacco stream left the spittoon largely untouched and his voice slurred. "Are you one of them profiteers, Barnwell?"

"I admit it, brave boys. Readily, I admit it. Whilst you brave boys faced mortal perils, I purveyed blankets to the Army of the Potomac. None of your shoddy! No, sir! If I exacted a fair price, I delivered a warm blanket.

"A substitute served in my place. A new arrival to our fair shores, Mr. Phineas Ryan, accepted my price, fought as you did, marched as you did, and fell in my stead at Little Round Top. Gentlemen, if I did not fight bravely—as you did—my money fought and died as gallantly as six hundred honest dollars ever could!"

Corporal Smithers grinned like a fool. Though Private Hayward kept his eyes fixed on Charles Chepstow, his kinsman ignored him.

"Boys, you see me as I am. One would not call me 'fat,' but I confess to 'portly.' My constitution is robust, but I dare say any of you could throw me.

"Boys, to my disgrace, I confess that Eben Barnwell is not . . . Eben is not valorous. When Jubal Early's confederates neared Washington—was it just a year ago?—my portmanteau was loaded atop my carriage, my servant slept fully dressed, and I had rooms reserved in Baltimore.

"Valiants like yourselves deride cowards like Eben Barnwell, but would you enlist him?" Eben's hands framed his verbal picture. "You are in ranks as the sun rises through the fog. Ahead: the dreadful redoubt of the implacable foe. In your breast pocket: the Testament your mother pressed upon you the day you enlisted. Inside that Precious Book: a tear-stained letter to your sweetheart—inscribed 'to be delivered in the event . . .' " Eben's shudder amplified this detail. "Look sharp, boys! The bugle sounds! Your captain cries, 'Load your rifle! Fix bayonets!' But take comfort, boys! On your right hand—why it's Sergeant Wilson—a lion of a man. On your left—Private Hayward. Now, Hayward may have his head in the clouds, but when the drum rolls he's present for duty. In the second rank—why, it's Corporal Smithers—perhaps Smithers is too familiar with 'masked batteries' "—Wilson guffawed while Smithers reddened—"but brave Smithers will assault Confederate batteries as readily as the battery beneath a bawd's skirts."

Sergeant Wilson put an elbow into Smithers's ribs. "Ha!" he said.

"Boys, which of these brave fellows would you swap for portly, puffing, frightened Eben Barnwell? Eben's money will rush in where Eben will not. Eben's money is valorous, and as you surmount the rampart, at your side, fluttering beside our glorious flag, will be Eben Barnwell's bloodstained, battle-tried greenbacks!"

Private Hayward had asked his Washington cousin, Charles Chepstow, for postwar employment and Chepstow's disinterest had clouded Hayward's afternoon. Despite this, he couldn't be downhearted in this jolly fellow's company. "Mr. Barnwell," Hayward began.

"Oh, no!" Eben refused the unmerited honor. "It is for me to call you 'Mister.' Your countrymen are eternally grateful. You've sacrificed everything!"

"We ain't sacrificed so much." Corporal Smithers shook his head. "Some is dead. Some is walking on stumps."

Eben reproduced the expression he had worn last month at the Sainted President Lincoln's bier. "Terrible, terrible . . ." Eben murmured.

"We have all made sacrifices," Mr. Chepstow said, attempting to change the subject. "The great task for which we have labored is incomplete." His smile seemed to contain more than the usual number of teeth. "Death to traitors!" He emptied his glass.

Eben's smile faltered briefly. "The daunting task achieved, bright laurels fairly won. That's all the reason we could want for another tot of rum!" His finger shot up.

When Corporal Smithers shook his head, some of his brain parts weren't shaking at the same rate as others. The behinder parts came joltily.

"It was grand," Hayward said. "It was grand. Yes, there was terrible wickedness"—Hayward had been raised a Covenanter—"and often we were wearied or scared, but it was grand too. I don't believe we'll see its like again. "

A VIRGINIA UNIONIST who came north after Virginia seceded, Charles Chepstow became a legislator in the loyalist Virginia government-in-exile. After Lee surrendered, the Confederate legislature was disbanded and the loyalist governor took office in Richmond, but to Charles Chepstow's dismay, his legislators were not asked to accompany him. Worse, yesterday's rebels were seeking election to seats in the Virginia Assembly that loyalist legislators had assumed were theirs.

Now Mr. Chepstow smiled. "Thaddeus Stevens believes we should reissue rebel uniforms to inmates of prisons and lunatic asylums."

Eben winced. "Sir. In business, it is best to let bygones be bygones. Business looks to the future."

Private Hayward said, "They were wrong to seek disunion, Cousin, but I wouldn't like to see those uniforms on convicts."

"We must defer to you, sir." Eben trampled Mr. Chepstow's unvoiced objection. "For you have 'seen the elephant,' while Mr. Chepstow and I have been cleaning up after the beast."

Judging by his expression, Mr. Chepstow didn't find Eben's analogy as apt as Sergeant Wilson did. "You're a peculiar son of a bitch, Barnwell," Wilson said. "I'll say you are."

Eben replied more solemnly than the sally required, "I hold that good will, energy, and fixed purpose can improve a man. Yes, sir, that is my belief."

"After I'm discharged might be I'll go out West," Corporal Smithers said gloomily. "They say things is different out there."

"Didn't you say you had a wife?"

"Wife and two little 'uns. Two years since I seen Lizzie." Corporal Smithers stuck a forefinger in his rum and swished it. "It's a new deal out there. Out West, they don't give a damn who you are."

Eben sounded a happier note. "Boys, ours is the grandest century since centuries were invented.

"Soon, when we wish to visit San Francisco, we'll board that transcontinental railroad and whiz to the Pacific. Want to talk to the Queen of England, or the Czar of the Muscovites? Attach your telegraph machine to Mr. Cyrus Field's undersea cable and talk as much as you want to. We're done fighting wars. We won't have time for wars anymore."

"Mr. Barnwell, I hope you have the right of things," Private Hayward observed.

Eben squinted through his cigar smoke. "What do you know about Jay Cooke?"

"I know he's a rich son of a bitch," Sergeant Wilson drawled.

"Whereas General Sherman is a general of armies, Jay Cooke is a general of finance."

"You got another ceegar?" Sergeant Wilson asked.

When Eben shook his head, the sergeant found a lint-covered plug and settled it in his jaw. "What of this Cooke?"

Eben clapped his hands. "Where others see peril, Jay Cooke sees opportunity. Why, you boys couldn't have fought the war without him. His war bonds paid for this war, every bullet, uniform cap, and button. Ingenuity and capital—drop those ingredients in the pot, give them a stir, and they spell o-p-p-o-r-t-u-n-i-t-y."

"I don't spell so good," Sergeant Wilson said.

Eben pointed his finger. "What you think about the Confederate States of America?"

"Not much. We wrecked damn near everything we couldn't burn or carry off. Christ, Virginia looks like . . . like . . . ain't like nothin' I ever seed."

Corporal Smithers—whose eyes were crossing from drink—said, "My Lizzie wasn't but fifteen when we wedded. I'm sure gonna miss that gal."

"There's the opportunity," Eben said. "What do you think the South requires? Why, sir, it needs capital and ingenuity: banks, railroads, ports, plantations. Boys, you musn't neglect opportunity"—Eben rapped the table for emphasis—"on your doorstep. The former rebel states are a big plum."

Corporal Smithers said, "Damn, I'll miss that gal."

"Well," Eben said, irritated, "why not go back to her?"

"You ever had the pox? The surgeon looks at Willy and they wash him and then they pump him full of mercury, which hurts like blue blazes, but I don't pee like I ought and I got a rag pinned in my drawers. I'm gonna go west."

"The rebels have sown the wind," Chepstow intoned. "They must reap the whirlwind."

"Mr. Chepstow," Eben said. "What would you have us do?"

Charles Chepstow's smile was so deep his jaw seemed unhinged. "Hang them. Every rebel chieftain: Lee, Davis, all of them. The rebels must repent in sackcloth and ashes."

Sergeant Wilson drained his whiskey. "Ain't gonna happen." He burped and stood unsteadily. "We got no stomach for no more killin'. None of us Billy yanks do. Come on, Smithers. Time you took your Willy back to camp." The two soldiers pushed through the crowd.

Mr. Chepstow turned to his cousin. "I'm sorry I can't be of service. I am gratified to have renewed our acquaintance. Give my best regards to dear Cousin Rose." With a jerky bow, he was gone too.

Private Hayward rubbed his forehead. "Though he is only a distant connection I had hopes for Mr. Chepstow. I thought to find employment with him. Mr. Chepstow publishes a Richmond paper. The *New Nation*. Have you heard of it? Sir, might you have a position for a discharged volunteer?"

"You know I would!" Eben replied. "If I still had a firm, I'd hire you on the spot. Hayward, the market for one hundred percent virgin wool army blankets has gone. Poof! The United States Army has enough woolen blankets to last until the Second Coming!"

"I don't doubt it, sir. On behalf of my comrades and myself, I thank you for the pleasure of your company."

On a sudden impulse, Eben said, "Sit down, sir. Do sit down. Can you post a ledger, copy a letter book?"

"I was second teller at the Bank of Concord."

"Well, then, Hayward. I know a fellow over at the Treasury Department who fancies he owes me an obligation. Drop by tomorrow and ask for Undersecretary Robert Coalter. I'll speak to the man on your behalf."

Hayward's expressions of gratitude were effusive.

On his way home, in the pleasant twilight, Eben Barnwell reflected on how doing good was its own reward.

—

CHAPTER 5

INDEPENDENCE DAY

"WE CAN ACCUSTOM OURSELVES TO JUST ABOUT ANYTHING," Cousin Molly Semple testified

"Yes, ma'am," Jack the Driver said.

At Cousin Molly's request they dallied at the turn above Stratford, once the finest plantation in the Jackson River Valley.

"The mill wheel . . . ?" Molly observed.

Stratford's mill had ground the neighborhood's wheat, oats, and corn-meal. It had sawed the ties Samuel sold at the railhead.

Its millrace was stagnant, choked with sawgrass. Here and there, clap-boards had pulled away, dangling like broken pendulums. Whitewash, applied sometime before the war, endured in patches.

"Master wants to get her turnin' again. He surely do. But nobody got anything needs grindin'." Jack said.

Four years of war had reorganized Stratford's geometric fields into nature's softer, curvilinear forms: cedar splotches, tangles of devil's shoe-string, blackberry thickets advancing into unmowed fields. Though this remote mountain valley had been spared armies' passage, deserters and runaway slaves had burned its fence rails in their campfires.

One small riverside field had been planted in oats, presently knee-high. The field beside it had been plowed in long dark furrows that a man and horse were presently harrowing. The husbandry of these perfectly ordinary practices brought moisture to Molly Semple's eyes. She dabbed with her handkerchief. "Don't I remember two barns?"

"Yes'm, Miss Molly. Lightning hit the cow barn. Weren't no cows in it, though. When it burnt, Miss Abigail, she said she prayed we wouldn't have to make no more sacrifices, and I said amen to that. Master Thomas and Master Duncan—they wasn't home yet."

"Our prayers were answered."

"We was most as glad to see young masters' horses as we was to see young masters." Jack laughed. "Don't 'preciate no horse until you try to plow without one. Master Gatewood, he hitch Beulah to the plow, but Beulah been a milk cow all her days and weren't goin' to be no ox."

"How does Samuel fare?"

"Some better. In the morning he keen to get out and get doin' and he go to bed straightaway after supper. Master glad he boys home." Jack paused. "We glad you here too, Miss Molly. Be just like them olden times."

On her last visit before the war, Molly Semple had been wealthy, her competence managed by Mr. Jamison of the Planters Bank of Richmond.

Now? Molly Semple had heard rumors that some Richmond banks might receive an infusion of Northern capital and reopen, but apparently the Planters Bank was not to be among them. Molly had spoken with Mrs. Jamison in line for federal rations.

Ordered to burn warehouses before they evacuated Richmond, the Confederates had made too good a job of it and Richmond had burned from the waterfront almost to the Capitol. The fire had burned itself out two blocks south of Molly's home.

Some of Molly's acquaintances borrowed from Richmond's new money changers—the carpetbaggers—and Confederate currency (genteel Richmonders had trunks full of the worthless stuff) could not discharge debt. Carpetbagger courts ordered the debtors' homes sold at a twentieth of their value. To finance this journey, Molly had sold her last good jewelry, a fire opal necklace and white gold bracelet passed down from her grandmother. Throwing herself upon her Stratford relatives was distasteful, but leaving her Richmond home was the only way she could keep it.

The Jackson River ford had washed badly and Cousin Molly clung to her seat as her portmanteau rocked alarmingly.

Stratford House's porch railings and columns could have used a coat of paint and oiled butcher paper served for glass in several windows, but its pinkish brick glowed softly and to Molly, Stratford was an old friend whose smile may lack a few teeth but whose welcome is unmistakable.

Abigail Gatewood's hair had gone completely white and her face was gaunter than Molly remembered.

"Oh, my dear. Oh, my dear." The cousins were embracing and weeping while Jack, who had a knack for invisibility, shouldered Molly's portmanteau and disappeared inside.

"Oh, dear Molly, how we have missed you. Thank God you are safe at Stratford."

"Cuz." Molly wiped her kind brown eyes. "Some say we have been through a time of testing. What we have been tested *for* eludes me."

"You haven't changed, Molly. You are unalterable as Cheops's pyramid."

"I confess to similar girth," Molly noted ruefully.

"Samuel and Duncan are in the fields. Molly, they work so hard!"

When Jack unhitched the horse and departed for the fields. Molly understood that a good workman and horse had been detached for her during the busiest season.

"Dear cousin, how weary you must be. Come inside where it is cool and have water and a rest. You will sleep in our room. Duncan and Sallie have the old nursery, Pauline has Grandmother Gatewood's room, may she rest in peace. Thomas bides in town and—"

"Cousin, I do hate to impose . . ."

Abigail touched Molly's shoulder. "Imposition, dear Molly? We have begged for your visits."

"My visit may be rather extended." Molly's smile didn't *require* reassurance but didn't positively forbid it.

Abigail clapped her hands. "More's the better. Oh, Molly. We will be happy again. I know we will! Thank God we have Stratford to sustain us. Now you must rest. Your journey must have been frightful."

Although some Virginia Central track had been relaid, there were countless breaks over which passengers were conveyed in wagons of every description excepting only "new" and "well sprung," drawn by horses whose prominent ribs and weariness testified to prior Confederate service. In 1860, the trip between Richmond and Millboro Springs had taken two days—including an overnight stay at Orange's comfortable Depot Hotel. Today, the journey took six days, and if there had been a single easy mile, Molly Semple could not recall it.

Stratford had the pleasantly guilty air of a farmhouse whose inhabitants are outdoors working. The Gatewoods' bedroom was off the parlor.

"Molly, this shall be your bed. Will it suit?"

The narrow bed was set beside an open window that framed a glistening bend in the river fringed by sycamores. "Admirably, Cuz."

"There's fresh water in the pitcher, and soap—lye soap, I'm afraid."

"Samuel?"

Abigail perched on a love seat. "Samuel is Samuel, dear: unalterable, straight as a die. Do we ever change, Molly? Can we, if we would?"

Molly smiled and continued, "Tell me, dear Abigail, is Samuel reconciled?"

"To our conquerors? Oh, he tries to be. Did I write our Thomas is canvassing for Alexander Stuart? Stuart hopes to be elected to Congress this fall. Thomas believes he will win."

"Abigail, isn't it odd that we once celebrated this day as 'Independence Day'? Since we Virginians have so signally failed to achieve independence, July Fourth has acquired disagreeable overtones."

"Samuel says we are punished for our stewardship—that every time a master sold a negro family apart, God took notice."

When an odd look crossed her cousin's face, Molly knew Abigail was remembering that dreadful Christmas when Samuel sold Maggie and her infant son south. But what else could Samuel have done? Although Samuel had married Maggie to another slave, nothing had cured his son Duncan's unsuitable affections.

Molly brought her back. "How grateful I am, dear, we females needn't concern ourselves with such abstruse matters. I'm sure we have enough to worry about already! How is Sallie? She was such a comfort to our wounded boys. Winder Hospital had no better, gentler hands."

"When Duncan was restored, it seemed as if, like Lazarus, he'd risen from the dead." Abigail reconsidered. "Like all married couples, they take the rough with the smooth . . ."

Although Molly's smile invited further confidences, Abigail didn't offer them. "I have always loved this room," she said. "I hope you will be happy here."

Molly Semple believed that unconfronted difficulties would, like rice soaked in water, swell to unmanageable proportions. She glanced pointedly at the four-poster bed in which generations of Gatewoods had been born and died and, prior to those public ceremonies, in private been conceived. "You will tell me, dear, when my presence might be unwelcome," she said.

The tips of Abigail's ears glowed fiery red. "Oh. Yes. Molly. Excuse me. I positively must collect the eggs. Our hens are broody and settled on the nest, they take a hardened hand to dislodge them. " Abigail's smile was reminiscent. "Did you ever dream things could change so much?"

"No, dear. Like broody hens, I am bereft of imagination."

When the door shut behind Abigail, Cousin Molly slumped on the narrow bed and the starch leaked out of her shoulders. She repressed a sigh.

Molly's glance wandered to the beautiful river. The streamside sycamores were graceful and hopeful as young girls in spring dress. No matter what mortal men contrive, God adorns His world.

Cousin Molly Semple would get out of her traveling things, wash, and rest awhile. Then she would see about making herself useful.

THE ANTEBELLUM HARNESS smelled strongly of neat's-foot oil. With a trace strap borrowed from a unserviceable rig, it would serve. This afternoon they'd dragged chestnut logs into the yard to split for rails. Tomorrow, they'd harvest oats.

Oats were bringing seventy-eight cents a bushel at the railhead. Ready money!

Duncan Gatewood cut a diagonal slice through the strap Jack the Driver held against the stall divider. Jack seemed to know when Duncan needed him and when help might be resented. Sometimes their easy cooperation made Samuel think his son's amputation was perfectly healed. But after laboring all morning Duncan would disappear for a few minutes and on returning his eyes would be vague from laudanum.

On days they pried rocks from the plowed ground and rolled or levered them onto the stoneboat, Samuel Gatewood thought his son made overfrequent use of the remedy.

Earlier that spring, with no beast to pull the shovel plow but themselves, Samuel Gatewood and Jack had accepted their role as drafters while, dressed in man's trousers, blouse, and Sunday bonnet, Abigail Gatewood clung to the plow handles. Each cobble the plow sole hit jerked the traces into the men's sweat-soaked shoulders, but since complaint would have made hard work harder, a false, hearty cheerfulness sustained them. After the last tiny oat seed was tamped into the soil, they stumbled speechlessly out of the field.

News of General Lee's surrender reached Stratford that same evening. Since it was unpatriotic to feel the heart leap at such doleful intelligence, neither Samuel nor his wife Abigail remarked aloud. But as she helped Franky prepare their supper of boiled poke greens and grits, Abigail hummed one of Mr. Foster's sprightlier tunes and Samuel did not reprove her.

A week later when his grandson, Thomas Byrd, splashed his horse across the ford, Samuel felt such constriction in his chest he nearly stopped breathing.

"Hullo, sir." Thomas dismounted swiftly, carelessly, and beat dust from his uniform with his hat. A scrawny chicken dangled from his saddle. "Well, it's over." He looked around indifferently. "I never thought we'd get whipped but I 'spose we did. Duncan's all right. Not a scratch. He's fetching Sallie."

"Well, then," Samuel Gatewood said, able to say no more. "Well, then . . ."

———

MOLLY SEMPLE WAS AWAKENED by a tapping at her door and the aroma of warm cornbread.

"Hullo, Cousin Molly. Do you remember me?"

Molly sat bolt upright. "My eyes aren't as sharp as they were and you were a child when I saw you last, but if you ain't Pauline Byrd, I am sorely mistaken."

The young woman set down the tray and hugged her kinswoman. "It seems so long ago! I'm so glad you've come, Cousin. I'm so glad we're together."

"Sweetheart." Molly smiled. "My, aren't you grown."

"I'll be sixteen on my birthday."

Molly shook her head wonderingly. " You are a fetching young woman. You've your mother Leona's complexion."

The girl's face clouded. "Poor, poor Mama . . ."

"God bless your mama, child. She loved you so." Molly lifted the napkin that covered the tray. My goodness! Cornbread!"

"Oh, yes. There's cornbread and there's maple syrup—I lugged the buckets while Jack and Franky kept the boil. We made ten gallons. We have all the syrup we want! And here's milk and butter and here's an egg I boiled. Oh, Miss Molly, when I think of our poor negroes wandering the countryside with nothing to eat, it makes me so sad!"

"It is hard for them. Thousands have crowded into Richmond. They engage to work but then don't appear, they find drink—I suppose one oughtn't blame them. If these changes are difficult for us, think how much more difficult they must be for them. My Amelia has been with me since I was a girl and she knows no other work. My home has been *her* home. I told Amelia I had no money for wages but she could continue, as before, under my roof and share my food until I could pay her, but she said no, she wouldn't, she was free now so she'd leave. Amelia is sixty if she's a day, but could not be swayed from her purpose. Every night I pray for her."

As Cousin Molly poured syrup on her cornbread, she said, "Now, child. Tell me about your beaus."

On the cusp between womanhood and girlhood Pauline blushed to the roots of her hair. "Cousin . . ."

"Oh, dear, dear. Forgive this old spinster. We old maids take more pleasure from young people's courting than is altogether decent. Be assured, child, I only wish you happiness."

"Cousin, the truth is that no boy has come calling. Nary one. And I am not sure what I would do if one did." The girl continued in a rush, "Sallie is so smitten with Duncan she hasn't anything to say except, 'Duncan, Duncan, Duncan.' " She made a face. "If that is what love is, I think I shall find love disagreeable. To ignore everyone else in the world"—her gesture included Muscovites and the heathen Chinese—"for one man. Cousin Molly, are women always so moony when they find a beau?"

Cousin Molly had never married, but that was not to say she hadn't loved. "I believe we are, dear."

"It seems so silly. They are husband and wife and of course they love each other. But do they have to love each other so much?"

"He will be all the world to her until she has a child. Then the child will be the world to her. Women turn toward love as naturally as flowers seek the sun." She rested her fork. "That is the most satisfying meal I have had in ever so long. How is Thomas?"

She shrugged. "Oh, I don't know. I mean, Uncle Duncan lost an arm and his face was burned, but he never talks about the war. Tommy was only in the army six months and wasn't wounded, but he is so bitter. He says the scalawags and carpetbaggers are ruining Virginia."

Cousin Molly said, "I am sorry to hear that. Bitterness is one emotion the vanquished can ill afford."

"Poor Pompey. Some no-accounts—oh, they were Ira Hevener's friends—deserters like him—they were bothering the coloreds at the Botkin homeplace and when Pompey tried to run them off, they shot him."

Molly sighed. "How Pompey loved singing. His booming bass. The colored singers in the garret of that little church of yours made sure we whites couldn't hear our own voices."

"Grandfather buried Pompey and brought Aunt Opal home. She's changed, Molly. Opal's got her own house in the Quarters and eats out of our garden, but she doesn't help with the work and she's always cross when I speak to her. Why are people so awful to each other?"

"Child, our consolation is that no matter what we have lost—friends, family, riches—at last this war is over. " Molly clapped her hands. "Enough of sorrowful topics. Child, tell me about yourself."

Pauline had her mother's blue-black hair and (Molly noticed with a pang) Leona's gray-green eyes. But Pauline's eyes were more determined than poor Leona's had ever been.

"I am just a girl," Pauline said. "And . . . I am sometimes lonely here. Cousin Molly, will you be my friend?"

And Molly embraced the girl and murmured into her hair that of course she would, honey. Of course she would.

DUNCAN AND JACK rolled a chestnut log off the skid. Duncan set the wedges and Jack swung the maul while Samuel led the horse to the next log.

In the old days they'd taken an hour at noon for supper. These days, unless the horses needed a rest, they worked straight through, and when Jack turned to him now, Samuel cautioned, "I'll want these rails before sundown."

"Yes, Master. I'd be obliged for a word."

Samuel drank from his wooden canteen and offered it to Jack.

"It's Miss Franky," Jack said. "You know we been seein' right much of each other."

The couple had been living together in Jack's cabin since Christmas, but since Samuel wasn't supposed to notice, he hadn't. He registered appropriate surprise.

"We was thinkin' on gettin' married." Jack looked away. "I come to ask your permission."

"Why, Jack, you old devil. You? Married?"

"Yes, Master. Now I'm free I thought to get married. I never thought to marry before."

Samuel didn't intend to pursue that rabbit into the briar patch.

Heartily—falsely even to his own ears—he said, "Well, Jack, now you are freed you needn't ask my permission—or any man's. Should you wish to marry, you marry; simple as that. And I shan't be the one to marry you either. You won't be 'jumping the broomstick.' Preacher Todd will marry you."

"Preacher Todd's an upstanding white man, Master. And I ain't sayin' nothin' against him. But Franky is wantin' get married by the Baptists in Warm Springs. They got a colored preacher."

Samuel nearly protested that Stratford's people attended the Presbyterian church in SunRise, they always had. But he was changing a lifetime's habits, and contented himself with the observation, "What a new world it is, Jack."

"Yes, Master," Jack said, relieved. "It is for sure."

THAT NIGHT AFTER SUPPER, while the family caught up with Molly's Richmond gossip, Sallie and Duncan slipped upstairs. Through the transom above their closed door the couple heard faint voices and laughter.

Shirtless, Duncan lay sprawled across the bed on his stomach. Sally knitted on a chest beneath the window.

A framed lithograph from *Leslie's* magazine hung on the wall; roses in a jar on the bureau offered their aroma and the window was open to the night air. The lap robe Sally was knitting owed its ruddiness to the pokeberries she'd used to dye the wool. "It is good to hear laughter again," she said.

"I wonder, Sallie, if you'd rub salve on my stump. We hit a lick today."

She set down her basket and eased spearmint ointment on his puckered flap. It was hot to her touch.

"You must let others carry more of the burden." She kneaded gently.

"I do little enough as it is." He sat upright. "It seems strange that while we were fighting, when I might be killed in the next skirmish, my amputated limb didn't ache. Can we postpone pain?"

"Dearest . . . I know that some men suffer more from their amputations than others. Some have perished."

"I sometimes wish . . ." Duncan began.

"Yes, dearest?"

Sallie winced at Duncan's sardonic laugh. "What's the point of wishing? I lived. Many men did not."

"Do you still dream of becoming a horse breeder?"

He shrugged. "Oh, my dreams are real enough. Too real, at times. Damn the laudanum! I dream terrible things. You know how a wounded horse screams?"

"You are taking more laudanum."

"A bottle every three days. But what am I to do? Without it, the pain would keep me from doing my part, and at night, no matter how weary I am, I cannot sleep without it."

"You sleep better after our lovemaking." Sallie smiled.

This time his laugh was real. "Then let us put me to sleep."

CHAPTER 6

A HINGTY NIGGER

White Bull heard of a Hunkpapa wican who had cured a woman of Low Dog dreaming. The whiskey trader Pommerlau was traveling to the Yellowstone where this Hunkpapa had his winter camp. I went with him.

The third night, Pommerlau beat me with the butt of his whip and tied me inside his wagon. Because he was Catholic, he put his son outside the wagon before he raped me. I told him I had been baptized, that my Christian name was Mary, but he said that since I wasn't Catholic I was just another squaw.

After Pommerlau raped me, I knew he must kill me, because White Bull would make him cry when he learned what he'd done. I was always tied, even when I had to make water.

As we approached the Yellowstone, Pommerlau raped me more times.

One night, while the father was sleeping, the boy cut my bonds and I ran away. The boy had a snub nose and his breath was as sour as his father's.

Snow fell and covered my tracks. I found serviceberries and dug camas roots and snared a rabbit. I had no fire. One night, I slept in a bear's den—a cave in the riverbank.

That night I dreamed of my husband. He was as black as obsidian.

———

COLORED SOLDIERS STOOD at ease on the 38th United States Colored Troops' Galveston, Texas, parade ground. When one exuberant private boarded the wagon for the steamer, he tossed his forage cap high in the air. "Bottom rail's on the top these days!" he yelled.

Private Edward Ratcliff grumbled, "I swear to God, Burns, I swear to God Damned God. That nigger got his back pay, his uniform, and he goin' home to God Damn Charleston—Charleston!—thinkin' things gonna be different for him. Ten minutes after that boy come home he'll be shuckin' that fine blue uniform."

Sergeant Jesse Burns was big enough so strangers stared. Ratcliff was a short, hard man. Jesse read and wrote as well as most whites. When Ratcliff had been Top Sergeant (Sergeant Major) Ratcliff, Jesse had prepared his daily muster report. They became friends during the Petersburg siege.

Burns and Ratcliff sat in the rickety stand where the 38th's white officers reviewed their dusky soldiers. Jesse Burns had collected his pay, paid his small debts, and packed his haversack. The uniforms Jesse threw away would have clothed three slaves for a year.

Ratcliff filled his clay pipe and tamped it. "You goin' back to Virginia?"

"Edward, we must seize our chance. We have earned the franchise. We cannot let it slip away."

Ratcliff laughed. "You think they'll give niggers the vote? Hell, Jesse, everybody Virginia just elected to Congress is a reb or a sympathizer."

"Edward, though you accuse me of being too trusting, you are playing the innocent now."

Ratcliff snorted.

"Republicans are a majority in Congress until or unless the Southern delegations are seated, whereupon Democrats will be the majority. Edward, do you think Thaddeus Stevens will let that happen?"

"Those rebel congressmen were elected proper. What can Stevens do?"

"Mr. Stevens will think of something."

"Uh." Ratcliff lit his pipe and paused to draw in smoke. "Damn, Jesse, I thought I finally got to where I was runnin' to. First time I ran away from Master I wasn't but fourteen. Didn't get five miles. Second time I run, Master sold me to a master wasn't so tenderhearted. That bastard took a whip to me. Every blow he laid on my back made me worth less at auction, but he was singin', 'Hincty nigger, hincty nigger,' as he whipped me. Afterward he say how much pleasure it gave him. Next time I run, I got so near Ohio I could see the damn river, so I was sold south where I'd have farther to run. Finally Union General Butler gets to Hampton Roads and I signs on for the army. How many niggers got to be a Top Sergeant? How many niggers got a Medal of Honor?" He patted his chest. "I thought I'd surely got where I was gettin'. I'd stay in the army and fight Comanches or Maximilian's Frenchmen or whoever the army gonna fight. Instead they took my stripes and made me a damn mess cook . . ."

Jesse shook his head. "Edward, you know you cannot strike an officer. Certainly in this man's army, you cannot strike a Custer."

WHEN RATIONS MEANT for the 38th USCT disappeared in Austin, then–Sergeant Major Ratcliff had volunteered to ride to the Texas capital to sort things out.

Captain Nivens wrote the order himself. "Top Sergeant; volunteering? You?"

"Yessir."

The captain signed with a flourish. "Rations get misplaced or lost all the time."

"Yessir."

"They say there's some pretty Mexican girls in Austin."

"That's what I hear."

Captain Nivens blew on the ink and fluttered the orders in the air to dry. "Is that it?"

Ratcliff thought for a moment before he spoke. "Sir, what was you before you was a soldier?"

"I taught at Bowdoin College. Natural philosophy."

"I'll bet you be glad to get back to that natural philosophy; glad to shuck this hot wool uniform and put on civilian clothes."

The captain smiled. "I intend to resume a normal life."

"Bein' a field hand, Captain, was my normal life. 'Fore daybreak I'd go out with the gang and we'd hoe or thin or pick or sort or dry or pack tobacco until the sun drop out the sky. Master say, 'Nigger do this' or 'Nigger do that' and I done it. In the army I get my meals, my clothes, and they pays me too. Never used to pay us field hands nothin'. Other soldiers who ain't no sergeant major, they got to cook my meals and pitch my tent and they say, "Yes, Top, I'll get to it right away, Top.' White officers like you—the ones who know how an army really works—they comes to me and ask, 'What sort of soldier is Jones? Should we promote Jones or that rapscallion from E Company?' "

Captain Nivens folded his orders. "Ratcliff, the army is shrinking. Most of the officers who want to stay in cannot. Officers who were brevetted general for meritorious service or valor, are demoted to captains or lieutenants. Most white soldiers, and every colored soldier, are being discharged."

"Suppose General Grant was to put a word in for me, or General Sheridan."

"Perhaps, in that case . . ."

"Suppose Major General Custer . . ."

"He's Lieutenant Colonel Custer these days." Ratcliff's captain gave him his orders. "Good luck in Austin."

It was an easy three-day ride. Before he entered Austin, Ratcliff dallied by a meandering creek to wash and shave. He changed into his best dress uniform with the bright yellow sergeant major's stripes. Tom Custer, the General's brother, had won two medals of honor and Sergeant Ratcliff hesitated before pinning his medal on his tunic. Might be resented; might get him a hearing. On balance? Worth the chance.

Ratcliff rode through the dusty Texas capital as if on parade.

The tents in Custer's north Austin camp were laid out in military fashion, and the horses were well groomed, but the soldiers watched Ratcliff through dull incurious eyes.

Regimental headquarters were a one-story adobe ranch house with a shaded front porch. The United States flag and regimental colors hung in desultory folds in the windless morning air. A dozen officers, most in hunting garb, lounged on the porch and as Ratcliff approached made remarks he couldn't quite hear. He did hear, "My God, Tom, has the comic opera come to town?"

Stone-faced, Ratcliff dismounted and tied his horse to the porch rail. A slight, mustachioed lieutenant intercepted him on the stairs and returned his salute more casually than Ratcliff had offered his. "Sergeant Major. What's that you're wearing?"

Ratcliff barked, "Medal of Honor, sir."

The yellow-haired man in buckskins half asleep in his chair: that must be George Custer. He tipped his hat back to squint at the phenomenon. "Say, Tom," he drawled, "does that make you twice as brave as a nigger or merely as brave as a nigger two times?"

The officers snickered.

"Sergeant Major Ratcliff reporting to regimental headquarters," Ratcliff snapped.

"Jesus Christ! You're not joining the regiment?" Tom Custer blurted.

"No, sir. I've come to inquire about missing rations."

"Pity," the man in buckskins murmured, and Ratcliff's hopes leaped. "We officers and ladies do enjoy our theatricals. Tom, wouldn't this buck make a splendid harem guard?"

"Sir?" Ratcliff's attention was rigid as stone.

"I've always fancied the stage," Custer mused. "Tom, can't you picture me as Hamlet?" He stood, thrust his hand into his jacket, and peered across the landscape as if something more interesting than dust were out there. "To be or not to be, that . . . that gentlemen, is something we all got to figger."

Several officers applauded and he grinned infectiously. "And this boy here"—he pointed—"Othello the Moor!"

"Uh-huh," Tom Custer said. He pursed his lips and pointed down the tent street. "Quartermaster's tent's there, Sergeant. See him about your rations."

"Sir, I—"

"If you don't git, my brother'll put you in a turban."

Ratcliff executed a smart about-face and marched away. They probably didn't care whether he heard their guffaws.

He took a breath before ducking into the quartermaster's tent, which, like all such, was cluttered with barrels and wooden crates. The quartermaster was a sleepy, hatless fat man whose buttocks overflowed his stool. He thumbed through manifests. "Rations for the 38th USCT. Sure, they got here. That's as far as they got." The quartermaster read aloud. "They was two beef cows, twenty barrels of salt pork, hardtack, coffee, sugar, and"—he tapped the list—"five gallons of medicinal brandy."

"Well, Sergeant," Ratcliff said, "suppose you send our rations on their way."

"Can't. Beeves been et and Tom Custer got yer brandy. I never sent the salt pork nor hardtack because I figured you'd be better off makin' a fresh requisition." The man scratched his head and inspected his fingernails for louse eggs. "General threw a barbecue for the mayor n' the high n' mighty Texans. They ate all afternoon and then they danced. General's got the best band in Texas." He spat.

"What else he got?"

The quartermaster peered closely. "Be damned if you ain't a nigger! And here I was a-talkin' to you like you was a white man."

Ratcliff looked at him.

"Oh, it don't matter none. No offense. Top Sergeant's a Top Sergeant, I guess." He dipped his shoulder in a limp shrug.

Ratcliff thought the world was filled with white fools. "This Custer—"

"Which Custer you inquirin' about?" The quartermaster sneered. "The Custer that won't drink or the one that drinks too much? Both bastards favor the bullwhip."

"White soldiers?"

"We done wrote our senator. We got us up a petition and everybody signed. 'Deed we did."

Ratcliff yawned. "General Sheridan favors the Custers and General Sherman thinks the sun rises and sets on George Custer's ass."

"Ain't everybody thinks so high of 'em." The man sulked. "You heard about the victory parade?"

"How he lost control of his horse?"

The quartermaster snorted. "Lost control? He galloped the whole length of the victory parade and back again. Saluted the reviewing stand twict. Custer upstaged General Grant's entire army. That's one senior officer don't think too high of 'the Boy General.' " The quartermaster leaned forward. "He's a mean son of a bitch, that's who he is. Him and that damned brother of his." The quartermaster heaved himself off his stool and waddled to the front of the tent to pull the flap shut. He wagged his finger. "I'll swear I never told you nothin' . . ."

"Never heard a word," Ratcliff assured him. "Nary a word."

"Well, since you're a nigger, I 'spose I can tell you." He settled his rump on his stool and lifted his eyes to the tent peak and closed them. "It was payday, so I bought a jug. I'ze off duty. Ain't nobody's business what I do!"

"Just the same everywhere," Ratcliff assented.

"I drunk it. Now, maybe I shouldn't have drunk so much as I did. I was headin' for my tent, but I laid down and fell asleep. Wasn't like I was doin' anybody any harm . . ."

"No harm 'tall."

"Don't rightly know how long I was out. When I woke, it was pitch-black and kind of, you know . . . stiflin'. Close. It was stiflin'. When I reached out I strikes wood. There's wood on either side and atop of me and it's so tight I can't get my arms above my head. After a time inside I knew where I was. I knew *exactly* where I was." He licked his lips. "Top Sergeant, I was in a coffin. You can't be no soldier without you know about coffins, and that's where I was. Tom Custer had come upon me on the parade ground when I was passed out and helpless. He'd set a coffin over me and pegged it down so I couldn't get out. Then him and his brother and their friends stood around laughin' whilst I hollered and begged to get out." He licked his lips, looked down, and spoke quietly. "Oh, I reckon they had theyselves a big time."

—

SO FAR AS Sergeant Major Edward Ratcliff was concerned, Custer could upstage every victory parade and trap any number of drunk quartermasters under coffins: George Armstrong Custer could help him stay in the army.

At New Market Heights, after all the officers were killed, Top Sergeant Ratcliff took command. Hissing mortar shells had landed at his feet and failed to explode. He'd been shot at and stabbed at and knocked down by cavalry horses. He'd been buried alive when his bombproof collapsed under bombardment. He'd dug himself out that time, and by God, he was going to dig himself out now.

Still, it took nerve to walk down the street to Colonel George Custer's regimental headquarters and mount those stairs into the white officers' indolent stares.

Tom Custer was perched on the railing smoking a cigar. Ratcliff stood in front of the man. "Lieutenant. I figure we got something in common."

Another officer sang out, "Good God, Tom! Is the nigger claiming kin?"

Ratcliff touched his medal. "I hear you got two of these damn things," he said.

"What if I do?"

"Then you're a brave son of a bitch."

"I didn't know negro soldiers—"

"Got Medals of Honor? Not many of us did. General Butler give me mine."

"I suppose that makes you a brave son of a bitch."

"Suppose it does. I got somethin' to ask of you and the General."

The slightly built yellow-haired man uncoiled from the rail, yawned, and patted his mouth. "Every soldier's brave, Sergeant." His smile was as iridescent as it was unexpected. "Soldiers get medals if they're lucky. Unlucky soldiers get killed. Tell me, what's special about you?"

"Well, sir, four years ago I was a nigger slave and now I'm a Top Sergeant." Ratcliff touched his medal tenderly. "This proves I'm lucky *and* brave. Army's the only real home I ever had and they're going to throw me out on the street."

Light flared in Custer's eyes, like oil burning on water. "I was brevet-ted a major general and everybody calls me 'General Custer.' But I'm a damned lieutenant colonel now. That's how this army does things."

When the light went out of George Custer's eyes it left loneliness behind. Without caring much one way or another, he added, "Napoleon had a nigger marshall. Did you know that?"

"No, sir."

"So now you do." He spun toward his officers as if movement would energize him. "Boys, the sun is high in the heavens. What say we go hunting?"

His officers stirred.

Edward Ratcliff would rather have faced rebel bullets. "Sir, I—"

"Once the sergeant has finished, we'll see if we can't find us a buffalo. You finished, Sergeant?"

"Sir, I need your help."

"With your horse?" Tom Custer asked.

"What?"

"I asked if you needed help with your horse: mounting it and riding out of here."

George Custer shouted for his orderly. "Bring my Creedmore and plenty of bullets."

Ratcliff saluted the man's back, pivoted, and marched down the stairs to his horse. He swung his leg over the animal's back and settled into the saddle. His horse exploded in furious bucking and if Ratcliff had expected it, he might have stayed in the saddle, but he hadn't.

His head thumped Texas earth so hard, stars flashed before his eyes and he bit through his lower lip. He rolled to his knees and covered his mouth. Who would have thought one lip would hold so much blood? He ran his tongue around his teeth. His dress hat was mashed flat. His horse was sunfishing down the tent street as mildly curious white soldiers watched it pass. Custer's officers' laughter rolled over him like surf break-ing over his head.

Their voices were shrill as children at play. "Tom, I feared you'd spoiled the jest asking about his horse . . ."

"Don't get mad, boy," someone called. "Don't get a burr under your saddle . . ."

Tom Custer was doubled over with laughter. "Christ! A nigger pretendin' he's a soldier."

The Top Sergeant rolled onto his feet and brushed dust from his uniform. One pant leg was inside his boot, the other out. When he slapped his hat against his leg, that small dust cloud produced more laughter. His horse was gone. His back was sore. His right leg hurt. His head hurt. His mouth was thick with blood. He spat a gob.

He'd wanted to stay in the army. He wondered to himself, was that so much to ask?

He set his ruined hat on his head and marched up onto the porch to face Tom Custer and the red-faced laughing officers.

"I ain't pretending to be no soldier," Ratcliff said softly. "I is one."

SIX MONTHS AFTERWARD, Private Ratcliff dug dottle from his pipe. "Tom Custer was lucky I didn't hit him twice. Two hits would have killed the sorry bastard. Hell, maybe I'll go be an indian. My ma was half Cherokee. I know some of their lingo.

"Jesse, you think there's anyplace on this earth where a nigger gets treated like a man?" Ratcliff pocketed the pipe. "Heard from your wife?"

When Virginia newspapers resumed publication, Jesse had placed ads in the long columns of ads from former slaves seeking their families. Jesse had written the Freedmen's Bureaus too.

"No. Not a word," Jesse said.

Ratcliff figured he'd been married three times—depending on what counted as married. "Might be she's dead. Plenty niggers sold south into Mississippi didn't live through the first summer."

"I believe I'd feel it if Maggie was dead. I believe Maggie knows I'm looking for her and doesn't intend to be found."

"Friend Jesse, there's other women. There's plenty of fish in the sea."

"Friend Edward, I don't know that's true."

A few discharged soldiers still waited for wagons. A tenor began singing and other voices picked up his tune, their music sucked dry by the Texas air.

Ratcliff said, "Well, friend, we have had us some times." He shouldered his haversack and stuck out his hand. "Good luck to you. I believe I'll head west for a spell."

CHAPTER 7

THE ATLANTIC, MISSISSIPPI & OHIO

Eben Barnwell sat at Major General William Mahone's right hand. Mahone: famed around the globe as Robert E. Lee's most trusted lieutenant. Chestnut trees whose leaves were no bigger than a squirrel's ear shaded the veranda of the Warm Springs Hotel. Redbuds, dogwoods, forsythias, lilacs, and quince were in exuberant bloom along the promenade and the air was lush with scent. At Major General William Mahone's left hand sat Mr. Samuel Gatewood: distinguished proprietor of a venerable Virginia plantation.

As a boy, Eben Barnwell had milked cows in a Vermont barn so cold the milk froze into white rings on the iron hoops of his wooden bucket and he pressed into the cows' flanks for body heat.

These days Eben Barnwell believed he could become whomever he wished. That hope blazing in the man had barely flickered in the boy.

Mahone and Gatewood had offered Eben so many delicate courtesies Thomas Byrd's dislike was the hint of rue that makes sweetness sweeter.

General Mahone ignored Thomas Byrd and seemed amused by Eben's ebullience.

Eben vowed to emulate Mahone's detachment. Surely the General's ability to consider one problem while hip-deep in another was key to the General's wartime achievements.

Mahone shrugged. "Gatewood, if your mill was nearer Norfolk . . ."

"I can deliver any quantity of ties to the Jackson River railhead," Gatewood insisted. "Heartwood; no cracks or checks."

"But that is days from my Norfolk headquarters." Mahone tapped his newspaper. "President Johnson declares our rebellion ended. I thought it ended a year ago. Barnwell, does news travel so slowly in the North?"

Eben said, "Johnson's official pronouncement will encourage our English investors."

"I leave those details to you." A tiny dyspeptic man, "Little Billy" Mahone was fussy about diet and had kept a milk cow at his wartime headquarters. Though his soldiers joked about that cow, no one joked where Little Billy might overhear. After the surrender, William Mahone merged the Norfolk & Peters-burg Railway with the Southside to create the grandly named Atlantic, Mississippi & Ohio Railroad, which cynics promptly dubbed "All Mine and Otelia's."

As agent for A.M.&O. securities, Eben Barnwell had sailed to England courting investors who'd made fortunes in British railroads and were considering America.

In gentlemen's clubs, country houses, and quiet, paneled investment banks, Eben spoke about William Mahone and the Great Dismal Swamp, that impenetrable wilderness which in 1856 had thwarted the construction of the Norfolk & Petersburg Railroad: "Meandering streams, sawgrass islands, lakes, and bottomless mud. How," Eben asked rhetorically, "do you lay tracks across the Great Dismal Swamp? How, gentlemen, do you walk across water?"

Eben sustained his knowing smile until the potential investors confessed ignorance; whereupon Eben imitated the axeman's swing. "Submerged trees, gentlemen, cannot rot! William Mahone had trees felled, one atop of another, forming a submerged vegetative mass to support his roadbed.

"The A.M.&O. trains cross Dismal Swamp to this day: level grade, nary a bend, straight as an arrow.

"Gentlemen, long before he embarked on his military career, William

Mahone was the ablest railroad president in North America."

Potential investors dutifully examined the A.M.&O.'s optimistic prospectus but asked about Mahone's wartime exploits. Eben obliged, citing General Lee's entire reliance upon Mahone, who, had Lee been slain (according to Eben), was Robert E. Lee's chosen successor.

Eben concluded with a desanguinated description of the Crater Battle. "Grant mined Confederate defensive lines and blew them, men, horses, iron cannon—to kingdom come! Grant pushed three divisions into the tremendous breach. Opposing them? A single understrength Confederate battalion. General Grant's victory was assured. He would cut the Confederate line in twain, as a farmer hoes a serpent.

"But Ulysses S. Grant had underestimated his foe. For the man commanding the battalion was none other than Major General William Mahone!"

Eben found the money Mahone needed and some of it stuck to his fingers. That Eben's account of Mahone's Crater battle had been drawn from *Harper's Weekly* magazine and was less privileged than his English listeners may have believed didn't trouble Eben. Eben asked Mahone about the Crater once. Mahone wouldn't talk about it.

EBEN'S FATHER HAD BEEN a Vermont peddler. Jack Barnwell had mended pots and pans and sharpened knives, but never stepped inside the farm wife's kitchen door. Eben's mother was dead or absconded— Jack Barnwell never talked about her.

Sometimes when the Barnwells clattered through tiny villages at night, young Eben heard singing or a pianoforte behind lighted windows. These glimpses of better lives made the boy wonder if he and his father weren't aliens passing through the habitations of another race.

Jack Barnwell's morose silences could fill days and the only remark Eben remembered was, "Rich man never let the poor man get up"; which sentence became Eben's entire inheritance when Jack Barnwell died. As Eben was without known kin, the twelve-year-old fell onto the mercies of the county. The county commissioners thought tinkers a half step above gypsies.

The boy trembling before the commissioners might have stirred their consciences. On the other hand, while Eben Barnwell housed at the county poor farm would cost the county twelve cents per diem, that same fellow fostered to a farmer in need of an able young man would fetch the county two dollars a month and honest work was morally improving.

Eben went to work for Daniel and Ezekiel Knapp. These bachelors, never having had children themselves, presumed children were small varieties of grown men, as a pony is a small variety of horse. Since for their weight ponies can pull better than a horse, the brothers thought Eben's chronic exhaustion was obstinacy. Daniel Knapp beat the boy until he wet himself and then beat him for filthiness. Eben feared Daniel Knapp, but when he finally ran away he fled not blows but words. Eben Barnwell ran from Ezekiel Knapp's oft-repeated judgment: "Boy, you ain't nothin', and you ain't ever gonna be nothin'."

STRATFORD'S LADIES HAD COME to Warm Springs to greet General Mahone and bathe in healing waters, which had erased the troubled lines on Abigail Gatewood's face and restored her complexion to the glow Samuel Gatewood had first admired so many years before.

General Mahone assisted his wife, Otelia, to a rocker and tenderly laid a lap robe across her knees. Pauline took the rocker beside Mr. Barnwell and Cousin Molly settled in a swing.

Sallie set her hassock aside to lean against Duncan's knees.

Duncan had served under General Mahone, and when General Mahone became A.M.&O. president, Duncan wrote offering Stratford's Mill railroad ties, best quality, the same ties they'd sold the Virginia Central before the war.

Welcome news came by return mail: William and Otelia Mahone would be taking the waters at Warm Springs. Since that spa was no great distance from Stratford Plantation, perhaps Duncan could call upon them.

The A.M.&O., Mahone wrote mysteriously, had "a great many needs." Excited by the prospect of restarting Stratford's mill, Samuel Gatewood and Jack worked up a price list.

In the first postwar election, Thomas Byrd had canvassed for his mentor Alexander Stuart, and when the congressman-elect went to Washington City to be sworn in, Thomas had accompanied him. Like Stuart, the Southern congressmen who traveled to Washington City in December 1865 were moderates who had opposed secession.

During his campaign, Stuart had asserted that "Virginia still has rights under the Constitution of the United States, which have only been suspended during the abortive effort to sever her connection with the United States, and it is my duty to try and have those rights recognized and respected."

THOMAS BYRD HAD been in an ill humor after he returned from Washington City, and Samuel had hoped this outing might raise his spirits. Unfortunately, Thomas had seen Eben Barnwell as a living symbol of Virginia's humiliation. Now he asked about Barnwell's regiment.

"I left military affairs to bolder men. If I have a knack, it is for commerce."

"Will we have commerce in Virginia?"

"Yes, sir." Eben's broad gesture directed everyone's attention to commerce's glories. "If you cannot find opportunity in Virginia, you cannot cast a shadow in the noonday sun."

In the United States House of Representatives, on December 4, 1865, the clerk of the House had called roll without naming any of the duly elected Southern congressman seated before him. The radical Republican Thaddeus Stevens lounged in his seat, legs crossed.

One brave Democrat protested the roll call. "If Mr. Maynard is not loyal, who is loyal? During the darkest period of the war when he was an exile from Tennessee, his eloquent voice urged my state to discharge its whole duty to the Union; and yet here are honorable gentlemen who will not permit him to be heard, though he holds in his hand a certificate of election from the governor of Tennessee. Neither has the clerk read the names of members from Virginia. By what right has the Virginia delegation been excluded?"

The clerk replied, "If it is the desire of the House, I will give the reasons."

Thaddeus Stevens glittered with revenge. "The House knows it all and don't want the reasons."

As one by one Southern congressmen rose from their seats and left the chamber, Thaddeus Stevens never uncrossed his legs.

Walking behind Alexander Stuart, burning with humiliation, Thomas Byrd would have reignited the War if he could have, and now he said as much to William Mahone.

"The War is ended," General Mahone said. "We lost the War. We needn't enjoy our circumstances, but we must accept them as they are."

PAULINE BYRD'S SKIN had been ruddied in the warm mineral bath and her customary tautness slackened. She seemed lazier and more languorous than a young Christian virgin should.

Eben bowed to Samuel Gatewood. "Sir," he announced, "if Miss Byrd would consent to promenade, I would be grateful for your permission."

After her wordless appeal to Cousin Molly failed, Pauline Gatewood accepted Eben Barnwell's arm and the couple strolled down the garden lane beside the brook that gave Warm Springs its name. The brook steamed in the cool morning air.

MAHONE TURNED TO Thomas. "You were instrumental in Mr. Stuart's election."

"You are well informed, sir."

"Had the Southern congressmen been seated, they would have combined with congressional Democrats to thwart Mr. Stevens's legislation."

"Under the United States Constitution—"

"I am no lawyer, sir, I am a railroad man. If recent events have proven nothing more, they have shown that our revered Constitution is no protection against power; that powerful men like Congressman Stevens can bend that Constitution to their purposes and, while idealists fill the ether with dolorous howls, judgeships and postmaster's positions are filled with Stevens's supporters. Now tell me, young Byrd. How does Alexander Stuart stand on railroad consolidation?"

ON THIS COOL SPRING morning, Eben's future arrived in a rush. Vaguely, Eben had thought he'd one day wed, one day own a house, one day rear a family. When he'd envisioned that prospect, his wife's eyes (he could see nothing but her eyes) were entirely approving and his child adored him.

Eben was tongue-tied while Pauline chattered inconsequentially about forsythia, laurel, and the lilacs, whose scent was as sensual as languorous women are thought to be. "Would that every flower was tended as these." Pauline touched a rhododendron. Its tiny buds were potent as red-tipped bomblets. "Alas, *our* flowers take second place after useful vegetables. As my grandmother oft reminds me"—Pauline imitated Abigail's tone—" 'You cannot eat flowers, dear.' Mr. Barnwell, don't you wish we could?"

At once—although he had never previously imagined himself a flower eater—Eben became a devotee. "Indeed. Indeed I do. I suppose you garden a great deal?"

"If I removed my gloves, Mr. Barnwell, you would remark the coarse hands of a laborer. I am not what I seem."

Eben blurted, "To me, you seem beautiful!"

"Kind Mr. Barnwell. I am a plain girl, with the plainest ambitions."

"I shall be very wealthy," Eben blurted. "Presuming the natural increase of my fortune, I shall, one day, be someone to be reckoned with."

"Are you not presently someone to be reckoned with?" Pauline asked. "I do not mean to smile, sir, but having a fortune is beyond my expectations. Grandfather hopes to persuade General Mahone to buy our crossties. With the General's order in hand, he could reopen our mill. There are plenty of willing hands, negro and white. Nobody's got a cent, except the carpetbaggers . . . Oh, dear!" Her blush would have melted a sterner heart than Eben's.

"Miss Pauline, am I a fool? Am I unaware what some Virginians call us?"

"I . . . It is fearfully rude . . ."

"If I were to call this lilac an orange, would that make it an orange?" Eben gestured at the hotel. "If I were to call the Warm Springs Hotel a shack, would it become one?" As Eben's rhetoric mounted, his gestures expanded. "If I were to call General Mahone a coward, would that officer show the white flag? . . . Miss Byrd, you smile at me!"

"Mr. Barnwell, I cannot help myself. Forgive me! Please, weren't you about to render another comparison?"

He grinned, "As ridiculous as the others?"

"Sir! I did not say so."

"Miss Byrd, are you always so sharp-tongued?"

"No, sir. Present company has whetted my wit."

"Miss Byrd, may I ask you a personal question?"

Pauline pouted. "If you must."

Eben had the bit in his teeth. "Miss Byrd, what are your ambitions? What do you desire?"

"Me? Why—what every girl wants: marriage, children, a home. Love, if I am blessed with it. I do wish to be good. During the War, I wore my knees out praying. Dear Mr. Barnwell, don't be frightened. Young women are not *just* like young men, you know!"

"I didn't mean . . ."

"You are a Christian, sir? Then you must understand my wish to be good. You, sir; don't you hope to be good?"

He took her hand. "If you wish it of me."

She extracted her hand. "You grant me far too much authority, Mr. Barnwell."

"I am no thinker, dear Miss Byrd. The furnishings of my mind are spare and shabby—like a boardinghouse." Eben meant to expand his metaphor by describing the worn stair runner, the overflowing spittoons, and the stink of cooked cabbage, but caught himself in time. He coughed.

"I am no thinker, but I am a doer—like General Mahone. Whatever the hazards, Mahone will combine his railroads."

"If you say so," Pauline said. "In our Virginia experience the bravest, most steadfast human will was inadequate. My grandfather, Samuel, believes we are suffering God's punishment."

"With due respect to Mr. Gatewood, miss, I think a disproportion in capital did more to win the War than any defect in Confederate morality. Capital is a great lever. With enough capital judiciously applied, you can shift the world."

"You would know better than I about that, sir," Pauline said. "I am a plain girl." Her smile, Eben noticed happily, was anything but.

COUSIN MOLLY SET her knitting aside. "Ah, the young people return. Mr. Barnwell seems pleasant enough." Directing her eyes to General Mahone, Molly added, "For a yankee."

"Barnwell is energetic." He turned to Thomas. "How does Stuart stand on negro suffrage?"

"With every patriotic Virginian."

"I believe 'patriotic Virginians' are divided on that issue."

"Sir, I believe, with Mr. Stuart, that one day the negro may rise to equality with the white, but presently his illiteracy and poverty make him unfit to decide his own course, let alone the course of his betters."

Otelia Mahone grimaced. "Isn't this morning too glorious for politics? Don't we have enough of politics at home? Night and day, Billy. Night and day."

Mahone inclined his head. "My apologies, dear."

Sallie drew Duncan from his chair. "Dearest, let us promenade. I wish to be courted afresh."

General Mahone raised a hand. "A moment, Major?"

Cousin Molly persisted, "General, please tell more about Mr. Barnwell. I conclude our Pauline approves of the young man."

Mahone paused for thought. "In '65 the Atlantic, Mississippi & Ohio owned two serviceable locomotives and four cars. Our bridges had been destroyed and much of our track. We paid workers with bacon and corn-meal. There was no money to be had in Virginia and Northern financiers favored railroads they could control. Young Mr. Barnwell promised to sell A.M.&O. bonds. Mr. Barnwell had no credentials, but he was the only applicant for that job and he paid his own expenses." General Mahone steepled his fingers. "In February, our James River bridge was completed. Despite a disappointing wheat harvest, we have met operating expenses, are paying cash wages, and making our interest payments. Mr. Barnwell's sale of A.M.&O. securities has made everything possible."

Cousin Molly smiled. "You have answered me more entirely than I deserved, General. I merely wished to know Mr. Barnwell's antecedents."

A redwing blackbird sang and industrious bees tended the flowers. The sun dipped behind a cloud. "Antecedents? I believe he has none. I believe the girl who marries Eben Barnwell will be well provided for." Mahone abandoned Molly for Duncan. "What do you think of our prospects, Major?"

"General?"

"We've laid forty-three thousand new crossties on the south side."

Gatewood Senior heard his cue. "General—"

But Mahone stilled him with a gesture. "We've reconstructed two turntables, rebuilt seven locomotives, and purchased three miles of new iron rails. Major, I remember you as a resourceful and imaginative officer. I have need of such a man."

Duncan said, "Sir, I am a planter now."

"Sallie," General Mahone inquired, "do you think your husband will be satisfied with that occupation? War was the most dreadful thing I have ever endured and I pray to never know another. But the War elevated us. Major, I am building a railroad and would drive you mercilessly. Northern railroads covet our routes and our traffic." After a moment of Duncan's silence, the General turned to his father. "What was your price per thousand?"

"Why," Samuel stuttered, "they . . . they . . . five hundred dollars, at the railhead. Only five hundred dollars, sir."

"The planter's joys and triumphs are quieter than the soldier's, sir,"

Sallie said. "His is a work of patience and courage too. Some find a terrible beauty in brave men charging enemy guns. But beauty can be well-sown rows of green wheat emerging through warm soil. My husband's honest coat, sir, bears no insignia."

Mahone's smile dismissed Sallie. "Major, you will need to move to Norfolk. At present, Norfolk is our terminus."

CHAPTER 8

ADDRESS FROM THE COLORED CITIZENS
OF VIRGINIA TO THE PEOPLE OF
THE UNITED STATES

Fellow citizens:

The undersigned have been appointed a committee, by a public meeting of the colored citizens of Virginia, held June 5th, 1866, in the First African Baptist Church, Richmond, Va., to lay before you a few considerations touching the present position of the colored population of the southern States generally, and with reference to their claim for equal suffrage in particular.

We do not come before the people of the United States asking an impossibility; we simply ask that a Christian and enlightened people shall concede to us those privileges of full citizenship, which not only are our undisputed right, but are indispensable to that elevation and prosperity of our people, which must be the desire of every patriot.

The legal recognition of these rights of the free colored population, in the past, by State legislation, or even by the Judiciary and Congress of the United States, was wholly inconsistent with the existence of slavery; but now that slavery has been crushed, with the rebellion sprung from it, on what pretexts can disabilities be perpetuated that were imposed only to protect an institution which has, thank God, passed away forever?

It must not be forgotten that it is the general assumption in the South, that the effects of the immortal Emancipation Proclamation of President Lincoln go no further than the emancipation of the negroes then in slavery and cannot touch the slave codes which having passed before the act of secession are presumed to have lost none of their vitality. By these laws, in many of the southern States it is still a crime for colored men to learn or be taught to read, and their children are doomed to ignorance; there is no provision for ensuring the legality of our marriages; we have no right to hold real estate; the public streets and the exercise of our ordinary occupations are forbidden us unless we can produce passes from our employers, or licenses from certain officials. In some States the whole free negro population is legally liable to exile from the place of its birth, for no crime but that of color. We have no means of making or enforcing contracts of any description; we have no right to testify before the courts in any case where a white man is party to the suit; we are taxed without representation, and so far as legal safeguards are concerned, we are defenseless before our enemies. While this is our position as regards our legal status before the State laws, we are more unfortunately situated as regards our late masters. The people of the North have heard little or nothing of the blasphemous and horrible theories formally propounded for the defense and glorification of human slavery, in the press, the pulpit, and legislatures of the southern States; but though they may have forgotten them, let them be assured that these doctrines have by no means faded from the minds of the people of the South; they cling to these delusions and only hug them the closer for their recent defeat. Worse than all, they have returned to their homes with all their old pride and contempt for the negro transformed into bitter hate for the new-made freeman, who aspires to the exercise of his new-found rights, and who has been fighting for the suppression of their rebellion.

Fellow citizens, the performance of a simple act of justice on your part will reverse all this; we ask for no expensive aid from military forces: give us the suffrage and you may rely upon us to secure justice for ourselves and to keep the State forever in the Union.

It is hardly necessary here to refute any of the slanders with which our enemies seek to prove our unfitness for the exercise of the right of suffrage. It is true that many of our people are ignorant, but for that these very men are responsible, and decency should prevent their use of such an argument. But if our people are ignorant, no people were ever more orderly and obedient to the laws; and no people ever displayed greater earnestness in the acquisition of knowledge. If anyone doubts how fast the ignorance, which has hitherto cursed our people, is disappearing 'mid the light of freedom, let him visit the colored schools of this city and neighborhood in which between two and three thousand pupils are being taught. There, in the evening after the labors of the day, hundreds of our adult population, from budding manhood to hoary age, toil with intensest eagerness, to acquire the invaluable arts of reading and writing and the rudimentary branches of knowledge.

In concluding this address, we would now make a last appeal to our fellow citizens of all classes throughout the country. Every Christian and humane man must feel that our demands are just; we have shown you that their concession is to us necessary, and for you expedient. We are Americans. We know no other country. We love the land of our birth and our fathers, we thank God for the glorious prospect before our country, and we believe that if we obey His laws He will yet enthrone her high o'er all the nations of this earth, in glory, wealth, and happiness; but this exalted state can never be reached if injustice, ingratitude, and oppression of the helpless mark the national conduct, treasuring up God's wrath for a day of reckoning. The path of justice is ever the safe and pleasant way, and the words of Eternal Wisdom have declared that the nation shall be established only by righteousness and upholden by mercy. With these reflections we leave our case in the hands of God, and to the consideration of our countrymen.

Signed on behalf of the colored people of Virginia

JUNE 26TH, 1866

Dr. T. Baynes, Chairman of Committee

COMMITTEE:

Lewis Lindsey

J. D. Harris

Jesse Burns

William A. Hodges

ADVISORS:

Rev. Fields Cook, First African Baptist Church, Richmond

Rev. James Whitestone, Catherine Street Baptist Church

Mr. Charles Chepstow, Publisher, The New Nation

CHAPTER 9

THE COCINERO

I wintered with prospectors, Carl Shurtz and a blond man, Matheson, in a dugout by the Wind River. They laid with me in turn, but after they ran out of tobacco, Matheson said I belonged to him only, so Shurtz stabbed him in the heart and put his body out for the Real Dogs. Carl Shurtz's Testament was written in a language I could not read, but when I held it between my hands and prayed to Lord JesuChrist, I dreamed less.

After Carl Shurtz drank the last of his whiskey, he had worse dreams than mine. The creeks were high from melting snow when I left him and walked to Virginia City.

THE TWO MEN WAITED AT THE SMALL TABLE TUCKED INTO THE back corner of the Alamo Saloon. After the westering sun dropped behind Fort Worth's false fronts, before the bartender lit the lamps, the men were nearly invisible. A rawboned brushpopper shied. "Jesus Christ. What the hell you doin' sittin' there, scarin' a man half to death?"

Nelson Story, who had been a vigilante in Montana, opened his big hands and said, "No offense intended."

"You could have been Comanches, sittin' so quiet. Damned Comanches."

"I suppose you would have found out if we was," Bill Petty said.

"The hell with you too," the brushpopper said, and stepped out the back door to relieve himself.

The two men wore leather chaps over tightly woven denim trousers, checked flannel shirts, wide-brimmed hats, and bandannas. Neither carried a revolver, though a ten-gauge Greener leaned against the wall beside them. The shotgun belonged to Bill Petty, who worked for Nelson Story.

Every evening Nelson Story bought a bottle and sometimes they had a drink or two, sometimes not. Sometimes they invited a brushpopper to take a drink with them and they would talk intently and sometimes they'd shake hands with the man. The brushpoppers they hired were tough Confederate veterans and Ben Shillaber, the toughest man they'd hired, had commanded a sharpshooter battalion.

Every Saturday, the brushpoppers rode into Fort Worth to sell beeves they'd gathered that week. Civilization was no thicker on the brushpoppers than on the wary, mean, long-horned cattle they lassoed out of the cholla and mesquite.

This Saturday night began quietly. One man had cleaned out his patch of Texas underbrush and was looking for new territory. Another wondered why the beeves' horns had grown so much longer than before the War. Familiar theories were ventured.

It had been a wet spring and slick ground made dangerous work worse. One brushpopper's bronc had broken a leg. "I'd still be out there if I hadn't run into Ruiz." A luckier man bought him a drink.

A bigmouth proclaimed that the Committee for Reconstruction was ruled by Thad Stevens and the radical Republicans. Since some of the brushpoppers had fought on one side of the War, some on the other, a peacemaker broke in to say that cows in Sedalia, Missouri, had brought six dollars, double what Fort Worth buyers were paying.

"Yeah, *if* you get them there. Sedalia's two hundred miles."

A man wiped beer foam from his mustache. "I heard some damn fool wants to push a herd north to Montana. They say he's bought eight hundred head and aims to buy a thousand."

A cavalry officer jeered. "Let's hope the lunatic keepers catch him first. Why give a thousand cows to the Lakota?"

Conversation turned to indian outrages along the Montana Road. Someone proposed a toast to the transcontinental railroad, whose completion would bring civilization and prosperity to the plains.

That was how it went for an hour or so. When the whores showed up, they were greeted happily, even gallantly, and after a decent interval to renew or make acquaintances, couples went upstairs and, after fifteen minutes or so, the men came back down, their companions following some minutes later.

"Ain't it funny," Nelson Story said, "how a fella takes hours primin' for the act and once he's done, he runs like his pants are on fire?"

"That's our man." Petty nodded at a burly man taking a stool at the bar. "Chisholm says he's the best cocinero he's ever seen."

"Jesus Christ, he's ugly enough. You got anything against niggers?"

Nelson Story approached the burly negro. "Chisholm says you're the best cocinero in Texas."

"I've done that work."

"He says you're handy with a gun."

Ratcliff shrugged. "Ain't nothin' I'm proud of."

"Nelson Story." He offered his hand. "I'm putting an outfit together to trail beeves to Montana."

"I've never been to Montana," Ratcliff said.

CHAPTER 10

LETTER FROM MRS. DUNCAN GATEWOOD TO MRS. SAMUEL GATEWOOD

NORFOLK, VIRGINIA
JULY 29, 1866

Dear Mother,

I pray you will not object to the familiar endearment from one who retains no memory of her natal mother and loves you as a daughter.

Duncan and I are now established in Norfolk. Unlike Richmond and poor Petersburg, Norfolk was spared the War's ravages. I do not believe I have ever seen so many Federal uniforms. It is as if they cannot believe we are utterly conquered and fear they must conquer us again!

We have taken a small house on West Bute Street, which was a fashionable address before its better dwellings were confiscated by our Yankee visitors. The modesty of our home amongst its grand neighbors provides a sunny space in the back for my garden. Norfolk enjoys a warmer climate than our dear mountains: our peas are done bearing and we've enjoyed tomatoes for a week!

Many say that Norfolk is vulgar and there is vulgarity enough. Saloons, gambling halls, and palaces of vice are so numerous, some ladies don't venture out of doors. Having become too familiar with the dreadful wounds men inflict on one other, why should I fear some drunken man, suffering a wound he has inflicted upon himself?

Addiction to drink would be understandable in our poor maimed Confederates, but usually the sot wears a new blue uniform which has never been within cannonshot of battle.

I have news of our old servant, Jesse Burns! After his discharge from the Federal army, Jesse moved to Richmond to learn the printing trade. There has been no recurrence of April's unfortunate disturbances. Negroes claim a score of inoffensive colored men were killed before Federal soldiers stopped the riot our civilian officials did nothing to quell. The Negroes were marching for suffrage.

We do not get out in society—such society as Norfolk has—with Southern patriots in mourning and carpetbaggers and scalawags trumpeting their righteousness.

We do see Eben Barnwell when that whirlwind touches down in this town. Mr. Barnwell speaks of London and New York as if they were just down the street! He conscripts Duncan's telegrapher and fires message salvos to other merchants situated beside similar machines in Philadelphia and Boston. "British Government Bonds at 9%! You must buy all you can! Erie Railroad at 7%! Sell before the speculators dump the issue!" Mr. Barnwell exults about the laying of Mr. Field's telegraph cable under the Atlantic. Barnwell honestly believes commerce and swift communication will cure mankind's every ill. I cannot imagine what all this telegraphing costs.

Though doubtless he is a carpetbagger, Mr. Barnwell is an amusing carpetbagger. He has a wonderfully self-deprecating air and possesses as high regard for our Confederate heroes as Federal ones. Though he reminds me of Mr. Dana's Man Without a Country, if rootlessness discomfits him, he never complains.

Mr. Barnwell is enamored of our Pauline and sings her praises endlessly!

Duncan had supposed he would be doing clerk's work at the A.M.&O. but the General had more confidence in Duncan than we had supposed. and has made my husband his Confidential Agent in Norfolk and Richmond.

Duncan's is a position of discretion and trust and sometimes Duncan acts where General Mahone does not wish to be seen acting. Doubtless General Mahone's confidence is a great honor, but I worry Duncan's own honor may be compromised. There—isn't that a briar patch?

Having consolidated three railroads, General Mahone now covets the Virginia & Tennessee. He intends to create a continuous railroad from the port of Norfolk to Bristol, Tennessee.

Duncan says the Baltimore & Ohio is our fiercest rival. Dear Mother, legislators and railroad men gather in our parlor and talk and talk until I hear locomotives huffing and puffing through my brain!

General Mahone demands absolute fealty from his employees. If I didn't put my foot down, I believe Duncan would work Sundays as readily as those days God has appointed for labor. As it is, he comes home at week's end exhausted and is hard-pressed to rise for Sunday services.

Norfolk's Presbyterian churches outnumber the Baptists! Today, Church Street was melodious with bells. Reverend McCall's sermon was on predestination, a doctrine best left to stronger heads than mine.

As always I prayed for everyone at Stratford. Tell me, how is Aunt Opal? Does she still mourn Pompey?

I do have one more tiny bit of news, dear Mother. If I read the signs aright, in the allotted period of time, you will become a grandmother anew. There! Now I've told it!

Your devoted daughter
(in-law and in-fact),
Sallie

—

CHAPTER 11

COURT DAY

AS THEIR RIG LURCHED AROUND THE TURN, COUSIN MOLLY clutched her bonnet. "Mr. Barnwell, if you smash his carriage, the livery-man will empty your pocketbook. Sir, please rein in!"

When Eben hauled the reins, the livery's best horse snorted, flung his head from side to side, and champed the bit.

"After Augustus Belmont drove his coach-and-four down Fifth Avenue, all us city sports took up driving. I've been taking lessons." Eben Barnwell grinned. "Ain't terrible accomplished, am I?"

Pauline Byrd said, "The horse hasn't been born Opal couldn't drive."

Eben laughed. "Perhaps Aunt Opal will become my instructor. What a yarn that'd make in the city."

"Aunt Opal does need something to distract her. She's been terribly despondent since she came back to Stratford."

Eben patted Pauline's hand. "You are so good."

"Bravo, sir," Cousin Molly said. "Didn't Lord Chesterfield write that flattery must win any woman's heart?"

Eben slumped like an emptying balloon. "I am sorry. I am not acquainted with Lord Chesterfield. My father was an itinerant Vermont peddler."

"Tush, Mr. Barnwell! I merely chided you. I did not denounce you from the pulpit."

Eben reinflated, reassuring Pauline, "But you *are* good. Kind and good."

Eben had visited Stratford thrice that summer. Initially welcomed as General Mahone's confidant, it became apparent young Mr. Barnwell's visits were romantic.

Pauline was of two minds.

After Pauline's father, Catesby, killed himself, her grieving mother followed him into the grave. The daughter prayed until her knees were callused. Surely if she fulfilled her Christian duty to perfection, God would forgive her father for failing his.

Although her religious ardor had cooled, Pauline Byrd was still a serious young woman. Pauline may not have been "humorless," but "solemn" wasn't far off the mark.

Eben Barnwell's ethical distinctions were more sanguine than precise and he seemed to believe commerce's commandments were as binding as the familiar Ten.

However unlikely it seemed, the young man's indifference to moral concerns recommended him to Pauline. Respectable girls from good families sometimes do run away with highwaymen, as many jolly songs attest.

And, though Pauline never could have admitted it to herself, she wasn't indifferent to Mr. Barnwell's money. During the bleakest months of the War the Gatewoods hadn't starved; they always found game, wild greens, and cornmeal to put on the table. But throughout Pauline's childhood, servants had cleaned, cooked, and done every task her mother hadn't wished to do. One could not blame Pauline for thinking that circumstance "natural."

Pauline didn't yearn for bright yellow gold, but she hated to worry about money. Why should she fret when General Mahone's promises were readier than his payments? Why should she lie awake because Grandfather Samuel must beg the First National Bank of Warm Springs for yet another loan?

If one had enough money (so Pauline imagined), money would disappear; getting and spending would become as thoughtless as breathing. And absent the mundane, one could devote oneself to sublimer pursuits. (Even solemn Presbyterian girls entertain such fancies.)

Apparently the two women's minds were chasing the same rabbit, because Cousin Molly now asked Eben about General Mahone's arrears. "Samuel has shipped him twenty thousand crossties, but Samuel has just been paid for the first thousand. Samuel Gatewood has two gangs in the woods and Jack and his workers at the mill. These men must be paid, sir, or they will forsake us for work that does pay."

Eben said, "If Mahone could pay, he would. The harvest was poor, tobacco planters complain about free negro labor, and white workers cannot be found. Mahone's legislative squabbles are dear. I rented this horse and rig for fifty cents a day. The least influential legislator costs fifty times that."

Pauline was shocked by Eben's matter-of-factness. "Sir, do I understand . . ."

"Innocent child, that's how business is done. If the Virginia Legislature lets the Baltimore & Ohio lay track south, they will connect with the railroad Mahone covets. Mahone must match his rivals' legislative expenditures dollar for dollar, legislator by legislator. To do otherwise would be folly."

"If the General doesn't pay his bills, his crosstie supplier must dismiss his workers and shut down his mill," Cousin Molly insisted. "Everyone says the General is an honest man."

"He has that reputation."

"And your reputation, sir?"

"How do you see me, Miss Semple? Am I greedy? Cruel? Might I be someone who'd beat a child until it wept in pain and terror?"

"I do not know your people. I do not know you well enough, sir"— Cousin Molly was uncomfortable at this conversational swerve—"to judge your merits."

"But madam, you have been judging me, and if I am not mistaken I haven't come up to the mark."

THEIR CARRIAGE BREASTED the rise at the county courthouse, where today Ira Hevener was to be tried for the slaying of the negro, Pompey.

Pauline drew a sharp breath, "What are they doing here? They were never here before!"

Hundreds of dark eyes watched the whites' approach. Negroes in Sunday clothing thronged the courthouse lawn and steps.

Court Day, the second Tuesday of the month, was when business was done in Warm Springs; in the courtroom or in lawyers' offices, informally on the courthouse steps or in Mr. Alphin's excellent tavern. There must have been black faces at Court Day before the War, servants and coachmen and such, but Pauline—who had often accompanied her lawyer father here—could not recall them.

Eben tossed his reins to a boy who ignored his implicit command, and the reins fell to the ground. When Eben cried, "Boy! A dime to hold my horse," three boys (including the boy who'd previously rejected the task) dove to retrieve them.

"Once, they wouldn't have demanded a dime," Pauline sighed.

Like St. Paul outside Damascus, some must be driven to their knees to admit that life has utterly changed. Others receive gentler instruction: an unfamiliar inflection in a familiar voice, three negro boys scrabbling after a silver dime.

Cousin Molly said, "Once they had plenty to eat."

Eben jumped down to place Cousin Molly's foot on the mounting block. "Like us, the best will rise on their merits, the unworthy will fail."

"Sir, that is too harsh!"

"Miss Pauline, you hope the world is kind?" Eben spoke plainly. "I was twelve years of age when my father died. Since, Miss Semple, I have no *people*, the county commissioners put me out with dairy farmers for my labors. They did not actually freeze or starve or beat me to death. I suppose that is to their credit."

"Poor boy," Pauline said.

Eben shrugged off her tenderness. "When I ran from that place, I left that half-starved, cowering, runny-nosed boy behind me. I do not recall him today."

The negroes opened a lane to the courthouse doors and some turned their backs.

Pauline shivered. "I begged Grandfather to come."

Cousin Molly said, "Before the War, no man would have dared harm Samuel Gatewood's servant."

"Remember, Cousin Molly, oh, before the War, when Samuel put up our Christmas tree—the first Christmas tree ever in our valley? Remember how Pompey thought the candles would burn the house down and when we looked away for an instant, he'd . . . he'd snuff one out . . . ?" Pauline burst into tears.

Aunt Opal was waiting at the head of the courthouse stairs.

She and Pompey had been an odd couple. How little Pauline knew about people who had made part of her family for so many years. "Aunt Opal, I am so sorry."

Aunt Opal looked past Pauline's shoulder, "That boy Ira Hevener, he shot Pompey. Shot him three times in the chest when one shoot would have killed him. Us coloreds was there that night and seen Ira Hevener take his pistol and shoot Pompey three times, but we can't testify against no white man. Only ones testifyin' be the white boys was with Hevener. They white. Judge white. Jury white. Miss Pauline, what you think gonna happen here?"

"Aunt Opal," Molly said, "Pauline isn't responsible for Ira Hevener's misdeed."

"I expect we gonna find out Ira Hevener ain't responsible neither!"

Pauline's worried gray-green eyes sought Aunt Opal's cool brown ones. "Auntie, all those years we lived together—were we never friends?"

CHAPTER 12

RAINY DAY STEW

14 pounds beef soup bones
5 pounds onions
half cup vinegar
peppercorns
handful of salt

Crack bones. Cover with water in large pot, boil. Take off fire,
skim. Return to fire, boil four hours. Throw away bones, gristle,
and fat. Shred beef some. Pour into greased bread pans. When it
hardens, slice onto biscuits.

THEY STRUCK THE ARKANSAS RIVER AT DUSK AND THE VAN FORDED, but the gap between van and main was too great; the tame steers in the van were clambering up the far bank before the longhorns reached the turbulent river. Though Story's riders hollered and lashed them with rope ends, the longhorns swirled like a bovine merry-go-round and could not be persuaded into the water.

Nelson Story had provided his cocinero a new Bream and Company Dallas cookwagon with a fold-down table, two twenty-five-gallon water casks, and bins for flour, salt, baking powder, coffee, sugar, and white beans. Ratcliff's thick-shouldered, short-coupled gelding, Pedro, was tied behind. Inside, frypans and Dutch ovens hung from the wagon bows, and tin plates, knives, forks, and spoons were contained in deep drawers. Each cowboy stowed his bedding in the rear compartment and when a bedroll wasn't neat enough to suit him, Ratcliff threatened to boot it off, which was when George Dow started calling him "the nigger."

The failure to ford the Arkansas put Ratcliff out of temper. He liked to reach the night's bedground by late afternoon so he'd have time to build his cookfire and start supper before the riders arrived. If he couldn't get his cookwagon through the longhorns, he couldn't get his biscuits made. He had a buffalo tenderloin salted down; how was he to cook it? He yelled, "Unless you boys untangle those damn beeves, you'll be eatin' Rainy Day Stew tonight!"

They didn't untangle them and come dark they bedded the main on the near shore. Nelson Story stayed across the river with the van. When the riders dismounted at Ratcliff's cookfire, the coffee was hot, but the stew was as cold as the biscuits they spread it over.

"Christ almighty," George Dow muttered. "Who said niggers could cook?"

"Who said you knew how to push cows?" Ratcliff snapped.

George had the pinched face and rotten teeth of a man who'd grown up poor. "Wish't I had a hot meal in my belly."

"Well," Petty said, "I got a bellyful of your bitchin'. Shut your yap."

"Why's the nigger sayin' we don't know how to push cows?" George asked. "Might be before this drive is done I'll find out just how much he does know."

"Don't let Mr. Story hear that bullshit," Bill Petty said.

"Believe I'll ride with you tomorrow," Ratcliff said. "I believe I'll show this white boy how to push beeves across a river."

"Mr. Story won't like it," Bill Petty predicted.

"Believe I'll ride with you anyways."

An hour before sunrise Ratcliff banged his triangle and the nighthawks came in. A wrangler brought in the remuda, and Story's hands saddled up in a melee of dust and whoops and bucking horses. Ratcliff threw a saddle on Pedro.

A couple hands swam their horses across the Arkansas, roped some leader steers, and after they were dragged into the water, the van swam back to the shore they'd left yesterday.

They withdrew both main and van a quarter mile behind a rise where the critters couldn't see or smell the river and let them graze for twenty minutes. Then Nelson Story stood in his stirrups and waved his hat and all hell broke loose: pistol shots, popping rope ends, the shrill Confederate yip-yip-yip. The wide-eyed van thundered toward the river, and the main—nine hundred panicked Texas Longhorns—followed close on their heels.

If the van swam the river, the main would follow. But should the main pause for second thoughts at the water's edge the merry-go-round of beeves would open for business. Van, riders, main, riders stretched out at full gallop.

The longhorns weren't fifty feet behind Ratcliff and he put the spurs to Pedro. The beeves gathered momentum coming down the bank and as Ratcliff and Pedro hit the water, a Niagara of beeves tumbled in behind them.

Heads and broad horns out of the water, they swam mightily, eyes bulging, bawling in terror.

Eight or ten clambered onto a sandbar, Ratcliff swam Pedro to bump them off, and a longhorn charged Pedro, who couldn't duck, since the longhorn had four feet on the sandbar and Pedro was swimming. The horn hooked Pedro behind his rib cage and jerked him up and Ratcliff went into the water.

Ratcliff was eye level with swimming longhorns. Their six-foot horns glistened with muddy water and clacked like castanets. The river water tasted like gritty coffee grounds. His hat was gone; when his boots filled, he kicked them off.

He blew out his breath and sank under a steer's horns, and when he surfaced the steer's buttocks were churning past, so Ratcliff grabbed the tail. When the steer felt the drag, he swam harder—so hard he set his front hooves on another's back like he meant to climb over him. Ratcliff puked muddy water.

When Ratcliff's longhorn got his feet on solid ground, he thought to spin and hook his uninvited passenger, but Nelson Story galloped up and offered Ratcliff a stirrup.

When they were clear, Story said, "If they'll fit, I've a spare pair of boots."

Ratcliff said, "That'll be all right."

Nelson Story said, "I got twenty-five cowboys. You get paid twice their wages account of you're the cocinero. If there was something you had to prove, I suppose you proved it. Now on, you'll stay with the cookwagon."

A hundred yards downstream, Pedro stood shivering. Blood and muddy water pooled under his midsection.

"Pedro was a good horse," Ratcliff said. "I'll thank you for the loan of your pistol."

CHAPTER 13

THE LOYAL LEAGUE

Jesse Burns and Charles Chepstow were in the third pew of Richmond's First African Baptist Church as its deacons decided Brother Maxwell's fate. Charles Chepstow checked his watch and sighed.

"You were drunk," the Reverend Fields Cook said.

The reverend and the deacons were in the front pew, facing the miscreant standing awkwardly before them. "Master—"

" 'Brother,' " Reverend Cook corrected him.

"Brother Cook, I worked on that d . . . darn track gang four days and every day I ask where is my pay and Captain say pay ain't until Friday, so I say then I start workin' on Friday. That's fair. Day's work, day's pay. That's fair. Captain say there's plenty niggers in Richmond and he don't have to hire no saucy one, and he pay me for three days but not the fourth day, which it was noon already, two dollars and a silver quarter, so I goes to the Southside Cafe."

"Brother Maxwell, the Southside Cafe is not a respectable establishment. Did you gamble?"

Brother Maxwell shook his head. "No, sir."

"You did drink."

"Sir, ever since I left Edgeworth Plantation I look for work and I sleep on the streets. When I finds work they don't pay me one day and they don't pay me the next day or day after that. And when I ask them for my money, they tell me they got no more work for me 'cause I 'saucy.' "

Before the War the First African's congregation had been free blacks; some modestly prosperous. Freedmen flooding into Richmond tripled the colored population and strained Christian charity. Richmond's tobacco factories had resumed production but only hired white males. Some negroes worked on the railroad track gangs, but most freedmen found no work and slept, like Brother Maxwell, in the streets.

"You have attended First African Baptist awaiting your letter of transfer from the Farmville congregation."

"Back home, I was never no trouble. I'm a good nigger. I come to Richmond to make my way, but they ain't no work in Richmond and what work they is, Richmond niggers got it. I say—"

"And I say you were drunk in public and your actions disgraced the congregation to which you sought admittance. Brothers, how say you?"

Six deacons of the First African Baptist Church murmured assent.

Reverend Cook stood. "Brother Maxwell, you are expelled from the congregation. Upon genuine repentance and six months' good conduct, you may apply for readmission."

"I been comin' every Sunday. Been comin' to Sunday school too."

"I am sorry, Brother Maxwell. But we negroes are scorned by our former masters and your actions justify their scorn."

With many a supplicating backward glance, the ragged young man made his way down the broad center aisle, and though he paused at the door for a reprieve, when none came, he closed it quietly behind him.

"We'd have made a soldier out of that boy," Jesse whispered to Chepstow. "Worse boys than him made their mark."

Chepstow closed his watch with an audible snap.

Reverend Cook addressed his deacons. "Brothers, congregational business is concluded, but I trust you will stay for the Loyal League meeting. Brother Chepstow and Brother Burns have brought us a report from Philadelphia."

Charles Chepstow's lank black hair needed trimming and his lips were set in a prim line. He bustled to the altar to unwrap a long canvas parcel containing the Loyal League symbols. He laid a gavel and a rolled-up United States Constitution beside the pulpit Bible and carefully placed a ballot box on the other side. He jerked a cavalry saber from its scabbard and pronounced, "Union steel! Down with the traitors, up with the star!" Reverend Cook flinched from Chepstow's glittering blade. Chepstow laid the sword reverently beside the ballot box and intoned, "The negro must have his franchise."

This sentiment produced perfunctory amens as older deacons got up to leave. Before the War, a Richmond free black's prosperity, and sometimes his life, depended on the patronage of powerful whites; patronage that insisted upon the freed black's scrubbed, unwavering, asexual "respectability." For many "respectable" blacks, negro emancipation challenged a lifetime's provident habits.

Deacon Hanley's livery business depended on white custom. In 1860, when Deacon Johnson's boy was picked up by the Richmond police for curfew violation, Johnson's white patron saved the boy ten lashes. Deacon McIlwaine disapproved, on principle, of assertiveness by colored men. "Dangerous foolishness," he muttered.

"Dangerous?" Chepstow's eyes flashed. "Certainly it's dangerous. No week goes by I don't receive a death threat. I spurn them. I stamp them under my feet." As he spoke, Chepstow mimed a death threat received, opened, scanned with indignation, crumpled, and trampled. "What are threats to the Loyal League?"

Mr. Chepstow's dramatic presentation tempted two more deacons to follow their elders, but Reverend Cook's frown fixed them in their seats.

The twenty who stayed were younger men, and most, like Reverend Cook, had been free before the war. Some, like Deacon Lewis Lindsey, had political aspirations.

Reverend Cook said, "We are honored tonight to welcome two authors of that famous address from the colored citizens of Virginia which Mr. Stevens and our Republican friends have used to such good effect in Congress. Brother Charles Chepstow and Brother Burns are returned from the Philadelphia convention of Northern Republicans and Southern Unionists. Brothers, let us welcome them with prayer." Lowering his head, the reverend continued, "Lord, bless our deliberations this night. Bless those who dare to speak up for the right. We pray you will make us citizens as surely as you have set us free."

"Amen, Reverend Cook. Amen to that." Jesse's suit had been tailored for a smaller man, but it was brushed and his shoes were polished. "Deacons, I b'lieve that being *inside* Richmond looking out is better than being *outside* Richmond looking in. 'Specially if you're being shot at by Johnnies."

Chepstow overrode the deacon's chuckles. "First, Sergeant Burns fought with the United States Colored Troops. His fight continues at my side. Burns is a devil." Chepstow smiled indulgently. "A printer's devil, not a Baptist devil."

Nobody chuckled and Cook's "Amen" was halfhearted.

"Welcome to First African, Brother Burns. Will we see you on Sunday?"

"If I can get here."

"You do honor the Sabbath?"

"Yes, sir; when I'm able to. Mr. Chepstow and me, we print the *New Nation*. It's the only Republican newspaper in Virginia. Until the *New Nation* reported it, Richmond police were whipping blacks for being 'uppity.' The *Richmond Whig* didn't report these whippings. They never saw them or, perhaps, they thought whipping 'uppity' negroes was acceptable. The *Richmond Examiner* didn't have space to report such a trivial affair—police whipping blameless, respectable free citizens. No, sir. And the *Richmond Dispatch* was too busy worrying about the 'negro criminal element' and the possibility that somewhere, someday—they are never clear how or where—a respectable white woman might be 'insulted' by a negro.

"The *Richmond Examiner* says I'm a 'fancy man.' Mr. Chepstow, he's a 'yankee carpetbagger,' and that's the kindest thing they say about him. Yes, Reverend. You'll see me in church Sunday—after the *New Nation* is printed!"

"Brother Burns," Deacon Lindsey said, "you talk most as good as our preacher. Maybe you after his job!"

Reverend Cook smiled. "I understand Mr. Burns hopes to be a delegate to Virginia's Constitutional Convention, where his oratorical abilities will be tested."

Deacon Lindsey's skin was so taut, the bones that made up his skull were visible. "Perhaps one of you will tell me somethin'. I been wonderin'. I been wonderin' why the Virginia Assembly is ex-rebs. They was traitors and rebels once and they still is. I wonderin' why negroes and white Republicans like Brother Chepstow ain't sittin' in the Virginia Assembly."

"A profound question, sir." Chepstow unlipped his teeth. "A profound question. Traitors cling to power because we have not united with Mr. Stevens and our congressional allies to purge them. But purge them we shall."

"Brothers." Reverend Cook returned them to the business at hand. "Please tell us about the Philadelphia Convention. Did Frederick Douglass attend?"

Placing each word as carefully as a mason places capstones, Mr. Chepstow said, "Wonderful. Unparalleled. Stupendous. For five glorious days Northern and Southern patriots debated the principles of our Republican Party!"

"Mr. Burns, how many negroes were there?"

"There were Pennsylvania and Ohio negroes and a few from Georgia. Frederick Douglass entered the hall arm in arm with Mr. Theodore Tilton, who is a white man.

"I cannot say that every white delegate applauded Mr. Tilton, nor that they took my hand as readily as they would have taken a white's, but they did vote for negro suffrage, and that's enough for me. We cannot ask more from whites who learned negro hatred at their mother's breast.

"Mr. Douglass's eyes are sharp and penetrating. He has a blacksmith's handclasp." When Jesse shook his fingers as if they'd been squeezed, he drew laughter.

Charles Chepstow recaptured the floor with an account of their audience with Thaddeus Stevens . . .

———

STEVENS'S HOTEL ROOM reeked of ointments. Asafetida leaves roiled in an open pot atop a roaring coal stove. A handsome mulatto woman admitted them to the aged, sickly ruin who was the most powerful man in America.

Stevens's black wig had been chosen with indifference to appearance and was too ugly to be amusing. His clubfoot rested on his footstool like a challenge.

"Ah, Mr. Chepstow, we meet again. And you, sir? You are?"

Jesse swallowed a hard lump in his throat. "Jesse Burns, sir. I work for Mr. Chepstow."

Chepstow said, "You look well, Congressman."

Stevens's grin was ghastly, "Chepstow, it is not my *appearance* but my *disappearance* that troubles me."

"Is there anything I can get for you, Mr. Stevens?" Jesse asked.

"Ten more years of life. I believe that in ten more years I would see the colored race enjoying full citizenship."

"Thad, you'll outlive us all," Chepstow said.

"Mr. Chepstow, I haven't time for weary commonplaces. Tell me: will the Virginia Legislature ratify the Fourteenth Amendment?"

"They will not. The Old Masters are too proud."

Stevens lowered hard brows. "Are they, then!"

"Sir," Jesse began, diffidently, "if I might speak . . ."

Stevens's voice softened. "Speak, man."

"Sir, I was a slave on Stratford Plantation and until the War I thought I'd be a slave all my days. Then Master Lincoln, he made the War and set us free. I was a sergeant with the United States Colored Troops and I fought my old masters. They drew my blood with the bullwhip and I drew their blood with my Springfield. I reckon I know the Old Masters as well as anyone.

"One of my masters, Uther Botkin, was fond of quoting Mr. Jefferson: 'The man who keeps a slave has a wolf by the tail.' Mr. Stevens, sir, imagine yourself in Virginia, dependent on the labor of slaves for your prosperity and your family's happiness. What might you have done to preserve that wicked, un-Christian, but by your understanding necessary institution? Slavery, sir, was a great evil, but not all slave owners are wicked men."

"Mr. Burns, your distinction is too subtle. If we do not prevent them from doing so, your Old Masters will reenslave you. Surely you understand that."

Jesse considered for a long time. "As a Christian, I must think better of them than that."

———

CHAPTER 14

SON-OF-A-BITCH STEW

veal heart	*brains*
tongue	*kidney suet*
sweetbreads	*flour*
kidneys	*salt*
marrowgut	*pepper*
liver	

Be on hand with a bucket when the calf is slaughtered to cut out the organs. Discard connective tissue and soak in cold salt water. Cut up the meat and render suet. Flour and fry, one piece at a time. The heart will require longer cooking and should be put in first, then the tongue; the brains go in last. Use only a pound or two of liver. Add salt and pepper and an inch of water. Cover and cook for several hours.

DAWN WAS A RED LINE ON THE HORIZON WHEN NELSON STORY'S crew worked the buck out of their cow ponies. Before the sun had much heat, the herd had walked three miles. Some mornings steam rose off the horses, other mornings were milder.

A Mormon train of wagons and handcarts preceded them five miles ahead and a forty-wagon train kept the same distance behind. Sometimes horsemen passed through the herd and Story's hands kept a sharp eye that a beef or two didn't pass with them.

The cookwagon kept to the long ridges above where the ravines formed. Twice, when wagon ruts petered out over rock, Ratcliff mistook the trail and lurched down and up gullies and wobbled across sharp-banked dry creekbeds until he regained it.

Sometime around three o'clock Benjamin Shillaber, the scout, rode in to confab with Story. After the two chose that night's bedground, Shillaber saddled a fresh horse and Ratcliff followed with his wagon. The scout circled the bedground once and rode out. Shillaber never came in to eat until the nighthawks were on duty and he always ate his dinner silently, back to the fire.

After Ratcliff unhitched and watered his mules, he hauled water, started his fire, and mixed biscuit dough. Sometimes, while he waited for his coffee water to boil, he thought about the places he had been and the women he'd been with.

So many trains had traveled the Oregon Trail that year, the graze was poor and sometimes Shillaber found a waterless bedground with better grass.

By now the beeves were accustomed to the drive and marched north without prodding. They splashed nonchalantly across summer-shallow rivers.

Six weeks and three hundred miles north of Fort Worth, Nelson Story rode off to Fort Leavenworth for supplies.

Bill Petty had been a good segundo but was fretful in Story's absence. Bill fretted about the remuda, the pace they were traveling, even, one evening, the cocinero.

"Ratcliff," he remarked, "I believe my mother made better biscuits."

Ratcliff smiled. "Good thing your mama's ridin' with us, then," he said. "'Cause any biscuits you get tomorrow, she'll bake."

"I didn't mean nothin'," Petty said.

"Day without biscuits improve your manners," Ratcliff replied.

A delegation from the Mormon train came to buy beeves. Bill Petty would sell them for thirty dollars.

The Mormon negotiator had a skimpy beard. "Cattle were eight dollars in St. Louis."

"They'll fetch a hundred at Virginia City."

"First you got to get them there," the Mormon said.

Nelson Story rejoined them at the South Platte crossing and pried open a narrow wooden case. "Brand-new Remingtons, boys. One for every man."

When Ratcliff took a rifle, George Dow said, "Oh, my. Darkie with a rifle. What has this sorry world come to?"

"I might need to do some fool-killin'," Ratcliff said, sighting along the barrel.

"How the hell you work this thing?" Petty asked.

Story cocked the hammer, thumbed open the breechblock, inserted a brass cartridge, and closed the breech. He lowered the adjustable rear sights. "If they're comin' at you, fixed sights will do." He handed the Remington to Shillaber.

The muzzle loaders they'd carried during the War could be loaded and fired three times a minute.

George Dow set out a buffalo skull, a fibula (ox? buffalo?), a broken cinch buckle, two medicine bottles, and a green biscuit box.

Shillaber fired and the cinch buckle jumped in the air, a second shot set it spinning, the third shot disintegrated it.

Impatient men snatched up their new rifles. Flames spat from their muzzles—twelve, fifteen, seventeen times a minute—the targets disappearing in dirt spouts until the herdsman galloped up. "Quit your damn foolishness, less'n you want to chase a stampede!"

Next morning when they mounted, empty brass cartridges glistened under their horses' hooves like gold nuggets.

Although it was late in the season, Story couldn't push his herd through the Mormon train, so they loafed along, taking three days to cover two days' ground.

The trail kept to the west bank of the North Platte and every bedground was well watered. Some earlier pilgrims hadn't bothered to dig cat holes and on moonless nights a cowboy might step into a mess and blister the air cursing immigrants: unbelievers and Brigham Young's followers alike.

Five miles south of Fort Laramie they quit the trail for a dry camp on the bluffs above the river and the cattle disappeared in big bluestem grass that had previously known only antelope, mule deer, and buffalo.

Since they were in indian country now, Story left a strong crew with the herd.

Luckier men passed through the makeshift village outside the fort: log cabins, robe traders' sheds, two dozen scruffy indian lodges.

"They ain't no stockade 'round this fort," George Dow remarked.

"'Spose they don't figure to need one."

Frame and stone buildings faced Fort Laramie's parade ground.

The boardwalks were thronged with traders, soldiers, immigrants, dark-clad Mormons, and indians whose traditional buckskins were augmented by white man's discards.

Story told the men to have a drink at the post sutler's. "Ratcliff, keep 'em out of trouble while I have a word with the boss soldier."

Inside the two-story white clapboard bachelor officers' quarters and post headquarters, Colonel Palmer, Fort Laramie's commandant, was writing reports. At a pigeonhole desk beside a silent telegraph apparatus, Palmer's orderly transcribed the letter book.

Story said he planned to take a herd up the Montana Road; what about indians?

The Colonel rubbed his eyes. "The Crows will steal cattle if they can, though they'd rather steal your horses."

"I hear the Lakota are on the warpath."

The Colonel's face tightened. "In June, at this fort, Blue Horse and Big Mouth and Swift Bear signed Commissioner Taylor's treaty. Even Spotted Tail of the Brulé signed it."

"I take it some didn't."

The Colonel shrugged. "Malcontents, troublemakers. A few hundred of Red Cloud's Bad Faces. Have you ever known a dozen indians to agree about anything?"

"So me and my beeves got no worries?"

"Sixty miles to the north, Fort Reno is garrisoned by two companies, Colonel Carrington makes good progress building Fort Phil Kearny on the Little Piney, and Fort C. F. Smith protects the Bighorn crossing. The Montana Road is not without hazards but is negotiable."

"That telegraph work?"

"Indians get bored or drunk and pull down the wires."

"Uh-huh."

"Sir, last year the Pony Express was our fastest communication." The Colonel eyed the silent telegraph proudly. "The Union Pacific has reached Omaha. Had you postponed your journey twelve months, you might have come by railroad."

"That's a comfort."

"Last week, my wife's garden frosted. Winter snows are a worse hazard to travelers than the Lakota. We don't want another Donner affair."

"I sure as hell hope not. I'd hate to cut a steak off my boys. They're tough as whang leather."

"Sir, I do not appreciate your humor."

"I don't expect you'd appreciate sending some soldiers with us either?"

AT THE SUTLER'S Ratcliff bought flour and lard, onions, sugar, and apples while Story's riders lined the wide wooden counter where the sutler filled their glasses with brandy which was the worst Ratcliff'd ever tasted.

It was a week shy of army payday, and only traders were drinking tonight. One gap-toothed trader introduced them to Lakota customs. "First they cut off your hair, then they cut off your pecker, and afterwards, if they're feelin' kindly, they'll kill you."

In response to the brandy Ratcliff bought him, the trader described the failed treaty conference. "That Red Cloud jumped up like he'd set on a bobcat. I never seen no indian so damned mad. He came here to sign a peace treaty which—Red Cloud thought—was gonna close the Montana Road, and whilst he's jawin' with the peace commissioners, Colonel

Carrington comes marchin' in with seven hundred men. Never seen nothin' like it. Red Cloud's a Shirt Wearer—there's four Wicasas amongst the Lakota and they are *the* big men. That stiff-necked Carrington's got orders to march up the Montana Road through Red Cloud's prime hunting ground, and he's supposed to build forts there. Red Cloud was so mad I thought he was gonna cut Carrington's throat. When Red Cloud stalked out, all the big chiefs went with him."

After another brandy, the trader opined, "Safe? *Safe?* Jesus H. God-almighty Christ, no, it ain't safe. Ain't been one wagon train go north all summer didn't get hit, and some of the smaller ones got kilt altogether: man, woman, and child."

At the trader's elbow, Ben Shillaber downed brandy like a thirsty man.

"Mormons headin' for Salt Lake, indians don't trouble them 'cept they'll steal a milk cow or a mule, and they don't pester folks much on the Oregon Trail 'cept for beggin' and petty thievery. But them who goes to Montana through Red Cloud's country might die tryin'."

The trader leaned to Shillaber confidentially. "Can't say I blame 'em. White men ain't no different than redskins. Bobby Lee pestered General Grant and pestered General Grant until General Grant got fed up and laid him low."

Shillaber pushed his hat on the back of his head. Though eight empty glasses lined the plank bar before him, Shillaber's speech was precise. "Sir, I had the honor of serving under Pettigrew. Are you insulting General Robert Lee?"

"My name's Meredeth, Bill Meredeth. I was talkin' about indians. Didn't mean to get in no discussion of the War. That's over. We got to put that behind us."

Shillaber's dark eyes were hot. "Sir, were you a gentleman, I'd seek satisfaction."

Meredeth outweighed Shillaber and had the reach, but when he said, "You can have any damn satisfaction you damn well want," Shillaber smiled gratefully.

A minute later, the two men were circling like fighting cocks. Shillaber's scarf was wrapped around his leading left arm. He held an

Arkansas toothpick in his right. The trader jabbed the air with a bone-handled buffalo skinner.

Shillaber's faint otherworldly smile meant murder.

When Ratcliff fired into the plank ceiling, dust and dirt fell onto men's hair and into their eyes. Their ears rang. "That's enough," Ratcliff said. "Put away your pigsticker, Mr. Shillaber. Mr. Story thinks you are one hell of a scout and I 'spose you are. Sutler, give this trader a brandy." With his left hand, Ratcliff slid a two-bit piece down the bar.

Next morning when Shillaber returned his cup to Ratcliff's wash-board, he murmured, "Day after this drive is finished, we'll have a little chat."

For four days they trailed along the North Platte until they forded for the last time at Sage Creek. The Oregon Trail's broad thoroughfare marched west toward South Pass; the shallow ruts forking north were the Montana Road.

Five miles along, Sage Creek petered out and the soil became granular with alkali patches. Grama grass gave way to bristly, purple sagebrush. The sky seemed the eye of a remote God and the western mountains the rim of the world. Fresh snow adorned the peaks.

Nelson Story assigned extra riders to the remuda and told Shillaber to pick another man to scout with him. Shillaber said, "The darkie."

"Nope. Ratcliff's the cocinero."

Shillaber shrugged and picked George Dow.

Story rode alongside the cookwagon. "Ratcliff, I don't want you gettin' ahead of the herd anymore. "

"How can I set up supper if I don't get to the bedground first?"

"You'll manage."

"I hope you're particular fond of Rainy Day Stew," Ratcliff said.

The beeves' plodding hooves stirred alkali into dust and the riders tied handkerchiefs over their faces like road agents.

There were four graves, simple, low mounds, at Dry Fork Creek. Those who'd survived that attack—or perhaps found the slaughtered party—hadn't fashioned markers.

The streambed just produced enough seepage for the horses. The men drank from Ratcliff's barrels and ate Rainy Day Stew. Shillaber shot an antelope and Ratcliff hung the gutted animal from his wagon bows.

Five nighthawks circled the herd, three more the remuda. Distant wolves howled and near wolves called back to them. The nighthawks sang to the cattle. They sang "Old Brown Rosie" and "Liquor in the Jar" and "Lorena." No telling what the wolves were singing.

AT NOON THE NEXT DAY, Shillaber came in from his scout and dismounted for a plate of cold beans. "We're alone on the road," he said. "If there are other trains ahead, they are far ahead. I found water. More graves."

"How's the graze? "

"Fine along the stream banks."

Springs dribbled into a dry streambed that disappeared among brush-covered hillocks. The herd spread out and as the sun dropped behind the Bighorns, Story's crew rode among the beeves two by two, rifles over their saddlebows. At midnight when the first watch came in, Ratcliff had coffee and dried apple pie waiting.

Tom Thompson said, "Three fresh graves on yonder hogback."

"Four more by the spring."

A wolf lifted its howl and others took it up.

George Dow warmed his hands with his tin cup of coffee. "I hate that damn sound. Damned if I won't kill ary wolf I see."

"Tom, who was in the graves?"

"Dearborn, Campbell, Will Bothwell, another I disremember."

"I found three graves beside the creek," Bill Petty said. "They wasn't buried deep enough, so wolves dug 'em up. I think one was a kid, but couldn't tell for certain. Wolves ate everything but his head."

"You bury him again?" Ratcliff asked.

"I got to thinking, if I was a Lakota lurkin' out in the sagebrush, how happy I'd be if Bill Petty dismounted and started to digging. Why, I could slip up right close and might be I'd shoot an arrow clean through old Bill. That kid's already been buried onct. First buryin's what counts."

Tommy Thompson said, "Sergeant back at Fort Laramie said indian can shoot four arrows before his first one hits you. You suppose he was yarnin'?"

"How many graves that make?" George Dow asked.

Nelson Story looked up from his coffee. "Add the three I found, makes thirteen. Jesus Christ. Boys, there might be unfriendly indians in these parts. That make anybody want to piss his pants? No? Good. Think I'll roll up in my bedroll. I'd hate to lose shut-eye on what might be my last night on earth."

Noon the next day, they forded Stinking Water Creek. Behind them, Pumpkin Butte reared above the alkali flats, floating on its shimmering base like it might skitter away.

Powder River was a shallow muddy-white stream, shaded by alders and cottonwoods. Ratcliff knelt and dunked his head underwater. "Pfffahhh!"

Bill Petty pulled the boots off soft, shockingly white feet and waded in.

Nelson Story swiveled in his saddle. "Company's comin'."

A rickety wagon rolled down the rise, hesitated, and came on. When his skinny horses smelled water, the teamster, who wore a buffalo coat and black stovepipe, braced against his dashboard to hold them to a walk. A small head poked out of the wagon but withdrew.

"How-do," Story said.

With his horses' heads immersed in the river, the wagon wasn't going any farther. "Bonjour. You have so many cows."

"You're a Frenchy."

"I am Pommerlau. Pommerlau and my son, Joseph," he indicated the closed canopy. "We progress to Fort Kearny."

"Join up with us. No sense traveling alone."

"Pommerlau know the Lakota many years. Pommerlau treat them fair. They not harm him, I think."

"We've twenty-five riders and twenty-five new Remingtons. You'd be welcome . . ."

"Oh, I think we go by ourselves, sir. I wish you *bon chance*, yes?"

He lashed his team to bring them out of the river and the rickety contraption was soon lost to sight.

"Might be he had a daughter in there 'stead of a son," Bill Petty had overheard the tail end of the conversation. "Might have thought she wasn't safe with us hardcases."

"Likely his wagon was full of indian whiskey," Story said.

Ratcliff fried antelope steaks with the onions he'd bought at Fort Laramie.

The night was brilliant cold and the full moon white and bland, and the brilliance made the cattle restless. The nighthawks' songs promised there wasn't a thing for a cow to worry about.

The nighthawks kept one eye on the cattle, one on the sagebrush hills. Sometimes the brush seemed to move and sometimes a silhouette might have been a man crouched low, and when a rider saw something that spooked him, he'd bring a pal for a look-see, but it always was just a shadow or a patch of sagebrush.

A half hour before sunup, Tommy Thompson could smell Ratcliff's biscuits baking. Bill Petty gestured and the pair rode out in wide arcs coming at a suspicious shadow from east and west, slow, as if they just happened to be coming that way. Each had his Remington across his saddle and each had his thumb on his hammer and when the warrior rose up and his bow twanged and the arrow *whupped* into Bill Petty's shoulder, Bill jerked off a shot that startled the warrior, so his second arrow went wide and Tommy Thompson fired and the warrior fell and the cattle were clambering to their feet bawling and a dozen indians rode over the ridgetop in full cry, which was more than enough for the beeves, who stampeded, and Ratcliff screamed, "God Damn it to hell!" when the frantic animals overran his campfire and trampled his biscuits into the coals and if Ratcliff hadn't dived under the cookwagon might have flattened him too.

The indians made plenty of racket and the nighthawks' Remingtons sparked, but the indians were hunkered down on their horses' necks among running longhorns, so a man was as likely to shoot a cow as a man. Nelson Story yelled to guard the remuda and men surrounded the horses as dust settled where their cows had been.

Ratcliff's coffeepot was trampled into tinplate and his Dutch oven was in two pieces. The antelope ham had been breaded in cowshit and his stewpot was lost. "Sons of bitches!" he howled. "Oh, you sons of bitches!"

Story's men regathered what cattle they could. Bill Petty drank a cup of whiskey before Ratcliff cut the arrowhead off and pulled the shaft back through the segundo's shoulder. Jack Blascomb had an arrow in his upper thigh, but the point was lodged in bone and Ratcliff didn't want to dig for it. He cut the shaft off and bandaged the wound.

By eight o'clock, they'd finished their tally and were eating cornbread, sowbelly, and beans. Nelson Story said, "They got thirty head. Jackson, Petty, Thompson, and Ratcliff stay with the herd: everybody else saddle a fresh mount."

Ratcliff roped a horse anyway. "They busted my Dutch oven."

Tracks beelined for Pumpkin Butte. Bright sun, warm day, purple sagebrush, and chalky alkali.

"What if we're riding into a thousand indians?"

"Be a thousand sorry indians," Nelson Story snapped. "Unless they got cash for my beeves."

At noon they watered their horses at a brackish spring cows had muddied not long before. They drank from canteens and ate Ratcliff's cornbread.

"Wonder what Petty and the boys are eatin'," George Dow said. "Might be they're rootin' through the nigger's stores."

Ratcliff smiled. "They're cowboys, so naturally they're dumb. Even a cowboy ain't *that* dumb."

The riders smelled the woodsmoke before they saw it. Smoke haze shimmered above a rise and at Story's gesture they dismounted. Two stayed as horse holders while the others climbed through bristly sagebrush, stooped low, moving in silent dashes. They belly-crawled the last fifty yards to the top.

A dozen Lakota sat around the fire, eating one of Nelson Story's beeves, reliving the excitement of the night before. They wore hunting garb, not the elaborate finery of a war party, and likely had stumbled on the herd by accident. The indian perched cross-legged on the partially skinned beef was doing most of the talking.

The talker was gesturing with a marrow bone and Ratcliff drew a bead on his chest. When Nelson Story fired, Ratcliff's man flipped backward as if he'd been clubbed with a singletree.

Indians scattered and dove for cover, but the Remingtons barked and dirt spouted and men fell and one warrior charged until bullets punched his chest and lifeblood stained his vest. His bow dropped and he fell on his face in the alkali.

When the firing stopped, the silence rang in Ratcliff's ears. He swallowed.

Nelson Story dispatched the wounded. One dying man's heels drummed, another man voided his bowels.

"I'd hoped I was quit of this work," Shillaber said.

"Yes," Ratcliff said.

"You were a soldier."

"Edward Ratcliff, Sergeant Major, 38th United States Colored Troops."

"Top, there were three reasons the Federals whipped us: Abe Lincoln, Jesus Christ, and you niggers."

Ratcliff took that as an apology.

Skinning knife in hand, George Dow bent over the warrior who'd rushed them. Dow pulled back the scalp lock, stabbed a gap into the flesh of the forehead, pushed his fingers between skin and skull, and jerked the scalp free. He hung it from his belt.

Through the afternoon they chivvied the cattle and indian ponies toward the herd. One calf had a broken leg, so Ratcliff shot it and saved its organs for Son-of-a-Bitch Stew.

The Frenchy's camp was upstream from their bedground. His scalped skull gleamed like a bloody bowl. Iron wheel rims and wagon bows remained of his burned wagon, and his horses lay dead in their traces.

"Frenchy wasn't lyin' about him bein' a boy," Ratcliff said.

Tommy Thompson said, "Was a boy. Poor kid was too young to use it for anything but pissin'."

They dug graves deep enough so wolves wouldn't dig them up.

The next day they hit Fort Reno, which was a low stockade, a few tents, and a cemetery. Its captain wondered if anybody at Fort Laramie had mentioned reinforcements. They left Bill Petty and Jack Blascomb there with the army surgeon.

In the next three days they found graves at Soldier Creek and Crazy Woman Creek. It snowed and the earth was dusted white.

Fort Phil Kearny's seventeen acres were inside a pole stockade. Blanket indians came begging until they saw the scalp dangling from George Dow's belt.

George laughed. "Probably a friend of theirs."

"They look like they wouldn't mind eatin' some hundred-dollar beeves," Story said. "You fellows stay with the herd. Ratcliff, come with me."

Thirty cavalry horses stood ready-saddled just inside the gate. Though the horse brasses were polished, the animals were gaunt and dispirited.

"You fellows expecting trouble?" Story asked.

"Wouldn't be the first time." A corporal pointed at a steep, bare hill to the south. "Signalmen on Pilot Knob tell us what redskins are doin'." He pointed north. "Redskins on Lodge Trail Ridge signal them what we's doin'. Ain't a louse stirs don't somebody squeal on him."

Headquarters was an unpainted, single-story building facing a wide gravel walk where two shirtless soldiers were adzing a pine log into a flagpole. From a lookout platform atop headquarters, a sentry kept his spyglass trained on Lodge Trail Ridge.

"Get on down to the sutler's," Story told Ratcliff. "See what you can find out."

The pine steps Story mounted were so new-sawn they still oozed pitch. Like the horses at the gate, the sentry was polished but tired. "Colonel's inside doin' paperwork," he said. "Colonel Carrington never met no paper he couldn't whup."

The small man at the big desk had a beard, high forehead, and colonel's shoulder boards.

"Name's Story," Nelson said. "I come from Texas."

The Colonel's pen scratched. He dipped fresh ink and scratched some more.

"You got a few indians hereabout," Nelson Story noted.

The pen poised like a heron stalking fish. "Have you news of the Lakota?"

"We was hit south of Fort Reno. Two men wounded and they took some beeves. We got 'em back."

"How many cows are you trailing?"

"Thousand, near enough."

"I see." He wiped the nib on the cloth reserved for that purpose, before laying the pen in its tray. He blotted his report and slipped it into the top drawer. He extended his small cold hand. "Henry Carrington. I'm in command."

"Looks like they got you surrounded."

The Colonel gave him a sharp look. "Reinforcements are due."

"I never saw so much indian sign."

"They cannot take this fort. They cannot prevail against our how-itzers." He unlocked a tin chest for two small glasses. "I neglect my hospitality, sir." The whiskey decanter was full and remained near full after he poured.

Nelson Story rested his glass on his knee. "Obliged," he said. "I'll want to get up the Montana Road before snow flies."

"How many in your party?"

"Twenty-three top hands, every one armed with new Remington rolling blocks. We can get off five bullets to one for a Springfield and drop a buffalo at a thousand yards."

Carrington steepled his hands. "Mr. Story, because of the indian dan-ger, no parties can proceed up the Montana Road without forty armed men. You will have to wait for the next train to make up your party."

"Colonel, there weren't no train in front of us and far as I know, there ain't any train coming behind. We're the last this season. My men are crack shots, ex-soldiers to a man, and if the indians come at us, they'll surely wish they hadn't."

RATCLIFF SAT ON A BARREL in the post sutler's. A Crow indian hun-kered silently against the wall, Colonel Carrington's old negro servant lifted his coattails to the potbellied stove, a graybeard wearing a slouch hat of considerable age but no distinction occupied the only rocker. "My friend here"—the graybeard indicated the Crow—"says Brulés hit you on the Powder."

Ratcliff said, "News travels fast."

The graybeard said he was Jim Bridger, army scout. He asked how many Brulés. "I've heard ten, I've heard fifty."

"We killed ten. I thought we got them all."

"You're lucky one got away with the news. Reputation for orneriness could save your hair. Colonel buyin' your beef?"

Ratcliff said Story expected a good price in Virginia City.

Bridger cackled. "Son, it's many and many a mile twixt here and Virginia City."

"Many a mile from Texas too," Ratcliff replied. "Indians killed a Frenchy; Pommerlau and his boy. Cut 'em up bad."

"Them Frenchy traders never did think nothin' of sellin' guns to the Lakota. Lakota figure a mutilated enemy can't hurt 'em when they are passing through Shadowland."

"Reinforcements come soon," the Colonel's elderly black servant announced. "Colonel Carrington glad. Not glad 'bout their officer."

"I hear it'll be Captain Fetterman," Bridger said.

"You hear plenty," Ratcliff said.

Bridger shrugged. "I draw officer's pay, but I don't got to drill and I don't got to clean my quarters and I don't got to salute. All I got to do is hear plenty. I hear Red Cloud been talkin' to the Crows, bringin' gifts, bein' polite, and I think, my that's surprisin' on account of how Red Cloud has counted coup on a passel of Crow warriors and most times a Lakota runs into a Crow, gonna be one or t'other killed. And I hear the Arapaho, who was peaceful until General Conner attacked their winter camp and killed twenty or thirty of 'em, the Arapaho, they're steamed up and talkin' to Red Cloud too. My friend Black Dog"—he indicated the mute indian—"he says the Northern Cheyenne are signed up. I hear this Captain Fetterman was brave in the War. I hear Fetterman thinks by rights he should outrank Colonel Carrington. I hear this Fetterman's said, 'Give me eighty regular soldiers and I'll ride through the entire Sioux Nation.' I do hope he didn't say no such damn thing, but if he did, I hope he don't say it when he gets where they're at."

Nelson Story marched into the sutler's and snapped, "Ratcliff, let's ride."

Ratcliff put down his drink. "First, I got to buy me a Dutch oven," he said.

WHEN STORY GATHERED his crew, he said, "Colonel Carrington says he can't spare any graze near the fort. We'll camp on Rock Creek. "

"Boss, if indians hit us, these soldier boys might as well be in Fort Laramie."

"Colonel offered to buy our beeves. Appears indians have run off most of theirs."

Ben Shillaber smiled. "I'll wager he offered top dollar."

"Ten bucks a head."

Ben Shillaber whistled. "Yankees are such a generous people."

Three miles north of the fort on the banks of Rock Creek, they erected a cottonwood corral. "If I'd have wanted to be a carpenter I'd have stayed in Texas," Tommy Thompson complained. "Damned if I don't hate fellin' trees."

RATCLIFF BAKED DRIED apple pies that night, Sheep Shearer's Delight and Dirty George the next. Shillaber shot an elk and Ratcliff was tenderizing steaks with the butt of his revolver when the soldiers arrived. Their mustachioed lieutenant chuckled at the flimsy corral. "I suppose that will keep the Lakota at bay?"

"Might slow 'em long enough so we can shoot 'em," Ratcliff said. "Mr. Story's with the cows."

"Immigrants on the Montana Road depend on us for protection. Story has a duty to sell us provisions."

"You're doin' a fine job protectin', yes, sir," Ratcliff said.

The lieutenant offered Nelson Story the same ten dollars a head and added the unsurprising news that no wagon train was expected anytime soon. When the lieutenant leaned forward, his saddle creaked satisfaction. "Damned if I don't smell snow in the air."

Story's eyes were stone.

Shillaber found indian sign all around them and everybody saw indian mirrors flashing from the ridges. Twice they heard distant gunshots.

They grazed their animals by day but brought them into the corrals at dusk. Three days and half a night passed before the indians struck.

Except for hat and boots, Ratcliff slept fully dressed and at the first screeching, he grabbed his Remington and rolled out of the cookwagon. The night was indifferently lit by a half moon, the darkness punctuated by conical muzzle blasts. Running hard, Ratcliff dodged through swirling, panicked horses. The corral rail caught Ratcliff in the midsection and he gagged and his eyes swam as he sucked for air. Two warriors raced past full-tilt and an arrow snapped past his ear as he fired into the near horse's gut and the horse stumbled and its rider dropped his bow. Ratcliff fumbled for another cartridge, but he'd left his cartridge pouch behind. Nelson Story was yelling. Ratcliff hobbled back to the cookwagon for his boots and bullets. He'd whacked into something in the darkness and torn a toenail off.

The shooting stopped; men came out of the darkness to stand around the cold cookfire. "I hit one of the bastards," George Dow said. "I swear I did."

"I shot a horse," Ratcliff said.

"One, two, three, four . . ." Story counted his sentries. "Where's Reid?"

There were snow flurries in the air next morning when they found the missing man.

"Wouldn't have thought they had time to do all that." George Dow turned aside to vomit.

"Get a shovel," Shillaber said.

Nelson Story recited the Twenty-third Psalm over Reid's grave. He replaced his hat. "We're thirty days from Virginia City and winter's comin'. There'll be no more immigrant trains and I've come too far to sell my beeves for ten damn dollars."

Ratcliff's foot hurt.

"We can go on without the army or wait here until we're snowed in. We go on, I imagine we'll fight some indians. Those who want to go on to Montana, put their hands in the air."

"Jesus H. Christ, that's . . . why, that's plumb crazy." George Dow pushed both hands behind his back lest they suddenly develop minds of their own.

Ratcliff's hand went in the air by itself, just got lighter and lighter until it was floating like a hot-air balloon. Ratcliff was surprised; he always thought his hand had better sense. Excepting George Dow, nobody else's hand had good sense either.

George Dow said, "Mr. Story, you're plumb crazy. How many miles to Virginia City? Three-fifty?"

"Closer to four," Story said.

"Christ, Red Cloud's got him an army of prime warriors out there, and ain't one of them wouldn't like to fall upon a thousand beeves and a hundred prime horses and twenty-three scalps, theirs for the takin'. When we was fightin' Johnny Reb and Johnny had you surrounded and outnumbered, you waved a white flag and surrendered. Them Lakota don't let you surrender. Mr. Story, they slice a man's privates like the nigger slices a ham."

"We'll ride at night, hole up at daybreak. We can't have no cookfires. Ratcliff?"

Ratcliff enumerated, "Got pies and cold biscuits, Son-of-a-Bitch in a sack, jerky, cold sowbelly and beans, and a couple gallons of Rainy Day Stew. You boys won't like cold grub, but there'll be plenty of it."

"Shillaber, you and Tommy take hold of George. Lash him across his horse. I don't want him blabbin' to the fort."

That occasioned a tussle, but George Dow was trussed hand and foot and hung across his saddle like a sack of grain.

THEY RODE ALL NIGHT. Next morning, Nelson Story untied George and said he could ride back to Fort Phil Kearny if he had a mind to, but George didn't want to travel alone. He rubbed his hands to bring back the circulation and, when he thought nobody was watching, flung his Brulé scalp into the sagebrush.

By the waning moon, they passed east of the massive Bighorns. It was easy to lose sight of the dim wagon ruts and afterward Ratcliff would have nightmares of traversing steep coulees with horsemen roped to his cook-wagon to keep it from toppling over while his pans jangled and banged loud enough to be heard for miles.

Ratcliff thought he was a dead man who hadn't had occasion to lie down—a thought which buoyed rather than depressed him. He didn't owe debts to anyone and no man owed him. In this wide world, no man or woman would shed a tear to hear of his passing. He had had friends, wives, some kids. He hadn't loved any of them. Might be he was one of those fellows who couldn't love anybody. Ratcliff was learning that a dead man can admit things a living man can't.

His Remington was at his side, his cartridge pouch under the seat. He was wrapped in his heavy buffalo coat, his reins clamped inside his buffalo mittens. Since any patch of shadow might be an indian, he ignored the shadows. In the cold air, his mules' breath lifted like locomotive plumes.

He wondered when a dying man stopped feeling pain. He wondered how long Reid had hurt, whether Pommerlau's boy—Jacob? Joseph?—had felt the knife when it slashed his penis. He remembered a lifetime ago on the plantation. It was November—butchering time. Two great white sows hung on tripods above the scalding water. Two others had been killed and their life's blood was draining into pans when Master rode up. "Don't kill that last sow. We'll want her for breeding."

When the sows had been crammed into the shambles they'd squealed—like hogs always do at anything unfamiliar—but they fell quiet after the first one was killed.

Ratcliff and another boy dragged the pardoned sow out of the shambles by her heels and instead of the knife's hot bite at her throat, she was turned loose. She tottered like she was sick and they had to help her stand. As she stumbled off a child could have caught her.

Maybe that sow had died with her mates, her soul separated and roaming the ether. Maybe that sow's soul couldn't reinhabit her body.

Ratcliff's soul perched on his shoulders; not too heavy, companionable as a pet raven.

His eyes were sharper than usual and the night air was cold and clear as a mountain stream. Fog billows hid the base of the Bighorns.

On this leg of the Montana Road, most immigrant trains watered at the South Fork of the Tongue River, but near dawn, Nelson Story brought his outfit off the ridgetops into a dry bowl an hour shy of water. He set half the men around the perimeter and told the others to catch some sleep.

Ratcliff put out cold biscuits and sowbelly. No fire. No coffee. "I'd like sugar in my coffee this morning," Shillaber said.

"I thought only niggers liked sweet coffee," Ratcliff said.

Shillaber poured cold water into his cup and sipped. "Damned if I don't miss my coffee."

"Yes," Ratcliff said.

The next night, they watered at the South Fork near four fresh graves.

They came out of the Tongue River Valley onto a high waterless plateau. Easy travel, but ten thousand indians could be lying in the low places.

Clots of buffalo lifted their heads, antelope bounced soundlessly away.

Nobody slept more than four hours. Though they didn't talk much, they were unusually courteous. One morning, after he'd caught his own mount, Ben Shillaber helped Ratcliff hitch his mules. One night when the shadows seemed unusually menacing, Nelson Story rode alongside the cookwagon. "My wife is Ellen Story," he said.

Ratcliff said, "I never had no luck with women."

THEY PASSED NORTH of the Bighorns and next morning Ratcliff made a cookfire. After a couple hours' rest and a hot breakfast they resumed their journey, and late that afternoon, with horses roped behind as drags, the wagons skidded down the rocky slope into the Bighorn River Valley.

As the day warmed, Fort C. F. Smith appeared across the river and everybody started cracking jokes.

The ferry was cottonwood logs lashed together and caulked with rags. The lashings were hemp and rawhide—some frayed, some furry, some blackened, some green.

"My wagon was made in Dallas by Bream and Company," Ratcliff said. "I ain't trustin' it to that thing."

The ferryman said, "God Damn you for a hincty nigger. Nothin' wrong with my ferry."

"River's high and fast," Ratcliff said. "I'd despise continuin' to Virginia City without my cookwagon."

"Pull the ferry ashore," Ben Shillaber commanded.

"And just who the hell are you?" the ferryman blustered.

Shillaber's smile was icy as a January morning, "Just another humble pilgrim. Sir, pull your ferry."

While they relashed and recaulked the ferry, Nelson Story swam his horse across to the fort. Colonel Bradley, Fort Smith's commanding officer, shook his head and said, "Somebody in your outfit knows how to pray." He let Story use the bathtub in his quarters.

The herd swam the turbulent river without mishap and Nelson Story rejoined them. "We're burnin' daylight," he said. "Winter's comin' on."

Tommy Thompson sniffed the air. "Jesus Christ, boss. Is that rose petals I smell?"

Nelson Story blushed.

For two days they trailed the herd across the high country and when they descended to the Clarks Fork River, ice glossed the rocks in the shallows.

"I'm a Texan," George Dow complained. "My hide ain't thick enough for this weather."

Headboards on the riverbank read, "Reverend W. K. Thomas, age 36 years, of Belleville, Ill. Chas. K. Thomas, age 8 years, of Belleville, Ill. James Schultz, age 35 years, of Ottawa. C. K. Wright. All killed and scalped by Indians on the 24th day of August, 1865."

George Dow blew into his cold hands and checked his rifle.

Next day, near the Rock Creek crossing, Shillaber met twenty or thirty indians, coming at a gallop. Shillaber aimed his first shot, snapped the second and third before he raced back for the herd. The indians came on his heels, pell-mell.

Shillaber dashed through the cowboys his shots had alerted. Twenty-three Remingtons made a hullabaloo. Two indians fell and their fellows took them away.

"Who the hell were they?" Story asked. "What tribe?"

Shillaber grinned. "Indian tribe, I reckon."

Nelson stared at his scout for a long moment before adjusting his hat and clucking to his horse.

To the south, the Absaroka Mountains were white as sugar and the wind spun plumes of snow from the high ridges into clear blue air. Ratcliff burrowed deeper in his buffalo coat and wished he were in Virginia.

The Stillwater was frozen from bank to bank. Ben Shillaber and George Dow waded in to break trail. Their horses broke the ice for the beeves.

On the far bank an earlier pilgrim had carved a message into the bark of a cottonwood tree: "Jenny S.—bound for Virginia City in the Happie Land of Canaan."

The hills were covered with jack pines. Snow persisted on the north slopes and in shadows.

When Shillaber and Dow struck the Yellowstone ford, Shillaber went back to advise Story. It was a dangerous ford, its current so strong they angled the swimming beeves upstream. Roped to four riders, Ratcliff's cookwagon almost rolled over. They found George Dow on a gravel bar below the ford. He'd been scalped and had thirty-eight arrows in his body.

"George didn't want to make this trip," Shillaber said.

"He guessed right," Ratcliff said.

ONE DAY'S JOURNEY LATER, the wagon ruts they'd followed for so many miles deepened, proliferated, and became a real road. Children ducked back inside a homesteader's soddy. Soddies soon lost their novelty. When the cattle got into the crested wheatgrass, the cowboys needed rope ends to keep them moving. They stowed their Remingtons in the cookwagon.

Nelson Story tied his horse to Ratcliff's wagon and took a seat.

"Good country," Ratcliff said.

"Oh, hell, man. It's great country. Good soil, good water, good grass." Story stretched his arms from horizon to horizon. "Think how many cows I can run in this valley. I'll buy some Oregon herd bulls and make some real calves. The mining camps are crying for beef. Ratcliff, I swear to God. The Gallatin Valley is the land of milk and honey. Every man dreams there's a place, somewhere, where the mistakes he made don't matter anymore, where he can start over. John Smith don't need to be John Smith no more, he can be Bill Brown. Don't got to be Nigger Ratcliff, he can be Aloysius J. Parkman if that's who he wants to be."

NELSON STORY HAD five thousand acres between the Yellowstone and Shields Rivers. He left Tommy Thompson and five men with most of the herd and instructions to throw up a bunkhouse before the snow flew.

It was bitter cold when the rest of Story's crew and a hundred fat steers trailed into Bozeman City, Montana Territory. The metropolis of the Gallatin Valley had a main street of frozen mud, a flour mill, Fitz & Son's General Store, a score of one-story log buildings, twice that many tents, and the two-story City Hotel. In the Tivoli Garden Saloon, Story paid his crew and offered them their Remingtons for half price. He wished them good luck and opined that good luck generally sought the man who worked for it. Shillaber, Ratcliff, and the teamsters would continue with Story to Virginia City.

After a night of convivial leave-taking, no man was in a good humor when Story cursed them out of their bedrolls at dawn. Only Story was one hundred percent sober.

This road was graded for the coaches that sped between Virginia City and Bozeman City; but the graze was poor and that night a hundred cows spread out over five acres. Ratcliff made biscuits, bacon, and coffee.

When they woke it was snowing soft fat flakes and the sun glowed pink inside the low clouds. At midday they crossed the Madison River and the snow intensified. Ratcliff unhitched his cookwagon and saddled a mule.

Snow pelted Ratcliff's eyes. The cows turned their backs to the blizzard and started drifting.

When Ratcliff rode at the cows' faces and popped his rope end, they broke around him. Since the cows couldn't be turned, Ratcliff followed them, holding his reins inside the sleeves of his buffalo coat and retracting his head into the collar like a turtle. It snowed every minute of that long night and Ratcliff didn't know whether he was following the main herd or a few stragglers and he didn't see another rider until an hour before daybreak when the snow stopped and the cows quit drifting.

"Mornin', Ben," Ratcliff said.

"Mornin', Top. Sure wish't I was in Charleston," Shillaber said.

"Wonder where we got to."

Shillaber stood in his stirrups to inspect the soft white mounded hills. "T'ain't Charleston," he said.

Ratcliff stepped down to take a piss and while he was dismounted his mule took a piss too. The sun struck the new snow incandescent and hurt his eyes.

It took most of the day to push the herd back upstream to the cookwagon. Shillaber built a fire and Ratcliff made coffee and biscuits, bacon and beans. That night they didn't post a nighthawk. The cows were too tired to stray.

Next morning they made slow progress through the snow, but by three o'clock they'd descended into a wide valley where the wind kept the slopes clean and the cows could get to the bunchgrass.

They crossed a sulfurous, steaming creek.

Nelson Story said, "There's a hot springs up that draw. Supposed to be good for what ails you."

One teamster brightened. "Think it can cure the joint evil?"

Which was how it happened that five white men and one black man lounged in a steaming pool surrounded by untracked snow that stretched to the distant, sharp-toothed mountains.

Their clothing soaked too and sometimes a man's drawers would drift away into the steam.

"Tomorrow we'll be in Virginia City," Nelson Story said. "Lord, I'll be glad to see my wife."

"Sometimes I wish I had a wife," Shillaber said. "You married, Top?"

"Not so I noticed," Ratcliff said.

Their heads were sleek as beavers above the steaming water. Vapors curtained them and sometimes they couldn't see the fellow directly across.

"What's that medal hanging from your neck?" Shillaber asked Ratcliff.

"My mojo."

"I don't believe I ever seen so many bullwhip scars on one nigger's back. You must have been one hincty nigger."

The setting sun poised over the Tobacco Root Mountains like it might hang forever. Each man was encased in steam, suspended within the warm flesh of his own body.

Ratcliff said softly, "I'd run. They'd catch me, but I'd run again. I never knew where I was runnin' to." He added, "Might be I was runnin' here."

Next morning was sunny. The snow got sticky and rivulets filled the wagon ruts. When Nelson Story's Texas cattle drive arrived in Virginia City, the cookwagon was festooned with men's shirts and socks and drying underwear.

—

CHAPTER 15

AN OPIUM EATER

I stood at a distance, and aloof from the uproar of life; as if the tumult, the fever, and the strife, were suspended; a respite granted from the secret burdens of the heart; a sabbath of repose; a resting from human labors. Here were the hopes which blossom in the paths of life, reconciled with the peace which is in the grave . . .

THOMAS DE QUINCEY

". . . THESE UNREPENTANT REBELS," MR. CHEPSTOW CONTINUED, "don't believe in the legality of the Congress of the United States to make laws for them. 'So help us God,' they say, 'we won't be governed by Congress's laws.' It would be lunacy to let these rebels vote."

"Yes, sir," Duncan Gatewood said. Duncan's mouth was dry, and though Chepstow wouldn't offer brandy, he might have offered water.

Four Chandler and Price presses occupied the *New Nation*'s cramped premises in Shockhoe Bottom, which was "cheek by jowl" (as Mr. Chepstow liked to remark) with the "infamous" Libby Prison, where Union prisoners had been jailed during the War.

The only chair in the editor's tiny office held a tottering stack of unsold newspapers.

"Mr. Gatewood, you were a secessionist?"

"I've come to offer the A.M.&O.'s custom," Duncan said. "General Mahone needs timetables, freight rates, tickets, our annual report to the Public Service Commission, and so forth. Our custom will amount to three thousand dollars annually."

It was raining a soft spring rain and when he was concluded with Chepstow, Duncan would walk to the Capitol, half a mile. Perhaps the stroll would loosen his bowels.

"Yes, yes," Chepstow said impatiently. "And the quid pro quo?"

"Sir?"

"Is General Mahone a friend to the Republican Party? Hasn't General Mahone forbidden his employees from Republican activities on pain of dismissal?"

Duncan imagined he was assailed by a feist. The little dog barked, circled, and threatened his trouser legs, but he dare not kick at it because the feist would redouble its efforts. Duncan smiled.

"You find Mahone's denial of political rights amusing, sir?" Chepstow snapped. "I don't find it amusing. Nor does the governor."

Duncan's mind conjured a skirmish line firing plugs of tobacco instead of minié balls, but the image drifted away.

The floor thumped when Chepstow's pressman closed his press. Outside, the trolley bell dinged. Instead of walking, perhaps Duncan would ride the trolley.

Chepstow shook his head. "Confederate General Mahone seeking to curry favor with a Republican leader. Shameless!"

Duncan had fought under Mahone at the Battle of the Crater and sometimes dreamed of that day. When colored soldiers were being slaughtered like beasts in a shambles, General Mahone's red-hot curses had stopped the massacre. There'd been gore in Duncan's hair; his eyebrows had been pasted to his forehead by gore, the hair on the back of his hands had been glossy with stiffening gore. "Excuse me, Mr. Chepstow; my mind wanders."

"I love liberty. All our colored friends should have it. Every *loyal* man must have the right to vote."

"And the man who was a Confederate officer?" ex-Major Gatewood inquired.

Chepstow went to the door and called, "Jesse, come in my office. Please."

The pressman wiped his hands on an inky rag before offering his hand.

"Hullo, Jesse. So this is where you're working."

"I'm setting type. All the government notices and Mr. Chepstow's editorials."

"I hear you'll be a delegate to the Republican convention. You've come far."

"This is your old master," Chepstow said wonderingly. "*Master* Gatewood."

" 'Young Master Gatewood,' " Jesse corrected his employer. "Duncan's father was 'Master Gatewood.' "

"But he had absolute authority over you. He could do whatever he pleased."

"Not entirely," Duncan replied pleasantly. "If I had murdered Jesse without provocation, I might have been held to account. Certainly Preacher Todd would have remarked it. But since servants like Jesse were so valuable, we only murdered them on festive occasions."

"I don't get your meaning, sir," Chepstow said.

"No, sir, I believe you don't."

Jesse half turned to exclude Chepstow from the conversation. "Maggie's in Richmond. I saw her goin' into a bank on Broad Street. She was in black and wearin' a veil, but I knew her like it was yesterday. I didn't say nothin'. Didn't know what to say."

"Yes," Duncan said, nodding to the puzzled Chepstow. "A mutual acquaintance. Her husband was killed in the war. He was a Confederate hero."

As interest faded from Chepstow's eyes, Duncan said, "I'm glad to see Maggie has prospered. I do not believe she wishes to be reminded of unhappier times."

Jesse brightened. "I married my Sudie in January. It gave me a start, though, seein' Maggie that way."

Duncan had a sudden vivid memory of how Maggie had looked nude, on a particular winter day in the milk barn. "Sometimes," Duncan said, "it is best to forget." He took a breath and added, "My Sallie is well and we have been blessed with an infant: Baby Catesby."

Jesse nodded. "We got rooms off East Fourth Street. Down from the gasworks. My Sudie is a little bit of a thing. She's got a son."

Chepstow sighed dramatically. " 'What is to be done? What is to be done? The negroes forgive those who enslaved them. Virginia negroes would forgive Satan himself!' "

"Mr. Chepstow, he's for negro rights. Congressman Stevens hates Rebels and Senator Sumner hates Rebels and Secretary Seward hates Rebels and Mr. Chepstow believes that when those men die, others who hate Rebels as much as they do will take their place. Mr. Chepstow is an educated man and maybe he's right." Jesse shrugged. "There's near as many Virginia negroes as Virginia Rebels and in the south side there's more of us. If we get the vote and Rebels get the vote, I b'lieve we can sort things out."

Duncan went to the window. "Ah, the rain is stopping." He touched his stump gently. "Aches like hell when it's damp."

Chepstow stared at Jesse as if betrayed. "You'd undo our great work?" he asked. "You'd give these traitors the vote?"

"I've the late edition to print, Mr. Chepstow." Jesse's eyes were blank as a slave's.

Chepstow's wave sent Jesse back to work and soon the press was thumping again. Chepstow shut the door, which was scuffed at the bottom as if it had been kicked a time or two.

Outside, pedestrians strolled through the mist and trolley horses clattered on the cobblestones. Duncan picked up his green-and-black carpetbag. "Sir, you are a busy man. I shan't trouble you again."

Chepstow lifted his eyes to the pressed tin ceiling and intoned, "We've more business than we can handle."

Duncan had heard every circumlocution with which men cloak their greed. He set the carpetbag down. The street sounds, the regular thud of the press, the bright smell of ink: why did this print shop remind him of a child's playroom?

"Mahone astonishes me," Chepstow said. "Employing you as agent— a man apparently indifferent to his interests."

"And what are General Mahone's interests, sir?"

"Passage of his railroad bill. The Baltimore & Ohio's agents are offering two thousand dollars for . . . due consideration."

Duncan raised innocent eyebrows. "As much as that, sir?"

"Elections cost money," Chepstow said. "Republicans mustn't be outspent by their enemies." He wouldn't meet Duncan's eyes.

Duncan placed his carpetbag atop the unsold newspapers and unbuttoned it.

Chepstow shook his head wonderingly. "General Mahone must be daft; sending a man like you to persuade men of conscience."

"Yes, sir. Mahone would be daft to do so," Duncan began extracting greenbacks.

CHAPTER 16

WHAT RAVEN SAW

The Lord JesuChrist and whoring kept Low Dog from my dreams.

My crib was in Wong's Saloon. Sundays I worshipped JesuChrist so eagerly that Mrs. Evans, the reverend's wife, invited me to supper, but when she heard about Wong's Mrs. Evans said I shouldn't come.

Low Dog is too clean to visit me where an unwashed miner has rummaged and JesuChrist's songs drive him, howling, into the night.

It was not long before the Lord JesuChrist's birthday. Ice crystals skittered over the bare ground and the miners made bonfires on the gravel bars so they could keep digging their yellow metal. It was my time of the month so the miners used other women. I tried to stay awake. I prayed and sang JesuChrist songs.

But when I closed my eyes Low Dog said, "There you are. I was afraid you wouldn't come tonight." Low Dog's companion, Raven, rode his back.

"Why do you show me these things?"

Low Dog acted hurt. "Haven't you traveled far? Haven't I showed you your husband?"

"He is ugly like a black bear."

Low Dog licked his anus. "He will give you children and will not beat you. What more do you want?" He quit his anus to lick his lips and smile. "My friend Raven will carry you."

Raven cannot smile. He only opens his beak to speak or take food. "Get on my back," he said. "I will show you deeds Lakota will sing about forever."

Raven flew south to where the Montana Road left Fort Phil Kearny, crossed Big Piney Creek, and followed Lodge Trail Ridge onto a spur above Peno Valley. Snow lay in its wagon ruts.

Some Lakota had attacked a wood party north of the fort and army semaphores waved and Raven flew over the parade ground where a company of Seizers was assembling. Some of the Seizers were eager and made their horses dance, but the other Seizers were untried warriors and could not conceal their trembling.

Their Chief told the mounted Seizers they must not cross Lodge Trail Ridge, they must not.

The Seizers hurried out of the fort, racing to catch the Lakota and make them cry.

Raven croaked and flew higher until the Seizers looked like ants going to honey. When Raven glided over Lodge Trail Ridge I saw more warriors than I had ever seen in one place: Oglala and Miniconjous, Lakota, Bad Faces, Arapaho, and Northern Cheyenne.

The great war chief Red Cloud was leading them.

The Seizers hurried to cut off the Lakota decoys, but the Lakota fled toward Lodge Trail Ridge. The Seizers paused. Maybe they were remembering the Seizer Chief's orders, maybe they feared an ambush.

Just inside long rifle range the warriors taunted the Seizers and called them cowards.

The Seizers came on cautiously. The Lakota became more daring and more insulting. Young Crazy Horse stood on his horse's back and lifted his loincloth and showed disrespect. The Seizers fired at him and Crazy Horse fell. Thus encouraged, the Seizers came up Lodge Trail Ridge. The wounded Crazy Horse built a small fire and sat slouched before it, ignoring the bullets kicking dirt up around him. The Seizers advanced to kill him.

Three times Crazy Horse tried to mount his horse before he succeeded and crossed the ridgetop. The Seizers rode after him

Atop Lodge Trail Ridge they saw rolling prairie, the ruts of the Montana Road, tall grass, the familiar expanse of pale blue sky, and a Raven cawing overhead.

Crazy Horse was escaping toward Peno Creek. Companions held him on his horse. Angry Seizers spurred after.

When Crazy Horse and the other decoys crossed Peno Creek, Crazy Horse recovered and raced his horse in a circle—the signal—and so many warriors appeared that the Seizers were like a thread of blue dye in a brown river.

The roof over their heads was a roof of arrows.

Lakota war cries were louder than blackhorns shaking the earth and the Seizers stank with fear.

On strong wings, Raven lifted higher into the air as Seizer souls rose to JesuChrist.

CHAPTER 17

DISPATCH FROM COLONEL HENRY CARRINGTON,

COMMANDING FORT PHIL KEARNY,

TO THE ADJUTANT GENERAL, DEPARTMENT

OF THE PLATTE, OMAHA, NEBRASKA,

DECEMBER 22, 1866

Do send me reinforcements forthwith. Expedition now with my force is impossible. I risk everything but the post and its stores. I have had but today a fight unexampled in indian warfare; my loss is 94 killed.

I have recovered 49 bodies, and 35 more are to be brought in, in the morning, that have been found. Among the killed are Brevet Lieutenant Colonel Fetterman, Captain F. J. Brown, and Lieutenant Grummond. The indians engaged were nearly 3,000, being apparently the force reported on Tongue River, in my dispatches of 5th November and subsequent thereto. This line is important, can and will be held. It will take four times the force in the spring to reopen it. I hear nothing of my arms that left Leavenworth September 10. The additional cavalry ordered to join us has not been reported; their arrival would have saved us much loss today.

The indians lost beyond all precedent. I need prompt reinforcement and repeating arms. I am sure to have, as before reported, an active winter and must have men and arms. Every officer of this battalion should join it. Today I have every teamster on duty, and but 119 men left at post. I hardly need urge this matter; it speaks for itself. Give me two companies of cavalry, at least forthwith, well armed, or four companies of infantry exclusive of what is needed at Reno and Fort Smith.

I did not overestimate my early application of a single company. Promptness will save the line, but our killed shows that any remissness will result in mutilation and butchery beyond precedent. No such mutilation as that today is on record. Depend on it that the post will be held so long as a round or a man is left. Promptness is the vital thing. Give me officers and men. Only the new Spencer carbine should be sent; the indians are desperate; I spare none and they spare none.

Henry Carrington, Commanding

CHAPTER 18

LETTER FROM EDWARD RATCLIFF
TO JESSE BURNS

VIRGINIA CITY,
MONTANA TERRITORY
JANUARY 1867

Friend Jesse,

My wife She Goes Before writes this for me.

It's snowing again. Snow drifts halfway up our dugout window. We're lucky we got us a dugout. Plenty miners living in tents.

All the trees for miles outside Virginia City are felled for sluice boxes and pit props. Paydirt is twelve feet below the surface so props keep the trenches from caving in. Firewood is dear. She Goes Before has an elk stew on the stove. Elk meat tastes better than buffalo.

There's five or six thousand men here trying their damnedest to get rich. I guess it can be done. Bummer Dan swapped a Sharps carbine for his claim and Dan's bar produced a half million before it played out.

Virginia City smells like Petersburg bombproofs. I guess dug dirt all smells the same.

Gold dust is money. A pinch for a haircut or shot of whiskey. Two pinches for a girl.

I don't guess I'm a prospector. After three weeks digging, I sold

my half of our claim to my partner Ben Shillaber. Ben sold out
too and plays poker. He says poker is a better gamble than mining! I
couldn't find a cook's job so I hired on for a bouncer in Wong's
Saloon. I sit on a stool at the end of the bar and give toughs the evil
eye. Before they got law here, road agents robbed and killed whoever
they had a mind to. Biggest road agent of all was this Plummer—
and he was the sheriff! The vigilantes hung him.

Sometimes the vigilantes hung somebody who hadn't done much
but mostly they hung them what needed it. The toughs who stayed
are too scared to be tough anymore.

Jesse, I got me a woman. She Goes Before is a Santee Lakota.
She was taught by missionaries to read and write. She is teaching
me Lakota lingo.

Soldiers strung up her father during the '62 Santee rising.
When I met her she was a whore. She says living with me keeps her
from dreaming.

There aren't many women in Virginia City so I'm lucky. I like
her pretty good. Yesterday, Wong asked if he could borrow her back
just for Saturday nights. Ha, ha!

Virginia City is getting civilized. There's a telegraph to Salt
Lake so we get news soon as it happens. I hear the Virginia
Legislature won't ratify the 14th Amendment. I've seen chickens
with more sense!

If you got to be a nigger, this is better than Texas or Virginia!
Some out here hate us, but niggers are a damn sight better off than
chinks. White man shoots a chink don't think nothing of it. Indians
neither. Whites are too busy killing indians and chinks to fool with
niggers! Some coloreds have started a social club—just like the
Masonics.

I expect you heard about Fetterman losing his hair. He was a
damn fool. She Goes Before's people call that fight A Hundred in the
Hand. A month before they killed Fetterman, I helped bring Nelson
Story's beeves through that country. We were lucky. I guess luck's
what it comes down to.

She Goes Before says things are better across the Medicine Line in the Grandmother's land. In Canada whites and indians and niggers live in peace.

How are things with you? Write me your news.

Your Okola (that's Lakota for friend)
Ratcliff

CHAPTER 19

A FORMER LOVER

THE VERY PREGNANT MRS. DUNCAN GATEWOOD DISMISSED HER CAB outside 376 Clay Street. A few blocks from the Confederate White House, Clay Street had been among Richmond's best addresses. Carpetbaggers owned most of the mansions now.

376's wide front porch had no chairs, no porch swing, nor glider. Its drapes were pulled. The house seemed to be facing inward.

Although this was the last place on earth she wanted to be and she dreaded the information she sought, Mrs. Duncan Gatewood stiffened her spine, heaved her bulk up the steps, and spun the door pull. Twice for good measure.

Orioles were clamoring in a tree across the street. A ragman's wagon creaked by. A horseman tipped his hat.

Mrs. Gatewood heard a door slam somewhere down the street. A Mammy shouted, "Tommy! Tommy! You get's yourself back in this house right now!"

This sheer ordinariness made her mission ridiculous.

The door jerked open and a sharp-featured negro maid eyed her suspiciously.

"Mrs. Duncan Gatewood, to see Mrs. Omohundru." Sallie offered her card.

The maid put her hands behind her back. "Mrs. Omohundru ain't receivin' today. She don't hardly never receive."

The entry hall behind the woman was dim and the hall chairs were shrouded.

"It think it best Mrs. Omohundru decide whether she'll see me or not," Sallie said. "Assure her I will not embarrass her."

The maid rolled that thought around in her mouth like a child with a hard candy. Her hand darted to the card and she shut the door in Sallie's face.

Sallie heard the Mammy down the street calling, "Tommy, you come out of where you're hidin'!"

A squad of blue-clad cavalrymen trotted past and their captain saluted. Many Southern women snubbed the yankees, but Sallie nodded. What did that captain have to do with her? Was he faithful? Did he love his children?

Sallie had waited almost long enough to change her mind when the door opened as suddenly as before and the maid stood aside to let Sallie enter the high-ceilinged, chilly house. A wide staircase mounted to the second floor. The maid opened a door off the hall. "Mrs. Omohundru, she be 'long shortly. You can wait in the parlor."

The room was formally arranged with high-backed horsehair settees and chairs. The lithographs on the wall were indifferent renderings of city scenes. The fireplace looked as if it had never held a fire. The room's liveliest object was a plain-faced clock in an ebony case that hesitated as if the clock were taking a breath between each tick and tock.

A familiar Southern lithograph, *The Burial of Latane*, had the place of honor over the mantel.

Though there were several sconces, the gaslights were turned so low they almost sputtered.

Sallie rubbed cold hands together.

A moment later the maid returned with a sherry decanter, two glasses, and a cup of tea: no milk, no sugar. Sallie tasted bitter, tepid tea.

Although she was listening for footfalls, the turning latch startled her. Silent as a cat, the black-clad widow slipped into her parlor. Sallie rose. "Mrs. Omohundru."

"Mrs. Gatewood." Mrs. Omohundru's black garb was unornamented by ribbon or flounce. Her buttons marched up her corseted bosom like funeral coins. Her veil was attached to a small old-fashioned hat.

When she poured two glasses of sherry, ordinary hospitality seemed almost shocking; as if one were not supposed to eat or drink or smile in this grim house.

"Thank you," Sallie said. The sherry was wildly sweet with a sour metallic aftertaste. Sallie washed it down with bitter tea.

When the widow lifted her veil, Sallie was astonished at how young she was: Twenty? Twenty-one? The woman had been beautiful as a child and now she was a nubian princess. Sallie's heart cried out for her husband. Duncan had loved this woman once. Did he still?

Mrs. Omohundru's stare was too direct for politeness. Sallie put down her sherry and her cup.

"More?"

"No. Thank you so much."

"I searched the Tidewater for that particular sherry."

"It is . . ."

Mrs. Omohundru arched an eyebrow. "Indescribable?"

The word was so unexpected and the other woman's stare so intense, Sallie didn't know if the woman had meant what she'd said. She took a deep breath and relaxed. "Only a poet could do it justice."

"You and Duncan grew up together," the widow said bluntly. "I suppose he and I grew up together too. You know all about that. You were at Stratford that Christmas . . ."

"When you were sold south. Yes, I was."

Her eyes were dark and very cold. "I have become Marguerite Omohundru," she said. "Officially, I am the white widow of the Confederate hero Silas Omohundru. I own a majority share in the Farmers and Merchants Bank. I was born in Nassau, the Bahamas, the daughter of a Methodist minister. My parents are, alas, deceased."

"I can see why you would prefer that history. You can trust me, Marguerite. I won't reveal your secret, no matter . . ."

"No matter what?"

Sallie'd gotten off on the wrong foot. To gain time, Sallie took a sip of sherry, and choked.

When Marguerite's face lit up, years dropped away with her discarded hauteur. She enthused, "It is vile stuff, isn't it?"

Sallie thought, Lord, she is so beautiful. She asked, "Do you always serve this potion to your guests?"

"Invariably. Men who call on me see me as a potential acquisition, and as you may know, Virginia laws permit a husband to make whatever disposition of his wife's wealth he wishes. Several would-be suitors have assured me they can handle my money better than any widow can. Hence the *Latane*." She indicated the painting. "Faithful darkies mourning a fallen Confederate hero—if the scene doesn't remind my suitors of my heroic husband Silas, I direct their attention to it and ask, 'Where, sir, did you serve?' knowing full well that whatever privations they endured in the War, Silas's sacrifice was greater than theirs. My callers drink my tea and since the parlor is cold they have a second glass of sherry as I explain that Silas laid down a cellar of the elixir which I prefer to any other." She put a finger to her chin. "My most persistent suitor—a Carolina gentleman on the verge of ruin—visited three times before he accepted bankruptcy rather than one more glass of my wonderful sherry."

She laughed so merrily Sallie nearly laughed too. Abruptly, Marguerite changed tack. "Neither you nor Duncan can see my son. If you believe you can force the issue, you are mistaken. My Jacob would suffer dreadfully were his parentage revealed. You cannot wish that any more than I do." Pointedly she eyed Sallie's pregnancy. "Surely you will not want that!"

"That's not why I came," Sallie said.

"Can I believe you? But dare I? Jacob . . . he . . ."

"My husband calls your name in his sleep," Sallie said bluntly.

Could Sallie credit her puzzled frown?

"Lovers? Duncan and I? Good Lord. I have not seen your husband since . . . Mrs. Gatewood, I have not been with your husband since Master Gatewood, his father, sold me south."

"You swear? Oh, I'd prayed . . ." Sallie dropped her face into her hands.

"Sallie . . . May I call you Sallie? I cannot imagine what gave you such a notion. I remember you as sensible."

Sallie's head jerked up. She stiffened.

"Perhaps your condition?"

She stood. "Thank you for your hospitality, Marguerite. We shan't be seeing each other again."

Marguerite's smile was softer. "You do know why he calls my name. I can see it in your eyes." She cocked her head. "Don't you think you owe me an explanation?"

"I've been a fool."

Marguerite dismissed that. "No. You are gravid. Like myself, you have never been a fool. Forgive me, Mrs. Gatewood. I knew your husband in another life before I became who I am." Impulsively, Marguerite put out her hands.

"Will you join me in my garden room? It's a pleasanter place to talk. We'll have some hot tea."

"It is the laudanum, you know," Sallie said slowly. "It is the laudanum. I am a good wife, but I cannot produce better dreams than laudanum."

CHAPTER 20

THE SUPPLICANT

No person shall be a Senator or Representative in Congress, or elector of President and Vice President, or hold any office, civil or military, under the United States, or under any State, who, having previously taken an oath, as a member of Congress, or as an officer of the United States, or as a member of any State legislature, or as an executive or judicial officer of any state, to support the Constitution of the United States, shall have engaged in insurrection or rebellion against the same, or given aid or comfort to the enemies thereof.

FROM THE FOURTEENTH AMENDMENT TO THE
CONSTITUTION OF THE UNITED STATES

ON THE TENTH OF JANUARY, THE OLD GENTLEMAN HAD RETURNED when the clerk unlocked the office. "Morning, sir. It is almighty raw."

The clerk hung up his wool overcoat wondering how the old gentleman bore the cold without one. Excepting that lack, the gentleman was an exemplar of fashionable attire, albeit from an earlier decade: the high collar beneath which the elaborately rumpled cravat presented its solemn flourish; the narrow-shouldered, broad-lapeled frock coat that ended below the knees, on his silk waistcoat—my goodness, were those faded yellow butterflies? The gentleman's ruffle-fronted shirt (the same shirt the gentleman had worn the day before) had been the height of fashion during the Mexican War—as had the gentleman's silver-headed ebony stick and the black silk gloves whose limp fingers splayed against the yellowed silk lining of the stovepipe hat clamped under the gentleman's arm. His high boots were shone to a fare-thee-well but broken behind the toe caps and the insteps.

The gentleman's calloused hands bore faint hints of bootblacking.

Leading the way into William Mahone's offices on the second floor of the A.M.&O.'s Petersburg depot, the clerk repeated yesterday's caveat. "Sir, I cannot promise you the General will come in today."

"Surely he must—*one* day." The gentleman reclaimed the high-backed wooden chair he had occupied from yesterday noon until the clerk had snuffed the lamps and gone home.

The clerk's office was lined with blueprint cabinets. Tall windows overlooked the railroad yard. The clerk knelt to fill the potbellied stove and said, "As I explained yesterday, the General is supervising repairs. I telegraphed him you were here."

The gentleman smiled wearily. "Since you say my invoice needs General Mahone's signature before I can be paid, I shall wait for his signature. Tell me, sir: do Mahone's creditors often collect here? I fancy a gathering of creditors relating tales of destitution. Some testifying how their children are adapting to the county poorhouse, others how their homes stink of lye soap—now their wives are taking in laundry from families who are not General Mahone's creditors."

Water was seeping from the gentleman's boots and puddling under his seat. Mahone's clerk coughed. "I'm sure I couldn't say, sir."

The fire crackled and chuckled in a self-satisfied manner, but its warmth did not travel far from its ornate casting and the old gentleman's lips were blue.

ANNOUNCED BY HIS FOOTFALLS, a plump young man clattered up the stairs and strode directly to the stove, hands extended to its glow. "Whew! Cold? I'll say it's cold! Even we yankees call this winter! Paul, where's Little Billy?"

"High Bridge, Mr. Barnwell," Paul said. "You know the General—he doesn't give a hang about paperwork. He goes where the engineering needs done."

"Billy's a 'live man,' all right. Samuel Gatewood, damned if I saw you there, quiet as a church mouse. How are you, good sir! How are you! How is Pauline?"

"Good day, sir. Have you business with General Mahone?"

Eben waved his hand. "T'ain't important. Say, Paul, fire off a telegram to the General. We must have a meeting—tonight, if possible. Sir, what brings you to Petersburg?"

"My inability to satisfy my creditors."

"Ah."

The clerk threw the brass switch so electricity could pass from his batteries to his instrument. Hunched over his device, he produced the clicks and clacks that serve telegraphers for introductions.

"Is Pauline in good health?" Eben inquired.

"Sir, since postal service has resumed, Pauline can write you whenever she wishes."

With hands set firmly on his hips and his open, cheerful countenance, Eben Barnwell resembled a jolly Toby jug. "Dear me, sir. I'm afraid I have offended Miss Pauline. I intended no offense, I assure you."

The clerk's machine emitted a spate of clacks, which he translated for Eben Barnwell.

"Satisfactory. Mahone will sup with me tonight. Have you tried the Ballard's oysters, sir? I heartily recommend them."

Unwittingly, Samuel Gatewood licked his lips. "I am fond of oysters. Before the War, I often repasted on oysters."

"Well, then," Eben cried. "That's the thing. You must beard the lion. Mahone won't set foot in Richmond while the legislature is in session. But having refused to ratify the Fourteenth Amendment to the Constitution, our farsighted legislators have decamped to their districts."

"Do I understand you disapprove?"

"Sir, the Southern states seceded from the Union and Thad Stevens and his congressional Republicans believe Virginia was the lead state in that rebellion. Mr. Stevens has authored an amendment to the United States Constitution to disenfranchise those who recently attempted to break up the Union—and haughty Virginia has refused to endorse it. I am no politician, sir, I am a businessman. But business suffers when political vision falters. Sir, what will Mr. Thaddeus Stevens do now that Virginia has rejected his amendment?"

"It is vile legislation, sir. Under its provisions, those who defended their state would lose their franchise. Under this legislation, Duncan—my son Duncan—could never vote again. Why, under its provisions, General Mahone would be deprived of his franchise."

Eben laughed. "That is funny! The president of the Atlantic, Mississippi & Ohio unable to vote? Dear, dear me."

"Sir, I find your humor distasteful."

"Have I got in wrong with you? Pray accept my apologies. If we can't make jokes, we would be awfully gloomy. Please forgive a simple fellow who wishes no man harm. You know, sir, I would be your friend. I can't think of when I met a gentleman I so admired. Won't you forgive me, please?"

"Sir, I do not know what to make of you."

"Me? I am a simple fellow, certainly no saint. My vices so outweigh my virtues that if set in the balance, vice's pan would thud to earth while virtue's would soar into the heavens. I am a foolish lump of a man, but I can provide oysters!

"Please accompany me, sir. Little Billy will come to the Ballard Hotel and straight into your ambuscade."

THE TRAIN BOASTED a blue car, a red, and a third which may once have been green or gray. The locomotive was wrinkled, as if it had been bashed by a gargantuan baby and indifferently mended by indulgent parents. Iron patches covered bullet holes in its boiler.

That locomotive's stack spewed cinders and smoke. Stoves in the car contributed to the fug. Wet wool and unwashed flesh persuaded Samuel Gatewood to sit beside the window, which he forced open a crack.

At four cents per mile, the eighteen miles from Petersburg to Richmond, Samuel's ticket had exhausted his cash. Samuel Gatewood could not—would not—ask his son Duncan for help. He'd no return ticket to Stratford and should he fail with General Mahone, Samuel faced a one-hundred-seventy-mile walk home.

"Mr. Gatewood, since Miss Pauline has not replied to my entreaties, I must inquire of you. How is the dear child?"

"My niece is in good health. Ought else she must tell you herself."

Samuel was biding at Cousin Molly's Richmond house, which would have been warmer with coal for the fireplaces and brighter if the illuminating gas were connected. Last night, swaddled in quilts, by candlelight Samuel Gatewood had read Ecclesiastes. "Barnwell, this is not a smoking car."

Eben promptly pushed his cigar out the window. "Is Pauline affianced to someone else? I have confessed my error. I have repented and, sir, my offense was less than you think!"

Stratford's mill wasn't turning. Stratford's people lived on stored potatoes, turnips, winter squash, and the squirrels or rabbits Jack the Driver trapped.

Samuel hadn't met a payroll since September and owed three hundred dollars to his workers. His workers or their wives often came to Stratford to beg Samuel for their due.

The First National Bank of Warm Springs had refused Samuel more credit and demanded the money he owed.

Samuel Gatewood understood that he had been wealthy once, but he could not actually recall that happy state. His confidence in the future, in his ability to restore his family competency; that confidence belonged to a younger man. Someone like this Barnwell fellow.

That young man noted that the Central Pacific Railroad had passed entirely through Wyoming. "The railroad will change everything, sir. It will civilize the indians and everyone will be happy."

" 'In all points as he came so shall he go: and what profit hath he that hath labored for the wind.' " Samuel Gatewood cleared his throat. "A Bible verse. Do you believe God is punishing us?"

"Sir, why would He?"

When they reached Richmond, Samuel would walk the half mile or so to Cousin Molly's house, where he would remove his boots and stuff them with dry rags. He would eat an apple.

"Pauline has uncommonly strong moral sentiments," Eben ventured. "That day, after the Hevener trial (you'll remember, sir, we did ask you to accompany us), after Hevener's charges were dismissed, I approached Aunt Opal and, thinking to console and turn her thoughts to happier matters, I asked if she'd give me driving lessons. That's the offense for which Pauline punishes me. My, she was angry! Eben Barnwell was 'heartless,' he was 'unfeeling.' I tried to make amends, but Pauline would have none of it. Sir, those driving lessons were Pauline's own idea!"

The air was so brisk at the Richmond depot it took Samuel's breath away. From the platform, men and women dispersed to homes or places of business. Samuel envied them their destinations.

"Mr. Gatewood, would you join me, please? After we sup I'll send you home by carriage and this evening fetch you back. I don't know if you can extract your full due from Little Billy, but I'd bet you can get payment on account."

Samuel pictured a rich broth of fresh Chesapeake oysters. There was something corrupt about an oyster stew—so many creatures' lives, each precious in God's sight, given for one man's supper. Samuel said, "Pauline has been unhappy but would not say why, and Miss Semple does not betray her confidences. Pauline's mother, Leona, was delicate. Semples are more sensitive than Gatewoods. Abigail's favorite aunt, Elizabeth Semple, passed on at nineteen. She wrote poetry. Reams and reams of poetry. Strong morals and delicate sensibilities are a difficult combination. Have you ever stopped to think, Mr. Barnwell, how insignificant we are?"

Eben said, "Be assured, sir, we'll feel more significant after we dine!"

New owners had restored the Ballard Hotel to its antebellum splendor and the servants were familiar. The claret made Samuel Gatewood's head hum and the oyster stew was as good as he remembered.

Thus it happened that Eben Barnwell would lend Samuel Gatewood two thousand dollars until General Mahone was able to pay, and as surety, Barnwell would accept Stratford's mortgage. It was such a familiar, pleasant meal, Samuel could not think why he had ever disliked the young man.

—

CHAPTER 21

MILITARY DISTRICT #1

By proclamation of the United States Congress, March 2, 1867:

Whereas *no legal state governments or adequate protection exists in the Rebel states of Virginia, North Carolina, South Carolina, Georgia, Mississippi, Alabama, Louisiana, Florida, Texas and Arkansas; and* whereas *it is necessary that peace and good order should be enforced in said states until loyal and republican state governments can be legally established; therefore.*

Be it enacted by the Senate and House of Representatives of the United States of America in Congress assembled, *that said Rebel states shall be divided into military districts and made subject to the military authority of the United States as hereinafter proscribed, and that for that purpose Virginia shall constitute the first district . . .*

CHAPTER 22

INCIDENT ON THE RICHMOND
& DANVILLE RAILROAD

On the fifth day of April last year as the easternbound passenger train was passing the switch of the branch track leading to the coal pits, about 12 1/2 miles from Richmond, a pin which secured the lever by which the switch rails are moved gave way just as the engine and all the cars of the train, and the first truck of the last or "ladies' " car, had passed the point; as the pin broke, the switch lever fell downward, causing the switch rails to be moved from their proper place, by which the wheels of the hindermost truck of the ladies' car were thrown off the track; no chance being afforded to give notice to the engineer, nor for him to stop if notified, the train continued to move forward for a distance of about three hundred feet, when the car broke loose from the car next in front and was precipitated down the bank, which at this point is about fifty feet high, making in its fall about one and a half revolutions, by which the following named persons were injured:

Killed— Mrs. Trotter of Pittsylvania County.
Injured—Mrs. Green T. Pace, daughter of Mrs. Trotter, seriously.
  Mrs. S. E. Hayward of Richmond, arm broken.
  Mr. & Mrs. J. C. Harkness of Washington, DC, both slightly.

Mrs. J. C. Hobson of Richmond, slightly.

Mrs. M. B. Anderson of Richmond, slightly.

Mrs. L. H. Dance of Richmond, slightly.

Mrs. R. A. Denier of Richmond, slightly.

Mrs. C. E. Melcher of Germany, slightly.

Mr. Robert Green of Richmond, slightly.

Mr. J. Heineker of New York, slightly.

Bishop John Early, seriously.

Mr. Isaac Overby of Charlotte County, seriously.

Mrs. Samuel Gatewood of Highland County, seriously.

All the injured parties have recovered except Mrs. Gatewood, whose injury was a fracture of the spine, which caused her death one week after the occurrence of the accident, notwithstanding the most skilled medical aid procured. No blame could be attached to any of those employed upon the train, which was, in accordance with orders, moving at a moderate rate of speed in passing that point. The construction of the switch fastening was of the general and uniform pattern which had been in use upon the road from its opening.

From the Richmond & Danville Railroad's annual Report to the Virginia Railroad Commission

"HE RIGHT, YOU KNOW," AUNT OPAL MUTTERED. "PREACHER BUY a first-class ticket. Why he got to sit in that smoking car with the riffraffs?"

Abigail felt her headache returning. Every mile of this interminable journey had been lengthened by Aunt Opal's opinions. "Reverend Cook has justice on his side," Abigail said tightly. "But must he insist on it?"

April 5, 1867, the two women waited on the Petersburg Depot platform to board the Richmond train. Abigail hadn't traveled for years and this trip to visit her new grandchild might have been happier if Abigail hadn't given way to Christian impulse and invited Aunt Opal to accompany her.

Now Opal smiled her emancipated smile—a smile rich in irony; a smile that saw the world as bleak as it was and anticipated no improvement. "We ain't 'sisted on justice since we was drug to these shores," she observed. "Would have got whipped if'n we 'sisted."

Negroes who had been polite before the War had become so disagreeable. Sometimes Abigail believed negroes had been freed principally to try the nerves of polite white ladies like herself!

The car directly behind the cinder-belching locomotive, the smoking car, was assigned to sports and negroes. Whites traveling with a body servant were often dismayed when respectable servants were ordered into the malodorous car with the drunken whites who actually preferred such accommodation. The third car of the train was reserved for ladies and whites.

"I am a minister of the Gospel of Jesus Christ," Reverend Fields Cook repeated, "serving Richmond's First African Baptist Church." He coughed. "I will be a delegate to the Republican convention, twelve days hence."

White passengers were impatient and the engineer was leaning from his cab to assess the delay.

The harried conductor ran fingers through his thinning hair. "Don't matter who you are," the conductor said. "Like I said: ladies' car is for whites, which you ain't."

A portly white man offered mediation: "Sir, I am Bishop Early of Farmville. Although I am Episcopal, Reverend Cook is my brother in Christ. We do not object to his presence among us."

A middle-aged planter demurred. "I object, sir. A negro male among our wives and daughters?"

The bishop said, "In 1861, my own dear daughter was escorted to Southern Seminary by our negro coachman, Jim. Jim discharged his responsibilities to my entire satisfaction.

"That was then and this is now," the planter retorted. "Niggers ain't what they was."

"I remind you, sir, that we are equal in the sight of God."

"Maybe so," the conductor said, "but not in the sight of the Richmond

& Danville. My orders are, 'No niggers in the ladies' car.' If you don't like it, take it up with the superintendent."

Bishop Early spread his hands. "I'm sorry, Reverend," he said. "We cannot expect Christ's justice in this sinful world."

Unsmiling, Reverend Cook said, "Sir, your conscience is clear."

"Same like that Hevener boy," Aunt Opal muttered. "Pompey kilt, and that boy don't spend one day in jail for killin' him."

This particular observation had sauced every discomfort, large and small, during this tedious journey. The noonday sun made Abigail's headache throb.

Reverend Cook said, "I will inform your employers of this outrage."

"Tell whoever you damn well want to," the conductor muttered so everyone could pretend they hadn't heard.

Aunt Opal and the Reverend Cook went to the smoking car while the white passengers boarded the ladies' car, where the planter expanded his discourse on negro morals pre- and postwar with ladies too courteous to avoid him. Bishop Early fluttered his newspaper disapprovingly.

With a squeal, lurch, and Vesuvian blast of cinders, the locomotive shouldered its load. Abigail took her knitting from her reticule. Her grand-child's socks would be identical to those she had knitted, goodness—was it so many years ago?—for her infant children Duncan and Leona. Baby Catesby Gatewood—what a touching tribute to Pauline's father. Duncan and Catesby had been more like brothers than brothers-in-law.

After Catesby died (Abigail's mind shied—as it always did—at the dreadful words "took his own life"), Leona did not linger long. Abigail believed her daughter Leona had been too disappointed in life to want more of it.

The train swayed, the stove hissed and rattled. One could be suffo-cated by the stove or open the window and be suffocated by cinders.

The War had taken Abigail's daughter and son-in-law, maimed her son Duncan, and reduced Stratford's rich competence to poverty. Only Eben Barnwell's mortgage money kept the Gatewoods from bankruptcy. Abigail's niece Pauline had resumed correspondence with the man. Before the War Eben Barnwell would have been beneath the Gatewoods' notice.

Firmly, Abigail set these realities aside in favor of happier thoughts. Duncan and Sallie had moved into Molly Semple's Richmond house. Duncan was so busy with the legislature! And a new grandson: Catesby Gatewood! Abigail daydreamed about Stratford's grand Christmases, when her house glowed with warmth and hospitality. She recalled Sabbaths at SunRise Chapel; servants in the garret upstairs, the Gatewoods in the sanctuary below. How the coloreds could sing!

As the train chugged toward Richmond, Abigail's fingers automatically counted stitches in her grandson's tiny socks.

If Abigail Gatewood readily switched onto the well-worn tracks of reverie, avoiding present woes in favor of a pleasanter past, who can condemn her?

CHAPTER 23

TERRAPIN À LA DELMONICO

The diamondback Chesapeake terrapins are considered the best.
They must be freshly caught. Long Island terrapins are also
much liked by epicures, some averring that they are as fine as the
Chesapeake, but this is not a fact.

Drop the terrapins in sufficient tepid water to allow them to
swim, and leave them thus for half an hour, then change the
water several times and wash them well. Scald by plunging them
into boiling water, and take them out as quickly as the skin (a
small white skin on the head and feet) can be removed with a
cloth, then put them to cook in water without any salt or season-
ing for thirty to forty-five minutes. Press the feet meat between
the fingers and if it yields easily, they are ready. Let them get
cold, cut off the nails, then break the shell on the flat side; detach
this shell from the meats, empty out all the insides found in the
upper shell, suppressing the entrails and lights, and carefully
removing the gallbladder from the liver, then place the liver in
cold water. Remove the white inside muscles as well as the head
and tail; separate the legs at their joints and divide into inch-
and-a-quarter pieces—the lights, entrails, head, tail, heart,
claws, muscles, and gallbladder to be thrown away. Lay the terrapin in a saucepan with its eggs and liver cut in thin slices, sea-

*son with salt, black pepper, and cayenne, and cover with suffi-
cient water to attain to the height of the terrapin, then let boil
and finish the cooking in a slow oven for twenty or thirty minutes. Remove from heat. For each quart of broth, add a half pint
of cream, reduce to half, season with salt and cayenne pepper,
thicken with five raw eggs diluted with half a pint of cream, and
two ounces of fresh butter, toss the terrapin while adding the
thickening; this must not boil, finishing with half a gill of very
good sherry wine or madeira. The sauce should be thick and
served very hot.*

Pauline Byrd exclaimed, "Manhattan is a sublime prospect!"

Cousin Molly Semple asked, "What is that frightful stench?"

"It *is* sublime, isn't it?" Eben Barnwell exulted.

Pointedly, Molly Semple coughed into her handkerchief and jutted a forefinger at smokestacks on the Brooklyn shore.

"That's Pratt's. Pratt refines Pennsylvania petroleum. They say he's made five million."

Pauline enthused, "I did not know the world contained so many ships! Why, the whole world is here."

The Brooklyn ferry hooted past great sailing vessels, shouldering aside steam tugs, fishing smacks, and lighters.

"Isn't it, though!" Eben was as proud as if New York City were his invention.

Eben Barnwell's invitation had reached grieving Stratford like a gift from heaven. Samuel Gatewood wandered his demesne in a stupor, closeting himself every evening with a demijohn and not reappearing until the next noon, unshaven, red-eyed, and reeking. Sometimes, in the midst of her duties, Molly Semple was overwhelmed. She'd be sweeping or churning and she'd weep until she couldn't distinguish butter from buttermilk.

Pauline was glad to escape Stratford's troubles for a time.

Jack the Driver met General Mahone's mounting demands for ties and twenty-foot by twenty-four-inch bridge timbers. Although the General's payments were regular now, he was a year in arrears.

Stratford's mill workers were negroes. Timber cutters and the teamsters who hauled logs to the mill and sawn lumber to the railhead were white men working under Billy Hansel. Hansel had been a slave patroller before the War and Jack called him "Mr. Bill," while Hansel called Jack, "Jack."

Cousin Molly told Samuel they must refuse Barnwell's invitation, that an unmarried young woman visiting a yankee bachelor might be misunderstood, but Samuel insisted she go. "Abigail would have wanted it. October fourteenth it was, Sunday, October fourteenth, eighteen and thirty-eight, we resolved upon matrimony. What children we were! I promised Abigail that one day we would visit England. Abigail loved reading about London! How she admired London fashions! Abigail and I never went." Samuel's mouth trembled. "There was always too much to do."

Franky's marriage, motherhood, and her husband Jack's elevation to deacon of the Warm Springs Baptist Church had transmogrified a disreputable kitten into a gratified cat. Franky's brisk step had slowed and she'd become sedate. "Mrs. Mitchell," Molly advised her, "while I'm away, you'll be in charge of Stratford House. Mr. Samuel will want looking after. Please cook his favorite dishes. Do encourage him to eat."

After she wished them safe journeying, Mrs. Mitchell warned that Lucifer himself resided in New York City and Miss Molly and Miss Pauline should beware his snares.

On a bright July afternoon Sallie Gatewood met Pauline and Molly at Richmond's Virginia Central depot. Duncan was away on General Mahone's business.

Pauline wished to see sites associated with the Confederacy: its office buildings, statehouse, and the mansion where, through so many tribulations, President Davis had made his home. The three ladies paid their respects to flower-bedecked Confederate graves in Hollywood Cemetery.

After supper Pauline retired, and Cousin Molly and Sallie—two old friends—took sherry in the parlor. Hard scrubbing had restored the room to its prewar cheerfulness. Its heart-pine floors glowed and Sallie had rescued an ancient Aubusson from the attic. A handsome swirl of blue and lavender; the carpet's moth-damaged corner was under the coal bucket.

"My dear," Molly said, "you've brought my old house back to life. And Aunt Opal—hasn't baby Catesby improved Opal's disposition?"

"She spoils him terribly!" Sallie mused. "I believe Aunt Opal and Abigail must have quarreled before the accident; Aunt Opal acted as guilty as if she'd caused the derailment. So long as poor Abigail survived, Opal wouldn't leave her, nor would she let another do for her."

"Oh, my dear . . ."

After tears were shed, Sallie dabbed her eyes, blew her nose, and took a deep breath. "I've news, Molly, I could not trust to anyone but you. My Duncan, he, well . . . in the beginning, the laudanum salved his pain, but then . . ."

Molly simply listened.

"Then it, the laudanum, became Duncan's master. Duncan performed the duties his employer demanded and he never fell out of temper with me, but Molly . . . it was as if my living, breathing husband had been swapped for one of Madame Tussaud's wax replicas. Duncan's opium delusions were so vivid he frequently—while waking—even whilst conversing with me in this very room—my husband drifted away. Even now, I shudder to recall his remote, indifferent gaze."

After visiting Marguerite Omodundru, Sallie had resolved to bring matters to a head, and the next morning, before Duncan took his first dose, she confronted him.

Duncan countered with complaints about his work. He said that respectable men avoided private meetings with "the notorious Major Gatewood" lest their own reputations suffer. He said, "The Assembly has passed Mahone's bill and General Mahone has shaken my hand on it. That is as close as Mahone will come to those hands I have had to shake!"

Sallie said, "Duncan, I have loved you because you were hopeful and brave. Though I feared for you, I was proud of you. I would rather have had you dead than a coward."

"So, Sallie, are you proud of me now?"

She resumed tenderly, "Duncan, I regret your present indifference to our marital relations. Some say a woman should disdain conjugal duties, but I married a man, Duncan, and our relations were my delight."

Her candor stripped him of pretense. "Dear God." Eyes brimming, Duncan knelt at his wife's feet. "I will change. Please God, I will!"

Now Sallie told Molly Semple Duncan had resolved to quit laudanum and had found a Philadelphia physician who had success curing the opium craving.

"Oh, my dear. I am so glad for you."

"There! Now I have said it! Thank you, dear Molly, for listening to me. When I lost my Duncan to laudanum, I lost my dearest listener."

NOON SHARP the next day, Molly Semple and Pauline boarded a James River lighter, which conveyed them to their deep-water steamer.

Though young Pauline enjoyed the voyage, Molly Semple was afflicted by seafarer's complaint, and as Pauline was admiring the ever-changing coastline from the deck her chaperone stayed below.

Hence, as they entered New York Harbor and Pauline enthused about "billowing white sails," "sailors in the rigging like human beads on strings," and et cetera, an exhausted, queasy Molly Semple saw little to approve.

Eben Barnwell bounded aboard and before they could protest he'd collected the ladies and their baggage. Once aboard the ferry, Eben repeated his invitation to stay in his home.

"Two unmarried women in a bachelor's domicile? My dear sir!"

"Miss Semple, I'll warrant Manhattanites wouldn't give it a thought."

"As you will recall, Mr. Barnwell, we are not Manhattanites. We are Virginia rustics. We've secured accommodations at the St. Nicholas. My Richmond connections assured me it is respectable."

THE RIVER'S STENCH was overwhelming and the flotsam best ignored but Molly's spirits lifted as the ferry approached the Fulton Street slip. The lower deck teemed with men and women of every class and dress. Immigrants called to one other in a perfect babble of languages.

The trio were seated in Eben's carriage before the ferry docked and when the gate opened, their driver whipped his steeds as if at a starter's gun. Other carriages, wagons, beer wagons, and drays had a similar notion, but despite rude cries and gestures, no driver gained any particular advantage.

Clopping along Fulton Street, Eben Barnwell pointed out the newspaper publishers: the *New World*, the *Democratic Review*, the *Literary World* . . .

"So many!" Pauline exclaimed.

"Why, I'll say there are. That's the *Herald* there. Mr. Barnum's museum had that corner until it burned. One of Barnum's curiosities, a whale, blocked Broadway for two days."

"Is that why we proceed so slowly?" Cousin Molly inquired sweetly. "Are we impeded by roasted cetaceans?"

"Oh." Eben jammed his fingers into his waistcoat pockets. "It's always slow downtown." He brightened. "Everyone wants to be here and there ain't room for everyone."

Pauline said, "At Stratford months pass without strangers. How can you stand it, Mr. Barnwell—all these strangers? Do you recognize anyone?"

Eben thumped the roof with his walking stick. "Flynn, are you awake? Pick up their heels, man!

"It's a big old place, all right. In this city, a man earns his right to be known. Why, everybody knows Jay Cooke, and Commodore Vanderbilt, and Fisk, and Boss Tweed. Everybody knows Morgan and Jay Gould." He pointed, "That's Niblo's Gardens," he said. "Niblo's coryphees play to packed houses."

"What is a 'coryphee'?" Molly inquired.

"A dancing girl." Eben coughed. "Uh . . . Arabian."

"Arabian? Are these Arabian women decently clothed?"

"Ah . . ."

"Have you attended these uplifting performances?"

"Miss Semple, this is Manhattan. The most influential gentlemen in the city attend these performances."

"And in Manhattan, they are called 'gentlemen'?"

Although Madison Square's west side was unfashionable (its townhouses had been converted to rooming houses and apartments), the east side (Eben Barnwell assured them) was tip-top.

As they drew up at the curb, Eben exclaimed, "Here we are! Eben Barnwell's humble home!" and before coachman Flynn could climb down from his box, Eben had their door open. "Have a care where you step, ladies! The street cleaners have not been by this morning!"

Barnwell's home was severely rectangular and fronted the square behind a stern reddish stone facade. Barnwell clattered his door knocker, greeted his maid, and returned her curtsy with such a bow she blushed in confusion. Entering, Eben Barnwell announced he had paid "fifty" for the house. "I 'spose it's worth more now." He named his servants (besides Flynn and Mary, the housemaid, he employed Bridget Reilly as cook). Eben directed his guests' attention to the "pièce de résistance" (whose installation was completed at midnight last night thanks to Eben's frantic pleas and lavish bribes): "It is Croton water. Pure as a maiden's fancy."

A sullen stone cherub overlooked a marble basin into which he spewed water. The fountain apparatus occupied so much of Eben's modest foyer his visitors were splashed.

"Italian workmen," Eben informed the ladies. "The sculptor is descended from Michelangelo! Isn't it splendid!" On a more practical note he added, "You can turn it off with a valve in the coal cellar."

"Have you an umbrella?" Cousin Molly inquired.

Eben Barnwell's formal parlor was furnished with an elaborately carved sideboard and armchairs in green and red velvet. The brocade drapes were open wide and when Cousin Molly asked they be closed, he said, "Don't you like to look out at humanity, Miss Semple?"

"Sometimes," she replied. "But there are so many here."

The seascape which hung over the mantel was so dark with aged, crazed varnish, one couldn't determine whether the represented vessels were steam or sail. Eben laughed. "It's awful, isn't it? But the dealer I had it from said it was 'an excellent example,' that Morgan himself owned one by the same artist, and that the price had been reduced. Apparently I am a man dealers find agreeable."

"Mr. Barnwell, you are a surprising young man."

"Miss Semple, I am merely the son of a poor Vermont peddler."

"Yes, yes. You've told us that. But exactly who are you?"

"Molly!"

"As your kinswoman, dear, it is my duty to ask disagreeable questions."

Eben smiled and shrugged helplessly.

Molly Semple refused Mr. Barnwell's supper invitation but accepted his coach, which conveyed the women uptown to the St. Nicholas Hotel, a block-long structure. Their luggage was passed from coachman to porter to the desk clerk, who assigned their room and produced a key. The porter then escorted the ladies to a novel device: inside a wood-paneled closet, a boy stood at attention beside a hawser which passed through a circular hole in the ceiling and a hole in the floor. "Think of it, madames," the porter suggested, "as a little parlor, going up and down by machinery."

After the trio got in, the boy tugged on the rope, and the lobby floor receded as the closet ascended. They passed the mezzanine and second floor to debark safely on the third, where the porter's assurance that the hotel had stairs as well as this "elevator" relieved Molly Semple.

Their small neat room overlooked bustling Broadway. Down the hall in the bathing chamber, valves delivered hot water, and after dismissing reservations about the hygiene of the strangers who might have used the tub previously, Cousin Molly bathed.

Affixed to the wall above a porcelain stool was a rectangular wooden tank from which a brass chain descended to a pull.

Cousin Molly had read about these "water closets" but had never seen one.

As they dressed for supper, Pauline asked about it.

The older woman whispered, "It produces a draft on one's underparts."

SUNDAY, COUSIN MOLLY had thought to attend Presbyterian services, but Eben Barnwell had other plans. "Dr. Beecher is the most celebrated preacher in America. Beecher speaks to the modern Christian."

To Beecher's Brooklyn tabernacle they went.

Pauline felt agreeably daring. Unfamiliar with Congregationalism's tenets, Pauline supposed that liberal creed to be somewhere east of Christianity, though not so far east as Muhammadism.

"Is there a funeral?" Cousin Molly whispered.

"No, no. Beecher loves flowers. Every Sunday is springtime in Beecher's church."

Pauline's Presbyterian God was impatient with human frailty. Beecher's church was so sunny! How everybody smiled!

When Beecher stepped into the pulpit his big face was sallow and his large eyes were half closed under heavy lids. He announced a hymn, offered a languid prayer, announced another hymn, another prayer.

But when he began his sermon, his voice, which had been flat as a finishing iron, became lyrical and his face began to glow. "A man has a right to stimulate himself for right purpose. All men recognize this need in regard to business, politics, social life—but if needful there, where the senses and selfishness have much influence, how much more needful when we rise into the realm of moral and spiritual things?"

Beecher seemed pleased by his question and let it hang for a breath before resuming, "When men have a great stone to move, they first dig away the earth around it, working moderately and taking care to reserve their strength. When the earth is removed, they apply their lever, and now all take hold. At the word, 'Heave!' "—at Beecher's bellow, Pauline flinched—"each man strains with nerve and sinew—he throws his whole strength into that moment's effort, and the stone is forced from its bed."

Seductively as a lover, Beecher asserted that the passionate Christian could shift every stone, however heavy; that he could alter the very firmament.

Beecher's cadences buzzed at Pauline like a persistent wasp. How could this jolly optimism explain her self-slain father? Dr. Beecher's assurances gleamed like a conqueror's boot.

After the service, Pauline made for a door where Dr. Beecher wasn't greeting his congregation, which disappointed Cousin Molly, who'd rather hoped to shake Beecher's hand.

On their drive uptown, Eben told them Beecher was a famous abolitionist. Beecher's sister had written *Uncle Tom's Cabin*.

"Mr. Barnwell," Cousin Molly groaned, "we are rustics, not ignora-muses."

"Beecher believes a man can raise himself by his own will," Eben said stubbornly. "We aren't fixed by accident of birth. Beecher's sermons have been published."

Pauline said, "Can't we talk about something else?"

Molly patted her hand.

"I . . . I'm sorry, dear Molly. Everything is so new to me!"

Farther up Fifth Avenue, chockablock residences gave way to trees and meadows. Harlem Lane fronted horse establishments: stables, white-painted inns, and clubhouses. Trotters—hundreds of trotters—walked, trotted, or cantered along the broad dirt lane.

"Why, that's Robert Bonner driving Dexter!"

"What a handsome animal!"

They were overtaken by the lightest, most delicate sulkies, and color returned to Pauline's cheeks.

One driver's nod was a challenge. Another nod: challenge accepted. Lashing their trotters to utmost effort, the contenders wove through slower rigs at breakneck speed.

"How do they avoid collisions?" Pauline asked.

" 'Live men' don't fear collisions. Dear Pauline, this makes my blood race. How I wish I possessed the nerve . . ."

Pauline began thinking Eben's carriage—which had previously seemed so up-to-date—was rather dowdy.

Eben said, "After I place Mahone's new bond issue, I shall buy a trot-ter. I already have subscribers for ten thousand."

Behind matched blacks, a driver silently lifted his stovepipe. Hastily Eben Barnwell reciprocated, "Leonard Jerome! Good day to you, sir!"

The other replied with an flick of his whip.

"Jerome," Eben confided happily, "is Commodore Vanderbilt's part-ner. In Jerome's stable—I have it on good authority—every stall is walnut-paneled and carpeted. Carpeting in a horse stall—can you imagine?"

Appetites whetted, they returned downtown to the northernmost of Mr. Delmonico's establishments, a converted mansion one block west of Union Square. "I usually eat at the Broad Street Delmonico's," Eben confessed.

"If you frequent a different restaurant," Cousin Molly wondered, "why are we dining here?"

"Oh, Miss Semple, you ladies are too fine to dine with us speculators. The uptown Del's is higher-toned."

They were escorted to a table in what had been the mansion's formal sitting room. The faux-marble floor was stenciled in a diamond pattern, the globes of gas chandeliers glowed, and though it was early afternoon, the drapes were drawn.

At another table, a balding, schoolmastery man rose and bowed.

Eben returned this bow. "Amos Hayward is with the Treasury. He fancies I did him a service once. Isn't this a grand establishment? When I was a boy I didn't dream such places existed."

"When you were a boy . . . ?" Pauline prompted.

Eben summoned their waiter. "Randolph, the young lady will have the *crème de volaille*—that's a cream soup, Pauline—and the *truites de Long Island*—that's a Frenchy way of spelling 'trout'—and the terrapin. We're lucky to find terrapin on the menu."

Cousin Molly said she would be content with soup and bread.

"I am so glad you came," Eben enthused. "I am grateful you have forgiven me. If I am thoughtless, Pauline, it is from exuberance, not malice. Life is so awfully fast, I can hardly keep up!"

Randolph brought champagne. "Mr. Hayward's compliments, sir."

The balding man was bowing again.

"Give the gentleman our thanks and regrets we cannot join him at his table. The ladies are in mourning." Eben returned to his guests. "When Hayward comes to New York to audit the Bank of New York's accounts, we dine together. Hayward's an undersecretary. He drops the names of *powerful* acquaintances and hints at information *too confidential* to be shared."

Cousin Molly eyed the champagne. "Sir. It is Sunday and, as you have reminded me—we are in mourning.

"If you don't care for champagne, Miss Semple, simply invert your glass."

Which Molly did while, markedly, Pauline did not.

Diced onions, carrots, and celery floated in the thick soup. Cousin Molly was hungrier than she'd imagined.

"I've never had champagne," Pauline confessed.

"You'll acquire a taste for it," Eben was confident. "At the Broad Street Del's when a speculator makes a coup, he buys champagne for everybody. How I'd like to be that man!"

Pauline wondered how many of their fellow diners were as rich as young Eben Barnwell. She checked herself: what was she thinking!

Guilelessly, with a hint of envy, Eben told them how Gould and Fisk had bested Commodore Vanderbilt.

"That man with the matched blacks? The carpeted stable?"

"Yes, Jerome is Vanderbilt's man. When Vanderbilt tried to gain control of the Erie, Gould and Fisk printed Erie stock faster than the Commodore could buy it."

"But that's dishonest!" Pauline was uneasy. Who was Eben Barnwell, really?

"Dear child"—Eben drank champagne—"it is only money."

Molly helped herself to Pauline's untouched trout. "Most men work for their bread."

Eben said, "Yes. But in our great country any man can rise. No American is confined by his antecedents. Our waiter, Randolph, came from good family, but he and his mother fell on hard times." That worthy attended Eben's raised finger. "Randolph, how long have you been employed at Del's?"

"I started five years ago, in the kitchen."

"Now you're a headwaiter. May I ask, what was your largest gratuity?"

"At his New Year's affair, Mr. Fisk gave me fifty dollars."

"Thank you, Randolph. Would I could be so generous."

The waiter smiled. "Would that you could, sir."

"Fifty dollars for a single night's service," Pauline whispered. "How can that be? Jack Mitchell works daybreak to dusk for a dollar."

"Our nation is made for getting and spending."

"And for the Christianity of happy flowers," Pauline said. "Cousin, please take my trout. My appetite has deserted me."

When the terrapin arrived, it smelled overpowering, and the first rich spoonful stuck in Pauline's throat.

Money. Money. Money.

With tears in her eyes, Pauline wondered how she'd gotten so far from home.

CHAPTER 24

—

IN THE HAYFIELD

In the day, our canvas lodge glowed with sunlight; at night, its thin walls seemed solid as logs. We lay between bearskins on a mattress of deer grass, and sometimes I'd hear a Real Dog howl on the bluff across the river and I'd curl deeper against Plenty Cuts and did not dream.

Plenty Cuts and Shillaber bought wagonloads of flour and potatoes from the Gallatin Valley to Fort C. F. Smith. The Blackfeet had been attacking travelers, but we passed through their country for fifteen days without seeing them.

Plenty Cuts and Shillaber took jobs cutting hay for the Seizers.

Although High Backbone of the Miniconjou, Two Moons and Roman Nose of the Cheyenne, and the Arapaho Sorrel Horse all led war parties against the Montana Road, Washitu newspapers named it "Red Cloud's War." Though wagon trains were afraid to use the road, the Seizers' forts guarded it and Seizers came and went as they pleased.

We were offered a cabin outside the stockade, but the cabin was dark and smelled bad, so I bought a Cheyenne widow's lodge and household goods for five silver dollars and a half pound of plug tobacco. The widow moved in with Grasshopper, her sister's daughter.

Three miles downriver, they were mowing hay and most of the haymakers and Seizers slept there in a willow corral, but every night *my husband came home to be with me. He told me, in the Lakota tongue, how happy he was. Crow, Arapaho, and Northern Cheyenne lodges sheltered under Fort Smith's cannons. They were blanket indians and I was the warrior White Bull's sister, but I walked with downcast eyes.*

Crow warriors came to say the Lakota were holding the Sun Dance and preparing to attack the forts. The Seizer chief gave them small gifts but did not believe their warning.

Little Brown Snake, a Crow warrior, told me that White Bull had quarreled with Young Man Afraid of His Horses. My brother was chief of his own village now. My brother had fought bravely at the Hundred in the Hand and became a Wicasa—a Shirt Wearer.

"A Seizer slashed him with his long knife, but White Bull dragged him off his horse. White Bull boasts about his scar and how the Seizer begged for his life."

When the blanket indians learned I was White Bull's sister I was invited into their lodges, where I drank sassafras tea while the women told me giving birth would hurt.

Long ago my husband had been a Washitu slave. His masters had whipped him. The children saw his scars when he was bathing and gave Plenty Cuts his Lakota name.

Plenty Cuts had won honors in the Washitu's Southern war. After that fighting was finished he wanted to be a Seizer, but they wouldn't accept him because his skin is black.

He returned to life—he told me—in my arms.

In Virginia City Reverend Evans married us and Wong gave me away, but I told Plenty Cuts I would not be truly married until he gave horses to White Bull, as is our custom.

He said, "If you like we can be married by the Baptists too. Then the Blackfeet. We can get married by every preacher and medicine man in the territory."

I swatted his big grinning face.

Although neither Washitu nor indians treated my husband as a complete person, the Crow children loved him. They showed him how to shoot their tiny bows and giggled when they were the better marks-men. They taught him how to ride indian fashion with a saddle pad and a nose bridle. Sometimes they treated him like a beloved uncle, sometimes like a favorite dog.

RATCLIFF'S STOLID MULES FORGED THROUGH RYEGRASS TICKLING their chins. Grasshoppers, dislodged from their perches, became meals for cliff swallows that swirled above the mower. It clattered and clunked and the reel squealed as it dragged grass into the sickle bar, whose teeth chittered like the grasshoppers but louder.

For eons, buffalo had migrated through here, but none came near Fort C. F. Smith in the hot August of 1867.

That morning, three mowing machines swathed the pasture between the bluffs and the Bighorn River. The pitman arm of Ratcliff's mower clacked and the sickle bar chattered and Ratcliff half turned to keep the ungainly machine tracking. When something *thupped* past Ratcliff's ear, he thought it was an especially bold swallow. The haymaker on his right lashed his mules into a run as indians appeared before the wall of unmown grass.

Swallows spun up. The fleeing mowers bounced and chittered until their overworked pitman arms snapped. Inside the willow corral, soldiers grabbed their rifles and fired.

Lakota scouts lay motionless along the rimrock on the dry bluffs behind the corral.

After the haymakers whipped their teams into the corral, soldiers rolled a wagon across the opening. The indians pulled up their blown horses just beyond easy pistol shot. Several slumped wounded. One—a chief, by his eagle feathers—stood on his horse's rump to flip his loincloth at the soldiers.

The swallows who were rearing their second hatch on the cliff face chirruped and dove at indian scouts sprawled on the rimrock. Hundreds of Cheyenne and Lakota in war regalia waited silently behind the scouts.

No male had ever exposed his privates to Lieutenant Sternberg. "Mount up!" he cried.

His sergeant yelled, "They're decoys, sir. Same damn trick they pulled on Fetterman."

"We shall chastise them," Sternberg shouted. "Mount up!"

But hesitation proved the sergeant correct, for, by a miracle, the wounded indians sat upright and the winded horses regained strength and more indian horsemen came out of the tall grass: a dozen, two dozen, fifty, a hundred, two hundred.

"Oh, Christ," the sergeant breathed. "We're for it now."

In their cliffside burrows the swallows spotted a Harlan's hawk: just a dot next to the sun. Men in the corral lay among horse and mule droppings facing outward like the spokes of a wheel.

Ratcliff set his rifle stock to his cheek and dug his elbows into the dirt. Sweat dripped off his forehead. His rifle barrel shimmered. The indian ponies' hooves floated on a mirage of superheated air.

Arrows buzzed into the corral.

"Lieutenant Sternberg," young Private Abbott called. "You must take cover!"

"Who spoke? I'll have that man bucked and gagged!"

Private Abbott, who hadn't been in the army long enough to learn discretion, was spared by the bullet which took Lieutenant Sternberg in the forehead.

Some indians screamed like foxes. Some roared like a mother grizzly. They blew their eagle-bone whistles. Their vests were beaded with porcupine quills dyed red or black or green or blue. His buffalo-hide shield bore each warrior's medicine sign. The eagle feathers in their headbands had been got by lying all day in a blind beside an eagle's nest to snatch feathers from a full-grown bird as it landed. Red-tipped feathers honored battle wounds.

Ratcliff fired, ejected the empty, inserted, fired again, ejected, inserted, fired, ejected, inserted, fired . . .

Warriors charged the willow corral like they meant to ride over it, and

Ratcliff aimed at the mass of them and touched off a round, another, and indians and horses were a flesh wall looming over him, their arrows slicing through the flimsy willow barricade.

The indians expected the firing to stop for reloading, but two weeks before, the soldiers had been issued breechloaders and never stopped shooting.

The Lakota broke and withdrew. Ben Shillaber dragged a wounded sergeant into a lean-to. A mule had arrows buried in its rib cage and back. Its white eyes rolled and bloody froth dripped from its muzzle. It brayed frantically.

Hunkered over, Ben Shillaber toured the corral, patting one man on the back, joking with another. Arrows flew from the alders beside the creek, and rifles spat back. They never had a clear target and shot at what might be an elbow, might be a quilled vest, might be a moccasin.

They heaped brass cartridges in their hats.

Indians slipped out of the alders across the mowed field, concealing themselves in the shallowest dips and declines, sliding toward the corral like a snake after a sparrow's eggs.

A soldier cried, "There! Over there!"

"God Damned! Where'd he come from!"

"Shillaber made a good indian out of him!"

"He's just playing possum. Won't somebody shoot that damn mule?"

"Why don't the Colonel send help?"

"Don't worry about the Colonel, boys," Ben Shillaber laughed. "He'll come soon's he's finished his supper."

"What's that smell? Oh! God help us!"

Wisps of smoke, then flame licked above the grass, with darker flames roiling the grass heart, then black smoke rolling toward the white men and their stored hay shocks—a ten-foot wall of flame. It was so hot men laid their faces against the cool earth and prayed.

"Forget the damn fire!" Shillaber called. "Watch for indians." As the flames writhed closer he cried the Confederate yell and Union men who had feared and hated that cry yelled it too; even Ratcliff emptied his lungs.

The fire wall loomed over the corral and horses jerked at their picket pins and whinnied and bucked with fear.

With the sound a man makes flailing a carpet—a tremendous *WHUP*—the fire extinguished itself and falling ashes blanketed the corral. Ratcliff sneezed.

The clicking like rosary beads was men counting cartridges.

"The fort will see the smoke. If they can't hear the shots, they'll see the smoke."

"The water barrel's empty. Christ, I'm thirsty."

Even the oldest swallows couldn't recall such an insect feast. Beaks agape, they swooped, gorging as they dove. The Harlan's hawk taloned a swallow and bore it to the scorched earth, where, as the swallow uttered terrified chirps, the hawk plunged its beak and extracted a string of succulent gut glistening white against the burned grass.

Flights of arrows arced into the corrals, wounded more horses, and killed another soldier. When a warrior jumped up at the corral gate, Ben Shillaber shot him. The haymakers cheered the man's death agonies.

At dusk, Ben Shillaber offered straws to each man. Someone must bring help from the fort. Private Abbott drew and flinched.

"Ride like hell, you'll make it," Shillaber said. "The indians won't be expecting you."

But when Shillaber saddled Lieutenant Sternberg's gelding, Private Abbott missed the stirrup.

"Hold up," Ratcliff said. "Ben, there's no use gettin' a white boy killed when you got a nigger." Ratcliff snatched the reins from Abbott and swung into the saddle.

"You sure, Top?"

"Christ, Ben. If you Johnnies couldn't kill me, no damn indian can!"

Ben Shillaber handed Ratcliff his Colts Patent revolver.

At full gallop Ratcliff spurred through the gateway and cinders whirled up where the gelding's hooves struck the ground. Ratcliff lay along the horse's neck, nearly as flat as a Crow indian boy.

Indian ponies came behind.

Ratcliff raced for Fort Smith on the wagon track. The indians couldn't spread out in the tall grass.

Ratcliff wished they'd yell. He'd know how near they were if they'd yell.

The fort's low stockade was still a mile ahead when Ratcliff sensed a shape looming beside him. An indian pony's white nose crept up on Ratcliff's right. A cannon blasted from the fort. The shell whistled far overhead and exploded.

The shape drew neck and neck and a war club rose and crashed down and the reins dropped from Ratcliff's numbed hands. He slid over his horse's shoulder into the high grass.

Ratcliff struck the earth on his left arm and rolled onto his back. Stunned, he rose on an elbow. His vision was blurred, but he could draw and cock Shillaber's revolver.

The indian jumped into the tiny clearing Ratcliff's fall had created. The Lakota's red-and-green buckskin shirt was fringed with hair; his two eagle feathers were notched and red-tipped. The man's face was scarred from forehead to chin and his left ear had been cropped, so his head seemed unbalanced. His knife was a cavalry saber broken below the hilt.

In Lakota, he sang his kill song, "I have counted coup. Now I will kill you. I, White Bull, will make you cry."

The two men were alone in the circle of flattened grass. The grass wall around them was horse-high. Through a blood haze, Ratcliff squinted over his pistol at White Bull's chest.

In passable Lakota Ratcliff said, "I am Plenty Cuts. My wife, She Goes Before, will cry if I shoot her brother."

PART TWO

THE ATLANTIC, MISSISSIPPI & OHIO RAILROAD

We notice that when the slave was emancipated an unprecedented state of affairs existed. Master and servant, the educated and the ignorant, the proudest and the humblest, the richest and the poorest were made to stand on one platform, theoretically equal—man to man. Naturally the master could not look upon the man so recently his slave with that respect the American Constitution demanded. The slave could not look upon his oppressor and forget entirely his oppression, none but a fanatic could expect them to rush into each other's arms.

—REVEREND HENRY WILLIAMS
GILLFIELD BAPTIST CHURCH,
PETERSBURG, VIRGINIA, 1866

CHAPTER 25

A PHILADELPHIA SANITARIUM

KIDDER'S FARADIC APPARATUS WAS CASED IN AN OAK BOX RESEMbling a tobacco humidor. Duncan, normally curious about mechanical devices, never asked how the Faradic Apparatus produced current. Dr. Parrish's soft, stubby fingers attached one wire to the batteries and the other to the iron pipe which fed the room's gaslights. The examination chair had stout arms which Duncan clenched, and thin leather padding through which he could feel every spline of the chair's ladder-back.

"There, Major Gatewood. How were your bowels today? Have you employed the rectal syringe?"

Dutifully, Duncan reported.

"Your appetite? Were you able to eat the beef at supper?"

"I was satisfied with a boiled egg."

Dr. Parrish turned to his guest, a New York physician here to learn electricity's curative properties. "Major Gatewood began taking laudanum, five drops daily, to relieve the pain of his amputation. By the time he determined to seek a cure his daily dose routinely exceeded two hundred drops. Sensitive or excitable men are more susceptible to opium than those with a more sanguine disposition. When Major Gatewood came to me, his skin was muddy, his appetite dull, and his digestion impaired. His muscular development was poor and his sleep was more dozing than true sleep. Often sleep was accompanied by terrifying dreams. Dreams which—he tells me—sometimes attend our sessions on the apparatus but do not otherwise trouble him."

One electrode was a brass ball at the tip of a rubberized rod. The other was a circular brass disk. "Major Gatewood, if you will hold the disk over the occiput, there, just behind your ear."

The gaslights provided the only warmth in the room and the electrode was cold. Though the doctors wore black woolen suits, Duncan was shirtless.

"It is well to apply the negative pole first," Dr. Parrish said. "The current from Bunsen's cells is interrupted with this simple telegraph key."

When Parrish touched the brass ball to his skull, Duncan broke a sweat.

Afterward his mouth was always dry and his ears always rang, but Duncan never felt the current. When the current struck, Duncan fell into memory, revisiting events he had not known were stored. One time he was a boy on his beloved horse Gypsy, jumping rail fences at Stratford, smelling Gypsy's sweat, feeling the great horse's muscles bunching under his thighs. Then it was Spotsylvania, the day after that terrible battle: servants loading bodies on wagons while kinfolk and friends sought loved ones among the dead. Through tobacco-stained teeth, Sergeant Fisher described the battle: how two armies had fought hand-to-hand for eighteen hours on opposite sides of a narrow breastwork. Sergeant Fisher pointed to a corpse that had been hit by so many bullets it was no thicker than a folded blanket, Fisher asking, "Got a chaw? It cuts the smell."

Duncan's brother-in-law, Catesby Byrd, lay with his back against a pine tree. Though his boots were gone, they hadn't taken his watch, which was still ticking. Absently Duncan wound it and put it in his pocket. He'd get it to Catesby's son, Thomas.

Duncan wetted his handkerchief and knelt to wash gunpowder from Catesby's face. The bullet hole wasn't large and hadn't bled much. Duncan cleaned that too.

"I reckon he jest got tired of fellas tryin' to kill him," Fisher said.

—

"THE SUPERIOR, middle, and inferior cervical ganglia may be affected by galvanism." Dr. Parrish removed the electrodes, bent Duncan forward, and thumped his spine.

While the negro nurse, John Bingham, helped Duncan from the chair, the doctors inspected the apparatus. When Dr. Parrish tapped the key, it produced a six-inch spark.

"Come along, Major," the nurse said. "You bath be ready."

Laudanum's ironical detachment had kept Duncan floating above his life. Though Duncan was Mahone's chief briber, he wasn't the only one. In a legislator's office one afternoon, when he opened his green carpetbag, the legislator laughed. "You biddin' agin' yourself, Major Gatewood. I already been bought: lock, stock, and barrel."

Before the War the Commonwealth of Virginia had financed plank roads, canals, and railroads and taken stock in these enterprises. Although canals and plank roads lost money, several railroads, including Mahone's, had been profitable and were returning to profitability again. Mahone wanted to buy Virginia's shares of his railroads. The Baltimore & Ohio coveted the same shares.

Mahone won. Despite military rule, despite negroes at the constitutional convention, white conservatives would not hand over the Commonwealth to Northern interests.

The day after Mahone's legislative victory, Duncan had told the General he needed a rest, that he had promised Sallie he would seek a cure for his laudanum craving.

General Mahone drummed his fingers. "That damned constitutional convention is meeting and our military rulers will appoint another governor. Major, these are trying times."

"Sir, I cannot serve you ably."

Mahone's smile was chilly. "I am aware of your infirmities, Major." He paused. "You should know I have increased orders for your father's crossties and"—he smiled—"I'm not so far in arrears. Eben Barnwell believes the British investors will respond to our recent success. I can spare you for a month."

"Sir," Duncan said eagerly, "when I return I'd like different work. I'd make a reliable stationmaster . . ."

"Major Gatewood, I have a glut of stationmasters. Do give my best to your wife. I will see you in December."

WHEN HE HELPED Duncan into the scalding tub, Nurse Bingham said, "Oh, I believe that's hot enough, Major. Hot enough, sure."

When he arrived at the Philadelphia sanitarium, Duncan had been searched for laudanum by a white nurse who sympathized with Duncan's war injuries and was glad when his inspection didn't find a hidden supply. Nurse Bingham was less sympathetic.

Although John Bingham had been born free in Philadelphia and never ventured south, he was obsessed with slavery. He reported lurid tales as gospel. Bingham was especially curious about girls sold into the fancy trade and girls ravished by their masters.

When Duncan told him their black servants were considered part of the Gatewood family, Bingham gave him a sly look. "That's why you havin' all them mulatto babies by them negro women, eh, Major Gatewood? On account of how you is all family?"

As a boy Duncan had had a son by Maggie, his father's servant. He held his tongue.

"You gettin' red in the face, Major Gatewood," Bingham observed. "That's healthy. Yessir, that's healthy. Major, if negroes was your family, how come you sell them to the fancy trade? You ever sell any of your white family?"

In his first weeks, Duncan had taken three hot baths daily. Now he only bathed at bedtime. "We tried not to sell our servants," Duncan said.

"Did you 'deed?" Bingham poured a bucket of icy water over his head. "I wished I could have seen one of them slave markets. Them big ones in Charleston or Richmond. All them pretty women on the block and a man could look 'em over before he picked his pick. Oh, I would have liked to see that. Is it true you could ask the auctioneer and the woman would drop her shift so you could see everything? Is it true what they say?"

After a second bucket of icy water, Duncan climbed nude onto a wooden table where Bingham dried him, pulled on a horsehide mitten, and rubbed briskly.

"Go to Virginia," Duncan advised. "Ask those who were slaves."

Bingham stopped rubbing.

"No, sir. No, sir. I born and reared in the North and I stayin'. Major, how much would a high yellow, fourteen years, how much would you pay for such a gal?"

DUNCAN'S ROOM CONTAINED a washstand, wooden chair, and iron bed. Its uncurtained window overlooked row houses across the narrow street. In the afternoons sometimes he watched the neighborhood children at play. He didn't want for anything, didn't miss his old life, didn't yearn for a new life. Under cotton sheets and a light wool comforter, Duncan Gatewood, lately major in the 44th Virginia Infantry, slept like a boy.

CHAPTER 26

LETTER FROM JESSE BURNS TO EDWARD RATCLIFF (ENVELOPE MARKED BY TERRITORIAL POSTMASTER: "RETURN TO SENDER: ADDRESSEE DECEASED")

RICHMOND, VIRGINIA
APRIL 8, 1868

Dear Edward,

I am only now answering your letter. Hello, She Goes Before! Don't take Edward's ill humors to heart. He has a kinder nature than he pretends.

I am wedded myself. I met a young woman at a church social and Sudie took my heart for her prize. She is a comely woman of twenty-seven years. Sudie's son, Jimson, is accustomed to a slack rein. Jimson's friends are "The Knockabouts": the rowdiest boys in Richmond.

Sudie was a house servant and her gentle manners point up my own clumsiness. Sudie forgives me with many endearments.

I have seen my first wife, Maggie. She now calls herself "Marguerite Omohundru," is passing for white, and owns the bank she was entering! My beloved Sudie rescued me from confusion and despair, for Sudie loves me as Maggie never did.

When I determined to turn loose of Maggie and all she once meant to me, an oppression was lifted off my shoulders. May God bless Mrs. Omohundru. May God bless Mr. and Mrs. Jesse Burns!

I am employed as a printer at Richmond's Republican newspaper, which subsists on state government business and donations from Northern Republicans. I am poorly paid. Sudie, Jimson, and I are obliged to dwell in two small rooms on East Third Street in a district which is boisterous at any time and dangerous after nightfall. But even here, Sudie has created a domestic paradise. She begged discarded fabric from her employers (Sudie is a laundress), and sewed neat curtains for our windows. Though the curtains are mismatched, they are stitched by the same hand and each sports bright tassels! Our marital bed once graced a suite in the Spottswood Hotel. New bed boards, ropes, and some nails made it good as new. Jimson sleeps in the kitchen beside our coal stove.

How cold Montana must be! How do you bear it? Richmond's winter froze me solid!

We have completed the great work of the Virginia Constitutional Convention. Negroes registered in great numbers to pick delegates and, by the grace of God, I was elected.

We met in the Virginia Hall of Delegates, that same grand hall where Thomas Jefferson and Patrick Henry once debated. I tell you, Edward, when I took my seat in that hallowed spot I did not feel grand; on the contrary, I felt wholly insignificant. Sometimes at night I wake with a start and must needs convince myself my life is not a dream, that come morning I won't wake in Stratford's negro Quarters for another day's toil. I have met eminent statesmen: Judge Underwood, who guides our constitutional work; Thaddeus Stevens, who is attempting to impeach President Johnson; Frederick Douglass, surely the greatest man of our race; and even General Butler. We negroes invited our Army of the James commander to speak before the convention. White conservatives gnashed their teeth as the affable General Butler—the man who had led negro troops against them—instructed them how to write a constitution! Edward, the General you and I once saluted has shaken my hand!

Stratford's Thomas Byrd is the Staunton delegate and if this young man possesses every good trait of the Old Virginian, he possesses every ill trait too. Thomas Byrd is honorable, educated, and implacable in his determination that authority should remain in the white hands who have always wielded it. Edward, they are afraid of us! They fear to yield the tiniest point and they are outraged when we ask our due. They mock our clothing, our hopes, our morals, even our speech. We are caricatured in the Richmond newspapers. Each conservative speech is reported as solemnly as biblical exegesis, but they report every negro utterance 'spelt out, like we was mo' ignorant dan Ol' Massa's mule.' "

Our leader Dr. Baynes rebutted them, "Do not the proprietors of these papers know that it is they and their people who have robbed the black man of education, who have taken the money and labor of the black man to support themselves in grandeur? And now they curse the black man because he is not a grammarian?"

White Republicans like my employer, Mr. Chepstow, flatter negroes and favor negro rights so we will elect them. They speak confidently for us, even when they are ignorant of what we are saying amongst ourselves. Our voices are faint as a man shouting underwater.

Dr. Baynes suggested we quit the white Republicans and start an entirely negro party, but cooler heads prevailed.

Despite our travail, from this chamber that has known such greatness, negroes and whites together produced a new constitution for Virginia. The Underwood Constitution (for such it is named) will go to the United States Congress and then to Virginia voters. We have shown every fair-minded man that negroes can assume the full duties of citizenship. Edward, it is a proud day.

> Your fellow soldier,
> Jesse Burns, Delegate to the Virginia
> Constitutional Convention

—

CHAPTER 27

LETTER FROM THOMAS BYRD TO
SAMUEL GATEWOOD

THE BALLARD HOTEL
RICHMOND, VIRGINIA
APRIL 17, 1868

Esteemed Grandfather,

Since my last letter, the farce of High Life Below Stairs *has been performed daily in the Capitol before the admiring crowd of idle blacks who crowd the galleries. The discussion concerns taxation, and Mr. Chepstow, that assiduous scribbler, asks for a minute on the floor.*

"No, I ain't gwine to 'low you nary minit." The very black Thomas Baynes proceeds to say that he has "sot here and hern 'em talk about taxation and he goes fer layin' the taxation on de land" (expecting by this means to force owners to sell or give away lands to the freedmen).

Mr. Baynes next advocates a capitation tax but is entirely opposed to a poll tax! A mischievous Conservative politely asks the speaker to explain the distinction and we are told that a capitation tax is on the head and a poll tax is on the roads! These are the same intellects who advise negroes that if they don't support Republicans their children will be sold back into slavery! These are our constitution makers. The

*Conservative looker-on is filled with indignation, disgust, and amuse-
ment all at one moment. Several yankees who have visited this
Convention of Kangaroos were aghast at the spectacle.*

*The charade winds down tomorrow. Although the delegates were
willing to extend an engagement which has delighted Richmond
audiences for so many months, General Schofield, our military governor, thought they'd rooted long enough in the public trough. The
Republicans have collected their emoluments and dispersed.*

*What has been accomplished here, after pettifogging wrangles
and endless disputes over protocol which any educated man would
have found beneath his attention, was, simply, the enfranchisement
of Virginia's most ignorant negroes and the disenfranchisement of
the Commonwealth's finest whites. Should the United States
Congress approve the Underwood Constitution, those who cannot
(or will not) sign the Ironclad Oath cannot vote.*

*When Federal troops entered Richmond in April of 1865,
negroes cried, "Bottom rail on top," and so it is today. The least
among us has become first!*

*Our own Jesse is Charles Chepstow's creature. Jesse, who served
us Gatewoods, affronts us at every turn. Grandfather, when Jesse
Burns approached me in the chamber hoping to ingratiate himself I
snubbed him.*

*General Schofield has found it impossible to find persons who
could take the Ironclad Oath and fulfill the duties of office. I quote
the General, "I have been able to find in some counties only one, in
others two, and others three persons who could read and write and
take the oath." Yet the proposed Underwood Constitution would gov-
ern the majority with this minuscule minority.*

*The new constitution proposes that all those capable of holding
office cannot, and those who ought not must. If this weren't so bitter
it would be laughable.*

*I dined last night with Duncan and Sallie. Duncan remains
involved in General Mahone's concerns. He is cured of the Soldier's
Curse, and I thank God for that! Sallie is great with child again*

*and interrogates me about my romantic attachments. I replied that
Miss Stuart and I are friendly, which never satisfies Sallie, who
brooks no ambiguity where wedlock is concerned.*

*Can it only be a year since we lost dear, dear Abigail? Truly, her
passing was the end of an era.*

*How is Stratford? Do the redbuds and dogwoods and lilacs and
scent bushes and apple trees and peach trees bloom as of old? How I
wish I weren't obliged to make my way through this tumultuous
Capital.*

*You may have read that Mr. Chepstow was arrested for inciting
the negroes to riot. Quoth Chepstow: "You colored people have no
property. The white race has houses and lands. Some of you are old
and feeble and cannot carry the musket, but you can apply the torch
to the dwelling of your enemies. There are none too young. The boy
of ten and the girl of twelve—can apply the torch."*

*As punishment, the legislature canceled his state printing con-
tract! Bless us, this will give Chepstow more time to campaign, as he
intends, for the Republican nomination for governor.*

O tempore, O mores,
Thomas Byrd

CHAPTER 28

THE IRONCLAD OATH

I do solemnly swear (or affirm) that I have never voluntarily borne arms against the United States since I have been a citizen thereof; that I have voluntarily given no aid, countenance, counsel or encouragement to persons engaged in armed hostilities thereto; that I have neither sought nor accepted nor attempted to exercise the functions of any office whatever under any authority or pretended authority in hostility to the United States; that I have not yielded a voluntary support to any pretended government, authority or constitution within the United States hostile or inimical thereto; and I do further swear (or affirm) that to the best of my knowledge and ability, I will support and defend the Constitution of the United States against all enemies, foreign or domestic; that I will bear true faith and allegiance to the same; that I take this obligation freely, without any mental reservation or purpose of evasion, and that I will well and faithfully discharge the duties of this office on which I am about to enter, so help me God.

—

CHAPTER 29

KI YA MANI YO

We heard the gunshots when the Cheyenne and Lakota attacked the haymakers. Later we saw a pillar of dark smoke and the Seizers closed the fort gates. The Seizers did not ride out to the hayfield until the gunshots were not so many. Though the haymakers had driven the Lakota away, the Seizers galloped back to the fort like frightened men and did not bring their dead with them.

Ben Shillaber came to our lodge to tell me Plenty Cuts had ridden for help and that neither Plenty Cuts nor his horse had been found. That night I prayed to JesuChrist and to Low Dog. If Low Dog would spare my husband I would dream for him whenever he wanted.

All next day the Seizers hid in their fort with the gate closed. That evening, a young Crow came with a message from my brother, White Bull. Plenty Cuts was alive.

It was a full moon when the young Crow and I crossed the Bighorn River and rode south. At first light we came to White Bull's camp and the camp dogs barked and the pony guards ran at us yelling. Although my Crow guide had boasted of his courage, he was afraid and cried that we were under White Bull's protection and that I was White Bull's sister.

The pony guards were not quite boys, not quite young men, and the eldest was proud to escort me into the village. The Crow rode off on the spotted pony that was his price for fetching me.

White Bull's village was in a grassy meadow beside Rock Creek, a circle of lodges with my brother's lodge at the northeast horn of the entrance. The village was neither the biggest nor the smallest; perhaps twenty lodges and a hundred Lakota. Their pony herd was about three hundred.

Alerted by the pony guards, they were waiting for me.

Plenty Cuts was grinning like a fool. His trousers were torn at the knees and instead of his fine new corduroy shirt he wore a buckskin vest and one of his eyes was purple-black and he had a knot on the side of his head. When he put out his arms, I slid off my horse feeling that everything was as it should be.

SHE GOES BEFORE BLUSHED, BASHFUL AS A MAIDEN. "IT IS NOT proper to embrace before others," she whispered.

"Oh, hell," Plenty Cuts said, and hugged her, and while the warriors looked off into the heavens, giggles came from White Bull's lodge where his wives were watching.

White Bull was thick-bodied and slightly bowlegged. He wore his hair in a single braid. His smile bent downward at one corner from the scar that ran from his forehead to his chin.

"Welcome to my tipi, Sister," White Bull said. "Come inside and eat."

She Goes Before wished to linger with her husband, but White Bull shook his head.

White Bull's lodge was distinctively Santee. The big ends of the lodgepoles were at the top. Inside was dim and faintly smoky. The liner depicted White Bull's brave deeds: every coup, scalp, and stolen horse. Rattling Blanket Woman and Fox Head were beading moccasins. Despite her desire to be with Plenty Cuts, She Goes Before made small talk.

Plenty Cuts had fought with the Washitu in the hayfield where several Cheyenne and Lakota had been killed, including Runs Him, a warrior from White Bull's village.

White Bull was a powerful warrior. Red Cloud himself had praised his bravery at the Hundred in the Hand. White Bull was a Wicasa, a Shirt Wearer, a counselor who could speak for all the people. But Runs Him was dead, his family walked through the camp crying their loss; his lodge throbbed with grief and one of those who killed Runs Him was White Bull's brother-in-law.

A young woman wailed in the street, hair hacked, blood dripping from her slashed arms and her mutilated hands.

"Runs Him's wife," White Bull said as he and Plenty Cuts hurried past. "I have met with the Big Bellies, the village elders. We counciled until the fire was ashes. You and I must go to Runs Him's family."

Outside their lodge White Bull called and waited for the invitation to enter.

Runs Him lay in the back of the lodge, his face painted red overlaid with blue stripes. His family had dressed him in his finest vest, softest leggings, and his funeral moccasins beaded on the soles. He wore four eagle feathers in his hair. The bullet hole in his forehead had been stuffed with grease and painted to match his face.

Runs Him's kin glared at their visitors. Their anger sucked the air out of the lodge.

Singsong, White Bull chanted, "Runs Him is slain. The brave Runs Him is slain. Runs Him, who stood with me against the Crows; Runs Him, who first counted coup on an Arapaho when a boy of thirteen." White Bull recited the dead man's war honors, giving each due weight. He concluded, "It is better to die in battle than to live to carry a cane.

"I am White Bull, I am the Wicasa, White Bull. I have come to smoke with you."

He filled the long decorated pipe, smoked, and offered smoke to the four directions. He passed it to Runs Him's father. The pipe made its deliberate way about the circle until it reached Plenty Cuts, who smoked as he'd seen White Bull do.

White Bull counseled Runs Him's family: the men were to hunt skillfully, the women were to fletch robes, bring in firewood, cook, and make clothing. White Bull promised that work would relieve their grief and would be good to have done after their mourning. He said they should demonstrate that Runs Him's family should continue to be held in high regard. He spoke quietly but earnestly.

Runs Him's brother, Shot in the Heel, reminded the Wicasa that until a scalp was taken in revenge, his brother's spirit could not cross the Shadowland. White Bull said that was true and that after the fall hunt White Bull would lead a war party against the Crows in Runs Him's honor.

Shot in the Heel was unmoved.

White Bull said, "My sister's husband, Plenty Cuts, was a Washitu slave. When he tried to run away, the Washitu cut his back with whips. Now he wishes to be Lakota. He grieves for Runs Him and gives his only horse to Runs Him's brother to express his sorrow."

For the first time, Shot in the Heel looked Plenty Cuts in the face. "His hair would make a poor scalp anyway," he said. One child laughed.

That night in White Bull's lodge, the Wicasa told Plenty Cuts that a man's soul lived in his hair and that Plenty Cuts's unusual hair would be a powerful scalp. Fox Head, who was in the corner playing with a puppy, said everybody had enjoyed Shot in the Heel's joke. That joke—White Bull said—meant Shot in the Heel had accepted Plenty Cuts's apology, but it would be well if Plenty Cuts accompanied the war party and took a scalp to help Runs Him through the Shadowland. That Crow scalp would replace his own.

WHITE BULL'S WAS a rich man's lodge. The draft screen was painted with fast horses and enemies shot with arrows. White Bull's medicine bundle and shields hung from the lodgepoles. The floor was covered with blackhorn robes whose crinkly hair tickled Plenty Cuts's bare feet. Rattling Blanket Woman had hung bells from the tipi tightening rope and these jingled with the least wind.

When the fire died down, White Bull and Rattling Blanket Woman spread a robe over themselves. Plenty Cuts and She Goes Before took their place on the other side of the lodge. Fox Head shared her robe with the puppy and once everyone was settled, two camp dogs slipped just inside and lay down to keep watch.

In the morning, after the men went out, Rattling Blanket Woman told She Goes Before, "It is not good to have sex when the baby is due." She pushed She Goes Before's nose with her fist and laughed until the tears came.

———

FOUR DAYS LATER, scouts brought news that blackhorns were nearby and the Big Bellies sent a crier through the camp announcing the hunt.

The scouts went out again to fire the grass and drive the blackhorns from the river bottoms onto a high bench. Smoke from these fires flowed down Rock Creek into the village and women complained. At noon all able-bodied Lakota started toward the blackhorn jump. Mounted scouts rode on both sides of the hunting party because enemies might have found these blackhorns too. Plenty Cuts went with the women and children, who were led by the winkte, Shivering Aspen.

The children played games, the dogs barked, the women gossiped, and in this manner they proceeded along Sweetwater Creek until they reached the jump. The rimrock was eighty feet above them. The rocky talus below the bluff was littered with bleached bones. Shivering Aspen was a man of forty dressed in a woman's dress; his warrior's hawk face and stern features were belied by elaborately quilled, delicate clothing. The wintke had been a young man until, one morning, he came out of the lodge wearing women's clothing. After another young man had him, the wintke's parents had set up a separate lodge as they would for a married daughter.

Now the wintke sorted the women and children: some would remain with him, others must take places on the jump above.

Shivering Aspen was famous. He'd prophesied the Fetterman fight. After Chief Gall threw the wintke into Peno Creek, Shivering Aspen waded to shore saying he had seen nothing, so Gall threw him in again. The third time he was thrown in the icy water, Shivering Aspen had seen a hundred Seizers in his hand, which was why the Lakota called the fight a Hundred in the Hand.

Blackhorns feel safe on high places where they can see their enemies far off, and the broad bench rose gently to the rimrock. White Bull and others crossed behind the herd, drifting quietly back and forth, making the blackhorns uneasy. They moseyed uphill to safety.

On the rimrock a V of rock piles narrowed to the jump. Men stationed themselves near the point and women and children waited at the wide mouth. Wearing a blackhorn robe with horned headdress, Shot in the Heel escorted Plenty Cuts to the tip of the V, the final post before the rimrock quit and air began. "It is the place of honor," he said.

"I thank you," Plenty Cuts replied.

Below, the wintke was joking, berating a wife for the frequency with which her husband had visited his lodge. The wintke said her husband would move in with him pretty soon. The other wives hooted.

Shot in the Heel signaled and like a ripple, fifty Lakota lay down beside their rock piles. Wearing his blackhorn headdress, Shot in the Heel, the Blackhorn Caller, walked the precipice as a blackhorn walks, with overladen forequarters, tiny delicate feet, and skinny buttocks.

In no particular hurry, pausing to graze, the herd leaders—always cows—ambled into the mouth of the V and White Bull and his riders withdrew, removing their pressure. The Blackhorn Caller began to dance, not as a man dances, but as a blackhorn might dance. He threw his head like a rutting blackhorn, he lowered his head and pawed like a herd bull accepting a challenge, he bent over his newborn calf and licked it clean with the rough-tongued fastidiousness of a new mother. The intrigued blackhorns came nearer and the Blackhorn Caller redoubled his efforts, grunting now, as a blackhorn grunts satisfaction from succulent grass, bleating the bleat that means "Where is my calf?" The lead cows were drawn to this creature who was more blackhorn than they were.

When the herd was inside the wings of the V, Lakota women stood silently. This caused uneasiness, and since, as every blackhorn knows, safety is within the herd and stragglers might be cut off, anxious mother blackhorns shooed their calves deeper inside the V, and the deeper they came, the more silent Lakota rose to their feet and the higher the Blackhorn Caller pranced. Shot in the Heel became the Vision Blackhorn, the black-

horn who would lead her herd to better pasture and water than they had
known before. The Vision Blackhorn could lead them to Paradise: no
wolves, no mountain lions, no grizzlies, no hunters—only lush prairies of
crested wheatgrass, ryegrass, and bluestem; higher than the grasses their
grandmothers had known. The Vision Blackhorn danced for an end to
danger, privation, and fear. He danced as a blackhorn who had never
been afraid.

As the blackhorns drifted toward the point, as more silent Lakota
stood, White Bull and his riders came behind and women fluttered their
robes and the blackhorns' uneasiness turned to fear.

The blackhorns fled and no blackhorn was willing to be last because
stragglers were cut off and killed, every blackhorn knew that. That fluttering robe-wall made frightening noises, like magpies, like grizzlies, like
wolves.

The blackhorns escaped toward the Blackhorn Caller.

When the leaders were almost on him, Shot in the Heel dropped his
blackhorn disguise.

The earth shook from a thousand hooves and Shot in the Heel told
Plenty Cuts, "Let us see if this is our day to die."

Some blackhorns might have tried to break through the waving Lakota
robes if they hadn't known with blackhorn certainty they must stay with
the herd.

The running that had satisfied them wearied their legs and emptied
their lungs and they ran toward that patch of clear blue sky uncertain why
they were running but knowing that they must.

The lead blackhorns saw the end of the earth and dug in their forefeet
and for an instant tottered on the brink with nothing but air between them
and the distant blue mountains.

What bellowing! What outrage and fear!

Not ten feet from where Plenty Cuts flapped his robe and yelled, the
leaders locked their shoulders and dug in their forefeet, but, pushed from
behind, they skidded, tumbling into space. The blackhorns were taller
than Plenty Cuts, but his flapping robe was taller still, fluttering over them
like an eagle's wing. Sometimes a blackhorn's eyes locked with Plenty

Cuts's, wishing to turn aside, to charge the fluttering wall, but Plenty Cuts stared him down.

The wings of the V collapsed inward and riders pushed and the blackhorn laggards could only think of escape. The Lakota cries were triumphant and when the blackhorn heard these, even the youngest calf knew it must die. The last few might easily have turned and run back, but they were resigned, and though two or three needed prodding with lances, they too escaped into the air.

The Lakota skinned and quartered blackhorns until dark, and dog-drawn travois hauled robes and meat back to the camp, where women cut meat into long strips for the drying racks and everybody feasted on blackhorn hump or tongue, even the dogs.

The next day's work was the same, from daybreak until dark, and the night was the same.

Though they took all the blackhorn skins, they left much meat for the Real Dogs.

"What will you do when the blackhorns are gone?" Plenty Cuts asked White Bull.

"Blackhorns are sacred and live under the earth. We summon them forth to feed our people. Blackhorns hate the smell of white men. If we keep the whites out of our hunting grounds, blackhorns will come when we summon them."

AFTER THE MEAT was dry and the robes scraped, the Big Bellies decided to move to winter camp on the headwaters of the Tongue where they had camped three winters previously.

Washitu traders came in the Moon of the Falling Leaves with four empty wagons for robes and one wagon with trade goods to exchange. They gave more for the cow robes because cow robes were softer and more pliable.

She Goes Before had prepared four robes, which Plenty Cuts exchanged for two cartons of bullets and a mirror for She Goes Before.

Though Plenty Cuts didn't trade for whiskey, others did, and that night was loud with howling and fighting, One drunken man stabbed his wife in the breast. Next morning, the Big Bellies told the traders they wanted no more whiskey. White Bull said he would kill them and take their goods if they sold any more. The whiskey drinkers cursed White Bull to his face.

Later, some said the traders had brought the white scab sickness to the camp. Others said Old Woman Horn brought the sickness from the Brulés' camp when she came to visit her daughter.

THE DAYS WERE MILD and though light snow fell, it lingered only where the sun didn't touch it. Shot in the Heel had a Real Dog dream and announced a feast honoring Runs Him.

Plenty Cuts was invited to take part. After they smoked and feasted, the warriors boasted of the scalps they had taken and the coups they had counted. After a time, Plenty Cuts couldn't remember which warrior had chased a Crow into the river and taken his hair and which had stolen an Arapaho's warhorse tied behind the enemy's own tipi. Shot in the Heel retold the Hundred in the Hand, how the Seizer bugler had fought until his carbine had no more bullets and his revolver had no more bullets and the Seizer beat a Miniconjou, Standing Bear, with his bugle until the bugle was flattened and Standing Bear howled. The warriors chuckled at Standing Bear's discomfiture. "I took that bugler's scalp," Shot in the Heel boasted, "for he was the bravest Seizer that day."

When it was Plenty Cuts's turn he said, "Seizers gave me a Medal of Honor for courage. It is powerful medicine."

"How many enemies did you kill?" Shot in the Heel inquired.

Plenty Cuts said he didn't know. "Several," he said.

This made everyone laugh because in Lakota, "several" can mean "two" or "a hundred."

"It is well." Shot in the Heel then sang, "The brother who flees the fighting is no longer a brother. Ki ya mani yo. Recognize everything as you walk."

The next morning, Plenty Cuts joined the warriors outside Shot in the

Heel's tipi. White Bull had given Plenty Cuts his second-best pony and a blackhorn-hide shield with a hawk emblem because the hawk never runs away. She Goes Before gave him elk grease and white pigment to streak his face like the cuts on his back. Plenty Cuts's pony was good but not as good as Shot in the Heel's.

They dismounted out of sight of the village. They would lead their horses so the ponies would have speed and endurance when needed. The Washitu traders had spoken of a Crow village in the mountains. A warrior from that village, Chasing Crane, had taken three Lakota scalps and during a pony raid he'd tapped Shot in the Heel with his bow, counting first coup, and though Shot in the Heel had escaped alive, he had been shamed.

In Lakota country they walked and talked openly, but in the land between the tribes, they put scouts out and spoke in low tones. In this manner they walked fifty miles.

Each night they built a small fire under a bluff or deep inside an aspen thicket and ate pemmican. They joked about Plenty Cuts's black skin, joked that in a night attack he would be invisible.

One of the young warriors had visited the wintke's lodge and they joked about that too, telling the young man he might lose his taste for women.

When they were near the Crow village, Shot in the Heel scouted the enemy. The Crow village was in the mouth of a draw, protected by steep ridges on either side. Every evening, the pony herd was taken through the village into the narrow draw behind it.

"These Crows must think some Lakota want their ponies." Shot in the Heel smiled.

That night Shot in the Heel had a Real Dog dream. In this dream, Real Dog looked up from the blackhorn calf he was eating directly into Shot in the Heel's eyes. When he told his dream, Shot in the Heel said, "We will be successful, but I will be killed."

The others said nothing. Shot in the Heel said, "Hoka hey. It is a good day to die.

That afternoon they climbed the east ridge above the Crow camp, and it was as Shot in the Heel had said. In the morning Crow warriors escorted the pony herd out and kept guards with them all day. Several hunting parties went out as well and some urged Shot in the Heel to follow and attack one of these, saying that the pony herd was too hard a target. Shot in the Heel said, "Ki ya mani yo."

That night the Lakota made plans. The young braves wanted to climb down from the ridges and stampede the horses straight through the village. If anyone saw them, they would pretend to be Crows.

"Be hard for me to pretend I'm a Crow," Plenty Cuts said. So they made a different plan.

CHASING CRANE'S TIPI stood at the village entrance. The next morning before sunrise his dogs started barking. Rising from his robes, Chasing Crane heard loud singing. It was not Crow singing:

> *We're gonna hang Jeff Davis from a sour apple tree.*
> *We're gonna hang Jeff Davis from a sour apple tree.*
> *We're gonna hang Jeff Davis from a sour apple tree.*
> *As we go marching on.*

Chasing Crane's wife shooed their children to the back of the tipi. The dogs' hackles rose and they ran outside barking. Chasing Crane took his revolver and followed them.

A naked black man astride a white horse rode back and forth in front of the village, singing. His chest and legs were streaked with white paint. Other warriors joined Chasing Crane at the village entrance. Some carried bows or guns, some did not. Soon all the warriors were watching the naked black man singing his Washitu song.

The women were watching too.

Gradually the naked black man worked in closer and finally reined up before the Crow warriors.

"Chasing Crane!" he shouted, first in Washitu, then in Lakota.

Most of the Crows had never seen a black man.

Chasing Crane said, "Who calls for Chasing Crane?"

The black man pointed at him rudely and sang.

> *Gwine to run all night!*
> *Gwine to run all day.*
> *The Camptown ladies sing this song.*
> *Doo-dah, doo-dah.*

He raised his face to the lightening sky and yelled, "Oh, doo-dah dey!"

The ground shook with the rumble of running ponies and a pony guard screamed as he died and the Crows turned to face this new threat and those who hadn't thought to bring weapons ran for their tipis. The pony herd burst through the village and flattened tipis. Shot in the Heel leaned over and struck Chasing Crane with his coup stick, but Chasing Crane fired and the bullet entered Shot in the Heel's belly and came out his back.

The Crows came after their horses.

The weakened Shot in the Heel clung to his horse until they reached the cottonwood grove, which was the second part of their plan.

Most of Shot in the Heel's warriors were hiding in the cottonwoods, and when the Crows came close, the Lakota rode out singing kill songs and shooting arrows and guns.

Since Chasing Crane had been humiliated by Shot in the Heel's coup, he rode in front. The naked black man charged at Chasing Crane and killed him with a single bullet.

Another Lakota took Chasing Crane's scalp and counted second coup on his body. The Lakota killed two more Crow warriors and scalped them.

The Crows thought the naked black man was the evil spirit Iktomi in human guise, so they didn't pursue. They regathered some of their ponies, but the Lakota made off with fifty. Shot in the Heel died before sunset and the Lakota left him where he lay because it is good for a Lakota to die in enemy country. Ki ya mani yo.

When my water broke, Rattling Blanket Woman commanded the men and children to leave the lodge and told Fox Head to fetch Brings the

Horses and Touch Dog because they were wise in these matters. This happened during the Moon of Frost in the Tipi.

When the Grandmothers came, they heaped the softest skins at the foot of the lodgepole and told me to kneel and grip the lodgepole. Rattling Blanket Woman lifted my dress and washed me. When the pains came, the Grandmothers knelt beside me and embraced me and drained the pains into themselves and breathed my breath and encircled my belly and pressed. When my sweaty hair stung my eyes, they washed the sweat away and bound my hair with yarn. Brings the Horses sang, "The old die / the new are born / the nation of men lives forever." The Grandmothers sang loudly when I cried out so my cry could not be heard outside the lodge. This continued for some time. Brings the Horses said it was because I was old to be delivering my first, but Touch Dog said it was because Plenty Cuts was a big man, so his child would be as big as he was. Brings the Horses disagreed, saying that big stallions sometimes threw small ponies. Rattling Blanket Woman told them to stop quarreling and make tea. As I knelt on the furs, a convulsion gripped me. From my lungs and heart I bore down and my daughter left my body and Rattling Shield caught her and bore her into the world.

For a time, I rested while the Grandmothers rubbed bear grease and beaver castor over my baby and dusted her navel with puffball dust. They wrapped her in soft deerskin before laying her at my side. She smelled of love and fresh-cut mint. I wished to give her suck but did not because first milk waters the newborn's bowels. They took her from me and Rattling Blanket Woman fed her a little soup from a bladder shaped like a nipple.

Brings the Horses knelt and massaged my belly until the afterbirth came. Since Rattling Blanket Woman was the eldest, she suckled my first milk until my aching breasts were empty.

IN THE FIRST DAY of her life, the women of White Bull's family gave She Goes Before's baby six handsome willow cradles, each the value of a horse.

In the second day, her mother suckled her.

On the third day of her life, her dried navel cord was placed in a tortoise amulet which was presented to She Goes Before with a second tortoise amulet, identical but empty, to decoy evil spirits from the child.

On the fourth day, Plenty Cuts gave the naming feast, where the child was named Red Leaf after her grandfather.

In the second week, Plenty Cuts gave a horse to a poor man in honor of his daughter.

In the fourth week of her life, it snowed every day. When Red Leaf started to cry, her mother pinched her nose because Lakota babies must not cry.

In the fifth week, Red Leaf recognized her mother and smiled.

On the first day of her seventh week, her mother discovered red sores on her eyelids.

On the third day of the seventh week, Red Leaf became so hot that her mother took her out of the cradle board and rubbed her with snow.

On the fourth day, she lost her suck.

On the fifth day of the seventh week, Red Leaf's life ended and her mother cut a lock of her kinky baby hair for the ghost-owning ceremony.

———

CHAPTER 30

MENU FOR A BANQUET HONORING
MR. CHARLES DICKENS, APRIL 18, 1868

Huîtres sur coquilles
Consommé Sévigné • *Crème d'asperges à la Dumas*

HORS-D'OEUVRES CHAUD

Timbales à la Dickens

POISSONS

Saumon à la Victoria • *Bass à l'Italienne*
Pommes de terre Nelson

RELEVÉS

Filet de boeuf à la Lucullus • *Laitues braisées demi-glace*
Agneau farci à la Walter Scott • *Tomates à la Reine*

ENTRÉES

Filets de brants à la Seymour
Petit pois à l'Anglaise
Croustades de riz de veau à la Douglas
Quartiers d'artichauts Lyonnaise
Épinards au velouté
Côtelettes de grouse à la Fenimore Cooper

ENTRÉES FROIDES

Galantines à la Royale
Aspics de fois-gras historiés

INTERMEDE

Sorbet à la Américaine

RÔTS

Bécassines • Poulets de grains truffés

ENTREMETS SUCRÉTS

Pêches à la Parisienne (chaud)
Macedoine de fruits • Moscovite à l'abricot
Lait d'amandes rubané au chocolat
Charlotte Doria
Viennois glacé à l'orange • Corbeille de biscuits Chantilly
Gâteau Savarin au marasquin
Glaces forme fruits Napolitaine
Parfait au café

PIECES MONTÉES

Temple de la Littérature • Trophée a l'Auteur
Pavillon International • Colonne Triomphale
Les armes Britanniques • The Stars and Stripes
Le Monument de Washington • La Loi du Destin

DESSERT

Fruits • Compotes de pêches et de poires • Petits fours
Fleurs ·

CHAPTER 31

LETTER FROM EBEN BARNWELL
TO MISS PAULINE BYRD

15 MADISON SQUARE
APRIL 20, 1868

Dearest Pauline,

I trust this finds you in good spirits. My fortunes have soared inversely to Erie bonds, which I sold short when so many "wise heads" wagered they would rise. Pauline, I do thank God every day for smiling upon me.

How is beautiful Stratford? How fondly I recall our conversations on its dear, dear porch while shadows gathered in the river valley and the sun sank majestically behind the mountains!

I'm no hand at letter writing. I am accustomed to business talk: "Buy this," "sell that," "Price per hundredweight." But when I write you, my beloved, my pen is flustered and lifeless and I cannot say what I mean. What I mean is that I love Stratford as you do and will do all in my power to sustain it. Please reassure your esteemed grandfather that when certain speculations bear fruit, I shall remit the funds he desires. In the meantime, should he wish, I'll give his banker my personal assurances. Do understand, Pauline, that bankers would rather have return on their capital than any planta-

tion, even a plantation as charming as Stratford. There are so many Virginia plantations on the market!

Northern businessmen have lost enthusiasm for Southern investments. Business languishes where there is no civilian government and mundane transactions must be approved by military officers. When Congress decreed that Virginia must fall again under military rule, men who had been buying Atlantic, Mississippi & Ohio bonds began selling. Capital fled to the Baltimore & Ohio, a railroad incorporated in Maryland, a state whose legislators don't wrestle with negro rights nor whether ex-rebels can vote.

Little Billy blames me because I can't sell his bonds. Am I the Congress? Do I give a "darn" whether negroes vote? I thank God my own eggs are not in the A.M.&O. basket!

Enough of dreary commerce! Saturday I supped with the august author Charles Dickens. No, dear Pauline; we were not tête-à-tête. Along with two hundred others—I attended a banquet at the uptown Del's—surely the gastronomical highlight of the year! Chef Ranhofer pulled out every stop in his culinary organ. My waiter, Randolph, attended me and me alone.

On his previous visit to these shores, Mr. Dickens complained about our food, manners, even the rate at which we ate! On this occasion, among glittering crystal, burnished silver, damask drapes, the patriotic pieces montées, Mr. Dickens was graceful enough to offer an apology for his previous remarks!

I am endlessly grateful for the opportunity in our American nation! I cannot believe I would have come to anything in Mr. Dickens's England. Our menu is enclosed so you might know what you might have enjoyed had you been there with me. It was, in every respect, a satisfactory, patriotic evening!

Dearest—for you are my dearest!—I am 30 years of age, portly, and partially deaf in my left ear from a blow I took in childhood. I have no kin with claims upon me. I am, in every respect, a free agent. In character I am energetic and determined.

As a husband I'd be dutiful and considerate. I'd tend to my busi-

ness and my wife would rule our roost. Should God favor us with children, I would be an indulgent parent, for I am something of a child myself! Ha! Ha!

You may not have remarked my faults. I must confess them. I have been discouraged! Sometimes I have been discouraged! At dreary moments, dearest Pauline, I've thought myself a sham, a frightened child in adult's clothing. I could see nothing in my fellows' faces that was not mean, petty, or cruel. For me, the world held neither charm nor grace. Happily, these dismal episodes are infrequent.

I am not a subtle fellow and am perhaps too plain-spoken. According to the phrenologists I have a strong amative bump!

I'd rather joke than weep.

I own my house in fee simple and it is furnished à la mode. My servants are capable and content. I have substantial capital of my own and can promise that if you accept my proposal, you shall lack for nothing.

There, I've said it! Though I am unworthy of you I shall try to become a better man should you consent to honor me with your hand. Dearest Pauline, you would make me the happiest man in old New York and I would walk these streets with a lighter step if you wrote that you feel—even in the least measure—as I do.

> *Anxiously awaiting your reply,*
> *I am your earnest suitor,*
> *Eben Barnwell*

CHAPTER 32

IMPEACHMENT

And now this offspring of assassination turns upon the Senate, who have thus rebuked him in a constitutional manner, and bids them defiance. How can he escape the just vengeance of the law? Wretched man, standing at bay, surrounded by a cordon of living men, each with the axe of the executioner uplifted for his just punishment.

—THADDEUS STEVENS AT THE
IMPEACHMENT TRIAL OF
PRESIDENT ANDREW JOHNSON,
MAY 8, 1868

"BUT MAMA," FOURTEEN-YEAR-OLD JIMSON BURNS PROTESTED.

"Boy, you best take your hands off your hips when you're talkin' to me," Sudie said.

"But Mama. The boys're going down to the canal. Might be they something to do."

"Them Knockabout boys never did nothin' but mischief. You bring this ironing to Miss Gordon. What she gives you for bringin' it, you gets to keep."

"Mama, that cross white woman ain't never given me nothin' 'fore. What makes you think she gonna start?"

When Sudie Burns smiled, the gap between her front teeth made her seem the girl she had been fifteen years ago when her master, Jimson's father, first had his way with her. "Sometimes you get loaves and fishes"— she grinned—"and sometimes you gets enough loaves and fishes to feed a multitude. Jesse home soon. If you don't want your father wonderin' why you pesterin' me instead of doin' what you supposed, you better git."

"Jesse ain't my father," the boy said, but left with the wicker hamper with Miss Gordon's washed, ironed underthings.

Sudie Burns's kitchen was her laundry and her big wash kettle was on continual boil. Finishing irons, large and small, crowded the stove's front burners and drying linens obstructed passage to their bedroom.

Sudie wished she had a separate laundry house.

The footsteps weren't Jesse's and Jesse wouldn't have knocked. "Why, Mr. Chepstow. I didn't know you were comin' by."

"Evening, Sudie. I've come to speak to your husband."

Jesse's employer had never visited her home before. "Mr. Chepstow, I 'shamed. This wet laundry and steam and nothing cooked 'cept Jesse's supper. Would you take a chicken wing, a nice cornbread?"

No, Mr. Chepstow didn't care for cornbread. Mr. Chepstow wondered if there was another room where he might wait more comfortably, so Sudie ushered him into their bedroom, which before his arrival had seemed larger and nicer.

"I kin make sassafras tea. You want some tea?"

Mr. Chepstow sat on Sudie and Jesse's marital bed. He didn't want any tea but wondered if they had another lamp, he supposed the city gas didn't come down this far.

"Oh, we don't use the gas," Sudie said airily. "Ol' kerosene lamp good enough for niggers." Then she flushed. "We ain't got 'nother kerosene lamp."

Chepstow hadn't removed his hat. He folded his hands on his lap. "Must I tarry long?"

"Oh, no, Master. Jesse come home in a wink. He's out doin' his politickin'. You want anything to read while you're waitin'? Jesse, he's readin all the time! Jesse readin' Mr. Garrison and Mr. Whitman.

"Mr. Whitman is a dangerous versifier," Chepstow said.

"Oh, yes, sir. Yes, sir. That's what Jesse says. I don't expect he'll be readin' that Whitman no more. You like to read Mr. Garrison's paper? I can't read myself. Jesse, he tryin' to learn me, but I swear the littlest child learn quicker'n I do."

"You musn't underrate yourself, Sudie," Chepstow instructed. "Those who enslaved you approve negroes with a low opinion of themselves. That is why they belittle your people. For if you do not feel worthy of your rights, how can you assert them?"

"Thank you, Mr. Chepstow. You kind to tell me what white mens do. Mr. Chepstow, Miss Hankins's things needn' ironing."

His eyes flickered, but he recaptured his pedantic tone. "Yes, Sudie. You must strike while the iron is hot."

Sudie ironed, exchanging cooled irons for heated ones. She heard Mr. Chepstow walking around her bedroom, inspecting things. A portrait of Abraham Lincoln hung on one wall, and a newspaper engraving of Frederick Douglass was glued above their headboard. A daguerreotype man had made an image of Sudie and Jesse and Jimson at their wedding and that picture stood on the old blanket chest.

Sudie heard Jesse's familiar footstep, gratefully. "Jesse, you'll never guess. Mr. Chepstow, he payin' us a call."

Jesse's eyes were tired. "Ah," he said. "You give him something to eat?"

"I have scant appetite." Chepstow spoke from the bedroom doorway. "I trust President Johnson's head will entirely satisfy my hunger, after sufficient boiling to extract the alcohol from it."

Sudie said, "Mr. President Johnson no friend to us coloreds."

"Impeachment is certain?" Jesse asked.

"Tomorrow, the glorious sixteenth of May, the Senate of the United States will send that scoundrel back whence he came: unfrocked, de-Presidented, the object of honest men's scorn."

"Some coloreds think Mr. Stevens can't bring it off."

"I give you my word and my hand upon it." Mr. Chepstow ducked under a damp nightgown to clasp Jesse's hand.

Mr. Chepstow was out of favor. Republican donations had dried up and the state advertising contract had not been renewed. Although Mr. Chepstow had campaigned vigorously for the Republican nomination for governor, that nomination had gone to another. At the same convention Jesse had been nominated for the legislature from Richmond's Marshall Ward.

"How do negroes see the impeachment?"

"Tell the truth, sir, they're more concerned about the Virginia election. There's twelve Richmond seats in the legislature—coloreds running against whites and the whites have the money."

"From Mahone."

"General Mahone is as quick to buy a black man as a white. He doesn't care who wins—just so long as the winner's in his pocket."

"You are acquaintanced with Mahone's henchman."

"Duncan Gatewood. Yes, sir."

Chepstow sighed and turned into a pair of hanging bloomers, which he pawed away from his face. "This afternoon prominent Republicans called at the office. They intend to establish their own newspaper in Richmond! They have employed an editor and pressmen. As an alternative, they offered to buy the *New Nation*. I am a realist, Jesse. A realist."

"Yes, sir."

"I am called 'radical,' but I am a realist. I made them a price."

"Yes, sir."

"You are a trained pressman, doubtless you can find work elsewhere."

"Sir?"

"I fear the *New Nation* has no more need for your services."

"Sir?"

Sudie's face went gray.

"When they impeach that traitor Johnson, Jesse, we shall be vindicated!"

"Sir?"

With a nod as stiff as his collar, Charles Chepstow left their home.

"Jesse, what we gonna do?"

Jesse took a deep breath. "I suppose we'll do what we have been doin'."

"I can't keep us goin' on what I makes washin'. How many white newspapers gonna hire a nigger pressman?"

Jesse looked at his ink-smudged hands. "Oh, I don't know," he said. "Might be I work cheaper than a white man would."

CHAPTER 33

A HAPPY OCCASION

COUSIN MOLLY SEMPLE WAS PINNING PAULINE'S HEM. "DEAR, dear. I don't believe I've ever seen a more beautiful bride. Leona's gown fits you perfectly."

"Eben wanted something extravagant, but when I said how much my dear mother's wedding dress meant to me, he acquiesced. Oh, Molly, tell me you like Eben a little?"

"Of course I do, dear." Molly had set aside her apprehensions. "My dear, I'm sure you will be happy!"

"Cousin," Pauline said, "if it is within a wife's power to assure family happiness, we shall be happy."

"Mr. Barnwell seems fond of Stratford. I hope we'll see more of him."

"I couldn't bear to be entirely separated from Stratford. Cousin Molly, how will I adapt myself to New York City? All those people. That awful hurly-burly! I shan't know a soul." The bride's mouth trembled. "Dear Cousin, all my expectations are unlike what they were. The fixed stars of my modest universe are out of their orbits. I so wish Sallie could be with me today."

"Dear—"

"I know, I know. Her newborn is ill, so of course Sallie cannot come. As a child I dreamed of my wedding day. I had play weddings with my dolls.

Abigail and my mother would be present and my father, Catesby, would give me away. I thought they would wait for me to become a woman."

Cousin Molly cocked her head. "Child, all your dear ones will smile down from heaven today. How can you doubt it?"

Pauline's brave face ached Molly's heart. She coughed to change the subject. "Now, as your nearest kinswoman, it is my duty to address a topic you might wish to avoid."

"Cousin Molly! Dearest Molly! If you mean to advise me on my marital duties, I have a fair idea."

"Many women, dear, find them disagreeable," Cousin Molly replied.

"I am certain I shan't. Eben has confessed to possessing a heightened 'amative' bump."

Molly raised an eyebrow. "You shall be the judge of that, my dear."

"WHAT DO OUR ENGLISH investors say?" General Mahone said.

Eben fumbled a jade link into his cuff. "General, they are shaken. Gould and Fisk made fortunes running up Erie stock, but when they took the Erie into receivership, many English investors were ruined. Now they tar every American railroad with the same brush."

Just two years ago, Eben had bought his Madison Square home with commissions earned selling Atlantic, Mississippi & Ohio bonds. Nowadays, he couldn't sell a hundred dollars in a fortnight. Despite Eben's candid, accurate explanations, General Mahone presumed this was due to Eben's indifference or indolence. Eben never came to Petersburg anymore and had stopped reading Mahone's angry telegrams.

His Pauline had wanted to be married in the little chapel she had attended all her life. Eben had to invite the General but had hoped he wouldn't travel to this remote mountain plantation. When the General accepted, Eben briefly considered postponing the wedding.

Eben Barnwell sometimes worried he mightn't accomplish his purposes, but since the Knapps, he hadn't been afraid of another man. Eben was afraid of William Mahone. He feared the tiny, furious General would hurl himself across the room and seize him by the throat.

"General, there is no enthusiasm for a new A.M.&O. bond—no matter what interest we are willing to pay. If we float a new issue but withdraw it unsold, the failure will put frightful pressure on our outstanding bonds."

Mahone snapped, "I have never defaulted on an interest payment! I am not Mr. Gould. Nor am I Mr. Jim Fisk!"

"No, sir. Of course not."

"The Virginia Legislature favors the A.M.&O. Major Gatewood assures me we have a majority."

"Sir, you are contesting with the Baltimore & Ohio Railroad, which is, after the Pennsylvania, the wealthiest railroad in America. I am loyal to your purposes. I am your man, but—"

"Are you, indeed?"

Eben could not manage his second cufflink. He spoke rapidly, without intonation. "If you do not believe that I am acting in your best interests, sir, it would be best if you engaged another agent."

Mahone eyed him, assessing Eben as coldly as he had assessed soldiers before suicidal assaults.

"You must do better than this, Barnwell."

Eben's cufflink fell from his fingers and he knelt to retrieve it. Though it had rolled beside Little Billy's tiny, highly polished black shoes, the General didn't move to help.

Eben stood and dusted his trouser knees. Quietly he said, "This is my wedding day, sir."

"You have Otelia's and my felicitations."

"The odds favoring success, General, have always been long."

Mahone's hiss was sibilant. "Sir, I fought beside General Lee. What do long odds mean to me?"

BY MIDMORNING, the dew had lifted. Stratford's mill wheel was motionless and its gangsaw silent. A breeze ruffled cattails in the millpond and shivered the mirrored water.

"This is a beautiful spot, Mr. Gatewood," Otelia Mahone remarked.

She turned her embroidery hoop to catch the sunlight streaming across Stratford's front porch.

"I have always thought so." Samuel offered to recharge Alexander Stuart's glass, but that gentleman covered it with his palm.

"I've no head for whiskey." Stuart smiled.

"Ah," Samuel said. "Perhaps unfortunately, I do."

Duncan Gatewood's eyes were bright. "Mornings like this I'd saddle Gypsy and disappear up the mountain. Father thought me a degenerate loafer."

Samuel Gatewood would have given anything for one more of those long slow mornings, watching his young son gallop Gypsy. He contented himself, as elders will, by inquiring about his newest grandchild.

"Baby Abigail is tiny, but Sallie says she has a will of iron."

Duncan's nephew, Thomas, had so immersed himself in politics that the vast universe outside politics and politicians had become somewhat unreal. Now Thomas fumed, "Just one honest senator's vote saved the President of the United States from impeachment. What was President Andrew Johnson's crime? He did not wish to obliterate the South. Thaddeus Stevens will concoct another excuse to impeach Johnson again."

"Stevens has shot his bolt," Alexander Stuart said. "The man is dying."

"Mrs. Mahone," Duncan said, "might prefer a different subject."

"Thank you, Mr. Gatewood," Otelia replied amiably. "What with this Underwood Constitution, which may or may not come to a vote, and candidates running for an election, which may or may not be held, and yet another military governor, I'm afraid my weak woman's head is spinning." She forestalled them quickly. "Don't feel under any obligation to enlighten me."

Mr. Alexander Stuart stretched out his legs. "There's one. There. A hummingbird in the honeysuckle."

EARLIER, THOMAS BYRD, Duncan Gatewood, and Alexander Stuart had strolled beside the Jackson River, admiring beneficent nature and determining how closely Stuart's and Mahone's interests coincided.

Stuart wondered if a negro candidate for the Virginia Assembly had not come from Stratford Plantation.

"Jesse Burns, yes," Duncan said.

"A Republican." When Stuart stopped, the others stopped too. "Will we ever wean the negro from the Republican Party?"

Thomas said, "The Republicans promise them everything ignorant men desire."

"Jesse Burns reads and writes better than most whites," Duncan said. "I've no evidence colored candidates are less able than their white counterparts, and they may be less corruptible."

"You would know something about corruptibility," Thomas snapped.

Duncan smiled, "Nephew, Nephew . . ."

Alexander Stuart stared at the misty mountains without seeing them. "Duncan, didn't you arrange for Jesse Burns's employment?"

"Jesse works at the Customs House. "

"Many believe that those whose bread they provide ought not act against their interests."

"Mr. Stuart, General Mahone is building a railroad. He will build it under a Republican governor or under a Conservative governor. He will build it under military rule if he must." Duncan knelt and cupped his hands to drink. "I have always loved this river. Downstream it joins the Cowpasture to form the James. The James is broad and powerful when it passes through Richmond, but the water is murky and no sane man would drink of it."

JACK MITCHELL, HIS WIFE, and their infant Mim set out for the wedding in a rickety wagon drawn by a mule that wore on its head a broken straw hat Mrs. Mitchell had decorated with white peony blossoms.

Mrs. Mitchell disparaged SunRise Chapel in favor of the African Baptist church they presently attended. "I hates to climb up into that garret," she said. "Nobody be there no more. Rufus, he gone, Aunt Opal in Richmond, Pompey dead. I despise sittin' up in that garret thinkin' 'bout them who is gone."

Jack clucked at the mule. "Missus, we come to show our respect for Miss Pauline and the Gatewoods. We don't got to care where they married, here, there, or somewheres else; we shows our respect."

"What kind of respect they show us, Mister?"

"Master Samuel, he come to our wedding. Miss Abigail, Miss Pauline, Mr. Duncan, Miss Sallie, even Miss Molly—all them Gatewoods come. They give us a teapot."

"They didn't stay ten minutes afterwards."

Jack smiled. "Missus, I don't believe we stayed ten minutes neither."

His wife punched his arm and they continued in silence until Mrs. Mitchell refreshed a familiar inquiry: why Billy Hansel, who worked for Jack, drew a dollar a day, same as Jack.

"On account of how we gets to live in our cabin for free and we gets all the mule feed we wants and picks apples and peaches and plums and rhubarb and horseradish whenever we needs some. Billy Hansel's a white man. You think Mr. Samuel can pay a colored more'n his top white man?"

"I wished we didn't live in the Quarters no more. It ghosty."

"I tell Mr. Samuel he should rent them cabins out. If nobody livin' in them, they be fallin' down. Think how it'd be, Missus. Be a town of col- oreds and you could get a Mammy look after Mim sometimes and Sunday evenings we'd sit on our front porch and rock and folks'd come along to pay their respects."

Franky sniffed. "Be just like them old slavery days. They's hirin' at the Warm Springs Mill. Pay a dollar and a quarter."

"That's what they payin' today. What be payin' in the wintertime when nobody got no wheat nor corn for to grind? Missus, we stay here. Might be more money somewheres else, but Stratford our *home*."

"Stratford might not be Master Samuel's no more. That Barnwell come pokin' 'round askin' questions: what 'bout this, how 'bout that, just like he's the Master. I hear Stratford mortgaged to him."

"Mortgaged": that dread word froze Jack's tongue.

"Master Samuel don't care 'bout nothin' but drinkin' since Miss

Abigail died. Miss Molly, she keepin' the books, and you doin' the mill. What use is Master Samuel anyway?"

"Missus, you got to remember he was a good man once." The mule picked up its heels as they entered SunRise.

AFTER THEIR NUPTIALS, Eben and Pauline accepted congratulations. Yes, they would reside in New York. Yes, they hoped to visit Stratford frequently. How could they forget their dear Virginia friends? No, Mrs. Mitchell, Manhattan isn't the Devil's principal abode, He has lairs everywhere.

Pauline lingered longer than Eben might have wished and her good-byes were more tearful. Eben meant to be a good husband and had asked a happily married friend, George Nutley, about his spousal duties. Patience, Nutley counseled, was a husband's gift to matrimony. Eben resolved to be patient.

Eben had a bad moment when their carriage moved off and his weeping bride waved desperately from her window, apparently more in love with what she was losing than the husband she had gained. Eben perched stiffly across the seat, wondering how anyone as unworthy as himself had captured such a prize.

Eben was married and determined on intimacies he longed for but dreaded. What if the Knapp brothers were right and he was nothing; nothing at all? What if Pauline—his wife—learned who he truly was?

Pauline used her handkerchief, wiped her eyes, and patted the seat. "Please do sit nearer, dearest. I need your strength. Whatever was troubling General Mahone? He was so distant and unfriendly. I was so glad Jack and Franky came." Pauline paused before continuing in the sweetest voice Eben had ever heard. "Dearest husband," she whispered, "I shall try to be a good wife to you. Will you forgive my mistakes?"

"Oh," Eben said happily, "I shall love you whatever they may be."

CHAPTER 34

CIRCLING THE KETTLE

*Kill a fat puppy, no more than three months old, skin and gut it.
Fill a buffalo-paunch cooker with water and when it is boiling,
immerse the puppy until the meat is tender. Fill bowls with broth
and meat. In the center of the lodge place four bowls for honored
guests. One bowl contains the puppy's head, the next his forefeet,
then his hind feet, and finally his tail. The most honored guest is
served the puppy's head, the next the forefeet, and so forth . . .*

After my child Red Leaf died, I put a lock of her hair in a soft buckskin bag with sweetgrass and mint. I tied this bag to our lodgepole
until the ghost lodge could be constructed. Because we were of White
Bull's family, our lodge was in front of my brother's and the ghost
lodge stood in front of our lodge for the same reason.

Every morning Plenty Cuts and I daubed our faces red before
coming out of our lodge.

During the Moon When the Grain Comes Up, Rattling Blanket
Woman, Fox Head, Blue Whirlwind Woman, and I beaded moccasins and pouches and White Bull and Plenty Cuts went off to steal
ponies. They stole fifty ponies from the Crows, but they stole horses
from the Snakes and Rees too.

The Crows hated Plenty Cuts for the trick he had played on them and for stealing so many horses, and their young warriors vowed to hang his scalp from their scalp pole. In the beginning young Lakota warriors rode with Plenty Cuts and White Bull, but they took such grave chances to steal horses and didn't care about scalps or counting coup, and soon even Sorrel Horse preferred to go with war parties that promised greater honors.

In the Moon of Ripening Plums, Plenty Cuts and White Bull rode to Fort Phil Kearny where Red Cloud and others had gathered to see if the Seizers would abandon their fort as they'd promised.

Red Cloud knew of the trick my husband played on the Crows and said it was a fine joke. He said it was honorable to own our child's ghost, that with Plenty Cuts's face painted red he was almost Lakota.

LODGE TRAIL RIDGE WAS DARK WITH INDIANS WHEN THE SEIZERS ran their flag up Fort Phil Kearny's flagpole, fired a volley, and lowered it for the last time. Their bugler played taps.

Red Cloud waited with Plenty Cuts and White Bull, an honor that made some Lakota jealous.

"Faugh, that is sad music," Red Cloud said. "I have spent too much time with the Washitu. Sometimes I think Crazy Horse and Sitting Bull are right. Make no treaties with the Washitu. Fight them until everyone is dead."

Plenty Cuts said, "Sitting Bull can fight the Washitu for a time, but when they decide to kill Sitting Bull they will bring more Seizers than there is grass on the plains and kill him."

"Washitu do not honor their treaties."

"They'll steal you blind. But if you quit fightin' maybe they won't kill every last one of your children."

Red Cloud was a squat, hawk-nosed man with the deepest chest Plenty Cuts had ever seen. In his forties, his black eyes could spark at a joke or turn hard and unrevealing as anthracite coal. He'd come up from nothing—

his father had been a drunk. Red Cloud had counted coup eighty times. Now he asked Plenty Cuts, "Why do you hate Washitu mules?"

Every morning Fort Kearny's horses and mules had come out of the fort to graze and, at Plenty Cuts's suggestion (seconded by White Bull), young braves had concealed themselves near enough to shoot an arrow and flee. Fatal to numerous Washitu mules, this practice didn't endanger the boys. After Captain Fetterman's example, no Seizer wanted to pursue a lone indian across Lodge Trail Ridge.

Plenty Cuts said, "Red Leaf's ghost told me to kill the mules."

The indian horde buzzed like bees ready to swarm.

In a column of fours, the cavalry rode out Fort Phil Kearny's front gate followed by infantry, guns, wagons, and a cavalry rear guard. The Seizer band played the "Garryowen" and "Marching through Georgia." The rear guard torched a log building and galloped after the column. Before the Seizers disappeared behind Pilot Hill, hundreds of hooting Lakota warriors raced down the ridge through the open gate into the hated fort.

Some galloped around the flagpole hollering, some dismounted onto the commandant's porch and rushed inside. One whose brother and uncle had been killed by Seizers went from window to window, smashing every pane of glass.

Warriors rolled a whiskey barrel onto the post sutler's porch, hatcheted it, and knelt to drink.

Plenty Cuts and White Bull raced for the burning log building: the post magazine. Plenty Cuts jumped down the stairs, kicked the thick door open, and began passing ammunition cases to White Bull. Fire roared in the sod roof. Wind streamered the smoke toward Pilot Hill.

Some indians donned abandoned Washitu clothing. One fierce warrior wore a bright green skirt below a mess boy's red vest.

Another dragged a rocking chair onto the parade ground and rocked solemnly. One hacked at Fort Kearny's flagpole.

As fire dripped through the roof planks, Plenty Cuts salvaged eleven cases of cartridges, eight forty-pound bars of lead—even a cask of gunpowder.

Younger warriors drank and yelled and rode ponies into the Washitu buildings and snatched fire from the burning magazine to ignite everything else.

Plenty Cuts warned that the magazine would explode, but two heedless young warriors were scorched and rolled when it erupted into the sky.

As White Bull and Plenty Cuts loaded packhorses with bullets and powder, Red Cloud sputtered with laughter. "The Washitu mules might have carried these goods away. Now I understand why you hated Washitu mules."

After they burned Fort Phil Kearny, the warriors returned to our big village on the Tongue River. We were a thousand lodges, the most since the Hundred in the Hand.

Although many warriors brought gifts for their wives, Plenty Cuts brought cartridges, lead, and powder for Red Leaf in her ghost lodge.

That night Old Man Afraid of His Horses held a feast to honor Red Cloud. White Bull, Rain in the Face, Roman Nose of the Cheyenne, and Chief Gall of the Hunkpapa were invited. Red Cloud invited Plenty Cuts because of his Washitu knowledge.

Two puppies had been killed in Red Cloud's honor.

After the men had smoked the pipe, Red Cloud recalled how he first learned the forts were being built and how he had then vowed to destroy them. When the Great White Father sent his peace commissioners, Red Cloud would not meet with them until the forts were abandoned and the Montana Road closed. Red Cloud recalled the honors won by the Lakota and Cheyenne at the Hundred in the Hand. He introduced Plenty Cuts, telling how he fooled the Crows and killed Chasing Crane. He asked Plenty Cuts if the Washitu would ever return to the Montana Road.

Plenty Cuts said the Washitu needed their Seizers to occupy their South country and protect the Union Pacific Railroad. Rich, powerful Washitu owned the Union Pacific and didn't care about the Montana Road. That was why, Plenty Cuts said, they had abandoned the forts and closed the Montana Road. His saying angered warriors who had fought bravely and had had relatives killed in the fighting. Red Cloud reminded everyone that Plenty Cuts had smoked the pipe and must speak the truth even when that truth was not what they wanted to hear.

Red Cloud said the Lakota needed meat for the coming winter. After the fall hunt, he would go to Fort Laramie and make peace.

Plenty Cuts said the Washitu would feel insulted, they would say they had abandoned the forts as Red Cloud wished, why was Red Cloud delaying? Red Cloud did not like this speech either.

Red Cloud said this time the Washitu would wait for the Lakota, which made all the Big Bellies laugh. When the puppies were served, Red Cloud and White Bull were given heads, but Plenty Cuts was given a tail.

CHAPTER 35

LETTER FROM MRS. EBEN BARNWELL
TO MISS MOLLY SEMPLE

15 MADISON SQUARE EAST
NEW YORK CITY
AUGUST 22, 1868

Dear Cuz,

I take this occasion to write happy news. Seven months hence I am due to be delivered of an infant. Eben is already furnishing our nursery! Every afternoon, between one and three, I must interview vendors of infant furniture and apparel, of which there is much too much! Eben has been true to his promise to leave domestic arrangements to me and I have indulged myself. Eben's dark bachelor establishment has become as light and airy as Stratford House. Despite his protests, I had his precious Italian fountain disconnected and workmen have hauled it away. I cannot think why he ever wanted a Niagara in our foyer!

In only one small matter is Eben insistent. At dusk, after our gaslights are lit, Eben opens our parlor drapes so our home is open to the gaze of any curious passersby. Eben says, mysteriously, that "it might give some poor boy hope."

Otherwise he grants my every whim. At my request, Eben sold his pew at Mr. Beecher's church in favor of one at the Fifteenth Street

Presbyterian. (I doubt his old pew was much worn.) To humor his
"dear little wife" Eben attends worship—often enough so Dr.
MacDougal no longer greets him after services as if Eben were a
complete stranger!

As it happens, Mr. Jay Gould also worships at the Fifteenth
Street Presbyterian. Mr. Gould appears to be a devoted family man.
Can pirates be devoted Christian family men?

"Please read that again," Samuel Gatewood asked.

Molly Semple did so.

"Does she say anything about Mahone?"

"Samuel, if you let me finish reading, you shall know everything."

Eben delights at the prospect of a child and promises to spoil our
child mercilessly! Although he is a good provider, he never can recall
where he set down his best hat nor where he laid his gloves! I some-
times think I am the mother Eben never had.

We do not go out much in society. Although George Nutley is
Eben's partner in several ventures, I rarely see Mr. Nutley and have
never met his family. Eben protects his "dear little wife" from the
vulgarity of commerce!

Eben is all business. When I told my husband that Thaddeus
Stevens had died, that Virginia's scourge now resided in regions best
not contemplated, Eben said only that Union Pacific stock must rise
on the news.

"Thaddeus Stevens, dead," Samuel Gatewood mused hoarsely.

On the anniversary of his wife's death, Samuel Gatewood had gone through Stratford House emptying brandy bottles and hadn't had a drink since. "Neither Grant nor Sherman nor Sheridan nor all the Federal generals taken together have done as much to ruin our beloved Commonwealth as that arrogant miscegenist. I pray we never see his like again!"

Molly checked an urge to touch Samuel's white hair. "Dear Samuel,

that is unworthy of you. Mr. Stevens was nothing to us. He never was anything to us. He was an angry hunchback who dwelled in Washington City
and made laws. Can't we forgive him?"

Samuel's lips tightened. "Three days ago, dear Molly, I asked you to
join me in matrimony. While ours would be a marriage of convenience, we
are affectionate toward one another. You replied you were not certain our
affection could survive matrimony.

"Since my invitation, you have examined my flaws. While I have many
flaws of character and temperament, I cannot think, dear Molly, that you
are much surprised by them. We have known each other too long. Mr.
Stevens cannot be harmed by my condemnation, nor, as you have imagined, can I.

"You and I, dear Molly, are too old friends to pretend we can do much
to reform one another. Correct morality is no substitute for marital con-
tentment."

Samuel held Molly's gaze for a moment before she returned to
Pauline's letter.

*Tuesday evening, Mr. Hayward invited us to dine. Amos
Hayward is a fussy sort of man who has invested his modest savings
with Eben, explaining earnestly (and often), "I don't know anyone I
trust as I trust you, Mr. Barnwell."*

*We dined at the Hotel Brunswick, which is across the street from
Del's and made a pleasant change. Though Mr. Hayward ate
abstemiously, he pressed extravagant dishes on us.*

*Mr. Hayward is chief clerk to Mr. Boutwell, the Secretary of the
Treasury. Some years ago, Eben helped Hayward obtain his position, and though Hayward's subsequent promotions were through
his own merits, Hayward hasn't forgotten Eben's kindness.*

*Cuz, too much deference and gratitude is just as wearisome as
too little!*

*Eben asked me to enclose this banker's draft for Grandfather.
On his most recent visit, he saw that Stratford needed repairs and
trusts this money will get them made. In November he'd like to bring*

*a few businessmen down to Stratford for a hunt. With
Grandfather's kind permission, of course!*

*Eben says that General Mahone's railroad hangs in the balance
and Mahone is devoting every resource to ensure that it does not
come to smash . . .*

"Please read that again," Samuel Gatewood asked.
"Samuel, please! Let me finish!"

*There are some promising developments. Eben says if Mahone
wins over the Virginia Legislature, he may yet carry the day.
Apparently Virginia's military governor, General Stoneman, is in
Mahone's camp.*

*Do write me all your news, Cuz. Tell me about Jack and Franky
(I will never get used to "Mrs. Mitchell"). Write about our neighbors
and friends. Is brother Thomas still working with Mr. Stuart? Is he
seeing very much of Miss Stuart? Tell me everything about dear,
dear Stratford.*

*Your loving cousin,
Pauline*

Molly folded Pauline's letter and slid it back into its envelope. "So,
Samuel." She handed him Eben's draft.

He glanced at it indifferently. "I now owe Barnwell more than
Stratford would realize. 'Lay not up your treasures here on earth, but in
heaven.'

"I thought I was the master of my fate," Samuel continued. "I thought
my obstacle was my own character: my pride and my temper. If I could
overcome myself, I would satisfy my duty, my dependents would be contented and, I supposed, grateful. Vanity, Molly. Vanity." He studied the back
of his hands. "I shall keep Stratford so long as I can. I shall engage an attor-
ney to sue General Mahone for his arrears. His custom has bled us dry.
Pauline's husband may invite as many yankee guests to Stratford as he

wishes. We will show Mr. Barnwell's friends the hospitality which Stratford once offered freely."

When they stepped out onto the porch, they were greeted by hundreds of fireflies, each briefly brighter than a star.

"Dear Samuel," Molly Semple said softly, "I will marry you. It is late in life for both of us, but we will be stronger together than apart. If we do not love one another yet, I trust love will come."

CHAPTER 36

A SQUAW MAN

THE LAKOTA CAME TO FORT LARAMIE TO MAKE PEACE WITH THE Washitu. The morning frost was eaten by the pale sun and the air was bright. The dead leaves on the alders were curled and black.

Plenty Cuts rode at Red Cloud's right hand. Plenty Cuts wore Washitu trousers and a vest with blue quills. In his broad-brimmed stockman's hat was a single notched eagle feather reddened at the tip, for he had killed an enemy and been wounded. His face was painted red for the ghost-owning. His Medal of Honor hung from a leather thong around his neck.

At Red Cloud's other hand was Old Man Afraid of His Horses, who'd been Red Cloud's rival before the Seizers abandoned their forts. Old Man Afraid of His Horses wore a chief's headdress and a vest quilled with white quills and brass bracelets on his arms. The Brulé, Hunkpapa, Sans Arc, and Blackfoot chiefs who rode behind wore their finest clothing to honor the occasion.

Red Cloud wore a dirty blanket and no eagle feather.

Fort Laramie's new commandant, Major Dye, was waiting on the parade ground; his infantry, mounted infantry, and cavalry formed a phalanx behind him.

Blanket indians and Washitu civilians crowded the boardwalks. As soon as the chiefs dismounted, Lakota warriors wheeled their horses and dashed, whooping, back across the river. They had brought many prime robes to the fort and were anxious to start trading.

The chiefs sat in the same tent that had been erected when General Sherman and the peace commissioners had come to make peace but Red Cloud had not come.

Major Dye introduced himself and his officers and each chief stood to shake hands except Red Cloud, who stayed seated, extending his fingertips to Dye.

"And he is?" Major Dye inquired.

Red Cloud said, "Plenty Cuts listens for me. So you do not say tomorrow what you do not say today."

"You're his interpreter?"

Ratcliff smiled. "The chief speaks the lingo pretty good. He just don't want to miss anything."

Major Dye pointed at Ratcliff's medal. "Where did you obtain that?"

"New Market Heights. I'm a hincty nigger."

Major Dye and his officers took wooden chairs and the post chaplain prepared to take notes.

Red Cloud asked, "Where are your chiefs? The peace commissioners? How can we make peace without Washitu chiefs."

"They came in August and you did not come. You did not come after we abandoned the forts on the Montana Road. Now I am empowered to make this treaty," the major replied.

"We need powder and bullets for hunting," Red Cloud said.

So it went. The major would assert his authority to negotiate for the Great White Father, and Red Cloud would inquire where the Washitu chiefs were and demand powder. Dye's restless officers smoked pipes and cigars until the tent was thick with smoke.

THAT EVENING IN the Lakota encampment across the river, some who had traded robes for whiskey careened through the village like mad dogs.

Outside Red Cloud's lodge, Plenty Cuts politely sang out his name. Inside he was offered blackhorn soup, which he tasted though he'd eaten twenty minutes before. After serving him, Red Cloud's wife, Pretty Owl, retired to the back of the lodge, where her daughters were mending moccasins.

The two men sat before the fire.

"What can we do at this place?" Red Cloud asked.

"You've been telling Major Dye you came for powder and bullets."

"They will not give us powder and bullets."

"Reckon not. Might be the Lakota could use those powder and bullets on Major Dye's soldiers. Why did Red Cloud come? So his young warriors could buy whiskey?"

"I hate whiskey. My father, Lone Man, loved whiskey more than he loved his son. Whiskey killed Lone Man. Washitu will give the Lakota all the whiskey they want." Red Cloud stirred the coals. "Washitu gifts are like a blade sharpened on both edges. As you cut your meat you cut your hand. We are few and they are many. Should we fight?"

Plenty Cuts said, "If it was just you and me, I'd say yes. We wouldn't win: there's too many of them and some are clever bastards. But it'd be some satisfaction to kill a few. But it ain't just you and me. It's all the Lakota."

Red Cloud said, "I am a warrior. How much humiliation must a warrior eat?"

Plenty Cuts said, "I reckon you're about to find out."

THE NEXT MORNING, while Major Dye was explaining that part of the treaty where the Washitu and Lakota promised to never make war again, a soldier delivered a telegram.

Ulysses S. Grant had defeated Horatio Seymour for President of the United States. All the soldiers seemed happy at this news and when Red Cloud asked why, Plenty Cuts told him Grant was a great chief who had been willing to sacrifice many warriors in battle.

Red Cloud asked again for powder. He said the blackhorns had run away and the Lakota needed more powder and lead.

Major Dye's officers smoked and the chaplain took notes with his scratchy pens.

That evening, Major Dye honored Red Cloud, Big Bear, and Old Man Afraid of His Horses with a feast. Plenty Cuts went to the sutler's for a beer.

A drunken corporal lifted a hand, palm outward, and said, "How."

"How, what?" Ratcliff replied.

"Hey," the corporal said, "we got us a squaw man, here."

Ratcliff stepped so near, the corporal took an involuntary step backward. "You've got Sergeant Major Edward Ratcliff, 38th United States Colored Troops. The Crater, New Market Heights, Five Forks. Might be you'd like to buy me a drink."

"Siddown, Corporal Peterson," a veteran sergeant spoke up. "Top, I'll buy you a drink. Least I'll buy your medal a drink. Can't say I ever saw a Lakota wearin' one. Can't say I ever saw a red-faced nigger either." The sergeant put out his hand and Ratcliff shook it awkwardly. He was out of practice.

"I was with the Bucktails myself," the sergeant said. "Thought I'd stay in the army for the pension and maybe settle out here."

"It's a big country. Might be room for everybody."

"That what you tell Red Cloud?"

"Red Cloud's no fool. He's looking for a treaty whites can't break."

The sergeant examined Ratcliff. "Ain't many niggers on the plains. Scout name of Shillaber was here in August. Said a nigger friend of his was in the Hayfield scrap."

"Shillaber say where he was bound?"

"Nope. He quarreled with a robe trader name of Meredeth and the night Shillaber left, Meredeth disappeared too. Talk is Shillaber did for him."

Plenty Cuts remembered when he'd been a different man with a different name: five white men and one black in a steaming pool surrounded by untracked snow that stretched to distant, sawtoothed mountains.

———

MAJOR DYE PROMISED that the Montana Road would never be reopened, that no new forts would be built, that annuities would be provided and instruction for those who wished to become farmers.

Red Cloud laughed. "We Lakota have already learned as much as we wish to learn about farming."

Major Dye agreed to Red Cloud's demand that the treaty could not be changed unless three-quarters of the Lakota wanted it changed. All the land between the Missouri and the Rockies would be reserved for the "absolute and undisturbed use" of the Lakota.

For the first time Red Cloud smiled. "Until the rivers do not flow," he added.

"Yes."

"And the sun no longer rises in the east."

"Just so."

"Until men cease to make war."

"Yes, the absolute, undisturbed use."

"Until all the Lakota cross over into the Shadowland."

"Yes."

Red Cloud laughed and washed his hands in the dust and took the pen the chaplain gave him and made his mark. The other chiefs made their marks. Major Dye passed out cigars.

—

MR. STUART ARGUES
FOR COMPROMISE

We now look with extreme aversion on negro suffrage, but may we not find upon actual experiment that it is not such a bad thing as we have been accustomed to believe?

The inherent inferiority of the race, and their want of education and property, will necessarily put them in a position of subordination to the superior race. Knowledge is power, property is power. Would it not therefore be strange if the superior intelligence and accumulated property of the superior race should not exercise a controlling influence over the ignorance and penury of the inferior?

—Alexander Stuart, in the *Richmond Whig*,
December 19, 1868

—

CHAPTER 38

LETTER FROM THOMAS BYRD TO SAMUEL GATEWOOD

RICHMOND, VIRGINIA
JANUARY 21, 1869

Dear Grandfather,

I have met with President Grant! On the 4th of January, I accompanied Mr. Stuart and his committee to Washington City. The tyrannical Underwood Constitution had been approved by the House of Representatives and was due for Senate consideration: hence our urgency. Mr. Stuart's compromise—universal suffrage for ex-Confederates as well as negroes—is bitter medicine, but Mr. Stuart believes (and I concur) that we will gain more than we lose.

We trod the halls of Congress, singly and in concert, trying to persuade Radical Republican senators that Virginia has no desire to secede again, nor to re-enslave its negro population. In this we were greatly assisted by Mr. Walker and Mr. Stearns. These moderate Republicans impressed skeptics within their own party.

Grandfather, I thank God Thad Stevens no longer sows his grapes of wrath. The author of the 14th amendment to the Constitution of the United States has been interred—as per his wishes—in a negro cemetery. If Stevens had chosen to be interred in Stratford's front hall, I would not quarrel—so long as he was interred.

We Virginians were treated so courteously on this occasion, I nearly forgot the humiliation Stevens inflicted at our last visit— was that only three years ago?

Wherever we went, we were dogged by Mr Chepstow and his Radicals chanting that only Radical Republicans can be trusted, that if white Virginians are enfranchised we will undo all the blessings of Confederate defeat and swiftly re-enslave our negroes by fair means or foul!

At Stratford, when a dog killed a chicken we tied the carcass around the dog's neck until it rotted and fell of its own accord. Grandfather, I understand how that dog felt!

From courtesy we met with President Johnson. Poor man! So beleaguered, despised, and powerless! He was grateful for our commendations.

But the man we most hoped to influence was the President-Elect, and General Grant kindly consented to an interview.

Grandfather, I had never thought to meet another to rival General Lee in my esteem, but Grant is that man. He received us in his rooms at Mr. Willard's Hotel, explaining that until inauguration, he remained strictly a military man and thus unable to comment on policy. Nonetheless, he was interested in hearing what we had to say.

Mr. Stuart and Mr. Walker made a compelling case—that should the Underwood Constitution be submitted to Virginia voters in its present form, it would be voted down, and that depriving Virginia of the services of her natural leaders was pernicious. "Must we give our Commonwealth over to the illiterate and unpropertied?" Mr. Stuart inquired.

Virginia's military government has had notable difficulty filling posts with literate men who can swear the Ironclad Oath and General Grant has a soldier's respect for worthy adversaries.

Mistaking the time of our appointment, two of our committee who meant to attend failed to attend. Chepstow promptly spread misinformation that Mr. Jenkins and Mr. Mayre had snubbed General Grant.

I was dispatched to seek a second interview. Two armed Treasury agents were stationed outside Grant's rooms and they searched my person for an assassin's pistol. When Colonel Porter, the General's aide, admitted me, they made to follow.

"I am sure the young man intends the General no harm," Porter said.

Nervousness prompted my impolitic reply, "Not since April 1865." Colonel Porter dismissed my raillery with the faintest smile.

The General was dressing for dinner and greeted me in shirt-sleeves. They say Grant is so tenderhearted he cannot abide to see a horse mistreated and eats no meat until it is thoroughly carbonized. Yet this tender man ordered twelve thousand Union soldiers to make hopeless charges at Cold Harbor!

I explained my mission and assured the General that every member of our committee held him in the highest regard, that Mr. Jenkins and Mr. Mayre had simply misunderstood the time of their interview.

With Colonel Porter's help he attached his collar. "I bear no animosity toward the South," he said, "and intend to be President of every region."

I cannot predict what General Grant will do when he becomes President Grant. He seemed to feel that universal suffrage for negroes and ex-Confederates is a worthy compromise, but I was more confident in his presence than the next morning when I woke realizing that he had not actually promised more than due consideration.

Mr. Stuart returns to Staunton next week and I will come home to Stratford. Mr. Stuart is urging me to run for the legislature.

Duncan is determined to quit General Mahone. Apparently Duncan has long dreamed of breeding horses, and Sallie is encouraging him to do so—in Montana Territory.

Relay my warm regards to our dearest cousin, your new wife, now my new dear grandmother.

Your obedient grandson,
Thomas

—

CHAPTER 39

THE CANDIDATE FROM MARSHALL WARD

AFTER HE LOST HIS JOB AT THE *NEW NATION*, JESSE SOUGHT work at the *Richmond Whig*, the *Examiner*, the *State Journal*, the *Dispatch*, and the *Inquirer* to no avail. The *State Journal*'s editor told him, "My printers would quit me if I hired a nigger for white man's work." Sudie's washing paid their rent and Jesse lined up for rations at the Freedmen's Bureau. The little family was lucky to have a home: many unemployed negroes lived in derelict canal boats or abandoned warehouses. Jesse found occasional work unloading freight or mucking out livery stables at fifty cents a day.

When President Grant scheduled the long-postponed Virginia election, Jesse Burns ran for the legislature from the Marshall Ward, as did Robert Patterson, a white, and Lewis Lindsey, the negro who in April celebrated the third anniversary of Richmond's fall with a rally and march through the city. Next evening the church where the march had originated burned to the ground.

Virginia male citizens would elect its state legislators, its governor, and they'd vote on the Underwood Constitution—as amended by Alexander Stuart.

Jimson quit his gang. "Politics ain't different than the Knockabouts, but there's more money in it," Jesse's new canvasser informed his candidate.

Jesse campaigned energetically, but Lewis Lindsey seemed to be everywhere. Though Jesse appealed to conservative negroes, Lindsey's rhetoric fired the young men. Robert Patterson's small bribes and whiskey won friends. His political barbecues drew a hundred voters at a time.

After the *New Nation* shut its doors, Charles Chepstow bolted the Radical Republicans (some say he was pushed) and campaigned among negroes for Robert Patterson.

Duncan clapped Jesse on the back and said, "You should have come to me sooner."

Thanks to Duncan's money, Jesse's barbecues and speeches began outdrawing his rivals'.

If he won, Jesse would vote General Mahone's interests. Had Duncan asked him to vote against the Underwood Constitution or negro suffrage, Jesse would have refused. But Jesse didn't care which railroad dominated Virginia.

Jesse had planned his last political barbecue for the first Sunday in July until Jimson reminded him Sunday was the Fourth, a holiday Virginia negroes ought not be seen enjoying too much. Jesse rescheduled for the last Sunday in June. Duncan Gatewood provided the barbecued hog, five dozen chickens, and a demicask of brandy for Jesse's two hundred guests on a beautiful afternoon beside the James River.

Boys fished in the lee of the small island while their mothers sat on blankets and gossiped.

Lewis Lindsey claimed Jesse Burns was the "white man's nigger." Since Lindsey hadn't fought in the war, Jesse wore his United States Colored Troops uniform to every rally.

The day was warm. Seagulls fluttered above the rapids.

Some whites had come to Jesse's barbecue, but they kept to themselves except at the cask, where Jimson ladled brandy and political exhortations with a balanced hand.

Jesse slipped five dollars to voters expecting to be paid.

Duncan Gatewood stretched, yawned, and turned to Jesse. "Thank God this will soon be decided. Lord, I'm sick of politics."

"You still going to leave Virginia?"

"There's nothing for me here. I'll resign after the election. I've bought twenty brood mares—approved by Aunt Opal. If Opal'd been born white, she'd be the richest horse trader in the Commonwealth.

"Good horses are scarce in Montana. The cavalry will pay a hundred fifty dollars for a clean-limbed gelding. Jesse, this is what I've always wanted to do. I often wonder why I ever did anything else."

Jesse said, "You might run across my army friend, Sergeant Major Edward Ratcliff, out there. Fine soldier, went west with a cattle drive and now he's living with the indians. He sent me a telegram from Fort Laramie. Edward Ratcliff has become Red Cloud's interpreter." Jesse laughed. "God works in mysterious ways."

"If he's riding with Red Cloud, I'd rather not make his acquaintance," Duncan said.

An old black man approached decorously. "Deacon Hanley, First African Baptist, Mr. Burns. You prolly seen Hanley's rigs 'round town."

"Surely have, Deacon Hanley."

"Mr. Burns, us respectable niggers, we don't want no trouble. That Lindsey nigger, he'll get our churches burned. I'm votin' for you."

"That's good of you, Deacon," Jesse said. "You ate any of our fine barbecue?"

"No, no. I didn't come to eat a thing. I come to say I supportin' you."

"Always glad to see you, Deacon." Jesse shook the man's wizened hand. "Mr. Gatewood and me, we was young'uns together. Mr. Gatewood's with General Mahone."

"Good to meet you, sir. Mr. Burns, he's got my vote. He'll have my teamsters' votes too."

At Duncan's inquiring glance, Jesse grinned. "No sense givin' money to a man who'll vote for you without it. That's what my canvasser, Jimson, tells me. That boy is cut out for politics."

Sudie Burns and Sallie Gatewood sat on the riverbank while their infants cooed and gurgled at one another and Aunt Opal trailed young Catesby, who was splashing in the riffles at the water's edge.

Sallie Gatewood said, "My father Uther was a schoolmaster and taught Jesse, Duncan, and me. We were like brothers and sister."

"Jesse don't talk much about them olden times," Sudie said. "Ain't it funny how we'uns and you'uns come up in the world together and when we growed up you all go one way and we go t'other?"

Sallie sighed. "Perhaps it will not always be so."

Sudie shook her head. "Nothin' gonna change this side of River Jordan."

Impulsively, Sallie took the other young woman's hand. "Mrs. Burns, isn't this a beautiful day? Can we not set aside for one day all that divides us?"

Sudie smiled her fine gap-toothed smile. "I can see why Jesse favors you, Miss Sallie."

Sallie replied, "Jesse is a fine man. A credit to his race."

"Duncan a credit to your race, Miss Sallie?" Sudie drew back.

"Oh, dear. I meant to praise your husband and instead I offended you. I am sorry. Mrs. Burns, I'd like to be your friend."

"Grand white lady like you befriendin' a washerwoman?"

Sudie's infant Sojourner and Sallie's Abigail inspected one another as solemnly as two buddhas.

"You are my old friend Jesse's wife," Sallie said softly. "If that position isn't grand enough, you may soon be the wife of a Virginia assemblyman."

Sudie had grown up expecting to live her life as a slave, to lie with Master when he insisted and to marry whoever Master chose for her. Jesse, who'd fought with the Union Army and might be elected to the Virginia Legislature, was pure miracle. To Sudie, Jesse was the unlikeliest thing that ever happened, and sometimes she studied him so avidly it made her husband uneasy.

Now Sudie said stubbornly, "Ain't gonna think about that!"

"Things will change as they must. Our children will know a different world than ours. I pray our animosities and misunderstandings will become mere curiosities like those in Mr. Barnum's museum."

"There's this ju-ju man back on the plantation. An' that man could prophesize. I asked him onct what would become of us and he said we'd have trials for a hundred years. Miss Sallie, what we done to deserve such tribulations?"

"If you call me Miss Sallie, I must call you Miss Sudie."

Sudie laughed. "You crazy as a bedbug, Mrs. Gatewood. 'Deed you is."

CHAPTER 40

GHOST-OWNING

In THE MOON OF RIPENING CHOKECHERRIES IN THE YEAR THE sun died, at White Bull's village on the Powder River, Plenty Cuts gave a good horse to Blue Cloud the healer, who painted a square of soft buckskin with Red Leaf's face and hung the buckskin on a spirit pole at the rear of her ghost lodge. Blue Cloud then crossed spirit poles in front of the lodge and draped a fine buffalo robe over the poles. White Bull set his chief's war bonnet on the buffalo's head, and the fine moccasins, leggings, shirts, and parfleches the women had made were laid beside this mock buffalo.

Blue Cloud offered the pipe to the four directions and to the White Buffalo Maiden who had taught the Lakota the ghost-owning ceremony.

Friends gathered inside the spirit lodge to feast on buffalo tongue and hump that had been boiling over the fire. When no one could eat more, Plenty Cuts gave a fine buckskin vest to Red Cloud. He gave a pair of fine moccasins to Old Man Afraid of His Horses. He gave a parfleche to Pretty Shield, the mother of Riding Bear, who had been killed fighting the Crows. He gave a horse to the winkte Shivering Aspen. He gave his Henry rifle to Iron Bear and his Colts revolver to White Bull. "I might have killed you with this, my brother," he said. That day, Plenty Cuts gave away fifty horses.

Blue Cloud sang and drummed through the afternoon while Plenty

Cuts and She Goes Before gave away possessions. After the sun set, Blue Cloud carried the spirit bundle to the open door and prayed as he opened the bundle.

When the healer opened the bundle, everyone shouted so Red Leaf would be accompanied by joy on her journey across the Shadowland.

Men congratulated Plenty Cuts and She Goes Before and Blue Whirlwind Woman beamed as She Goes Before and Plenty Cuts told their guests to take what they wanted from the lodge. He gave the lodge itself to a poor widow. He removed his trousers and beautiful beaded vest and She Goes Before took off her dress and her moccasins and pressed them on a young woman she didn't know very well.

When it was finished, Plenty Cuts and She Goes Before were naked. They owned nothing but Plenty Cuts's medal, Red Leaf's ghost, and their new life together.

CHAPTER 41

GENERAL MAHONE'S SIGNAL VICTORY

THE EVENING JINGLED AND JANGLED. CARRIAGES CLOGGED THE
street outside Richmond's Spottswood Hotel and Stephen Foster's jaunty
tunes poured through open windows to compete with the banjo players on
the porch. Those waiting outside to congratulate General Mahone wore
Sunday best, those already inside owned more than one Sunday suit.

It was sultry. Mist hung over the James.

At the door A.M.&O. railroad detectives separated the sheep from the
goats. Mr. Charles Chepstow sputtered. "I brought out the negro vote for
Robert Patterson."

"Yes, sir," a burly detective replied. "I already told the General what
you told me. Patterson lost. General was surprised you come. Evening,
Colonel Ward. What a triumph, eh, sir?"

Inside, General Mahone received admirers in the larger Spottswood's
reception room while Gilbert Walker, Virginia's new governor, held court
in the other. Duncan and Sallie sat on the stairs above the crush.

"Look, there's General Gordon."

"And General Hampton."

Thomas Byrd waved.

"Oh, dear. There's Thomas."

Duncan grinned. "Mr. Stuart's confidant? The esteemed legislator-elect from Augusta County? 'Oh, dear, there's Thomas' indeed. Come, we must pay our respects."

The one-armed gentleman and his wife excused themselves through the crowd.

"Duncan!" Thomas was all smiles. "Isn't this simply grand?"

"Congratulations on your election."

"You mean congratulations on *our* election. White men are restored to suffrage in Virginia!"

"Let us hope we are worthy of our franchise," Duncan replied.

"Come," Thomas said. "The General wants to thank you personally."

General Mahone and Alexander Stuart were sober. Otelia Mahone wore the strained smile of one who has heard too many outpourings from too many ardent, inebriated hearts.

"Well, Major." In his spotless white linen suit, the tiny General seemed a confection. "Thanks to your efforts we have won a signal victory."

"Sir, you musn't overestimate my contribution."

"On the contrary, General, you are welcome to overestimate my husband whenever you wish." Somewhat to her dismay, Sallie had learned charm's usefulness.

General Mahone bowed. "Are you certain, madam, that you cannot persuade your husband to remain in my employ?"

"Sir, when my husband was wounded, his hopes kept him alive. He has always loved horses and hopes to make our livelihood from them. Mrs. Mahone, I believe your husband knows 'hope'?"

Otelia Mahone was startled into candor. " 'Resolve,' perhaps. 'Hope' lacks luster for Billy."

Thomas Byrd toasted, "A new governor, a Virginia Constitution ratified . . ."

"And the Atlantic, Mississippi & Ohio," Mahone returned, lifting a glass he wasn't holding. Mahone caught Duncan's ear. "Major, Mr. Chepstow is making a commotion at the door. Please send him away." Mahone took his wife's hands. "Gentlemen," he said, "I give you the authoress of all my happiness."

THE RAIN WAS WHAT Virginia country folk call a "lady rain," gentle and persistent. The cobblestones glistened. Coachmen waited inside their rigs.

Those who would be admitted to the gala had been. The railway detectives leaned against the porch rail and smoked. The banjo players' circle of chairs was empty. Charles Chepstow's face was slick and pale.

"Evening, Mr. Chepstow. General Mahone thanks you for your efforts. I cannot think of many more deserving of Virginia's gratitude."

"I had hoped for more tangible gratitude. Do you know how difficult it is to persuade a negro to vote for a white man like Robert Patterson?"

Duncan Gatewood smiled. "Mahone asked you to campaign for Patterson? The General throws a wide net."

"I had expenses . . ."

"Sir, at one time you thought to become governor of the Commonwealth of Virginia. You are spared a duty many men would not seek and those who obtain often find onerous. General Mahone asks that you go home. Sir, you will not be admitted."

Chepstow opened and closed his mouth several times but found no sentences therein. The ex-editor disappeared among the carriages.

Sallie whispered, " 'Deserving of Virginia's gratitude.' Darling, you are a hypocrite."

"Dear, we ordinary mortals are indebted to men like Charles Chepstow and Thaddeus Stevens. They are living reminders that moral certainty must finally give way to messy, illogical kindness."

They walked through the July rain like newlyweds. What they said was unimportant; like mourning doves, they cooed.

Just a few blocks from the august Spottswood Hotel they entered that part of the city known as Marshall Ward.

JESSE BURNS'S VICTORY celebration had neither banjo players nor detectives. The victorious candidate received his constituents outdoors on a wooden chair underneath a tattered canopy. Men shook Jesse's hand, introduced their children, and though a few pressed for favors most had come from their pleasure that a fellow negro had been elected to the legislature of the Commonwealth of Virginia. Jimson Burns ushered them into their man's presence and, when that young man thought a constituent had overstayed, hastened him along.

Jesse rose to his feet. "Major Gatewood. Miss Sallie."

"The Honorable Assemblyman Burns," Duncan replied. "Jesse, we're proud of you."

Jesse grinned. "Reckon I'm proud too." He turned to his supporters. "Friends, there are some say, 'Never trust the white man,' but Major Duncan, Miss Sallie, and I grew up together. Sit down, Major, take my chair."

"Assemblyman Burns, your friends didn't come out in the rain to meet me. We've come to offer our congratulations."

"You and Miss Sallie slip on inside. I won't be much longer and Sudie will skin me if you get away without seeing her."

Sudie's laundry lines were empty tonight and chicken stew burbled on the stovetop. "Hello, Master Duncan, Miss Sallie. If I'd knowed you was comin', I'd of scrubbed this house."

"Mrs. Burns . . ." The two women embraced while Duncan went to the cradle and extended his fingers to baby Sojourner. "What a strong little thing! I don't believe I ever saw a baby with a stronger grip."

Duncan and Sallie were soon seated at Sudie's kitchen table. When Jimson came in, his mother asked if he had washed and the boy replied with the air of a man who cannot be bothered with trivialities that he had.

"We don't have no city water in Marshall Ward," Sudie said. "Just that hand pump down the street. No sewer neither. Mrs. Gatewood, what I liked about Jesse from the start: he don't swerve. He's like one of them locomotive engines on the track, it only got one way to go and if you're in the way, you better jump for your life. When Jesse says change will come, it will!"

Jesse entered, massaging his swollen hand. "Well, this here locomotive has shook more hands than any locomotive should have to. Even old

Deacon Hanley came to tell me I 'stand up for the negro.' Duncan, Miss Sallie. Will you take supper with us?"

Sallie said, "We'd be pleased. That chicken smells good."

"Wait'll you taste Ma's cornbread," Jimson said.

"Don't you go braggin' on me."

Sudie laid out mismatched plates, reserving the cracked ones for Jimson and herself. Jesse brought the chicken, pot and all, to the table and Sudie set cornbread beside it.

Jesse bowed his head and offered thanks for the food and for the opportunity to serve his people and for his wife and his son and his brand-new daughter, Sojourner Burns. He thanked God for his friends the Gatewoods and hoped there'd never be enmity between them.

After dinner they lingered, talking late into the night about olden times on Stratford Plantation. Because they would not think how unusual it was for whites and blacks to be eating together, it wasn't unusual at all.

CHAPTER 42

IMMIGRANTS

HIS SIGN HAD SEEN BETTER DAYS: "ELLAM OMOHUNDRU: DEALER in Full Task Hands, House Workers, and Sound Horses."

"He's supposed to have good horses," Duncan apologized to Aunt Opal.

The proprietor's vest was green, worn over a sleeveless shirt. His broad-brimmed hat perched on his ears. His odor was complex.

Duncan said, "A Silas Omohundru speculated in slaves . . ."

"Uncle Silas taught me the business. Said I should never forget they was human and I suppose they was, partly." Ellam giggled. "Uncle Silas was the hero of Fort Gregg. Tough old rooster. Didn't do to cross Uncle Silas. Don't do to cross Ellam Omohundru neither, if you get my drift." His suspicious glower skidded off Duncan's eyes. "Lost a wing in the War? I was in Richmond overseeing slaves on the fortifications. Lee wanted to draft them into the army. Imagine that: niggers fightin' side by side with white boys." Ellam rubbed his mouth. He ignored the stone-faced Aunt Opal.

Duncan said, "I am seeking a stallion."

Omohundru's establishment was a hodgepodge of brick stables and outbuildings outside the suburb of Manchester on the south side of the James. Stablemen barrowed dung onto towering heaps. Others exercised horses on a circular track.

"Uncle Silas's widow won't receive me. Twict I called on her and her nigger said she 'wasn't at home to the likes of me.' Some joke. Uncle Silas was a bastard, you know. Ellam's a Piedmont Omohundru."

Duncan said, "You do sell stallions?"

"Oh, hell, yes. Hell yes. Finest stallions in Virginia." He winked. "Yankee officer gets to drinkin' and playin' cards and pretty soon he's got nothin' to wager but his horse and next mornin' Ellam's got another horse for sale." With his thumbs in his vest pockets, the man resembled a banty in full crow.

"Mr. Omohundru . . ." Duncan said.

"You want to see them? Hell, I didn't know you was in no hurry. Olden days gentlemen had time for a little talk, maybe a tot or two before they got down to business. Yankee ways: these days everything got to be yankee ways."

Without further remonstrance, the dealer escorted Duncan through the stalls. Each of his horses had a baroque history. Many had belonged to a "real gentleman" fallen on hard times who'd been obliged to sell an animal dearer to him than life itself. "Had to pay fifty dollars gold for him," he said of one thoroughbred. "Officer's mother was dying and the gravedigger wanted his fee."

Twice Duncan entered a stall to examine teeth and feet. Once he asked that an animal be saddled. "Backer's a spirited beast," Omohundru said. "You'll want a martingale for him. He's a hell of a horse—wants a *real* rider."

Duncan gripped the left rein between thumb and forefinger, the right between third and fourth.

Aunt Opal watched critically while Duncan gaited the steed.

Ellam raised his voice. "You'll be wantin' brood mares too, I reckon. I heard about you, Major Gatewood, how you was buyin' up brood mares all over the Tidewater, roans and blacks, sixteen hands, well broke, no more'n six years. I was wonderin' when you'd get to ol' Ellam."

"I have purchased enough mares. Omohundru, what do you want for Backer?"

"You know"—Omohundru scratched his head—"You done picked the best stallion on the place. I was gonna put Backer out with my own mares."

"I suspected such might be the case."

Aunt Opal whispered in Duncan's ear.

"What's the nigger want?" Omohundru asked. "Tell her I ain't buyin' no more niggers. 'Gainst the law these days." He eyed Aunt Opal as he had his horses. "Don't expect I would have paid much for you, Mammy. You're past your prime."

Duncan's smile contained a warning. "As you say, sir. It is illegal."

Without breaking stride, Omohundru continued, "Backer belonged to a Massachusetts colonel. I'd take three hundred for him."

Duncan indicated a nondescript roan in the exercise ring. "My advisor fancies that one."

"But you ain't rode him."

"I defer to more knowledgeable opinion."

Ellam cried to the roan's rider, "Bring him here, Chief. Have a care! Have a care! That horse is a man-killer."

The rider's hair hung down his back in a thick black braid. Wordlessly he trotted the stallion toward them.

Ellam retreated. "Have a care, damn you!"

Despite his bored, solemn-faced rider, the roan reared onto his hind legs. Young horse—three or four years old.

"His price?"

"Brandywine ain't for sale. Was I to sell him to you, I'd be known all over Virginia as the man who sold Major Gatewood the horse what killed him."

As evidence for this proposition, the horse snorted and reared again. Despite Omohundru's alarmed squeals, his indian rider managed to contain him. Ultimately, Ellam Omohundru sold Duncan the roan for two hundred fifty dollars. "I'll throw in the bridle. It's worth an old bridle to meet a white man lets Mammy choose his stud horse."

The indian dismounted, dropped the reins, and walked off. The ground-hitched horse stayed put while Duncan counted out bills.

"Shinplasters," Omohundru complained.

"There is no gold to be had in Richmond."

"God Damned speculators. Hell, next thing you know, Chief there will be swapping his wampum for gold futures." The horse dealer cackled at the prospect. Then he confided, "He'll need all his wampum onct I send him down the road."

Duncan bent to make a stirrup for Aunt Opal. She rode bareback, her skirts flowing down Brandywine's flanks. When she clucked, the horse trotted quietly away.

"Well, I'll be damned," Ellam said. "I'll be damned."

"Perhaps not," Duncan said. "God is said to be merciful."

DUNCAN WAITED DOWN the street at an Irish workman's saloon which served a meager free lunch and cheap watery beer. He was nursing his second when Omohundru's grooms arrived, the indian in the rear. He sat at the end of the bar, away from the others.

Duncan set his beer down beside the indian's. "You've another name besides Chief, I expect."

"I was born 'Yartunnah'—that suit you better?"

"I figure a man's handle is what he says it is."

His eyes were blacker than a moonless night. "You wantin' to know 'bout that horse you bought?"

"No. I've never known Aunt Opal to misjudge a horse."

He nodded. "She's right about that one. Brandywine was the best in the stable. Even the fool was beginning to suspect his worth. He signaled me to have him act up."

"Your performance was unconvincing."

The indian shrugged and drained his beer glass.

"Another?"

"No." He grinned suddenly. "Drink is a curse."

"Omohundru fired you?"

Another shrug. "Would have happened sooner or later. Fools don't surround themselves with men who know more than they do."

"You're Cherokee?"

"When you white men ran us out of Georgia, my people stayed. Fought with Stand Watie's regiment in the war. Put on paint and feathers and scared bejesus out of the Federals. I was younger then."

"I'll need a good hand with horses in Montana," Duncan said.

"Montana? You ain't scared of gettin' scalped?"

"Not by my friends."

"Uh-huh. Some call me Joe Lame Deer. Means the same as Yartunnah, more or less."

DUNCAN RENTED COUSIN Molly's house to Colonel Elliot, who had commanded artillery but would now bribe legislators. Duncan introduced Elliot to Mahone's legislators and those who might yet be weaned from the B&O's pernicious influence. Colonel Elliot refused to meet with the black legislators he called the "Customs House gang."

In farewell to Duncan, Little Billy said, "Major, you were a brave officer," and "Our business is concluded."

INTO COUSIN MOLLY'S ATTIC went the little pine nightstand that was all Sallie had from their wartime home in Petersburg. Her father Uther Botkin's library of Thomas Jefferson, Thomas Paine, and Edmund Burke went up there too. Sallie wrapped Duncan's sword in his uniform and placed them in an old trunk under the attic window along with her father's spectacles, cane, inkwells, and bedraggled quill pens.

In that dusty attic, lit by narrow windows at either end, Sallie didn't know why she was crying. A new beginning—wasn't that what she wanted for herself, her husband and children?

They bought horse harness, shovels, axes, and two Winchester repeating rifles. Sallie wrapped her crockery in newspapers and packed each piece between sawdust layers in an oak cask. They bought horsemans' dusters and broad-brimmed hats. At the bootmaker Aunt Opal behaved as if being fitted for riding boots happened every day.

In August, Duncan and Sallie went home to Stratford.

Jack Mitchell met them at the depot and as their buggy negotiated the familiar road, every turn refreshed memories. Gangs were cutting corn and Duncan's hand curled instinctively as if holding a corn knife: twist the ear, snap the stem, slash the husk, toss the ear onto the golden heap in the wagon bed.

"Husband, will we ever return?"

"I wish I thought so."

Jack said, "We is sinners. We enjoys to sin. Old Adam and Eve, when they left that garden, they takes their sinnin' ways with 'em."

"Jack, you are a wellspring of encouragement."

"Plenty coloreds takin' themselves away. What good it do? What they gonna find we ain't got at Stratford?"

The fences had been repaired and the mill was painted. Sheep and a dozen cows grazed behind the barn. The mill wheel was turning and the air vibrated with the whine of the saw.

"General Mahone has paid his arrears?"

"Don't rightly know. Master Gatewood, he keeps the accounts."

In a checked vest and trousers slathered with saw oil, Samuel was supervising sawyers cantdogging a log into the whirling four-foot blade.

Duncan asked a young black his name.

"I'm Lockridge, Master. Pearly Lockridge."

"You look a lot like Rufus. Partisan rangers killed him in '62 or '63."

"Mama say Rufus was my daddy." The young man paused. "Mama say Rufus wanted to be a farrier. He wanted to better hisself."

Rufus's face filled Duncan's memory as vividly as if Rufus had just walked into the mill. He felt his throat constrict and thought: Everything here is connected to everything else. He said only, "Yes. He was a good man."

After the log was turned for the next cut, Samuel wiped his hands. "Jack," he said, "I leave you to it. Doubtless the men prefer your supervision."

Cousin Molly had supper waiting: smoked ham, new potatoes, beans, coleslaw, and peach pie. Molly complained the raccoons were climbing the peach trees for the ripest peaches, breaking laden branches as they climbed. "We chained Old Buck in the orchard, but those scoundrels calculated the reach of Buck's chain and rioted just beyond his reach. Poor dog barked himself hoarse."

While the ladies were cleaning up, Duncan and Samuel went to sit on the porch roof. "Remember—" Duncan mused.

Samuel cut him short, "I could spend the rest of my days remembering."

Mahone was paying current accounts, but Eben Barnwell was financing Stratford's improvements. "Barnwell is speculating in gold," Samuel said. "Everybody is speculating in gold. At the county seat, men of probity are paying a fearful price for it. It is this infernal telegraph. We hear more than we need to about matters which do not concern us."

That night Sallie and Duncan lay in the bed where years before the boy Duncan had dreamed of war and glory and horses.

THE NEXT DAY, it was raining and cold when they left.

They joined Aunt Opal, the children, and Joe Lame Deer in Baltimore. Joe Lame Deer slept in the horse pens. "Hell," he told Duncan, "my people'd kill for one of these ponies."

"We depart on the morning express," Duncan said.

As Aunt Opal was taking the children off to bed after evening prayers, her reticule clunked the door frame.

"Aunt Opal, what on earth?"

The black woman pulled an ancient pistol from her bag. "Them red devils come for these childrens, they wish they hadn't."

They left at six A.M. Two days to Indianapolis, two more to Chicago, where they paused to rest the horses off the cars.

Chicago was a one-story town with wide dirt streets. Young Catesby gaped as a wooden house on rollers, its owners sitting placidly on the porch, was drawn solemnly down the street.

Joe Lame Deer was fascinated by the stockyards. "They got a machine where a hog walks in one end and comes out canned pork!"

The family took rooms at a depot hotel. About midnight, bawling cattle pulled Sallie from sleep and she went to the window. Under a full moon, the stockyards stretched as far as Sallie could see; as if cattle, hogs, and sheep had built a beasts' metropolis.

The next day, Duncan secured berths in one of Mr. Pullman's sleeping cars and the horsecar was coupled behind. At nine o'clock Wednesday morning, September 8, 1869, they departed Chicago for the West.

The Pullman car had mirrors and an ornate coal stove. At night its seats could be converted into berths, like a ship's berths. Those ingenious devices intrigued little Catesby greatly.

They were an hour out of Chicago when one of the car's wheels ignited; a bearing had failed and set the oil in the wheelbox afire. The train waited while the crew put the fire out with blankets and sand. Not twenty minutes later, another wheel burst into flame and was extinguished.

After a third bearing failed, the engine abandoned Mr. Pullman's car. The passenger cars had been crowded before the Pullman passengers piled in, and despite his objections, little Catesby rode in his father's lap.

The boy quieted when the train rolled sonorously across the great wooden bridge that spanned the Mississippi.

On the western shore of the river they entered the Great Plains. A few farms were scattered here and there, but there were long spaces between them. Ducks and geese covered marshy sloughs and startled deer bounded away from their train.

Another Pullman car was waiting at Cedar Rapids, but the conductor warned that this car was the worst on the line and that spring floods had eroded the track ballast. "Might upset," he announced cheerfully.

Sallie slept with Aunt Opal and the children in the lower berth.

Though the train did manage to stay on the tracks, it lurched and bumped horribly. Nobody slept well, and at dawn the weary travelers were sitting in the Pullman's parlor watching the horizon redden.

The conductor pointed. "Them'll be Council Bluffs. I guess we didn't upset after all."

"Next time I ridin' in the horsecar with the redskin," Aunt Opal said.

THE CEDAR RAPIDS & Missouri Railroad terminated at the Missouri River, where their baggage and horses were ferried to Omaha City. Joe

Lame Deer said the horsecar had been comfortable; he'd slept in a manger of fragrant timothy hay.

Omaha City had more tents than wooden dwellings. The only hotel was a two-story building whose stairwells and rooms were so filthy, Sallie removed the straw ticks off the beds as a precaution against fleas.

Joe Lame Deer never left the horses, which became more valuable with each mile west.

While they waited for the thrice-weekly train, they met fellow passengers in the hotel lobby. They would be sharing their Pullman with "the Honorable Algar and the Honorable Snellie." Snellie was a wispy man who longed to hunt buffalo; Algar hoped to kill a grizzly.

Their youngest traveling companion was a boy, accompanied by a negress. Although the pair kept to themselves, young Catesby Gatewood refused to honor their preference and when Aunt Opal closed her eyes Catesby was tugging the boy's shirtsleeve.

"Why, hullo. Haven't you anyone to play with?"

"Master Jacob," the boy's servant warned, "you was told by your mama—"

"Not to consort with disreputable strangers. Yes, Kizzy. But this boy seems reputable. Can you do sums? How is your spelling? Can you spell 'indian'?"

Young Catesby set his thumb in his mouth, considering.

His mother intervened. "Oh, dear, is he bothering you?"

"Oh, no." The boy assured her that he was glad to make the acquaintance of young . . ."

"Catesby," Sallie furnished.

"I am Jacob Omohundru, and this is Kizzy. We are traveling to San Francisco. Do you think our train will be attacked by indians? I certainly hope so. Have you a rifle, sir? Sir, are you unwell?"

AS DUSK WAS extracting the last dim light from the western sky, Sallie and Duncan trudged the boardwalk that fronted Omaha City's main street. "I suppose there can be no doubt who he is," Sallie said. "He favors you."

"He seems well brought up. Christ, Sallie! Why now?"

"Dearest, taking the Lord's name in vain can't change the fact that that young man is certainly your son."

"Yes."

"Who believes, as I discovered after you fled so ingloriously this afternoon, that he is the son of Silas and Marguerite Omohundru; his father was a businessman and his mother is the daughter of a Bahamanian parson. Jacob intends to visit the Bahamas one day. I doubt Kizzy remembers me. We only met once."

When the boardwalk ended, they continued down the dusty street. Lanterns illuminated tent saloons and tent faro parlors and men weaved and hallooed and one drunk tipped his hat to Sallie.

"What will you do?"

"I cannot tell him who I am; I would expose his mother as a colored woman who could not have married Silas Omohundru and has no rights as his widow. I'd as soon put a revolver to his head."

"Then, dear, you must not tell him," Sallie said firmly.

THE PULLMAN PALACE Car Express contained sleeping cars, a dining car, a parlor car, and an open observation car. Joe Lame Deer and the horses would follow with tomorrow's freight. Duncan wanted to travel with the horses, but Sallie's smile was gentle and implacable. "Dear, you have often spoken about your son, lost to you as an infant. You have said you hoped to see him again."

THEIR TRAIN CROSSED the Platte River flats, a dreary featureless prairie interrupted only by brief stops for wood and water at stations guarded by soldiers.

The Pullman cars were the latest model and the parlor car had a pump organ upon which, after supper, the Honorable Snellie played and sang music-hall ditties of a nature unsuitable for children's ears. After Aunt Opal and the children retired, Duncan and Sallie sat up as Snellie's organ wheezed and blackness slipped past the windows.

At breakfast in the dining car, Jacob Omohundru marched to their table. "Sir, I must apologize if I said anything to distress you back in Omaha. Mama says my manners leave much to be desired."

"Jacob Omohundru, you've done nothing wrong. I was suddenly . . . indisposed."

"Oh, that's grand! Oh, not that you were indisposed, but Kizzy said I must have been rude because you left so precipitously. Are you well again? Isn't it splendid out here? I've seen forty-three antelope and I thought I saw a buffalo, but Kizzy says it was a rock."

At Sallie's suggestion, they went to the observation car. The open car's leather benches were dusted with the same cinders that crunched under their shoes. "Did you lose your arm in the War, sir? My father was killed in the War. Mama says that he defied the yankees to the end. I'm not sure that was a good idea. Defying the yankees to the end, I mean. If he'd compromised I should still have a father. Where are you bound, sir?"

Duncan said they would leave the train at Medicine Bow and take the Bridger Trail north to Montana Territory.

"Will you prospect for gold, sir? Mama says that gold is being bid up by speculators, that Mr. Fisk and Mr. Gould have a corner and own so much gold that if anyone wants gold they must buy gold from them. Look, sir, that is a wolf on the ridgeline. He is my first wolf ever. Isn't he splendid?"

As he stood on the seat, the wind blew the boy's hair off his face and Duncan gripped his son's leg to steady him.

Duncan said, "Men are buying gold because President Grant is friendly with Fisk and Gould. Grant's brother-in-law, Corbin, is in with Gould."

"That may be so, sir, but Mama says Grant doesn't like Gould as much as everybody thinks he does. Mama says Grant will release gold from the Federal Treasury rather than see Gould own it all."

"Your mama—is she always right?"

"About money, yes, sir. Always."

Duncan said he wasn't looking for gold but for land suitable for a ranch where he would rear horses.

"I think I should like that sort of work. Mama won't let me play or go to school with other boys. I must have tutors. Mama says I learn my lessons better from tutors. I believe I could learn my lessons and still play with other boys. What do you think?"

"I wouldn't wish to argue with your mama."

Jacob nodded. "She usually bests those who try."

"Yes," Duncan said, remembering the ferocious little slave girl he'd loved so many years ago.

After a time, Kizzy came, worried that Jacob might be bothering the gentleman. When Duncan assured her he was enjoying the boy's company, Kizzy plumped herself down with her knitting.

His mother had sent Jacob to San Francisco to Mr. Leland Stanford, who had constructed the western segment of this railroad. At a critical time for that enterprise, when others balked, Mrs. Omohundru's Farmers and Merchants Bank had provided financing. "Mama says Mr. Stanford may be of service to me one day," the boy explained. "I must be on my best behavior."

In the late morning, they stopped in Cheyenne for water. The boy was fascinated by the trappers, traders, and blanket indians on the platform. "Aren't they magnificent!"

"I don't know," Duncan said. "They look like loafers to me."

The boy settled into his seat. "I'm sure you're right, sir. I shan't admire them."

"They probably aren't so bad," Duncan relented. A drunken indian paraded along the platform, whooping. "He looks happy enough."

The boy set his mouth. "We are not meant to be happy, sir," he said. "We are meant to be good."

They passed through Sherman, which, though only a water tank, was, according to *Crofutt's Guide*, the highest point on the Transcontinental Railroad, eight thousand feet above sea level. As their train descended through narrow canyons and trestled rushing mountain streams, the boy stuttered with delight. "Look there, sir! Look there!"

The boy ate supper with the Gatewoods. "I hope to see Chinamen in San Francisco," Jacob said. "I have read about the Celestial Empire."

At dusk, they stopped at Medicine Bow, the rough railroad camp that was the head of the Bridger Trail. It didn't take long to unload the family and their luggage. The engineer blew his whistle in farewell.

The wind was cold. Baby Abigail was fussing.

The boy leaned out of the observation car. "Remember what Mama said about the gold," he cried.

"God bless you," Duncan shouted. The train grew smaller and smaller and vanished around a bend.

A man and wife, their two children, and a middle-aged negress stood on the empty platform on what seemed like the edge of the world. Wind-scoured sagebrush covered the hills behind a tiny settlement of shacks and dugouts.

"Dear husband."

"Dearest wife."

—

CHAPTER 43

BLACK FRIDAY

Telegram from Eben Barnwell to Amos Hayward,
8:02 a.m., September 24, 1869:
MUST KNOW WHAT G INTENDS STOP BARNWELL

Hayward to Barnwell, 8:33 A.M., September 24, 1869:
G AND B MET THREE HOURS LAST NIGHT
STOP HAYWARD

To Hayward (8:34 A.M.):
MUST KNOW WHAT G INTENDS STOP BARNWELL

To Barnwell (8:35 A.M.):
NO NEWS YET EXCLAMATION POINT HAYWARD

EBEN BARNWELL DROPPED THE CRUMPLED TELEGRAM ONTO THE littered floor of the Broad Street telegraph office. George Nutley, Eben's partner in the venture, gripped his shoulder and hissed, "Sir!"

Eben forced a smile. "Nothing yet, George. Would you breakfast?"

Nutley cackled. "You can eat? God, how I wish I could. I keep noth-

ing on my stomach, Barnwell. Nothing." Bumping past speculators and
messenger boys, he stumbled out of the crowded office.

Nutley's nerve was breaking.

At 8:35 on Friday morning, September 24, 1869, with gold prices
at one hundred fifty dollars an ounce, Eben Barnwell was holding contracts to deliver twenty-three thousand ounces—one thousand four hundred and forty pounds—of gold, at one hundred thirty dollars per
ounce. Eben's contracts were to be fulfilled at twelve noon Friday,
October 1, 1869. Eben had bought his contracts on margin, ten percent
down, with money loaned him by George Nutley's brother, Joseph, chief
teller of the New York Bank for Commerce. A messenger boy had just
informed Eben that Joseph Nutley was seeking him "on a matter of considerable urgency."

As security, Eben had pledged his house, his trotters, his securities,
even a call mortgage on a remote Virginia plantation. Eben's gold contracts
were in the safe in the office he shared with George Nutley. Eben could not
bear to look at them.

The Broad Street Del's was so crowded Eben couldn't find a seat at
the bar. He ordered champagne.

A stranger punched his shoulder. "I am buying," he pronounced.
"One fifty and a half."

"Who is selling gold today?"

"Hah! I will find that seller. Fisk and Gould can't buy all the gold in
America!"

In April when Jay Gould began buying, gold had stood at 130. In June
Jim Fisk jumped into the market—June being the same month Fisk and
Gould invited President Grant aboard Fisk's private steamer from Boston
to Providence. En route, naturally the financiers explained economics to
the new President. Patiently, Fisk and Gould mentioned the value of open
markets, that gold must float and that the invisible hand of the market
would set a fair price. Certainly Grant mustn't release gold from the U.S.
Treasury. On the first of July, President Grant enjoyed a performance of *La
Périchole* from Jim Fisk's private box in Jim Fisk's opera house, and in

September the President graciously accepted the loan of Jay Gould's private railcar for the vacation he and Mrs. Grant so richly deserved.

Later that month, Eben traveled to Washington City to see Amos Hayward, now private clerk to George Boutwell, the Treasury Secretary. Hayward told Eben that Secretary Boutwell was urging Grant to release Treasury gold but Dan Butterworth, head of the New York subtreasury, was making Fisk's argument: that national prosperity depended upon unregulated competition, that American entrepreneurs must have their reward.

Like every other Wall Street speculator, Eben had been buying gold. The western miners couldn't produce it fast enough.

Three days after President and Mrs. Grant returned Jay Gould's beautifully appointed parlor car, Amos Hayward telegraphed Eben that President Grant was wavering and Boutwell was getting the upper hand.

So Eben sold gold. He sold the gold he had and he sold forward contracts for gold he did not have. With the money he realized selling these contracts he sold more gold.

Friday morning, Eben Barnwell had five twenty-dollar gold pieces in his pocket. He was wondering how far he could get on one hundred dollars.

"Another champagne, sir?"

"Thank you, Randolph. It is you, Randolph?"

"Yes, sir. Mr. Delmonico has the uptown staff here today. I've never seen it so busy."

"You, Randolph. Are you buying gold?"

"Sir, I have purchased a few December contracts. My mother . . . sir, Mother once enjoyed a better station. I look forward to restoring her circumstances. Mr. Fisk says gold will hit two hundred before Christmas."

Eben drank champagne. "Randolph," he said, "this stuff seems awfully thin. I believe I'll have brandy."

At nine, when the Gold Exchange opened, gold stood at 152. By nine-thirty it was 156.

In his pocket, Eben slid gold coins over one another.

"What of Fisk?"

"Fisk is buying."

"Grant's brother-in-law—what's his name?"

"Mr. Corbin has not come out of his home today."

"Yesterday, Corbin was buying."

"I don't give a hang for Corbin. I'll take twenty at one fifty-seven!"

Inside the William Street Gold Exchange, the crush was so savage that if a man raised his hand to bid, it was difficult to bring it back down. The air burned Eben's eyes and at ten-thirty, with gold at 159, he stepped outdoors and stood panting like a dog.

Nutley sat in his parked carriage, his face the color of chalk. "One fifty-nine, Barnwell. One fifty-nine. I am a ruined man. Who will provide for my family?" He jerked the blind down and his coachman flicked his whip and the carriage rattled off.

Why hadn't Eben considered *his* family? Pauline, who loved and trusted him? Little Augustus Barnwell, helpless infant and Eben's pride and joy? Eben's few gold coins might pay a single man's fare west but never his family's. What work could he find? Without his money, who was he? Eben perfectly recalled the Knapp brothers' farm and the shivering, runny-nosed, frightened boy he had been. Why, he was still that boy! All Eben's adult life he had been playacting as the confident, amiable, energetic Eben Barnwell.

Eben squeezed his eyes closed and prayed, "Dear Lord. Please don't let Pauline find me out."

Nutley would do the honorable thing: the scrawled letter of regret, the icy muzzle of a revolver at his temple.

Eben did not wish to vomit into the gutter.

The telegraph office floor was awash with discarded buy orders from Boston, Philadelphia, even San Francisco—orders at yesterday's price: 145. At 145, Eben would lose fifteen dollars for each ounce of gold delivered. At 160, he would lose thirty dollars. At 200, clever Jim Fisk's estimate, he would lose seventy dollars. Why, that was a phenomenon!

——

TELEGRAM FROM EBEN BARNWELL to Amos Hayward, 9:45 A.M., September 24, 1869:

ANY NEWS STOP BARNWELL

Hayward to Barnwell, 10:16 A.M.:

G AGREES WITH B STOP
CONGRATULATIONS STOP HAYWARD

Eben Barnwell's heart leaped into the top of his chest and hung for an instant before resuming its everyday thumping. He gripped the counter to steady himself.

He stumbled into the street and flagged a jitney cab. "Driver, hurry! You must hurry! Here is twenty dollars. You will have a second twenty dollars from Mr. George Nutley of 27 Stuyvesant Square when you deliver my message. I am Eben Barnwell. You are to say Eben is vindicated. Just that. Vindicated. No more. Can you remember? 'Vindicated!' For God's sake, hurry!"

Speculators scurried between the Gold Exchange, Del's, and the telegraph office. Eben broke into a sweat. His teeth chattered. In London he always stayed at Brown's Hotel. He wondered if Pauline would like Brown's Hotel. He wondered if more land might be purchased for Stratford. Were any adjacent plantations for sale? He wondered where his young Augustus would go to college when he became a man.

Most of Del's tables were vacant, but speculators were three and four deep at the bar. Randolph attended him at a table beside a window. "One sixty, sir," Randolph said happily.

"I'll have the consommé. Please bring me a bottle of Sillery."

"Not too thin, sir?"

"I believe my palate—my palate was distressed."

"I'm fetching five glasses of brandy for one of champagne today, sir."

At eleven minutes to twelve, Friday, September 24, 1869, the telegraph announced President Grant would sell Treasury gold until the price had stabilized. The news flowed down the street to the Gold Exchange and into Del's, where it was disbelieved, contested, hotly denied, and rebutted as Del's emptied and men ran into the street, some to the telegraph office, others to the brokerage where Fisk and Gould had been all morning; where Jay Gould had been (as everyone later learned) selling gold.

The mob would have done Gould and Fisk grievous injury if the pair hadn't fled through a back door into the alley where their carriage was waiting.

Wall Street's anguish was worse than when Lincoln died. One man came into Del's, ordered a bottle of rum, and, hoisting it to his mouth, drank, recorked the empty, and walked out as sober as he had come in.

"Some bastards knew about this," a speculator screamed, his finger roving from bewildered face to bewildered face. "Somebody was in on it."

Eben poured himself more champagne. It might have been water.

"Gold's at one thirty and falling," someone shouted.

Eben had imagined that becoming rich would make him happy; that he would shout his good news and buy champagne for everybody. Instead, he felt as if he had robbed someone.

The weary, no longer runny-nosed, no longer frightened boy Eben Barnwell stacked four twenty-dollar gold pieces beside his glass as a tip for Randolph.

CHAPTER 44

—

WASHITU STRAWBERRIES

JESSE CLEARED HIS THROAT. "I HELPED BUILD THESE FORTIFICA-
tions," he said.

Assistant Secretary Methuen said, "That so?"

Jesse said, "In '63, I was paid twenty dollars a month to work on
Washington's defenses. Seemed all the money in the world."

"Um-hum," the assistant secretary said, consulting his watch.

"Then I enlisted—38th USCT. Fought on the Petersburg line."

"They should have been here an hour ago. We can't keep the river bot-
tled up forever."

An assistant secretary of the Interior, James Methuen, and Jesse Burns,
assemblyman from Richmond's Marshall Ward, waited beside a fifteen-
inch Rodman gun in a stone emplacement above the Potomac River. The
gun crew and its captain sprawled on the grass smoking and enjoying the
beautiful morning.

On the broad sweep of the Potomac, gunboats prevented a flotilla of
sail and steam vessels from proceeding downstream. Just visible through
the gun captain's glass, other gunboats performed similar service at the far
end of this makeshift firing range. From cap to muzzle, the Rodman gun
was twelve feet long. The largest rifled gun in the United States could hurl
a fifteen-inch missile four miles.

The assistant secretary fretted.

The colored tailor who had made Jesse's suit made the Virginia governor's suits, and Jesse's suit was the same cut though cheaper material. Jesse had admired a broad-brimmed beaver hat, but when the tailor rolled his eyes Jesse had purchased a bowler.

This morning, on the Richmond, Fredericksburg & Potomac train Jesse'd folded his jacket across his lap. Consequently his garment was unwrinkled. The assistant secretary's shirt collar was frayed, a jacket button hung loose, and his bowler had a quarter-sized grease spot above the hatband.

Yesterday, the Richmond Customs inspector personally delivered the telegram to janitor Jesse Burns.

EDWARD RATCLIFF ACCOMPANYING RED CLOUD
PARTY STOP SECRETARY OF INTERIOR COX
REQUESTS YOUR PRESENCE IN WASHINGTON STOP

"What they want you for, Burns?"

"Edward and I served in the army together, sir," Jesse replied.

"You'll provide a full report, on your return."

"Yes, sir."

"You'll commend me to Secretary Cox."

"Yes, sir."

When Jesse won election, Jimson had expected—Jesse didn't know what—that the new assemblyman would have a fine job with a fine title and Jimson Burns, his campaign manager, might have a fine job too.

When it didn't happen, Jimson went back to the Knockabouts. Sudie pretended nothing was wrong—"He all growed up now"—after Jesse surprised her crying.

When he told her he'd been called to Washington, Sudie asked, "Interior Cox, he important?"

"He reports to President Grant," Jesse said.

"Jesse, why they want you?"

"Because Edward is with Red Cloud and his Sioux indians, and I am Edward's friend."

"But why would they want you?"

Sudie's not-insensible question was answered by Assistant Secretary Methuen, who met Jesse at the depot. "Red Cloud refuses to move his people to the Agency. He has outraged Secretary Cox with his demands. Apparently your friend Ratcliff has Red Cloud's confidence. Chief Red Cloud won't trust us but trusts a renegade negro." Metheun shook his head. "I've seen Ratcliff's army record."

"Edward was cited for bravery," Jesse said.

"He was court-martialed for striking an officer." He grimaced. "Tom Custer, no less."

"Might be," Jesse said in a thick slave voice, "Tom Custer needed strikin'."

The fixed smile on the assistant secretary's face flickered as he registered then disregarded Jesse's insolence.

"We intend to show Red Cloud he cannot trifle with the United States. Jesse, you are an elected official and an employee of the United States Customs House."

"Assemblyman Burns," Jesse corrected him.

"To be sure," Assistant Secretary Methuen said.

In the Washitu year eighteen hundred and seventy, which Lakota call "the year when Many Strikes was killed," in the Moon of Ripening Strawberries we left the Tongue and came to the North Platte to meet Red Cloud. It had been a bitter winter and hungry spring. Though Plenty Cuts and White Bull hunted far, blackhorns were scarce.

Now, as I walked beside our travois, I put tiny, sweet strawberries into my mouth and the sky was as it always had been and the creeks flowed from the melting snow as they always had and my new baby stirred in my belly.

After Plenty Cuts and I owned her ghost, Red Leaf took Low Dog's place in my dreams and she told me my second child would be her sister. Dreaming with Red Leaf was as pleasant as my waking. One night Red Leaf took me to the great Washitu village where years before Low Dog had shown me the Seizers parading. So I was not surprised when Plenty Cuts told me Red Cloud would go to Washington City to meet the Great White Father and we would go with him

Seizers met us at the railroad outside Cheyenne. Red Cloud and the Seizer chief smoked the peace pipe. The Lakota cheered as Red Cloud, Plenty Cuts, Red Dog, High Wolf, Yellow Bear, Lone Wolf, and Black Hawk boarded the train. The only other wives were Whistling Duck and Falls Down Woman.

I had never ridden in a railroad wagon. The wagon swayed and shook and rattled like a wican's rattle and hard black cinders came in the windows and warriors knelt at Washitu spittoons to be sick.

Our wagon had hard benches for sitting and a tiny room where you could relieve yourself onto the speeding earth below. The wagon behind us carried fifty Seizers. The eating wagon in front had wallpaper and dark wood and brass lamps and it reminded me of Reverend Riggs's parlor at Yellow Medicine Mission. Men as black as Plenty Cuts cooked meat and potatoes, but Lakota do not eat potatoes.

Red Cloud and Plenty Cuts talked late into the night, Red Cloud asking Plenty Cuts about the Washitu, for surely they are a peculiar people.

Our train stopped at the Missouri River, where we left it for a ferry. Seizers kept curious Washitu away with their bayonets. The train waiting for us on the other shore made thick smoke like green cottonwood.

It was pleasant sitting beside the window as the grassland rushed by. When we stopped for coal and water, the Seizers wouldn't let us get off the train. They were afraid we would run away. Open prairie became Washitu farms. Washitu villages hurried past, each bigger than the one before. I shuddered. "They are so many."

Plenty Cuts took my hand. "We will be in Washington City soon."

As a girl I had lived on the edge of the Washitu empire and as a woman that empire stretched to the Yellowstone River. Knowing that something is and seeing it are different things. So many farms, so many villages, so many towns, so many miles of railroad track, so many Washitu. When a hunter kills a blackhorn but does not skin it,

*after a time in the sun its skin falls away and the pale worms under-
neath are as numerous as the Washitu.*

JOURNALISTS AND OFFICIALS surrounded Red Cloud's party as they
approached the Rodman gun.

Jesse put out his hand. "'Lo, Edward. I feared you were dead. My letters came back unopened."

Edward Ratcliff's arms bulged from his elaborately beaded vest. His
Medal of Honor lay on his bare chest and an eagle feather dangled beside
his cheek. "Mail service ain't worth much west of the Platte," he said.
"Damned if you ain't dressed just like Ol' Master."

"I am elected, Edward. Can we have imagined it? One of twelve
negroes in the Virginia Legislature. Negroes can vote like the white man
and Virginia's readmitted to the Union. We will yet achieve equality."

"You won't live that long."

"Then my daughter will harvest what I am sowing."

"Jesse, you ain't changed none. I ain't Ratcliff to the Lakota, I'm Plenty
Cuts. This here's She Goes Before."

Jesse lifted his bowler to his friend's small bright-eyed wife.

The gun crew assembled at the Rodman gun.

Plenty Cuts said, "She's shy, but she talks better'n I do. Reads and
writes too."

"I will be truthful, Edward. I am here to influence you to make Red
Cloud accept the government terms."

Plenty Cuts smiled. "Nobody makes Red Cloud do nothin'. He talks
with the Big Bellies and he talks with the Shirt Wearers and he doesn't say
nothing until he puts it all together and when he talks he makes so much
sense it's like you thought of it yourself. The Washitu—white men—can't figure him out. Red Cloud asks one thing then another thing and says no he
never promised this and no he never promised that and when he's got a good
grip on their privates, he yanks 'em and the Washitu sing Red Cloud's tune."

"Attention, please," the assistant secretary said. "Sergeant Ratcliff,
please interpret."

The gun crew were alert and confident.

"This Rodman gun uses Mammoth powder, which is, I dare say, unlike powder you are accustomed to. Mammoth powder produces a steadier, more regular explosion." The warriors fingered the fat hexagonal flakes. The women covered their ears.

The gun crew uncapped the gun barrel and rammed a charge home. The gun captain sighted down the long barrel, nodded his satisfaction, and jerked the lanyard. The big gun bellowed its projectile, which, as a black dot, was briefly visible high in its trajectory before it dove into a water spout miles downstream.

After the gun captain lowered the muzzle, the next projectile skipped four times—like a boy's stone in a pond. The gun captain grinned. When Red Cloud said something, the indians laughed.

The assistant secretary demanded, "Sergeant Ratcliff, what does Chief Red Cloud say?"

"Well, sir, Red Cloud says he could have four arrows in that gun captain before he could uncap the muzzle."

That evening, we rode in carriages to the house of the Great White Father. Plenty Cuts's friend Jesse came too. He had been told to influence my husband. What do Washitu think of the Lakota? Are we such fools?

We entered a long room where hundreds of candles in glass wheels suspended from the ceiling glistened and quivered and chased points of green and red and blue light around the walls. The Washitu have many powerful things, but this was the first beautiful Washitu thing I ever saw.

The Washitu came in while I was admiring the dancing lights. The men dressed in black, but their wives' gowns shimmered. Grant, the Great White Father, introduced his wife to Red Cloud. Grant's daughter, Nellie, gave Red Cloud flowers and Red Cloud smiled at her. He had daughters too. A bearded Washitu chief bowed to Red Cloud and said he was Lord Murray, and had the honor to be Her

Britannic Majesty's ambassador. He asked how many Lakota (he said "indians") Red Cloud represented. Red Cloud handed Murray the flowers and asked the Great White Father why the Lakota couldn't trade at Fort Laramie where they always had and why wouldn't the Washitu give them powder?

The Great White Father said, "Tonight we smoke the peace pipe. Tomorrow we talk of serious matters."

Perhaps Red Cloud had met his equal.

The Great White Father sat at one end of the longest eating table in the world. A Seizer officer wanted the Lakota to sit here and there, but we decided to sit together. Red Cloud took the chair facing the Great White Father. I sat between Plenty Cuts and his friend Jesse.

Jesse smelled like a Washitu and spoke like a Washitu. Plenty Cuts had told me Jesse was a Washitu chief, but the other Washitu chiefs ignored him.

I asked Jesse why he wanted to be a Washitu. "You must love the Washitu very much," I said.

My remark hurt Jesse and I was sorry I said it. When I apologized, he said, "We must learn how to live with one another."

The Great White Father stood to say that The New York Times *had called Red Cloud "the most celebrated warrior now living on the American continent," which made the Great White Father jealous. All the Washitu laughed.*

The man at the Great White Father's right hand began to make a speech, but Red Cloud stood and interrupted. My husband translated as Red Cloud said he sought peace with the white man and bullets and powder so his people could hunt the blackhorns and have plenty to eat. Red Cloud had been told the Great White Father was a great warrior. If the Great White Father came to Lakota country, Red Cloud would take him on a war party against the Crows.

A black robe made a prayer to the Lord JesuChrist.

The men who brought our food were as black as Jesse and Plenty Cuts. It is a great honor to serve chiefs and I wondered what these black men had done to deserve such honor.

The Great White Father's wine tasted like thin trade whiskey and his water had been drawn from a stagnant pond. The meat they put before us was covered with white slime and I couldn't tell what animal it had been. Lakota do not eat unless they know what animal it is.

Red Cloud said, "Maybe this is why the Washitu don't send us the food they promise. They cannot send it because their meat is spoiled." Plenty Cuts did not tell the Washitu why we were laughing.

My husband and I ate what Red Cloud ate: strawberries and ice cream.

The ice cream was so sweet it bit my mouth and though the Washitu strawberries were as fat as plums they had no flavor.

PART THREE

IN THE VALLEY OF
THE GREASY GRASS

Yellow Hair has never returned
    so his woman is crying, crying.
    Looking over this way, she cries.

Yellow Hair, horses I had none
    and you brought me many.
    I thank you. You make me laugh.

—LAKOTA KILL SONG

—

CHAPTER 45

LIGHT BROTH AND A CODDLED EGG

For chicken broth, when stock is boiling remove it from heat and add desired cream.

To coddle an egg, lower it gently into boiling water. Cover the pan and remove from heat. Cook for six to eight minutes.

MRS. EBEN BARNWELL TOOK HER CUSTOMARY TABLE AT HER usual hour: after the opera and theater crowd but earlier than fashionable Manhattan society dictated.

Gaslights cast their soft glow on embossed wallpaper and wine-dark swagged silk drapes. Delmonico's was almost empty and waiters were relaxing at a large corner banquette. Randolph folded his newspaper, straightened his bow tie, and draped his towel over his arm. "Sorry, Mrs. Barnwell." He laid Delmonico's morocco-bound menu at her elbow. "I didn't see you come in. Will Mr. Barnwell be joining us tonight?"

His voice was so empty of affect, he might as well have shouted that Eben Barnwell and his wife never dined together anymore. Pauline's husband dined with his friends.

"I'm afraid not," Pauline murmured. "Your mother, is she improved?"

"Thank you, yes. Mother isn't coughing so much and last night she slept through the night. Sunday we'll ride the ferry. Mother adores salt air. Her cheeks bloom like a schoolgirl's."

He filled her water glass. "The trout is particularly good this evening. How is young Master Augustus?"

Pauline smiled. "Merely the light of my life. I wish I could spend every minute with Augie. Sometimes I wish we didn't have servants so I could do everything for him myself. Augustus Belmont Barnwell is a spark! No fish, thanks; just light broth and a coddled egg. Green tea, please."

Randolph raised a disapproving eyebrow and tapped the thick menu. "If I might, Mrs. Barnwell . . . Pauline . . . please. Our Chef Ranhofer is a genius of cuisine and when regular patrons—like yourself—don't let him demonstrate his art, well . . ." With a glance to be sure nobody was in earshot, the waiter whispered conspiratorially, "Our prima donna sulks!"

Pauline covered her mouth to contain her giggle. Randolph's mock seriousness—he could be more waiterly than any *real* waiter—raised her spirits. Although she wouldn't have confessed it, not even to herself, Pauline felt more at home at this table than in her own home.

How she missed Stratford Plantation!

"I fear your prima donna will be obliged to sulk . . ."

Randolph covered her hand with his own and lowered his voice solicitously. "I'm to bring the maestro a request for broth and a coddled egg? May I tell him you're an invalid?" Hearing his own words the waiter flushed. "Sincerest apologies, Mrs. Barnwell. I completely forgot myself. In the spirit of my jest, I—"

She patted his hand reassuringly. "Randolph, Randolph . . ."

He straightened. "Broth and a coddled egg, madam. Can I persuade you to try a glass of wine? They say wine improves the digestion."

"Oh, very well." The waiter sped off on his vital mission while Pauline was thinking theirs was an *odd* friendship, odder here in New York than it might have been in Virginia, but friendship it was.

Randolph's father's had captained a New Bedford whaler sunk with all hands by the Confederate raider *Kearsaw*, with the consequent economic collapse of a cadet branch of the "distinguished" (Randolph's word) Howland family. Mother and son left Massachusetts for a modest cottage on Staten Island and Randolph took employment at Delmonico's. From Randolph's hints, Pauline guessed Mrs. Howland was unreconciled to their reduced status.

He was a complicated man, this waiter, and sometimes surprised her. When Pauline mentioned her distaste for Dr. Beecher, Randolph pronounced, "Beecher serves the rich man's Christ. Though he dines with us, he never leaves a penny for his waiter. The good reverend believes gratuities ruin a poor man's moral standards."

Every Saturday, rain or shine, at one o'clock Pauline brought Augie here for lunch, showcasing her special joy and triumph.

Pauline's table was directly beneath a gaslight where she could read and reread Cousin Molly's letters.

As always, Molly's latest began with Stratford's weather, presently too much rain: they had so much grass you couldn't see the lambs, and the woods roads were too muddy to work. How Pauline would have loved suffering such inconveniences: the "days too cool for oats," the "afternoons too wet for hay," even those hushed winter mornings when ice locked the ponds and snow covered the porches and the path to the sawmill and milk barn.

Everyone at home was well. Thomas Byrd and Miss Stuart were affianced. "Our Thomas is making a career as a politician. He cannot be 'pinned down.' " Samuel worked at the sawmill from dawn to dusk. SunRise Chapel's preacher had quit his church for the Dakota gold camps. "Poor Reverend Todd, " Molly wrote. "When God didn't favor the Confederate cause, He destroyed the poor man's faith—but the promise of Black Hills gold lying where any man could pick it up is faith of a sort, I suppose."

Pauline was dabbing her eyes when Randolph brought her wine. Through nostalgic tears, Randolph's friendly face prompted an indiscretion. "Has my husband been in tonight?"

The waiter hesitated. He murmured faintly, "Mr. Barnwell, madam? I can ask in the other room. Mayor Tweed dined with Mr. Fisk tonight."

She touched his sleeve. "Oh, no. Never mind. It doesn't really matter, does it?"

"Pauline . . ."

Damn it! The man was sorry for her! She stiffened.

"As you say, Mrs. Barnwell. I'll fetch your broth."

"Oh," Pauline said, "please don't hurry. My letters are excellent company." She laid her precious packet on the snowy tablecloth beside her wine. "Letters from home."

Randolph startled her by taking and hefting them as if verifying their importance. Gently, he set them down. "I envy you your home," he said softly.

She had met Randolph's mother just once; the day before Christmas when she arrived at her usual time, she happened upon the heels of the employees' holiday party. Mrs. Jacob Howland's clothes had been fine twenty years ago. She smiled, but not at anyone in particular. Her eyes were vague. When Randolph introduced Pauline, his mother said, "So nice," and coughed discreetly into her handkerchief. Pauline wasn't to notice the red spots staining the thin old linen.

THERE'D BE "ACTRESSES" if Eben was with Jim Fisk and Boss Tweed: "actresses"! Eben's "actresses" never played a bigger stage than a double bed!

Although Eben's "amative bump" had vanished, her husband indulged her to distraction. Eben Barnwell's wife could buy whatever trifle she wanted. Unlike most husbands, Eben relished visits from his wife's dressmakers and hatmakers.

"Eben, I cannot possibly wear what I already have!"

"Dearest Pauline, how can anyone ever have everything they desire?"

What was Pauline supposed to do with her life? Pray? Try on new gowns? Read novels? Wait for Eben to come home?

Always late at night. Tiptoeing up the stairs with his shoes in his hand. She'd feel their bed dip under his weight and she'd smell cigars and whiskey. Sometimes, underneath those masking odors, she smelled perfume.

Eben's faithlessness was impersonal and had nothing to do with her. She hadn't failed him as woman or wife. Eben Barnwell, who was utterly indifferent to music, attended the opera because Jay Cooke kept a box. Despite Pauline's genuine fright, the inexperienced Eben Barnwell drove their carriage four-in-hand because Augustus Belmont did.

Eben Barnwell lay with actresses because Jim Fisk lay with actresses. The sheer innocence of Eben's faithlessness made it harder to bear. If Eben had turned against her, perhaps Pauline could have done something about it—but how could she stand against the entire New York demimonde?

She made excuses for herself: Stratford had been so poor and so utterly vanquished. Poor Preacher Todd! If God could treat ordinary Southerners so harshly, how could He be the just God Pauline'd been taught to revere? If God could ruin Stratford, kill Pauline's father and mother, and keep Grandfather Samuel desperate, what sort of a God was He?

Her conscience rejected Pauline's excuses. How had she, who had so many convictions, married a man who had so few? Had she forgotten Christ's teachings: "For it is easier for a camel to pass through the eye of a needle than for a rich man to enter heaven"?

Poor woman: she'd grown to love her flawed, sinning husband. There, she'd admitted it! That grasping, careless, shallow child she'd married; yes, she loved him. She loved the frightened boy beneath that stiff celluloid collar and heavily starched shirt. She loved the silly bravado of the white rose boutonniere. She loved what Eben Barnwell was, not what he strove to become.

What did Pauline care for the "sophistication" Eben admired? Today's sham, smart understandings would be succeeded by tomorrow's sham, smart understandings. What did she care what the demimonde thought or promised or believed? Vanity; all is vanity, sayeth the preacher.

"Your broth, Pauline?"

"I'm sorry, Randolph." She smiled. "Lost in my thoughts. I didn't see you standing there."

The man smiled his better-than-a-waiter waiter's smile. "Delmonico's staff are inconspicuous, madam. From our first day in service, we train for it."

"I'm sorry, Randolph. We've got off on the wrong foot and it was my fault. I shouldn't have grilled you about my husband and I shan't again. I promise." Sudden tears flooded her eyes and fell unheeded on the linen tablecloth.

"Pauline . . . ?" Randolph hastily provided a glass of port. "Dear Mother drinks this whenever she's distressed. Will you . . . ?"

"Thank you." Pauline blew her nose into her handkerchief. Her fingers trembled as she lifted the glass to her lips. "I wouldn't want to make this a habit," she said.

"No indeed. Now, dear Pauline, do taste your broth. It'll do you no end of good."

THAT NIGHT, SHE WAS in her nightdress when Eben came home slightly drunk and ebullient. Her husband had attended a Century Club dinner honoring General Custer. Everyone had been charmed by the "Boy General." The famous indian fighter, frontiersman, author, and youngest (brevet) major general in the Army of the Potomac was considering a career change. "Custer's sick of the army," Eben confided. "He told me, and these are Custer's own words, 'Eben, my friend, the army's no place for "live men." ' The General might run for political office, but I hope he'll come into our line of work."

Eben kicked one shoe under the bed and dropped his necktie on their dresser, where it dangled like a flaccid snake.

"What, husband," Pauline asked, "might that work be?"

He blinked. He blinked again. "Dear wife." Eben's lopsided smile begged for understanding. "How would the Northern Pacific be built without Jay Cooke to finance it?"

Pauline felt a sharp headache coming on. "Why, dear husband, does the Northern Pacific need building?"

Eben's face fell and Pauline felt terrible. Disappointing Eben was too like disappointing little Augie. Eben rummaged for a cigar, lit it, and puffed until his head was wreathed in smoke.

He smiled at her like Emperor Maximilian must have, facing the black muzzles of that Mexican firing squad. "Pauline, dear, are you becoming an anarchist?"

CHAPTER 46

IN THE TERRITORY

"SURE YOU WON'T JOIN ME IN A LIBATION, GATEWOOD?" COLONEL Eugene Baker chafed his hands together.

It was a little after ten o'clock on a brisk Montana morning. Duncan, Aunt Opal, and Joe Lame Deer had started rounding up horses long before dawn to have them at Fort Ellis by seven: the appointed hour. Then they'd waited. "Little early for me, Colonel. Your remounts . . ."

The Second Cavalry commander poured whiskey into his coffee cup and downed it. "Starts the soldier's day right." He shuddered when the whiskey hit home.

Duncan persisted. "I only had eight grays in my bunch; I hunted up the rest in Virginia City, Helena, and Butte. Joe and I took the stage to Fort Benton for the last two." He chuckled. "Colonel, you have single-handedly cornered the gray gelding market in Montana Territory."

Baker waved that away as if six thousand dollars in horseflesh were beneath his consideration. "Gatewood, you lost your wing at Cedar Creek?"

Duncan, who'd discussed that fight with the man before, bit his tongue. "No, sir. I was at Petersburg when Cedar Creek was fought. General Early commanded our forces in the Valley."

Baker was bemused. "My God, what a day! What a God Damned day! We called it 'the Woodstock Races.'"

At Cedar Creek the Federals had whipped half their number of exhausted, starved Confederates. "You Johnny Rebs ran like rabbits."

Duncan Gatewood managed a wan smile.

Fort Ellis protected Gallatin Valley settlers from indian raids and Duncan's SunRise Ranch bred and broke horses to cavalry specifications. Ellis's commanding officer was Duncan's biggest customer and this requisition was the largest he'd ever filled.

Early that year, a Seventh Cavalry crony had boasted to Baker that the Seventh Cavalry troops were mounted on distinctive horses—E Company rode grays, C sorrels, L bays, and so forth.

Although some men balked at giving up known, trusted mounts, the Second Cavalry's bays and sorrels were reassigned, and Duncan easily found Baker's blacks. But Duncan and Joe Lame Deer had scoured the territory for thirty-eight gray geldings, and gray geldings ran through Duncan's dreams.

Colonel Baker's office was unpainted pine walls, two mangy wolfskins (one adult, one cub) on the floor, and stern daguerreotypes of President U. S. Grant, Secretary of the Army Sherman, and General Sheridan, commander of the military district. Baker's uniform was perfectly pressed, his slouch hat was brushed, and his epaulets gleamed. Despite his smartness, Colonel Baker often seemed on the verge of toppling over. His eyes were unfocused and his hands locked around his cup.

"Cedar Creek was hard-fought," Duncan said.

"Like rabbits," the Colonel repeated vaguely. As if some inner debate had been resolved, he refilled his cup and stepped to the window overlooking Fort Ellis's parade ground.

"The survey . . ." Baker announced.

"The Northern Pacific . . . ?"

"Next week, we'll escort Northern Pacific surveyors to the Yellowstone."

"The Lakota . . . ?"

"Overrated, Gatewood. They'll run before they fight." He downed his whiskey and glowered at Duncan as if Duncan might be one of those Quaker do-gooders who thought the Lakota could do no wrong.

Last January, when temperatures were well below zero, Colonel Baker's cavalry had attacked a Piegan Blackfoot village on the Marias River. The village had been friendly and most of the 173 dead were women and children. Although his own officers later testified Baker was drunk during the attack and had, in fact, attacked the wrong village, Montana settlers applauded him and he was cleared by an army board of inquiry.

After burning the indians' robes, supplies, food, and lodges, they shot the ponies. Then Baker marched two hundred prisoners toward Fort Ellis until told that some had smallpox. He abandoned them in the snow.

JAY COOKE'S NORTHERN PACIFIC RAILROAD was already carrying passengers and freight between Duluth, Minnesota, and Bismarck, Dakota Territory. The railroad's western segment had been surveyed from the Pacific Ocean to Bozeman, Montana Territory. But that country between Bozeman and Bismarck was six hundred miles of terra incognita: prime Lakota hunting ground, granted to them in perpetuity by Red Cloud's treaty. Although some Lakota lived at the indian agencies, many still roamed the grasslands between the Yellowstone and Powder Rivers hunting buffalo and feuding with their traditional Crow enemies. Their winter counts—Lakota tribal histories—described fights with the Crows or memorable hunts. The Washitu were too insignificant to mention.

So: the Second Cavalry would escort Northern Pacific surveyors from Bozeman to the Yellowstone River. Next summer, the Seventh Cavalry would escort a second survey party from Bismarck to the Yellowstone and the Northern Pacific route would be entirely surveyed.

Montana's gold boom was petering out and many camps were ghost towns where only patient Chinese remained, picking through the tailings dumps. Bozeman merchants who'd become prosperous supplying the camps were concerned about their future and, it goes without saying, the future of Western Civilization.

Every far-seeing settler knew progress needed the Northern Pacific, which couldn't come to Montana until the army moved the damned indians out of the way.

Duncan prompted, "Your remounts, Colonel . . ."

The Colonel blinked. "Grays? A troop of grays?"

A chill brushed Duncan's spine. "Yes, sir. 'Thirty-eight gray or dappled gray geldings, two or three years old, well broke and sound,' " he said, quoting Baker's requisition word for word.

"Grays?" Jabbing his finger. "Suppose you tell me, Gatewood, what the hell difference it makes what color a cavalryman's horse is." Baker stared at his finger as if he couldn't recall why he was pointing it. His hand dropped. "I captured a gray at Cedar Creek, but the damned beast foundered. Were you at Cedar Creek, Major? God, what a victory!"

"No, sir. I didn't have that honor."

Baker smiled knowingly. "Bet you're glad you didn't 'have that honor.' "

Duncan managed to say, "Yes, sir." Drawing a deep breath, he pictured his precious Sallie, Catesby, and little Abigail. Why, just yesterday Joe Lame Deer put Abby up on her first horse. "Your geldings are present for inspection, Colonel. As per your requisition, they're every bit as fine as General Custer's Gray Horse Troop. Maybe finer."

"God Damned Custer." Baker glowered. "Yellow Hair'! The 'Boy General'! 'Son of the Morning Star'! Christ almighty!"

He set his slouch hat at the correct angle and strode to the door. "Let's have a look at them, Gatewood. Let's see if they're half as good as you say they are."

The regimental farriers had already inspected every horse standing at the stable hitch rail. Joe Lame Deer leaned against the log wall chewing a straw. Arms folded, eyes closed in the pale October sun, Aunt Opal perched on a farrier's three-legged stool. When their officer approached, the farriers snapped to attention. Joe shifted his straw to the other side of his mouth.

"The Gray Horse Troop, eh?" Hands clasped behind his back, Colonel Baker strolled the line of remounts. He stopped suddenly. "I won't accept this one. He's a biter. Look at his eyes. He's a cribber and a biter."

"Colonel . . ." Duncan had trained this horse. He was easy-gaited and calm.

"Don't you argue with me, Gatewood. I don't have to take guff from any damn horse dealer."

Aunt Opal opened her eyes and blinked. She got up and pursed her lips. Duncan's frown and cautionary head shake quelled her protest.

Duncan handed her the reins. "No use trying to fool you, is there, Colonel?" Duncan laughed the laugh he'd used bribing Mahone's legislators. He had hoped he'd never hear it again.

"Can't pull the wool over my eyes, eh, Gatewood?" Baker cackled. "That's done, then. Captain Brisbin will prepare your draft." Colonel Baker smiled. "Now, Gatewood. Is it late enough in the day for a Confederate officer to drink with a Union officer? Command is a lonely job—but it has some prerogatives."

Duncan couldn't think of anything he'd like less. "Always a pleasure doing business with you, Colonel. Sorry about that drink. Another time."

Baker's smile dropped off his face as Duncan laughed his corrupt laugh. "Some of us can't hold our liquor like you, Colonel. Hell"—he smiled—"some of us have to ride home."

When Duncan thumped up the headquarters' steps and ducked under the low lintel, Captain Brisbin closed his letter book. "Colonel Baker sign off on your horses?"

"All but one. They're good horses, George."

Duncan knew the sharp-featured, sardonic captain from the low-stakes poker game at the Tivoli Garden Saloon.

"Thirty-seven fine remounts." Duncan didn't hide his satisfaction. "At one hundred and fifty dollars per."

The captain dipped his pen, wrote and blotted a draft. He extended it to Duncan but mock snatched it back before letting Duncan have it. "Our commander was sober, I presume."

"Sober as he ever is."

"Sober enough for the cavalry, at any rate." Captain Brisbin noted the transaction in his ledger and blotted that too. "The 'Gray Horse Troop,' dear, dear me . . . !" He threw back his head and roared with laughter. "Baker can't forgive Custer for getting famous when he didn't."

"Maybe Baker was drunk when 'famous' was issued. See you Saturday night?"

"'Deed you will, Mr. Gatewood. I'll be lookin' to relieve you of your ill-got gains."

The farriers were stabling horses while Aunt Opal comforted the rejected one. "Ain't one darn thing wrong with you, Badger. You fine! Ain't you, Badger boy?"

"We'll sell him to somebody, Auntie."

"That Baker, he a fool."

"He surely is, Auntie. But five thousand five hundred yankee dollars will take us through this winter in style."

Unimpressed, the old woman climbed onto the horse. "Come on, Badger. We leavin' this den of fools. We goin' home!"

Joe Lame Deer fell in beside Duncan outside the fort.

At first Joe's laconic ways had made Duncan uneasy. Work with a man all day and not say two words? But in time Joe's silence became natural; even comfortable.

Joe knew what needed to be done on a horse ranch without being asked. When Duncan had a change of plans—like these gelding purchases—he told Joe, and Joe quit what he had been doing and turned to the new tasks without comment. Every Friday, again without comment, he accepted his pay. Last year, once in July and again in August, he disappeared; the first time for a week, the second for ten days. He returned without explaining where he'd gone or why.

Very late in the fall two years ago, the Gatewoods' family wagon train arrived in the Gallatin Valley. Of necessity, they'd wintered in a dirt-floored, leaky-roofed homesteader's soddy. Sallie, Duncan, and the children slept under buffalo robes in the rear of what felt more like a cave than a house. Aunt Opal and Joe had pallets nearer the door. Aunt Opal complained she'd never been colder or more miserable in her life and if things didn't get better, and she meant *soon*, she was goin' back to Virginia.

Finally spring came and foals were born and Duncan was learning every byway in the valley and the honest and less-than-honest horse dealers in the Territory. Joe gave his son Catesby lessons in horseshoeing and together they foaled a breech birth. Although his father showed Catesby how to shoot, Joe taught him how to hunt. Joe taught Catesby sign language, the lingua franca that let Cherokee talk to Comanche and Lakota to Arapaho. At a cliff north of the ranch Joe and Catesby chipped arrowheads from the black glassy obsidian.

Duncan wanted to ask Joe: "Were you ever married?" "Where were you born?" "Do you like it here with us?"

But he knew questions would drive Joe Lame Deer away quicker than dangerous mavericks, bitter weather, and poor pay.

Now Joe grunted. "Good medicine."

"You betcha," Duncan said happily.

Just two years in the Territory with a draft for all that money. The paper simmered in his breast pocket. He wanted to take it out and make sure the figures were correct, but if he did the wind would grab it or a hawk would swoop down and bear his prize away. He patted his pocket. He whistled a few bars of "The Cavaliers of Dixie"—that jaunty tune. Joe Lame Deer grunted again. Joe thought whistling brought bad luck.

In the summer months, Bozeman's streets were dusty or muddy. Once or twice every spring, it took an eight-horse hitch to pull some unfortunate immigrant's wagon out of a mud hole. After three weeks of May rain, a wag posted a sign beside Main Street: "No Fishing!"

The cold weather had stiffened the streets. As they trotted along, Duncan nodded at friends he hadn't known two years before. Acquaintances became friends quicker here than they had in Virginia.

The First National Bank was the largest of Bozeman's three brick buildings.

Joe stayed with the horses while Duncan strolled into a small lobby fronted with gilded cashier's cages. He'd removed his hat when he'd come in to ask Harris, the head teller, for enough cash to buy his gray horses. On that day, Duncan was shaved and wore a fresh shirt. Today his shirt was rumpled, he smelled of horse sweat and manure, and his hat stayed on his head.

Harris hummed as he credited Duncan's account. "Has Colonel Baker set a date for his Yellowstone expedition? The railroad surveyors are anxious to get going."

"Next week, he says."

Harris stamped papers and handed Duncan a receipt. "Rather late in the year for such an undertaking," he observed.

"You know the Colonel," Duncan said vaguely.

Harris pinched his nose between thumb and forefinger and flashed a grin Duncan hadn't known the man possessed. "Rather better than I'd wish to."

Yes, it *was* late. Snow draped the Bitterroots down to the timberline. Duncan and Joe Lame Deer went next door to warm themselves at the Tivoli's potbellied stove.

Joe took his stein into the corner while Duncan made himself a corned beef sandwich from the free lunch on the bar.

Willem Schmidt was bald as a cue ball and his eyebrows were so pale they were nearly invisible. He owned the Tivoli Garden Saloon and had an interest in the livery stable. Schmidt helped found Bozeman's Masonic Lodge Number Six but quit it when most of its members were ex-Confederates. Now Schmidt was canvassing Union veterans for a second lodge.

Duncan asked him about the library fund.

"Mrs. Story kicked in twenty dollars, but Nelson says he won't put in a dime so long as Professor Vernon is involved."

"Vernon's a good teacher."

"Nelson thinks he's a four-flusher." Schmidt leaned over the bar confidentially. "Anor Rasmussen was in here whining about you last night."

Duncan's face hardened. "He knows where to find me."

"Anor says you cheated him out of his homestead."

"Willem, am I going to have to shoot that stupid son of a bitch?"

The saloon keeper chuckled. "I do not believe so. Anor is a blowhard, no more."

Snow was in the air when they'd first come to the valley and Duncan bought the first halfway suitable homestead for sale: Anor Rasmussen's.

When Sallie walked into Rasmussen's dirt-floored soddy with its leaking roof and smoky chimney she wept.

"Dear?" Duncan had said.

"Don't ask," she'd said.

They burned Rasmussen's straw ticks and scrubbed everything with lye soap.

In December and January Duncan and Joe shoveled the horse barn's too-low-pitched roof lest the snow buildup collapse it.

SunRise Ranch lay above the forks of the Madison River. Duncan filed homestead claims for himself, Sallie, Catesby, and Abigail on the dry grasslands above the river.

Charles Anceney's Meadowbrook bordered them on the south. Anceney had trailed two hundred Percherons from Salt Lake City to become the biggest draft horse breeder in the Territory. Although they weren't competitors and helped each other out as neighbors must, the Gatewoods and Anceneys were more polite than friendly.

Now Duncan told Willem, "If Anceney hadn't told Anor how much he'd have paid for Anor's place, Anor wouldn't have his dander up. Lord knows what Charles actually would have paid. It's easy to be a big spender when you don't open your wallet. Life is a puzzle, Willem, don't you think?"

"We are born, live a little while, and die."

"Business slow, Willem? Belly acting up?"

"Some of us will ride into Lakota country next week. Good men. Well armed."

Maybe fifty scrawny, sickly indians lived in tipis and shacks outside Bozeman. They hunted small game, picked through garbage, and begged. Come winter, one or two would get drunk and freeze to death in the street. Joe Lame Deer didn't look right or left when he and Duncan rode through their shantytown.

Territorial governors beseeched Washington to protect settlers against indian depredations. There weren't many depredations in Montana Territory and none at all in the Gallatin Valley, but vigilantes like Schmidt sallied forth every few months to take a few scalps, rape some squaws, shoot a few prime buffalo and lace their carcasses with wolf poison. The vigilantes were widely admired.

"Count me out, Willem. I didn't come to this country to kill indians. I saw more than my share of killing in the War."

At Burnett's Mercantile, Duncan bought a mother-of-pearl comb for Sallie and stick candy for the kids. Joe went on home for the evening chores while Duncan stopped at Black's Mill to see if his shingles were ready. The first summer they were in the Gallatin Valley, Joe and Duncan built a horse barn with a properly pitched roof and rooms (with stoves) for Joe Lame Deer and Aunt Opal, who wintered better than their boss and his family, shivering in Rasmussen's soddy a second year.

Black had most of Duncan's shingles and promised the rest Saturday. Two Scandinavian carpenters were building their ranch house. Sallie wanted a house like those she saw in *Godey's Ladies' Magazine*. Something with generous porches and elaborate trim. "A painted house," Sallie called her dream.

The house wasn't painted yet, but the carpenters promised—if the weather held—the family could move in by Thanksgiving.

A big western sunset was coloring the sky as Duncan rode toward his family's new homeplace.

Duncan Gatewood had never been a praying man. Even during the war, those times he believed he was certain to die, he hadn't prayed. It hadn't seemed right to trouble the Lord on such short acquaintance.

A gust rattled the sagebrush. The temperature was plummeting so fast, Duncan could feel it sink through his bones.

After fording the Madison, Duncan circled onto the ridge behind his homestead. He sometimes came up here to see the ranch as a stranger might, some pilgrim fresh off the Bridger Trail, anxious to get settled before the first snow.

Duncan mouthed the names of the mountains walling this rich green and gold valley: the Bridgers, the Gallatins, the Crazy Woman Range.

That pilgrim might say: "Here's a lucky man. He's got stockpiled graze on the ridges where the wind'll keep it clear all winter."

That pilgrim might say: "Well watered too. The bottoms will grow all the corn, wheat, and timothy a man might want. Bet that river's full of fish."

An antelope burst out of a thicket and bounced over a ridge out of sight.

A pilgrim might admire the new barn and horse corrals.

The carpenters were working late. A mile from the figures on the roof, Duncan saw a carpenter's arm rise and fall. A full second later, he heard the hammer's bang.

The low soddy was in shadow. Its open door framed a warm rectangle of light.

In the pasture beside the river Duncan's foals were frolicking, dashing toward the river only to brake, turn, and race back the way they'd come.

A pilgrim might go so far as to say: "It's a lucky bastard has all this."

Duncan Gatewood bowed his head and gave thanks.

CHAPTER 47

A TREASURE TROVE

That winter we camped on the Belle Fourche River. We moved slowly, slept long into the morning, and spoke no more than we had to. When my daughter Tazoo whimpered from hunger, I gave her a leather strap to chew. My brother's wife, Fox Head, turned her face away and died. One by one we ate our ponies.

Though our hunters ventured far from the village, they came back empty-handed.

In the Moon of Frost in the Tipi, Plenty Cuts and White Bull put on snowshoes to hunt deep in the mountains.

When they returned, their sled was heavy with meat. They'd discovered three blackhorn cows trapped in a snow-walled park the blackhorns had trampled. The animals had peeled and eaten tree bark as high as they could reach. The blackhorns didn't run back and forth or bellow. They stood calmly while Plenty Cuts and White Bull shot them down. The two hunters butchered the youngest cow and dragged her tongue, hump, loins, and hams back to the village. It was a half moon and the snow sparkled and they walked all night without stopping.

When our village heard about this, they backtracked to the park, but there was no meat left— just skeletons the Real Dogs had picked clean on the trampled, bloody snow. The hunters brought bones back to be cracked for marrow.

Our wicans summoned blackhorns from under the earth, but the blackhorns did not come. The wicans said the blackhorns didn't come because they hated the smell of Washitu.

As soon as the ice broke in the rivers and we were able to travel, Plenty Cuts and I came into the Agency for food. Inkpaduta had sent word there were blackhorns in the Grandmother's land north of the Medicine Line and White Bull and his family went north. I kissed Rattling Blanket Woman and we wept.

THE SOD AGENCY stood on the Platte River a short ride from Fort Laramie. The lodgepole pine stockade surrounded its blockhouse, well, and storehouse. Traders and the indian agent slept in the stockade protected by cavalry under Colonel David S. Stanley.

The indians called Stanley "Black Face" to honor his temper.

Cheyenne, Lakota, and Arapaho villages clung to the Agency like nursing puppies. The farther from the Agency the better the graze, and shabby villages rotated around the Agency like a wagon wheel around its hub. However often they moved, they pitched their lodges in old lodge circles among old campfires and dried dog and pony excrement.

Blanket indians pitched their tipis nearer the stockade. Indians who had once been warriors didn't own one pony. When they had no more buffalo hides to trade, they traded their burial moccasins for whiskey.

Red Cloud wished to return to Washington and the Great White Father reluctantly agreed to see him. Plenty Cuts expected to go as the Chief's interpreter, but Red Cloud invited the half-breed Rivière to accompany him. Plenty Cuts said he hadn't wanted to go, that he'd had his fill of the white man and white man's villages, and She Goes Before told everyone her husband spoke the truth.

A week after Red Cloud departed, Plenty Cuts went hunting alone, as was his custom now White Bull was gone. He rode east and south onto the high grasslands where the buffalo had been so plentiful some herds had taken three days to pass.

Twenty miles from the Sod Agency, the grass had recovered and his pony dropped his head to snatch at it. Plenty Cuts rode thoughtlessly. Insects lifted ahead of him and small animals ran through the understory, invisible beneath waving bluestem that touched his pony's withers.

Pollen and seed heads coated the pony's flanks and Plenty Cuts's legs and moccasins. An ocean of grass stretched for miles to the western snow-capped mountains. He didn't see any buffalo.

That night he camped on Horse Creek. He caught two trout, gutted them, and wrapped them in wet grass before he bathed. He sat naked before his fire until he dried. He tossed some kinnikinnick, Indian tobacco, into the fire.

Patience descended upon him. His hobbled pony spattered drop-pings. He ate his fish. The creek chuckled. Sap popped in his fire. The stars rolled overhead as they always had.

The next day, when he came to the water tower beside the Union Pacific track, at first he thought he'd found a snowbank. So late in the season? So far from the mountains? Was the white man hauling snow to the railroad so passangers could eat ice cream crossing the plains?

One wagon was departing and another was unloading bones as Plenty Cuts approached the snowbank: an eight-foot-high mound of buffalo bones, a hundred feet long glistening in the noonday sun.

A bearded man whose authority was belied by his filthy clothing stood in the shade of the water tower while a sweating teamster shoveled and hurled bones onto the pile. "Get me another load by Tuesday, Henry," he encouraged, "and you'll have two more dollars."

He glanced at Plenty Cuts and addressed him in a confidential tone. "There's fortunes to be made for any man who ain't afraid of hard work."

Plenty Cuts frowned.

"God's truth, pilgrim. Buff bones are bringing six dollars a ton in Omaha. They grind 'em up. Oh, they say buff bones is the best fertilizer what is. They say they'll turn a New Hampshire farm green again, though"—he shook his head—"I misdoubt that, seein' as I was born and reared in the Granite State."

For the first time he seemed to truly see his visitor. "Jesus," he said. "You're Lakota." He squinted. "No, you ain't. You're a nigger. Can't be both, which is it."

Plenty Cuts dismounted and led his horse to the watering trough under the tall wooden tower.

The teamster wrestled a skull from his wagon and dropped it with a crash. "Two bucks ain't enough, Posey. Hell, it took me two days to find these."

"I'll be movin' west Wednesday, soon as these are picked up. Archer stationmaster will tell you where to bring 'em."

To Plenty Cuts he added, "This country here was prime pickin'. Gentleman hunters shootin' from the train was a bonanza for the workin' man, but my gatherers got to go farther now." He sighed philosophically. "I expect my price will go up once the easy pickin's are gone. Which did you say you were?"

"Didn't."

"Well, you sure look like a nigger, but you're dressed like a redskin." He gestured at Plenty Cuts's breechclout and high moccasins. "Maybe you're a breed?" The man hitched himself onto the bone pile and offered snuff. Plenty Cuts shook his head.

The sweaty teamster brought his wagon around and the buyer gave him his pay.

"Scrip!"

"Ain't got no silver, Henry. Course, if you'd rather have my IOU . . ."

The teamster snorted and stuffed the bills into his shirt pocket. "See you in Archer, Posey," and he drove off.

Posey turned to Plenty Cuts. "Well, whatever you are, you can gather bones and I reckon in that outfit you can get 'em where honest white men fear to tread. I hear the Powder River country is a treasure trove. A real treasure trove."

He wiped his forehead with a surprisingly clean gingham handerchief. "Hot, ain't it? I swear these bones draw heat."

———

PLENTY CUTS LED his pony over the iron rails and the ties. He wondered how many forests it took to carry a railroad from the Atlantic to the Pacific.

Night was falling when he made camp in the sandy bottom where Lodgepole Creek ran, fifteen feet wide here, clear and cold from the distant mountain snows. It was grassland; no trees anywhere. Though there was driftwood on the stream banks, he didn't make a fire. He had food in his parfleche but wasn't hungry.

Plenty Cuts was not a reflective man. His instincts had never betrayed him. Often, more thought and slower reactions would have left him dead.

Tonight, his mind was as big as the universe, as big as the whiteness of sun-bleached bones.

Sitting cross-legged in the sand, in the twilight, he started composing a letter to his friend. "Jesse, I guess it's all over out here." He paused to reconsider. "Friend Jesse, I surely hope things are well with you and your good wife." He tried in vain to remember her name.

A strange memory intruded: what he'd said about women in Texas, that day they were discharged, how there were plenty of them, "plenty of fish in the sea."

"Jesus," he said aloud. His pony lifted its head at his voice but resumed grazing.

"I ain't doin' so good. Me and She Goes Before and Tazoo came in to the indian Agency. We get treated like we was idiot children. Feed us, pat us on the head, but don't make trouble."

Scratch that! Whatever he'd been, whatever he'd done, he'd never been a whiner.

"Nelson Story would have favored this land, Jesse. Good grass, good water, and no buffalo to eat the grass and the redskins locked up in the agencies. Oh, there's loose ones in the north around the Powder River and Yellowstone, but both sides of the Union Pacific is white man's country now.

"I believe Ol' Massa done caught up with me. Seems I can't get away from Massa no matter how far I run.

"Jesse, do you ever wish you were back in the army? When I think back on it, the army was the best I ever done. How about you?

"Or are you still a race man? Are you still hope-sick?"

That coinage pleased even as it shamed him. What if one's direst predictions came true? What kind of man could take pleasure in them?

Man like him, maybe.

Man like him.

He blinked and rubbed his eyes. The moon was up and the shallow creek shone like a silver ribbon.

"Friend Jesse, I thought I might see you again in Washington City, but Red Cloud took somebody else. I guess I told Red Cloud one truth too many."

"I guess I don't like the truth any better than he does.

"So here's the truth: I do not wish to lie with my wife anymore. I do not wish to do anything. I wish only to eat and sleep."

God Damned moonlight in his eyes. So bright it made him weep.

He stood and rubbed his arm across his face and, putting a finger to each nostril, blew snot onto the sand.

The hell with this damned letter. Who would he get to write it for him anyway?

TWO DAYS LATER, Plenty Cuts returned to the Agency empty-handed. He did not tell She Goes Before about the buffalo bones piled like a snowbank, though he dreamed about them.

Red Cloud came back from Washington, without significant concessions. Despite this, he sent a message to Sitting Bull and the other chiefs who hadn't come in to the Agency. Red Cloud said, "I shall not go to war anymore with whites. Make no trouble for our Great White Father. His heart is good. Be friends to him and he will provide for you."

It wasn't known what Sitting Bull thought of this message, since he did not reply.

———

We had come in because there was no game on the plains and here, at least, Tazoo could eat.

In the warm months some familes roamed the country as the Lakota had always done. In winter, they'd come in for the Agency rations. When I suggested we might too, Plenty Cuts told me, "It don't make no difference what we do."

When I asked him why, he said, "Might as well get used to the Agency. Here's where we're gonna be until we die. We're all blanket indians now."

I said it didn't matter that Red Cloud hadn't chosen him. The young men didn't respect Red Cloud anymore.

My husband listened as an adult listens to a child prattling.

My husband did not hunt. He rose long after the sun rose. He forgot to wash and sometimes he smelled bad. He did not lie with me. He would watch the young men playing the wheel and arrow game, trying to toss an arrow through a beaded wheel. In the evenings he went to the lodges where the gamblers played the bone game, singing and striking the ground with their sticks while the gambler considered his guess. My husband never gambled; he watched. I feared he might take his own life.

I went to Shivering Aspen, the wintke, for advice and told him everything.

He said I must pretend to be cheerful even when I was not and must not complain, no matter what Plenty Cuts said or did.

The wintke said that I must not feed my husband's demon.

The wintke prepared a lotion I was to rub between my breasts and on my upper thighs. He told me to bathe, anoint myself, and surprise my sleeping husband with caresses on a night when the moon was full and the canvas walls of our tipi glowed with light.

In the Moon of Ripening Plums, I anointed myself and caressed my husband awake and we lay together and everything was as it had been between us.

In the morning, he told me he had been sick but now he was well. He went to the sweat lodge and fasted. He prayed for success in the hunt. His voice was strained, like a singer's who has not been singing much lately.

He took his rifle, his best pony, and a packhorse into the mountains where the blackhorns had always been numerous.

He was gone ten days and when he returned he had one small parfleche on his packhorse. "The railroad's through the mountains too," he told me. "The blackhorns are bones."

He emptied his parfleche onto the dirt. His bullets had shattered five prairie dogs into bone shards, blood, and fur.

I said brightly, "I will clean them and make a stew. Fresh meat will taste good."

My husband turned over one of the small broken animals with his foot. "I ain't nothin' but a nigger pretendin' he's a redskin. I ain't nothin' in the world."

CHAPTER 48

—

A CADAVER

WHEN THE LEGISLATURE WAS IN SESSION, JESSE BURNS WAS "the Right Honorable Delegate from the Marshall Ward," a tireless advocate for free public education. On the House Internal Improvements Committee (the Railroad Committee) he voted as General Mahone's agent, Colonel Elliot, told him to. Jesse's five dollars a day when the legislature was in session and four dollars janitor's pay when not was more cash money than he'd ever had in his life—more money than he'd thought existed. After Sudie complained that her coffeepot was "plumb wore out," Jesse walked into a hardware store on his way home that evening and paid cash for a fine blue enamel pot.

He and Sudie rented three ground-floor rooms on First Street: the parlor, hall, and butler's pantry of an ancient, neglected family home. Two other negro families were on their floor, but they used the back door and the old walls were so thick, Jesse and Sudie never heard them. It was as if they had a house of their own. The butler's pantry became Sudie's tiny kitchen, Jimson slept in the hall, and the front parlor, with its grand windows and elaborate cornices above faded, faintly voluptuous French wallpaper, was their and baby Sojourner's bedroom. Sudie thought it was the "grandest room I've ever been in," and Jesse thought it was grand too.

During the War, the Richmond Customs House had housed the Confederate Treasury and President Davis had had an office on the second floor. Although Jesse kept his clothes in a basement locker he shared with two other janitors, sometimes just walking into that important structure on a brisk spring morning made him proud.

Times were hard. The tobacco warehouses only hired white men and many Virginia negroes had returned to the plantations they'd worked before the War.

Throughout the South, white Republicans were appointed postmasters and clerks and mail carriers. Even the crew of the Customs steam launch were party loyalists. After Jesse's trip to Washington, the Customs Inspector suspected Jesse might have some influence and Jesse did nothing to disabuse him of that idea. The Inspector apologized for the poor patronage he could give Jesse: one job on Mahone's track gang.

Jimson sneered at it. "That's nigger work. Ain't seein' no white men layin' track."

"Yes," Jesse explained as if to a child. "You may have noticed that we are *not* white men. We are colored men striving for equality. We have made progress. We can vote and there are negroes in the United States Congress. But until the day of Jubilo, Jimson, we have to earn our bread by the sweat of our brow. Many grown men would be grateful for a job laying track."

Honestly puzzled, Jimson shook his head. "Damn, Jesse! I helped you get elected. You can't do no better for me than that?"

"Your mother hates to hear you curse."

Anger chased surprise across the boy's face. He snapped, "Well . . . Well, then . . . the hell with her!" and stormed out the door. When Jimson came home, three days later, he was wearing the clothes he'd worn when he left and Jesse didn't ask where he'd been. Jesse thought Jimson needed a lengthy, reasoned talking-to, but he deferred to the boy's mother, who begged, "Don't bother him none, Jesse. He eighteen years old. He a man now! Don't make my son less than who he is!"

JIMSON WAS SULLEN and silent. Jesse was offended and silent.

Thanksgiving Sunday, Richmond's churches tolled worshippers to church. Although Jimson rarely attended, somehow Jesse had assumed

Jimson would accompany them that day. Sudie was dressing Sojourner in a new blue frock when Jesse heard the front door creak and he caught Jimson going out. "Don't you think it's time you start making something of yourself?"

"Like you done?" Jimson raised a young man's contemptuous eyebrow. "Yeah, you so damn smart. You can read and write good as any white man, so you a janitor cleanin' up white men's messes. When you was elected I thought you was gonna *be* somethin'."

In the weeks to come, Jesse would consider and reconsider what he might have said. Should he have humbled himself, or appealed to the boy's better nature?

But that morning the Right Honorable Member from the Marshall Ward was too angry to consider.

His stepson's fists were clenched. Jimson's mouth was twisted in a derisive sneer. Jimson Burns: who'd never fought a war, never been cut by a bullwhip, never lost his wife and child, never had friends murdered, never seen every hope broken and lying in shards at his feet—what kind of reply did *he* deserve? Jesse slapped his stepson so hard his hand stung.

The blow knocked Jimson slack-jawed against the door frame. He straightened slowly, touching his cheek.

"Jesus, son," Jesse said. "I . . ."

Jimson smiled bitterly. "God Damn! I been smacked by a broom-pusher!"

Though Jesse called after him, Jimson Burns ran into the clamoring of bells. Jesse never forgot the sound of those bells.

Monday morning after Jesse went to work, Jimson came home for his clothes.

When Jesse told his wife, "He'll be back soon as he gets hungry," Sudie was furious.

Jesse heard Jimson was sleeping in a dilapidated tobacco warehouse in Shockhoe Bottom. He was running with the Knockabouts, gambling and drinking and maybe doing things Jesse was better off not knowing. Jesse guessed Jimson came home sometimes and Sudie slipped him money. He and Sudie never spoke about that. They never spoke about Jimson at all. Every evening after he hung up his hat, Jesse asked about baby Sojourner.

One week before Christmas, his workday finished, an elated Jesse Burns stepped from the Customs House's clean, dry vestibule onto slushy Bank Street where the lamplighter was sparking the gaslights. There was a vacancy on the Customs steam launch, and the Inspector had asked Jesse to find a negro to fill it.

Jimson would be grateful.

Jesse paused outside Goldschmidt's Fine Tailors. In its window, a bolt of heavy blue serge was draped over a settee. An ebony walking stick leaned against the arm.

Jesse stuffed his hands in his pockets and shivered. Wasn't outdoors but twice a day anyway, just long enough to walk to work or home. Twenty minutes each way. Jesse didn't need a coat for twenty minutes—nobody could get cold in twenty minutes!

Tonight, he'd ask Sudie what she wanted for Christmas. He had eight dollars put aside.

The gaslights ended where Marshall Ward started. For three years, Jesse had tried to get gaslights to his district. By arguing a threat to white citizens' health, he had gotten sewers, but Marshall Ward's drinking water still came from water wagons or the dubious municipal well.

Lamps glowed behind house windows. The sky was overcast, the moon a splinter, low in the eastern sky.

When he saw the crowd in front of his house, Jesse broke into a run. Neighbors were gaping on his front stoop, and his front door yawned open in a terrible invitation.

Dry-mouthed, heart pounding, he shoved through, crying, "Sudie, where's my Sudie?"

His wife sat in a hall chair, hands folded limply in her lap. Kneeling at her side, Reverend Fields Cook's head was bowed in prayer. One hand rested on Sudie's shoulder.

"Sudie . . ."

When his wife looked up, she said plainly, "Jesse, it's my boy. They kilt him."

"Did what?"

"Richmond police come. Say Jimson been kilt. Then they go."

"But how?"

"Say he try to rob a white man, so white man shot him dead!"

"But, but . . . how?" Jesse repeated stupidly.

"Pray with me, Jesse," Fields Cook said.

"Said Jimson was with that gang of his."

"Where is the boy? Where is Jimson now?"

She blinked. Her eyes focused. "Jesse, I don't know. Police never said. Just knock on the door and when I come they say Jimson shot dead. Oh, Jesse. They didn't care nothin' 'bout my boy. They like they postmen bringin' a letter. When I asked where was my boy, they gets in their buggy and drives away."

"I take you to the police, Mr. Burns," a familiar voice at Jesse's shoulder.

Deacon Hanley owned a dozen cabs and thirty freight wagons. He'd been an influential supporter.

"Hanley's Livery" was in gold script on the carriage's black varnished door.

When Jesse started to climb into the driver's box beside the Deacon, the rich old man refused. "No, sir. No, sir. You rides inside. Might be you ain't payin' tonight, but you rides inside."

Jesse paused on the step. "Deacon. The Knockabouts. Do you know them?"

"Just your boy and that scamp Jelly Jones. He hitch onto my freighters and hangs there like a darn monkey." He paused. "I am tolerably sure Jelly Jones and his mother live in one of them canal boats."

"Take me, please. I must know . . ."

"Please step inside, Mr. Burns. We be there directly."

The leather seats smelled faintly of saddle soap.

It began snowing as the Deacon's cab descended narrow cobblestone streets toward the river. Lazy, wet flakes drifted in the beam of the carriage lamps.

By 1850, the James and Kanawha Canal Company was transporting goods and passengers up the James River to the Allegheny Mountains. In

'63, Stonewall Jackson's body was brought to Lexington by canal boat. Two years later, Sheridan's cavalry destroyed its locks, bridges, and towpaths and the James and Kanawha died with the Confederacy.

The few surviving canal boats were stranded in a basin beside the James. Most were sunk to their gunwales. The boats were long, with low cabins to pass under bridges. One occupied boat was swathed by tattered canvas from bow to stern so it seemed more tent than boat. A lantern glowed behind the canvas where a porthole might have been.

DEACON HANLEY OPENED the door for the younger man. "That's them. Mrs. Jones's husband sewed tents for the army. He sewed that roof too. Mrs. Jones by herself since he run off."

In the dim glow of Hanley's carriage lamps, Jesse picked his way across slush-covered black planks, some which gave alarmingly under his feet. Behind the boat basin the James River was a flat black carpet. The boat rocked when he set his foot on the stern and a woman cried, "Who that on my house? Best you sing out! I got me a pistol in my hand."

"It's Jesse Burns," Jesse called. "Jimson Burns's father."

He waited in the cockpit until she pulled a canvas flap aside where once the wooden door must have hung. Her face was smallpox-scarred and years ago her left arm had been broken and badly set. It jutted like a broken wing. Behind her, in the light of her lamp, Jesse saw heaps of old clothes, blankets, and rags.

"You that legislator man!"

"Yes, ma'am."

"I didn't vote for you and I didn't vote 'gainst you so you needn't be comin' 'round here."

"It's about my Jimson, Mrs. Jones. I am told . . . I believe Jimson was shot tonight."

The woman clapped a hand to her mouth. "Jelly, he never said nothin' 'bout that!"

"What did Jelly say?"

"Said it t'weren't nothin', what they done. T'weren't nothin'. Said him and them other boys was on Calhoun Street on that bridge and a rig was passin' and the driver was wearin' a top hat and so, boys bein' boys . . ."

"What did they do?"

"There ain't nothin' for them! Nothin'! White men gots all the jobs. They'd hire an Irish before a nigger!"

"What did they do!"

"They made snowballs and when he comes out t'other side, they smacked his hat.

"Well, they runs for a ways, you know. They figure the driver, he curse an' keep on goin', but he don't."

"He come after 'em, Mr. Burns. They walkin' down Grace Street when they hear this horse a-gallopin' and that's who it was, 'cept he ain't wearin' no stovepipe hat no more. He standin' up in his rig. He takes out his pistol and shoots. Jelly never tol' me he shot nobody. Mr. Burns, them boys shouldn't have done what they done, but there weren't no call for shootin'."

"I'd like to talk to Jelly."

Her face slammed shut. "Jelly ain't here."

"Where is he?"

"Ain't here. Jelly gone. I don't want no trouble, Mr. Burns." She withdrew her head and as her canvas door fell into place, she said, "I'm right sorry 'bout your boy."

Jesse hadn't felt like this since the war: everything up for grabs, life and death so interwoven you couldn't tell the one from the other.

When he came back to himself he was leaning against the cab, and the Deacon was saying, "You all right, Mr. Burns? You feelin' all right now?"

"Can you drive me to City Hall?"

Jesse climbed the familiar steps into City Hall and his heels clicked down the long marble corridor past "City Treasurer" and "Commissioner of Revenue" in gilded letters on frosted glass. Jesse had often come here before, helping constituents trapped in the white man's law. Sometimes they couldn't understand what they'd done wrong; some times they'd done nothing worse than attracting a policeman's notice. Jesse descended into the basement, which housed the police and the city jail.

SERGEANT MCBRIDE LAID his cigar in a soapstone ashtray some prisoner had carved. McBride was so pale-complected Jesse wondered if he ever came out of the basement. "Evenin', Assemblyman Burns."

"A white man shot my stepson, Jimson Burns, tonight."

"Jesus, Mary, and Joseph!" Hurriedly, the sergeant flipped through his record book, his fingertip skidding down the pages. "I just come on, you see," he apologized. "I ain't caught up with things yet."

"Grace Street. It happened on Grace Street."

He flipped the page and his finger stopped: "Commander E. B. Wetherell. With the Federal navy. Wetherell was driving down Grace to his hotel when he was attacked by several colored men. Commander Wetherell drove them off with his pistol."

"He . . ."

"Says here he fired his revolver and the coloreds, uh . . . dispersed." McBride swiveled the book. "Here. Read for yourself."

"Leaving my stepson dead."

"Assemblyman Burns, I wasn't there. I don't know the particulars, and the officers what looked into it wasn't present neither. Them Knock-abouts, that Shockoe Bottom gang—they tried to rob an officer of the United States Navy who defended himself. That's what it says." He tapped the register.

"Where is Jimson now?"

"It don't say nothing 'bout that."

"Where is Jimson now?"

McBride set elbows on the counter. "Assemblyman Burns, you're sorrowed and upset. If I was in your shoes I'd be sorrowed too. But the policemen who visited the scene and interviewed Commander Wetherell say he had the right of it and I ain't terrible surprised the Knockabouts have come to this. We been keepin' an eye on them boys."

"Sergeant McBride, where is my son?"

"Jesus wept, Mr. Burns. Wouldn't I tell you if I knew?"

THREE INCHES OF fresh snow covered the pavement outside City Hall and the gaslights illuminated circles of innocent snow. Deacon Hanley was tucked under robes beneath his snow-dusted hat, head bowed, asleep.

Jesse slapped the side of the cab.

"Deacon, please take me to Colonel Elliot's home. Corner of West Fourth."

Elliot was an ungracious, testy man who'd been wounded at Gettysburg and walked with a cane. When the legislature was in session he used the speaker's office to give Mahone's legislators instructions. On his way out, each man collected an envelope with his name on it.

When Duncan Gatewood and his family were preparing to leave for Montana, Jesse and Sudie had visited this same house to wish them luck. Its wrought-iron gate opened onto a narrow walk covered with glossy, untrodden snow.

The elderly negro who answered Jesse's ring recoiled. "You come 'round back!" he hissed. "Who you think you is?"

"I am the Honorable Jesse Burns, delegate for Marshall Ward, with urgent business with Colonel Elliot."

Recognizing Jesse's driver, the old negro called, "Deacon Hanley! Deacon Hanley! This man who he say he be?"

"Mr. Burns. He in the legislature!"

Partially reassured, Elliot's houseman let Jesse into the hall, but didn't offer to take his hat and didn't show him into the parlor. "You wait here, Mr. Delegate, while I fetch the Colonel. He decide whether he talk to you or don't."

Colonel Elliot wore a patterned moss-green silk dressing robe. His left hand clutched the stair rail as he descended, placing his cane before every step. "Burns, what do you mean, coming to my home? You know I don't discuss business—" When his eyes came level with Jesse's, the Colonel frowned. "What's wrong, Burns? Why are you here?"

"My boy Jimson. He . . . Jimson's been killed. My Jimson has been shot to death. I don't know . . . where my boy is lyin' tonight."

"The police . . . ?"

"Won't tell me anything."

Elliot sat heavily on a hall chair and eased his left leg straight before him. "Your son, you said?"

"My stepson. Jimson's not but eighteen. His mother is desperate."

The Colonel rubbed his leg. "It's snowing. You have a cab?"

"Yes, sir."

The Colonel got his leg back under him, but sweat popped on his forehead as he rose. "Wait until I am dressed. Burns . . ."

"Yes, sir?"

"Nothing. Nothing at all."

Twenty minutes later, in business attire, the gray-faced Colonel came back down the stairs. Jesse held the front door but didn't dare offer his arm.

In the closed cab, Jesse could smell the Colonel's bourbon. "Nothing?" He snorted at a private joke. After a while he admitted, "Had a son myself."

After a silence broken by hoof thuds and the jingle of trace chains, he continued, "First Lieutenant Peter Elliot, 14th North Carolina. We expected great things . . . great things. Peter Rexrode Elliot. Named for my wife's father. I remember . . ."

"Yes?"

"Too many things. Far too many things. God, how I hate remembering."

The cab stopped at a grand house on Church Hill.

Although the Mayor's houseman insisted his master was abed, the Colonel pushed past into the dark house while Jesse returned to the cab. Snow fluttered in the lamplight. He could see his breath.

Lamps flared in a front room.

Deacon Hanley shuffled his feet over Jesse's head. "Mr. Burns," he called softly.

"Yes, Deacon Hanley."

"I'm terrible sorry 'bout this. I was right hopeful for that boy."

Jimson's father had had no hope for the boy. Jimson wouldn't go to school. He wouldn't improve himself. He *wouldn't* . . . Jesse groaned.

"You poorly, Mr. Burns? You feelin' poorly?" The Deacon's anxious face appeared at the hatch. "Oh, you grievin'. That'll be all right, then."

Jesse had worked to improve the negro race, but he'd done nothing for the young man in his own home, the young man who'd eaten at his table, who'd campaigned for Jesse's election believing, trusting, that somehow the election would lead to something better for both of them.

All the while he thought he'd been helping the boy, he'd been casting him down. "Oh, Jimson," Jesse sorrowed. "Oh, my dear boy . . ."

Moments after the Mayor's door closed behind Colonel Elliot, the lamps in the house were extinguished. Elliott gave Jesse an envelope. "From Mayor Solney for the police."

"What is it?"

"Just hand them the damn thing."

They rode downtown silently. When the cab stopped again, Colonel Elliot said, "Burns, I've done what I could. You'll remember that."

"Will my remembering make any difference?"

The Colonel's eyes were bleak as cold ashes. "Not to me, certainly, but perhaps God will care. Burns? Whatever your reason don't ever come to my home again."

As Deacon Hanley took the Colonel away, Jesse climbed the City Hall steps for the second time that night.

He waited on a hard bench while McBride woke the duty captain. Jesse tried to stop thinking, but he couldn't.

When McBride came back, he said, "Mr. Burns, Captain says we ain't gonna charge Commander Wetherell on account of he was defendin' hisself." He returned the Mayor's letter. "Captain says they took your boy to the hospital. Dr. Hunter McGuire's got him."

Hope surged through Jesse. "Then . . . Jimson's . . . he's alive?"

McBride shook his head. "That's not what he's doin' there."

THE RICHMOND HOSPITAL was three blocks from City Hall, just beyond the dilapidated mansion which had been the Confederate White House.

After Richmond fell, Abraham Lincoln had spent the night in the house, sleeping in President Jefferson Davis's bed.

Until Jesse showed him the Mayor's letter, the hospital attendant denied knowing anything about "Jim-son? Jim-son Burns?" The young attendant's eyes were insolent. "Whew," he said. "Mayor Solney himself. Ain't you the Nigger King." He blotted pustules on his cheek with a handkerchief polka-dotted with blood. "Reckon your Jim-son'll be in the theater."

"Theater?"

"Oh, yeah. Boy's set to be a headliner!" The young man was amused.

They climbed two flights of iron stairs and passed down a dim hall lit by every third gaslight.

It was like a real theater, Jimson lay on a zinc-topped wooden table beneath a circular chandelier. Rows of seats rose into darkness behind the stage.

Jimson was naked and his clothes were nowhere in sight.

The attendant dabbed a pustule and pronounced, "Dr. Hunter McGuire was Stonewall's personal physician." He examined the handkerchief. "McGuire is reckoned the finest surgeon in Virginia."

Jesse approached the table reluctantly. Jimson had been a modest boy and Jesse had never seen him naked. He was smaller than he'd been alive.

"Most of our cadavers are negroes," the attendant continued. "Don't make no difference to Dr. McGuire. McGuire says there's not a 'lick of difference' 'twixt a white man and one of you, but I ask, how can that be?"

His stepson's forehead was the purely coldest thing Jesse had ever touched. The wound in Jimson's left breast was a small circular hole, blue-tinged at the edges. How could something so small kill a grown man? The gas jets sputtered overhead. Jesse's ears rang.

"You gonna take him?" the attendant asked.

Jesse nodded.

"I give twenty dollars for this boy. Who's gonna refund my twenty dollars? We get plenty infants and shriveled-up old birds, but we don't get many prime specimens like this one. I gave that cop twenty dollars."

CHAPTER 49

RATION DAY

Rations per indian person shall be: Daily: a pound and a half of beef (or in lieu thereof, one-half pound of bacon), one-half pound of flour, and one-half pound of corn; and for every one hundred rations, four pounds of coffee, eight pounds of sugar, and three pounds of beans.

Plenty Cuts never hunted again. Although he went with the gamblers from lodge to lodge, he never wagered. He had been known as He Who Fooled Chasing Cranes and He Who Speaks for Red Cloud. He became the man who watches the bone game.

It was no longer good between us. When he lay with me, it was like laying with a stranger.

He grew fat. He did not keep himself clean.

I talked to Tazoo. Tazoo talked to me. I talked to my husband. He did not talk to me.

The winter was hard and more Lakota came in to the Agency.

Yellow Hair's brother arrested Chief Rain in the Face and beat him, and Rain in the Face was shamed and vowed to eat Tom Custer's heart. Rain in the Face escaped. The Seizers laughed at Rain in the Face's promise and the Lakota laughed too. They weren't laughing at the same thing.

Black Face and Yellow Hair were to lead the Seizers to the Yellowstone.

They said this was a peaceful expedition, but it was Lakota land by Red Cloud's treaty and they had no right to enter it.

One morning I said to my husband, "We should join my brother in the Grandmother's land. Your soul is dying."

Plenty Cuts was so angry he struck me.

The next day I went to Shivering Aspen for the medicine that would kill the baby I was carrying. That night I had terrible cramps and the baby was not born. I lashed together sticks for a raft and sent my boy down the river to the Shadowland.

Every fifth morning, I'd stir the fire, boil water, and make Tazoo's mush. Tazoo would stay with Touch Dog while I went for rations. Plenty Cuts always pretended he was asleep and when I returned, he would be elsewhere, so he could pretend he didn't know about the rations. Our poor food appeared in our lodge as if by magic.

That morning—it was the Moon When Blackhorn Calves Are Born—I gathered with other women on the riverbank. A few of us at a time were admitted into the stockade, where we touched the pen for our rations.

Sisters called greetings to sisters, married women asked virgins why they hadn't gotten a man and advised others to leave the husband they had. Though we made many jokes, no woman joked about our husbands' inability to feed their families.

The Seizers' Ariska scouts wore indian leggings and breechclouts and blue wool coats. In tongues the Washitu didn't speak they named Lakota and Cheyenne warriors they'd killed. We women pretended we didn't hear their boasts.

I passed into the stockade with a Cheyenne mother and her daughter. The mother, Three Birds, sold herself to Washitu for whiskey, but her daughter had fourteen summers and had never known a man. Fast Water was hard-muscled from her vigorous childhood but awkward with new womanliness. She kept her eyes on the ground and clutched her mother's sleeve.

Dr. Daniels, the indian agent, was a minister, and Sundays he preached to the Seizers and the blanket indians who came to hear him. The blanket indians said listening to his sermons brought better rations.

Three Birds asked where we were camped and I lied because she had no husband and if she came to our lodge we'd have to feed and shelter her.

The sun warmed the top of my head. Agent Daniels and his half-breed interpreter Rivière sat before the storehouse. After Rivière decided the woman before him was from a registered household and this was her ration day, she would touch the pen, the agent would sign her name, and half-breeds would fetch her food.

Seizers were parading through the stockade. They said, "Hup, two, three, four."

Three Birds told Rivière her name. She was from American Horse's village.

Rivière asked if her daughter was betrothed. He walked around the girl, like a man who is buying a colt.

The indian agent yawned, filled his pipe, and folded his newspaper. The headline was: "Grant Nominated for Second Term."

I wondered if Grant ever looked into his daughter's face and understood that Lakota daughters were as dear to us as his was to him.

I did not think so. The Great White Father had been a great general in the Washitu's Southern war and great generals do not have hearts. Sitting Bull hated every Washitu: man, woman, and child.

While the agent read his newspaper, Rivière told Three Birds that he would give her two demijohns of whiskey to lie with her daughter. He gestured at the register as if asking about Three Birds's rations, but he was talking about her daughter.

The interpreter told Three Birds he could strike her off the rolls so she could never get rations again.

Three Birds's husband had been killed in a raid against the Crows. Her family had disowned her because of whiskey.

Now she cried and her daughter started crying and the agent looked up frowning from his newspaper.

"The squaw says she is from Chief Gall's village," the interpreter told the agent. He shrugged. "Maybe she is, maybe she ain't."

Three Birds knew Rivière was lying but could not speak for herself.

"He is trying to buy this virgin," I said in the Washitu tongue. "If her mother won't sell him her daughter, he will strike her from your ration book."

Rivière hit me so my lip bled. "Lying squaw!"

Agent Daniels jumped to his feet. "Now, see here, Rivière!"

A Washitu in fine buckskins came over. It was my husband's friend Shillaber. He was Black Face's new chief of scouts.

"I'll be damned if it ain't She Goes Before." He took my hands. "What's the fuss?"

When I told Shillaber what Rivière wanted, the interpreter lied. "This squaw got it wrong. I asked the other squaw if her daughter wanted rations for herself or a husband too, if she—"

"Give her rations, Rivière," Shillaber said in a voice that silenced the man. The soldiers said, "Hup, hup, hup." Rivière put Three Birds's hand on the pen and brought her rations himself.

"Do you want to sign the register?" Shillaber asked me.

"I am an ignorant Santee. I will touch the pen," I replied.

Shillaber said, "Bring this woman fresh beef. Not brined meat." I thanked him.

"I hear . . . I hear Red Cloud had a nigger interpreter."

He was making me nervous. "Yes, it was Plenty Cuts."

"But no more."

I shrugged.

Shillaber lifted his hat and smoothed his hair where the hatband had flattened it. He beamed. "I'll be damned. Old Top's still on top of the grass."

I said, "He hates the Agency."

"Can't say as I blame him. Might be I'll come see the old boy."

Shillaber had been my husband's friend. I did not wish to bring this Washitu to our lodge but could not think how to refuse him.

I loaded our rations into parfleches balanced over my pony's hips. Meanwhile, Shillaber went to the Seizer chief Black Face, who was watching Seizers drill. I heard Shillaber say, "United States Colored Troops" and "Medal of Honor." I did not hear what else he said.

We were camped at the Aspen Bend, which had always had good grass, water, firewood, and shade. But the grass had been grazed so bare the earth was big and little stones, the river water was brown with filth, and after the ponies stripped their bark the aspens died and turned as gray as a ghost forest.

The pony guards preceded us into the village shouting that a Washitu was accompanying She Goes Before. Warriors came out of their lodges carrying weapons, but Shillaber ignored them. We trotted down the village street chatting about matters of no consequence.

Ignoring my protests, Shillabar carried my parfleches into our lodge and when we came outside again, Plenty Cuts was waiting for us. I had forgotten my husband's smile.

How could his happiness produce my sorrow?

"God Damn it, Ben!"

"Top, you're fat as a hog!"

Shillaber opened his case and gave my husband a cigar. "I'm Colonel Stanley's chief of scouts. First Shillaber in history ever hired on with the winning side."

"They say the West changes a man."

Shillaber laughed. As generous as if he were Lakota himself, he gave cigars to all the warriors.

In Lakota, Plenty Cuts said Shillaber was a great warrior.

"He is Black Face's dog," one Big Belly complained. "He leads Yellow Hair against the Lakota."

In a loud voice, Plenty Cuts reminded everyone of Red Cloud's treaty. "Lakota and Washitu will fight no more."

They did not like to hear this. The Big Belly spat and a young man made a rude gesture my husband pretended he didn't see.

Shillaber understood more Lakota than he let on and said, "Red Cloud is in Washington again." He shook his head. "Wish you was there too?"

"Ha, ha."

Shillaber grinned his broadest grin and said, "How 'bout me and you take a little ride? Might be we'll find us a buffalo."

"You whites have killed all the blackhorns," my husband said.

"Well, then, if we don't find one I reckon we won't kill one."

I wished to stop my husband but had no words. The two men crossed the ford and climbed the river bluffs where Washitu settlers had first appeared in this country in canvas-covered wagons on what they called the "Oregon Trail."

Plenty Cuts and Shillaber had their heads together as if they were discussing something important. I felt weak. My knees trembled. Touch Dog brought Tazoo to me and I held her in my arms. Tazoo blinked her beautiful eyes and stared at me, as babies do, drinking me in. She sensed my distress and opened her mouth to cry. I pinched her nostrils shut because Lakota babies must not cry.

CHAPTER 50

ON THE SCOOT

CAMP AND GARRISON RATIONS
(PER CAVALRYMAN):

Meat: *12 ounces of pork or bacon, or*
         1 pound and 4 ounces of salt or fresh beef

Bread: *1 pound and 6 ounces of soft bread or flour, or*
         1 pound of hard bread (hardtack), or
         1 pound and 4 ounces of cornmeal

To every
100 rations: *15 pounds of beans or peas,*
         10 pounds of rice or hominy
         10 pounds of green coffee, or
              8 pounds of roasted (or roasted
              and ground) coffee
         1 pound and 8 ounces of tea
         15 pounds of sugar
         4 quarts of vinegar
         1 pound and 4 ounces of adamantine,
              or star candles

> *4 pounds of soap*
> *3 pounds and 12 ounces of salt*
> *4 ounces of pepper*
> > *30 pounds of potatoes. when practicable*
> *1 quart of molasses*

Desiccated (dehydrated) compressed potatoes, or desiccated compressed mixed vegetables, at the rate of 1 ounce of the former, and 1 ounce of the latter, to the ration, may be substituted for beans, peas, rice, hominy, or fresh potatoes.

MARCHING RATION:
> *Meat and Bread; same as above*
> *Coffee, Sugar, and Salt; same as above*

"CHRIST, TOP. YOU SAYIN' TOM CUSTER REMEMBERED YOU?" SHILL-aber asked.

"Most fellas remember the son of a bitch knocked him on his ass."

"You struck Captain Custer?" Mark Kellogg gasped.

"Hush, now, son." Shillaber spoke to the older man as if he were the younger. The three mounted men waited slightly behind Colonel Stanley's infantry officers. The Ariska scouts hunkered in the dirt, gambling. Unlike their Washitu masters, they had all the time in the world.

"Don't go writin' that down," Plenty Cuts instructed. "It ain't nobody's business."

Mark Kellogg had persuaded a Duluth newspaper to let him report the Yellowstone expedition. Although his boots were worn out and his jacket was clumsily patched, he had high hopes. He hesitated before returning his journal—folded sheets, written top to bottom—to his saddlebag. His mule brayed.

The two frontiersmen had adopted him as if he were a stray dog.

Shillaber wore buckskins and a broad-brimmed planter's hat. Shillaber's indian scouts wore army coats over leggings or breechclouts. Most troopers were dressed for comfort, unbuttoned shirts, bandannas—many tied their blue woolen coats behind their saddles.

Colonel Stanley snapped his watch shut. "Even the God Damned civilians are ready. Is this an army or a kindergarten?"

Stanley's officers murmured agreement.

The Custer clan was clustered around an empty ambulance with an open backboard. Tom Custer whispered in Captain Keogh's ear and they laughed, too loudly under the circumstances.

The sun rested on the Dakota horizon like a hissing golden ball.

Colonel Stanley's lips were clamped so tight they were invisible. He enunciated, "That God Damned stove."

Earlier that same morning, while soldiers boiled their salt pork and scorched and pounded green coffee beans into a brackish brew, Custer's negro cook, Mary Ward, had prepared ham, grits, and prairie chicken eggs for the General, Mrs. Custer, brother Tom, and a few of the General's favorites.

In Custer's commodious hospital tent they'd supped and yarned about other campaigns, other times. As a joke Tom Custer slipped salt into his brother's coffee. Everyone but George thought that was funny.

Hence, nineteen companies of United States Infantry, two field guns, ten companies of the Seventh Cavalry, seventy-nine officers, eleven indian scouts, and the Northern Pacific's three-hundred-man survey crew waited while Custer's iron stove cooled sufficiently to be loaded into an ambulance.

General Custer and his wife remained in their tent while the stove cooled and his commanding officer heated up.

"When I signed up for this whoop-up, Tom Custer looked me straight in the eye," Plenty Cuts told Shillaber. "He knew me, all right."

Shillaber shook his head. "Top, when you dropped Tom and put paid to your army career, you wore a sergeant major's uniform: Hardee hat, NCO's sword, gear spit-shined and pressed. Look at you today."

Plenty Cuts's ragged uniform coat hung over buckskin leggings almost to his high moccasins. A red-tipped eagle feather was tied in his hair. "Um."

"Don't 'um' me, redskin. I'd wager if you were to discard your heathen attire and appear before Captain Custer in blue uniform, complete with Medal of Honor prominently displayed, he *still* wouldn't recognize you. Yankees can't tell one nigger from another."

The scout continued mock-solemnly, "Worst mistake yankees ever made was freein' you niggers. You're a primitive people. 'Twas up to you, we'd not be escorting surveyors into Lakota country where we might get ourselves killed and scalped. Hell, 'twas it up to niggers there wouldn't be no Northern Pacific Railroad."

"Who you think gonna lay the track?"

"Micks? Chinks?"

"Always plenty nigger work, ain't there?"

"You think we want to do it?"

THE SUN WAS well up before the stove was finally stowed and the Seventh Cavalry band struck up the jaunty "Garryowen." General Custer's farewell embrace was so ardent it brought a blush to Mrs. Custer's cheeks and appreciative smiles from his favorites.

When the Boy General mounted his stallion Vic, the bored, irritated army stirred into life. Custer's buckskins were soft, buttery white. Buckskin fringes shimmered in the sunlight. His slouch hat was broad-brimmed (fair-skinned, he burned easily) and his carelessly knotted neckerchief bore black and white checks. The ivory-handled British revolver on his left hip balanced another on his right. No clumsy, regulation saddle for this rider: George Armstrong Custer rode a hunt saddle (so much kinder to horse and man). When Yellow Hair lifted his hat in the air to signal their start, even grizzled veterans found themselves believing there could be nothing finer than to follow, fight, and kill under this American Napoleon. Men stepped off and harnesses jingled and wagon wheels rumbled and sergeants bellowed and mules brayed and cannon limbers creaked and Martino, the Seventh's Italian bugler, added flourishes to the "Garryowen."

"We're on the scoot," Kellogg announced happily.

"God Damn that popinjay," Colonel Stanley said to nobody in particular.

As they departed Fort Rice that June morning, Colonel Stanley's men might have been mistaken for the sturdy farm boys of the Army of the Potomac where Stanley's noncoms and officers had learned their bloody trade. But an hour onto the plains, with sweat darkening their shirts and dust clotting their spittle, reality intruded. These weren't General Grant's stout citizen-soldiers: Stanley's men were ill-formed, ill-nurtured, and ill-educated. Many recent immigrants barely spoke English. In 1873, not many employers were as myopic as the United States Army. The army overlooked rickety bodies, pockmarked faces, and rotten teeth: the bitter marks of impoverished childhoods. If there was gallantry in the van of the expedition—and there was—misery trudged through the dust behind.

KELLOGG COULD NOT keep silent. Silence was as foreign to him as Paris, France. He didn't care if anybody was listening: his chatter was more song than sense. He'd worked for one paper. He'd worked for another. He'd married above himself. He'd loved his wife, but she'd died. His daughters were living with his wife's parents. He wrote them faithfully. He hadn't seen them in years.

LAKOTA WARRIORS COVETED Winchester and Henry repeating rifles. Tests by Army Ordinance proved the soldiers' single-shot Springfields were more accurate.

SCOUTS, INTERPRETER, AND chief of scouts rode in front of the column. Often the Custer clan were ahead of the scouts.

The first day became the second, the first week blurred into the next.

Kellogg's mule almost kept up. Plenty Cuts turned in his saddle. "He's crossed the creek. Now he's coming up the ridge."

"Don't worry 'bout that fool," Ben Shillaber said.

Plenty Cuts found himself thinking about the daughters Kellogg never saw.

The Custer clan went hunting. They bet who could shoot distant antelope. They killed and left as much meat as they brought back. From time to time Custer recalled his commanding officer toiling along behind and sent a deer or antelope ham. The clan played poker until midnight.

One morning Tom and George were so far ahead of the scouts they were two dots on the empty prairie.

Plenty Cuts said, "No tellin' what they might run into."

"That's what they come for," the chief of scouts replied.

"What?"

"To run into something."

INDIAN PONIES COULD survive on sagebrush and cottonwood bark. The cavalry horses needed grain. Indian ponies carried light riders bareback. Cavalry horses carried a soldier, saddle, weapons, and food and clothing for fifteen days. Indian ponies were a warrior's wealth. Cavalry horses were expendable.

THE CUSTERS RELISHED a joke. When it rained without letup for one, two, three days, a week, they joked about gumbo. Tom Custer deliberately bumped his horse into Mark Kellogg's rain-sagging shelter-half, and roared laughter when it deluged the reporter. Rain soaked through slicker seams and slouch hats drooped. George Custer chuckled that any man with saddle sores had earned them.

Colonel Stanley didn't see the humor, and chivvying a sickly, ill-trained army through knee-deep mud did not improve his chronically acid disposition. Stanley's miserable troopers were building a pontoon bridge across Muddy Creek when Bugler Martino, Custer's courier, delivered a note: Stanley's subordinate wanted grain for his horses.

The roaring creek was chest-deep on soldiers trying to lash the pontoons together. When soldiers lost their footing and were swept downstream, they were roped unceremoniously ashore while replacements crawled across the unfinished bridge, jumped in, and, like as not, were swept away too. They'd been working since daybreak, hadn't paused for dinner, and their bridge was twenty feet from the far bank.

Colonel Stanley tore the note into shreds and dropped them into the muddy water. "Tell Lieutenant Colonel Custer to report to me."

MARTINO, CUSTER'S BUGLER/COURIER, believed that God had put George Armstrong Custer on earth so men like Martino would have someone to revere. Martino swelled with Tuscan hauteur before producing an extremely disrespectful salute.

"God Damn that man," Colonel Stanley told the swollen creek.

That afternoon, Colonel (regular army rank) Stanley (who'd been brevetted a general during the War) had words with Lieutenant Colonel (regular rank) Custer (who'd been brevetted a major general during the War). Stanley ordered the Seventh Cavalry to ride behind the infantry. Custer's troopers could drag stuck wagons out of the mud.

The rain quit, the ground dried, and the cavalrymen clipped along, their excellent band striking up pleasant tunes. Since nobody was bringing him fresh meat, Colonel Stanley ate the same rations his soldiers ate.

Shillaber and Plenty Cuts were drinking coffee at their fire while, sitting cross-legged, Kellogg turned his notes into an article that would go with the morning courier. Behind the column of heat and embers, the sky was splashed with stars.

Tom Custer emerged from the smoke. In the firelight the scar on his cheek was deep and moody. "Major Shillaber. " Custer hunkered and put hands to the fire. He emptied Kellogg's coffee and refilled the reporter's cup from his flask.

"Something we can do for you, Captain?" Shillaber asked.

Tom Custer sipped and ran his tongue around his lips. Smiling, he turned to Plenty Cuts. "I been thinkin'." He laughed. "Mostly I leave thinkin' to my brother. You know what he told me once? He said I'd make a better general than him. How 'bout that? You seem familiar. Don't I know you from somewhere? Fort Sills? The Washita?" He chuckled. "You kin to my brother's cook?"

Plenty Cuts's eyes reflected the firelight.

"Or maybe you're her husband? You are married? You have the worn-out look of a married man. Nigger or squaw?"

"Suppose my wife is white?"

Tom Custer sputtered into the fire. He coughed and wiped his mouth. "God Damn, ain't you the one. Ain't you the one! Damned if you ain't!" He wiped the laugh off his mouth and got to his feet, pointing. "I'm keepin' my eye on you."

After he left, Kellogg asked breathlessly, "He really doesn't remember you, Top. Did you really knock him down? What will you do if he recognizes you?"

"Knock him down again."

TIRED OF WAITING every morning until Custer's stove was cool enough to load, Colonel Stanley informed that officer army ambulances were for sick or wounded soldiers, not cookstoves. The next morning, the expedition waited until the stove cooled and was loaded into a Northern Pacific wagon.

Soldiers soaked their salt pork and hardtack in alkali water. Those with money bought the sutler's tinned peaches and tomatoes.

It was eighty-five degrees during the day, forty at night. Sometimes before the poker players broke up, they sang "Annie Laurie" or "Drink to Me Only" or "The Lost Chord" under a black sky with so many stars it looked like a tin plate punctured by birdshot.

Plenty Cuts was staring into a dying fire when Shillaber hunkered beside him.

"Win tonight?" Plenty Cuts asked.

"Them pony boys can't play poker." Shillaber yawned and stretched. When he lit his cigar, his match flare extinguished the darkness.

Plenty Cuts said, "Makes a man think, night like this."

"Don't know that I care to think."

"I was thinkin' about baby Tazoo."

"Why the hell did you name your daughter after that murdering savage?"

"Tazoo was a Santee hero."

Shillaber puffed on his cigar. "Heard from She Goes Before?"

Plenty Cuts didn't reply right away. "Nary a word. She hates me bein' on this expedition. Thinks I'm betraying her people."

"Hell, Top. You're no Lakota."

"She thinks I ought to be." He sorted through memories. "Back in '64, I had a friend whose woman quit lovin' him. Jesse Burns was the sorrowfulest man in the United States Army. So I say to him, I say, 'Jesse, there's plenty of fish in the sea.'" He sneezed when Shillaber's cigar smoke tickled his nostrils.

"So," Shillaber asked, "are there?"

"Not so many as I thought."

THE NORTHERN PACIFIC crew shot elevations and determined gentle grades through the badlands' arid pinnacles. Shillaber's scouts found no fresh indian sign, hostile or otherwise.

One month after leaving Fort Rice, the expedition rendezvoused with the sternwheeler *Far West* where Glendive Creek emptied into the Yellowstone River. The *Far West* looked fragile as a wedding cake, but its powerful engines could shove thirty passengers and two hundred tons of cargo upstream in just three feet of water. All day long the *Far West* ferried men, horses, wagons, and guns to the western bank of the river: Lakota country.

EARLY MORNING. SILVERY RIVER. Fog in the trees. Clouds of gnats. Two ungroomed ponies were tied behind a poor man's lodge. The lodge flap was closed. Maybe somebody was inside, maybe the man's wives, maybe nobody.

"Lakota," Shillaber said.

"Brulé Lakota," Top defined the subtribe.

The old man fishing on the riverbank hadn't seemed bothered when a cavalry company galloped up. Plenty Cuts ground-hitched his horse and sat beside the old man. "Hello, Grandfather. Are the fish biting?"

"You Washitu have scared the fish away." The Brulé's face was lined with age and a ragged scar zigzagged across his forehead. His checked red wool shirt was buttoned to the neck. He didn't seem to notice the gnats sipping at his eyes.

Tom Custer stood nearby with his hands on his hips.

"I am Plenty Cuts. My wife is Santee. She is White Bull's sister."

The old man's bobber floated in an eddy behind a beached cottonwood. "So. Why do you ride with the Seizers?"

"I translate what the Lakota say so the Washitu can hear it true. I have translated for Red Cloud."

"Does Red Cloud ride with the Seizers these days?"

"Red Cloud stays at the Agency and eats food Washitu give to him. The young men no longer listen to Red Cloud."

"What's the old fool saying?" Custer demanded.

"We're getting acquainted."

"Get acquainted quicker."

"Rain in the Face has promised to cut that man's heart out. Rain in the Face says he will eat it." The old man chuckled merrily.

"So I have heard. Is Rain in the Face near? Is Sitting Bull?"

The old man lifted a shoulder in the tiniest shrug.

"Ask where the hostiles are camped," Tom Custer said.

The old man understood more English than he let on. In Lakota he replied, "They are where they are."

"We mean them no harm. Will they attack the survey expedition?"

Another shrug. "This is Lakota country. It is ours by right and by treaty. Do you think you can come into Lakota country whenever you want to? When I was young I would have fought you, but I am too old to fight now. Go away. Let me catch a fish so my wives can eat."

TOM CUSTER RODE with Plenty Cuts asking questions men never ask one another. "How many women you had? You ever count 'em? How many was niggers and how many was indians? Red women I laid with didn't do nothin' but lay there like they was dead. They play dead with you? Nigger wenches are more lively, but their private hair is scratchy. Like pressin' 'gainst a porcupine. Don't you think so?"

"Can't say I noticed."

"Why does Major Shillaber call you 'Top'? Ain't 'Top' a 'Top Sergeant'? Ain't a Top Sergeant a soldier? Why you so solemn all the time? I don't trust a man don't laugh."

"Niggers ain't got much to laugh about."

"Yeah, but you're a redskin." Tom Custer paused. "Hell, I don't know which is worse!" When he slapped Plenty Cuts's pony, the animal shied. Custer laughed. "Don't go getting no burr under your saddle."

With two companies, General Custer proceeded along the Tongue River. The scouts fell back on the cavalry while Bloody Knife and Shillaber searched the hillsides for an ambush.

Tom Custer was so excited he hummed like a teakettle. "Oh, I guess we'll get into it now," he said. "You scared, Top? I reckon I'm not scared. When I get myself worked up, I ain't scared of the devil himself. You ever think what it's like to be dead? Wonder how it feels when they lift your scalp. Think we'll find out? Lookee there! Bloody Knife is comin' hell-for-leather. Shillaber too. My brother's up in his stirrups. Oh, we're for it now!"

Bloody Knife had struck the tracks of a Lakota hunting party.

"Twenty, maybe thirty. We fight." Bloody Knife smiled. "Today or tomorrow."

George Custer chuckled. "Oh, we'll fight, will we?"

That night they doubled the horse guard.

The morning was clear and still. A bird was singing.

"Wonder where Stanley is," Kellogg said.

"Too far behind to do us any good." Shillaber checked the loads in his revolver.

"Do you think we'll fight?" Kellogg was scribbling furiously. "What's the bird, the one that's singing?"

Shillaber said, "Meadowlark. That's M-E-A-D-O-W-L-A-R-K."

"Hoka hey." Plenty Cuts yawned. "This is a good day to die."

Shillaber shook his head. "Redskins have the strangest damn notions."

THREE SUMMERS AGO, Plenty Cuts and White Bull had hunted this beautiful valley and White Bull had killed a blackhorn calf in the aspens beside the river.

Sweat trickled down Plenty Cuts's back. Sun glare shortened familiar shadows. The front horse's hooves stepped through shimmering heat mirages. Sun scorched the backs of Plenty Cuts's hands. His pony's neck was dark with sweat.

The valley was sullen. It had turned from him.

AT NOON, THEY RESTED in a cottonwood grove beside the river. While cavalrymen snoozed, Plenty Cuts watered his pony and filled his canteen.

Dragonflies skimmed the river. Horseflies buzzed his pony's head. A soldier yelled, "They're in our horses."

Somehow, Lakota warriors had slipped into the herd. They'd cut hobbles and were escaping with their prizes through a sputter of poorly aimed carbine fire.

Angry, exhilarated troopers mounted and gave chase.

The indians pounded through withers-high grass, exploding pollen.

They slowed outside a cottonwood thicket, which they entered at an insolent walk.

"Colonel!" Shillaber shouted his warning.

Custer reined up. "Yes," he agreed. "Martino! You and I'll go on ahead. Tom, take command here."

Two men trotted toward a cottonwood grove whose leaves shimmered faintly in the hot air. When angry ravens erupted from the grove, Custer reined up. Shillaber pulled his Winchester from its scabbard and jacked a round into the chamber. The metallic clack broke Tom Custer's stillness. He called, "Troop dismount! Form a skirmish line!"

Horse-holders—one to every four—took horses behind the skirmish line troopers formed in the tall grass.

Just ahead, General Custer was circling Vic, telling the Lakota he wanted to talk.

Then the cottonwood trees became flesh. Two hundred shrieking Lakota warriors broke from the grove while General Custer and the terrified bugler galloped for their lives. Shrill eagle-bone whistles. Kill songs.

Tom Custer was jittering, bouncing on the balls of his feet. His grin stretched his face. "Cock and take aim," he said. "Fire on my command! Kill their damn horses!"

His quirt failing, Yellow Hair stretched out over his horse's neck. Behind him, in the heat haze, his pursuers seemed bigger than life-sized. Sweat burned Plenty Cuts's vision and he blinked. The lead warrior's chest was covered with red wampum beads. Plenty Cuts didn't know him.

As Custer and Martino broke through the skirmish line, Tom Custer screeched, "Fire!"

Fifteen seconds later his troopers had fumbled new rounds into their carbines and Custer ordered "Fire!" again. The indians had been shaken by the first volley and lost momentum at the second.

The third volley broke them.

Yellow Hair ordered a retreat into a dry creek whose banks would serve as breastworks.

Tom Custer grinned at Plenty Cuts. "Ain't this stupendous?"

The Lakota crept nearer the surrounded troopers. Their arrows glinted in the air before plunging into the creekbed. Troopers fired at where they thought the indians might be.

Plenty Cuts's cheeks were white with sweat salt and his tongue was thick in his mouth.

Seemingly indifferent to indian bullets and arrows, George Armstrong Custer strolled to and fro as if promenading in the park.

After two hours of shooting at shadows, the troopers' ammunition was running low. When he heard the grim report, Custer didn't hesitate. "Horse-holders! Bring up the horses!"

Eighty-six men loaded their carbines, mounted, and burst out of that dry creekbed with Martino blowing his bugle like Gabriel at the last trump.

The Lakota ran. Custer's men pursued them for a mile, two miles, three—with no ammunition for a fight if they did catch them. When they finally abandoned the chase, the troopers were laughing.

"God Damn!"

"Didn't we show those heathens!"

Some shook hands.

Tom Custer danced his horse around Plenty Cuts. "How many you drop, Top? How many?"

"Dunno, Captain." When the interpreter levered his Henry, an unfired cartridge ejected. "B'lieve I forgot to shoot."

IN HIS FLATTERING article Kellogg accepted Custer's estimate of forty indians dead. Shillaber reckoned they might have killed ten.

ALTHOUGH THEY SKIRMISHED with the Lakota again, the Northern Pacific completed its survey, and at sundown, September 21, 1873, six months and twelve hundred miles after they had departed, the weary but satisfied expedition returned to Bismarck, Dakota Territory.

Where they learned that three days earlier, the Northern Pacific Railroad had declared bankruptcy.

CHAPTER 51

—

PANIC

September 18, 1873

To the Public—We regret to be obliged to announce that, owing to unexpected demands on us, our firm has been obliged to suspend payment. In a few days we will be able to present a statement to our creditors. Until which time we must ask their patient consideration. We believe our assets to be largely in excess of our liabilities.

Jay Cooke & Co.

IT WAS ONE OF THOSE FALL DAYS WHEN GRIMY MANHATTAN IS briefly a beautiful city. Last night's rain had washed the streets and granite cobblestones glistened. A breeze off the Hudson broomed coal smoke away. It was a day when old men smiled.

Over breakfast, Eben had agreed to a picnic with Pauline and little Augustus. Bridget was preparing their basket while Flynn brought the carriage around.

Last night, awakened by the drumming of the rain on the roof, Eben lay sleepless, feeling very much the sinner.

It had been a distressing year. Jim Fisk, who'd been so full of life, Jolly

Jim had been shot dead by a rival for an actress's affections. Jim hadn't been in his grave a month before his opera house was sold. Jay Gould had been forced out of the Erie and poor Boss Tweed—rumors circled Tammany's Boss like sharks.

Reform was in the air. Well, if reform was the coming thing, by God, couldn't Eben Barnwell reform?

Henceforth he *would* be faithful to Pauline. If the truth be told, he hadn't been much of a Don Juan anyway. It distressed him awfully when actresses begged him for money. Why must so many pretty young women have destitute mothers or sisters at the poorhouse door?

So that morning, when Pauline suggested—without much hope—that her husband might accompany his wife and son on an outing, Eben enthusiastically accepted her invitation.

While Pauline dressed Augustus, Eben tried on his new straw boater before the hall mirror.

When the doorbell rang, Eben sang, "Finish our basket, Bridget. I'll see who's at the door."

A gray-faced Amos Hayward was clutching a notice.

"Why, Amos," Eben said. "My, you are the early bird."

With trembling hand, Amos delivered it.

Which Eben read without comprehension, smiling brightly, "Oh, this is nothing. Cooke can't fail." Then he gasped, "My God!"

After the '69 gold panic, Amos Hayward left the Washington Treasury for the New York subtreasury, where he became—in a modest way—a man of means. His salary and cautious ventures—managed by his friend Eben Barnwell—had bought the lugubrious clerk a townhouse on Bank Street. Amos Hayward married and in due course—rather to Eben's astonishment—Mr. and Mrs. Hayward produced a daughter they adored.

Eben opened his watch: 8:14 on a beautiful Manhattan morning. He blinked rapidly. "Joke? Is this some kind of joke?"

"Oh, it's real enough, Mr. Barnwell. There's been a run on the Union Bank. E. B. Clarke has failed."

"Clarke? Not Clarke too." Eben peered up and down the silent street as if eavesdroppers might be hiding behind the plane trees or the wrought-iron fences. He snatched Amos Hayward's sleeve and dragged the man into his parlor, which he darkened by drawing the drapes. He turned to Hayward. "The Northern Pacific?"

"Bankrupt." Amos wore the smug gloom of a government employee whose livelihood is impervious to financial crises. "I came as soon as I heard."

"Who is that, dear?" Pauline called from upstairs.

"Nobody, dear. I'll deal with it."

"We'll just be a minute. Augustus is so excited."

"The street's a madhouse. There are so many men out of their offices, the horsecars can't turn around. There's a run on the Fidelity," Amos added. "But Fidelity promises to sustain."

The Northern Pacific's predecessor, the Union Pacific, had not merely made fortunes, it had made *men*. Who were Stanford or Crocker or Huntington before the Union Pacific? Every "live man" expected the Northern Pacific to repeat history. On Eben's advice even Amos Hayward had invested in Northern Pacific bonds.

Despite this shock, Eben felt a sting of anger at the man who had heeded his advice to buy Northern but refused to hold them. "Don't sell your bonds," Eben had advised Amos. "Don't buy a house. Houses don't earn a return on capital."

He had believed that Jay Cooke's promises were worth more than solid bricks, wainscoting, chimneys . . .

Bricks! Chimneys! Eben's eyes watered.

"You are diversified, aren't you, friend?" Amos inquired anxiously.

Eben dredged up his confidence. "General Custer is escorting the Northern Pacific surveyors! The savages can't stop the railroad now!"

"Eben? Eben, who are you talking to?" Pauline called.

Eben slashed the air with his hand. "Not a word, Amos. Not a God Damned word." In a milder tones he replied, "It's just Amos, dear. Baby Elizabeth is cutting teeth."

Pauline was backlit at the head of the stairs, which she descended so lightly, it seemed as if she floated down. Why, Eben thought, Pauline is truly beautiful.

She paused in the parlor doorway and shaded her eyes. "Eben, why is it so dark in here? Amos, is that really you?" She went to the drapes and opened them with a swish. Pauline frowned. "Is something wrong, dear?" With sunlight streaming over her shoulders, she answered her own question with a smile. "How could anything be wrong on such a glorious day?" She touched his cheek. "I am so looking forward to this, dear. We haven't picnicked in ever so long . . ."

By herculean effort, Eben was impassive. "Picnic. My dear . . . I'm afraid I can't, today. Business . . ."

At first his wife's smile didn't believe him, and when it did, it died. "Oh," she said. "Business. But Eben . . ." She turned her luminous gaze on him and said, " 'For what shall it profiteth a man to gain the whole world and lose his own soul?' " She persisted, "Darling, you haven't had a day off from work in ever so long, and Eben—I do miss you terribly. You know I do."

To disguise his turmoil, Eben spoke more coldly than he'd intended. "There will be other days just as fine."

She turned to his friend. "Amos, didn't your wife say Elizabeth was teething last month?"

Amos chuckled falsely. "Poor darling." He sighed. "Goes on and on, doesn't it?"

"Dear Eben," Pauline said, "are you sure you won't reconsider? It is such a splendid day and when winter comes there won't be more of them."

The ugliness of his charade gave Eben brute courage. "I said no."

"Ah, yes. So you did." The sorrow in her eyes changed to an indifference that chilled him to the bone. "I'll leave you gentlemen to your business. Good morning, Mr. Hayward."

Quickly Eben said, "I'm afraid I must go downtown, dear. We'll use Amos's carriage. You and Augustus will have your picnic. Don't let me spoil your day."

Eben knew the words trembling on her lips were, "You already have!" but she didn't utter them. Her face, which had been so glad, was an expressionless mask. How dare she be disappointed! Eben felt like shaking the disappointment out of her!

He was so angry he threw his front door open, stepped outside, and took deep breaths of air. He thought: She does nothing. She is an ornament. She is neither useful nor rich. Everything depends on me. Everything.

A diffident Amos joined him on the stoop. "Well, Amos," Eben Barnwell said, "let's go downtown and see what we can salvage."

When Eben urged others to diversify, he was preaching to ordinary folk who were more afraid of losing the little they had than gaining more. Like most speculators, Eben didn't heed this advice. Mr. Kellogg's reports from the Yellowstone expedition—the bright promise of Dakota Territory and the ease with which General Custer repulsed the Sioux—had convinced Eben to put his money into Northern Pacific.

In his thirty-fourth year of life, Eben Barnwell was a millionaire. This may seem a satisfactory sum to those who view money as something to be spent on food, clothing, or the roof over one's head, but in Manhattan, measured against Vanderbilt, Morgan, and Belmont and even the despised Jay Gould, Eben's fortune and hence Eben himself were inconsequential.

Eben had put his money into Northern Pacific in order to become the man his envy said he was.

Margin is a tool for canny men. Margin allows the speculator with ten dollars in his pocket to invest a hundred dollars, and when his securities appreciate, the buyer reaps the same profit as him who risked his own hundred.

In the remote possibility—all brokers agree the possibility is *extremely* remote—that instead of rising, securities fall, then the broker takes no notice of the man who invested the full one hundred dollars of his money to buy the presently distressed instruments, but takes hold of the margin buyer with a bulldog's grip lest the losses become his own.

BARNWELL AND NUTLEY'S offices were in the Merchants Exchange Building near the tip of Manhattan. Although Nutley had been dead for two years, Eben hadn't changed the firm's name. Firms with dead men's names were solid.

Eben's floor man, Tate, was in Nutley's old office, kneeling before the safe. After a glance, Tate knew his employer understood their position. "Didn't we keep some Standard Oil?" Tate asked

"I don't recall. Perhaps ten thousand."

"I'll have to take them to the Union Trust. They've called their margin accounts."

Eben sat at the mahogany desk, which was as free of dust as when poor George collapsed over it.

"Who else?" Eben asked quietly.

"Is asking for collateral? Everyone except First Chemical, and they're so busy dealing with this damn panic they haven't got around to us yet. You can be sure they will."

Eben's floor man pulled thick sheaves of Northern Pacific bonds from the safe onto the floor.

Eben reached for a certificate. As beautifully engraved as an oversized banknote, it bore the superscription: "Authorized by Act of the Congress of the United States of America, July 17, 1868."

A locomotive steamed magnificently across a rural landscape beside telegraph poles. Dully, Eben wondered if they had telegraphs in Dakota. He supposed they must. Duncan Gatewood—Mahone's man and Pauline's uncle—had moved somewhere out there. From time to time, Pauline read Eben bits from her aunt's letters. Didn't they have children? Two children? Yes, Eben believed they had.

Tate was ignoring the beautiful certificates for certificates—fewer— with oil wells on their face.

"Authorized by Act of Congress" . . . didn't that mean Congress wouldn't let Jay Cooke fail? How could they let Cooke fail?

"President Grant?" Eben asked.

His floor man snorted. "*Him?* What do you expect *him* to do?"

A few oil wells were laid tenderly beside the heaps of railroad trains crossing rural landscapes. Eben wondered if the artist had worked from life or just made things up.

"Anything in your safe, Mr. Barnwell? Didn't we buy Cunard?"

"Sold it," Eben said.

"The twenty-five thousand in Augustus Belmont's receivables?"

"Collateralized at the Union Bank."

"Mr. Barnwell?"

"Yes, Tate?"

"Are we finished, then?"

Tate was married. He sometimes spoke of a wife. Did Tate have children? Eben didn't know. He examined the certificate. Signed by Jay Cooke himself. Eben had dined with Jay Cooke. He knew Cooke's bold signature. Behind each Northern Pacific bond stood—well, Jay Cooke stood behind them, and who could want better security? Hadn't Cooke single-handedly financed the Union war effort? Cooke's signature had made engraved paper more valuable than a thousand locomotives or ten thousand oil wells. "Of course we're not finished." Eben swallowed.

He let the bond flutter to the floor. "We must buy time until Cooke reopens. This is just a panic. Those who outlast panics will profit. I've done so before."

He sent Tate to the banks, with promises to meet their margin calls. He went himself to the New York Bank for Commerce, where George Nutley's brother was president.

Alas, as a wise man once noted, "There is nothing more cowardly than a million dollars—unless it is two million dollars." Although Joseph Nutley owed his present position to Eben, and though there was no run on the Bank for Commerce—which was reputed to be, next to Morgan's, the soundest bank in the city—Joseph Nutley would only loan Eben money on collateral of his house, his furnishings, his artworks, and a remote Virginia plantation—at forty percent of their value.

For a time it was enough. The Fidelity sustained and the Union Bank sustained. But at one o'clock Friday, the exchange bell rang and a white-faced clerk cried, "The First National Bank of Philadelphia regrets that it can no longer meet its obligations." A groan like a wounded animal's rose from brokers and clerks on the floor.

At two-thirty, the gong rang again. "The Merchants Bank of Richmond has closed its doors."

First the clearinghouses went under, then the railroads. The Erie declared bankruptcy. Virginia's Atlantic, Mississippi & Ohio went into receivership. Commodore Vanderbilt poured money into the market to sustain his holdings. J. P. Morgan bought gold.

Bankers and brokers wept with relief at the closing bell, after which no more business could be transacted and no more defaults could be declared. Bullies shoved protesting investors through the bronze doors and bolted them.

At five o'clock, Eben Barnwell rode the elevated railroad to the 29th Street station.

He descended the iron stairs one at a time. His hair was disheveled. He'd left his coat in the office—or was it at the exchange? Eben opened his Waltham watch, which was accurate to three minutes a week. A marvel of American ingenuity. Time is money.

Eben had plenty of time. Of money he had none.

Eben wondered if the man who coined that nostrum had envisioned an exchange: how much per minute, per hour? How much for a lifetime?

For what shall it profiteth a man . . .

The dusk was as lovely as the morning had been. There was a pink cast in the western sky. How proud he'd been of his house in Madison Square. How proud he'd been of owning a house. How proud he'd been.

Eben Barnwell walked tiredly down the street—on the opposite side of the square.

Windows glowed through drapes opened on what had been Eben Barnwell's home, his things, his achievements.

Was anything finer than a respectable family's home?

In his rumpled clothes, Eben Barnwell felt dirty. He wiped his nose with his sleeve.

For a full half hour, he crouched beside a spindly elm tree contemplating the wonderful life someone else owned.

CHAPTER 52

MRS. S. T. GATEWOOD'S BOARDINGHOUSE
BRUNSWICK STEW

*Boil two chickens in water. Cook one pint butterbeans and one
quart tomatoes, cook with the meat. When done, add one dozen
ears corn, one dozen large tomatoes, and one pound butter.*

*Take out the chicken, cut it into small pieces, and put back;
cook until it is well done and thick enough to be eaten with a fork.*

"AUGIE, ISN'T THIS GOOD?" PAULINE TASTED THE DISH MORE
enthusiastically than it deserved.

"Not hungry." The little boy shrank as far from his bowl as he could
without abandoning his chair altogether. He banged the rungs with his
heels.

Samuel Gatewood's glance stilled them.

Molly Gatewood chattered, "Well, dear. If you're not hungry, you
won't want Amelia's apple pie. We'll put your piece out for the boarders'
breakfast."

As if it were his portion of hemlock, the boy jabbed his fork into the
stew and stirred it around.

Molly continued cheerfully, "I'm so glad the house is full and our
boarders are accustomed to our ways."

How Molly wished Samuel and Pauline wouldn't bring their political disagreements to the dinner table. No abstract quarrel should imperil good digestion and a pleasant night's sleep.

At awkward moments like this, Mrs. Gatewood restated the comforting and pacific.

Awkward moments they'd had when they opened Mrs. S. T. Gatewood's Boardinghouse. Their first boarders had been Irish working-men, yankee peddlers, and Virginians dispossessed by the War. Some smuggled whiskey into the house. Drunken boarders had banged on the front door after midnight although that door was locked from ten until seven-fifteen in the morning. One miscreant cracked a door light banging. The prohibition against whistling was widely disregarded. But it was a Virginian, "Captain Beasely, formerly of the Lynchburg Rifles," who nearly put paid to their venture when one Saturday night he slipped the front door lock and tiptoed a woman upstairs into his room: the largest front bedroom in the house. The woman's indiscreet cries wakened Amelia, who scurried to the carriage house to fetch Master Gatewood.

His climb up the stairs toward the couple's hushed giggles in what had been his wife Molly's bedroom tested Samuel Gatewood's battered pride. "Reduced to this! Reduced to this!" After he evicted the amorous couple and double-locked the front door, Samuel took down Pauline's sign, which had peeked discreetly through the drawn curtains of their parlor window: "Room and Board for Gentlemen: $1.50 weekly."

"Gentlemen!" Samuel had snorted.

Next morning when Samuel informed his wife of his irrevocable decision to evict their boarders, move back from the carriage house, and reclaim Molly's house as their own, his wife sighed, "Well, Samuel, if you must, you must. I suppose Pauline, Amelia, and I could take in laundry. We could sell Grandmother's dining room table—did I tell you Washington once took supper at its head?—and buy an agitator washing machine. You can hang the necessary clotheslines. Will our well suffice for a laundry or must we connect to city water?"

"Molly!"

"Samuel," she replied calmly, "as Christians we must believe that God knows how much we can endure."

"You should have heard that . . . *woman*. She howled like a cat in heat!" Samuel replied.

Was that a grin on his wife's face? "Samuel, perhaps I should have *been* her."

"But Molly—"

She touched his lips. "You have put them out, Samuel. Henceforth, we'll have to be more careful choosing boarders. We've only been in this business two months and have much to learn."

Learn they did. A year and eight months after they'd arrived in Richmond, Mrs. S. T. Gatewood's Boardinghouse was a model of decorum. After Thomas Byrd won election to the Congress of the United States, he'd directed his Irish canvassers to his grandfather's boardinghouse. If these men drank, they did not do so in the Gatewood house. If they enjoyed women's favors, they enjoyed them elsewhere. Their rent was paid Monday mornings without fail. After one remonstrance, they never again whistled in the house. What Mr. Curry, Mr. McNeil, Mr. Sullivan, and Mr. Houlahan did was argue politics every evening when they took coffee in the parlor after dinner. Alas for the comforting and pacific, Pauline and Samuel involved themselves in their disagreements while Molly retired to the kitchen to help Amelia prepare the family dinner.

BY LUCK, MOLLY had been with her husband the first time Samuel saw General Mahone driving down Broad Street behind his handsome team of matched bays. "Samuel." Molly caught his sleeve, whispering urgently. "Please don't make matters worse than they are."

"How could they be worse?" Samuel growled as Mahone's rig clattered away.

"Samuel, we have each other. We have a roof over our heads. We are not destitute. We have Pauline and little Augustus to think of."

"The boy is hopelessly spoiled, Molly. If he were at Stratford—"

"We are not at Stratford, Samuel."

"I thank you for the reminder." He bowed.

"Little Augustus believes his failings drove his father away and forced them from their home. If it hadn't been for that waiter's kindness . . ."

"Eben Barnwell's speculations ruined them. The boy had nothing to do with it."

"Samuel, dear. He's just a child."

"Eben Barnwell's recklessness cannot excuse the son. It cannot. The father's vices must not flourish in the son. Augustus Barnwell is spoiled and has unrealistic expectations!"

"He is six years old! That child had so much and has lost it all. You and I . . ."

"You and I?"

"We have been too long in the world to be flabbergasted by misfortune."

As usual, Molly was right. Though Samuel Gatewood had had bad nights after the First National Bank of Warm Springs finally and officially informed him that Stratford had been foreclosed—sold to yankee merchants for a quail-hunting preserve—Samuel had known the dread day was coming and had mentally discounted General Mahone's promises to pay. When Jay Cooke failed and General Mahone's railroad was forced into receivership, Samuel submitted his claims with faint hope of recovery.

When Granddaughter Pauline wrote that her husband Eben had decamped and she was coming home destitute, Samuel had worried more about Pauline's troubles than his own. Thank God they still had Molly's Richmond home, empty after Colonel Elliot returned to his homeplace in the south side.

Her journey financed by a waiter she knew, Pauline came back to Stratford the same day the new owners (three amiable yankee sportsmen) took possession. When Pauline understood what was happening, she walked to the family graveyard and sat for a time beside her mother and father.

The next day, Sunday, as Samuel and Molly were dressing for church, the last time the Gatewoods would worship at SunRise Chapel, Pauline had announced, "Grandfather, I won't attend church anymore. In good conscience, I cannot."

They'd sold some furniture to Stratford's new owners and stored the rest in the barn loft. The yankees had been solicitous of family feelings: the Gatewoods should visit anytime. Yes, certainly, they'd keep up the graveyard. Although they hadn't had personal dealings with Eben Barnwell, they'd heard of the man. Barnwell had utterly vanished. They thought California. Cuba? South America?

On Samuel's recommendation the yankees hired Jack Mitchell as their caretaker.

Samuel's trusted retainer helped load the wagon with the personal goods they'd take to their new home.

"Goodbye, Jack. I am sorry things have come to this. I will send you your back salary as soon as I am able."

When, as was his custom, Jack removed his old felt hat his gray head seemed painfully vulnerable. How many years had they been master and man?

"Yes, Mister Samuel. I knows you will." Jack's eyes flicked to the ruined sawmill: a few blackened posts, the jumble of blackened misshappen machinery.

Though there was no proof of arson, that's what it had been, and Samuel couldn't blame them. He hadn't paid his workers in months.

"They just hurtin' theyselfs," Jack muttered.

Samuel agreed in principle, though a tie sawmill without a railroad to buy ties wasn't worth much.

"I'll pay the men too." Samuel clicked to the horses and drove off without a backward glance.

In January of 1874, three Gatewoods crossed the Blue Ridge Mountains and the Piedmont's snow-dusted red clay. In Richmond, after modifications to the house and carriage house (Duncan sent money to Molly without his father's knowledge), they put out their sign and opened the doors of Mrs. S. T. Gatewood's Boardinghouse.

Amelia, Molly's old servant, turned up one evening and without explanation resumed the duties she'd always done.

Occasionally they saw Molly's Richmond friends. Most were reduced in status and some were impoverished.

Their new rooms had been the hostler's quarters over the carriage house. Sometimes Samuel woke to Pauline's pacing in the next room. Often the light glowed under her door half the night.

A scant year after they left Stratford, Samuel had sent Jack twenty dollars, and ten dollars toward the workmen's wages. At this rate, by Samuel's seventieth birthday, he'd be free of debt.

Every weekday morning, promptly at six forty-five, the dining room doors swung open on a sideboard where eggs, bacon, oatmeal, ham, sausages, bread, butter and jam, and metal pots of strong coffee were laid out. Those doors closed promptly at seven-thirty and were not reopened until five-thirty for dinner. Sunday breakfasts were at six-fifteen for the benefit of those who wished to attend early Mass and the doors stayed open until ten for the Protestants, Mr. and Mrs. Gatewood (Presbyterian) and Amelia (Baptist).

On nights when Thomas Byrd held political rallies, the front door was left open until the last man locked it behind him. Cheeses and pie in the parlor awaited Congressman Byrd's canvassers.

Molly and Amelia cooked meals, Pauline and Amelia cleaned, and Pauline took evening coffee into the parlor, although Samuel believed that Mr. Curry, a young railroad driver, appreciated Pauline rather too much. Pauline was altogether free and easy with these men; boldly taking part in their political discussions, an activity, Samuel believed, properly reserved for men.

Samuel bought groceries, arranged for coal to be delivered, kept the books, and collected rents.

He was fierce about rents and each boarder understood that if his rent was late by a single day, if on Monday morning one dollar fifty cents was not put in Mr. Gatewood's hand, that evening the defaulter's worldly goods would be out on the front porch and no entreaty, no heartfelt excuse, no extenuating circumstances would readmit him.

Every morning Gatewood appeared downstairs in frock coat and tie. When he took his regular constitutional, he wore a stovepipe hat, carried an ebony walking stick, and, summer or winter, always wore gloves.

Samuel was head of the household, but Molly was its heart. Sometimes a boarder needed a button replaced. Sometimes he needed a good woman's advice.

AFTER AUGIE HAD pushed his stew around his bowl and eaten his pie, his mother carried his plate to the wet sink. "Kiss Grandpa good night."

The brush of the child's lips on his cheek reminded Samuel of his own children's kisses so many years before. He said, "Good night, dear boy," and cleared his throat. Molly's knowing smile irritated him. The child would be a man one day, and if Samuel Gatewood had anything to say, he wouldn't be like his father!

Wise enough not to utter his thoughts, he removed his plate.

"I can do that," Molly protested.

"Damn it, I know you can!"

"Don't be cross with me, Samuel, just because you're cross with Pauline."

Earlier that evening when Samuel entered the parlor, his boarders were considering an agreeable subject: how the discovery of gold in the Black Hills had helped the Northern Pacific emerge from bankruptcy. Mr. Curry voiced his opinion that the railroad's resurrection would return the nation to prosperity. Gratifyingly, Curry looked to Samuel's expertise on all things "western," since Molly and his son's wife Sallie corresponded faithfully and sometimes Duncan or Samuel added a postscript.

Relying on his special knowledge, Samuel asserted that Manifest Destiny required "settling the indian question."

Mr. Curry condemned the indians in the strongest terms, but Pauline disagreed. "After all," she said, "it is *their* country."

"Aye, lass," Mr. Curry shot back. "So long as they can keep it."

"Like the British in Ireland, Mr. Curry?" Pauline inquired guilessly.

Since the Irish boarders were united behind Home Rule, Curry replied sharply, "It's not the same, lass. Not the same at all. The Irish are civilized, the indians are savages. Brutes."

Pauline's raised eyebrows reminded Curry of similar insults the Irish had suffered.

The parlor was sparsely furnished with Federal and Queen Anne pieces which the boarders respected more than Pauline, whose housekeeping left much to be desired. The hunt table held Molly's Georgian silver coffee service and third-best cups below daguerreotypes of Abigail Gatewood, Catesby, and Leona Byrd.

Mr. McNeil, who always attended two Sunday Masses, found a safer subject. "That Beecher fella . . ." he suggested.

"Protestant, isn't he?"

Samuel found Mr. Curry's smugness offensive. "Falsely accused," he snapped. "Man of his stature."

"Oh, I don't know," Curry replied. "He is a very *liberal* Protestant."

"Tilton's lying," Samuel said. "The Reverend Henry Ward Beecher seducing Tilton's wife? Preposterous!"

"Oh, I think he did," Pauline intervened again. "I think he must have. I have been in the man's church, you see. I have heard him preach. He is . . . Oh, he is hard to describe. Beecher . . . he serves the rich man's Christ."

"Tilton's accusation is an assault on decency itself," Samuel shot back.

"And decency," Pauline contended, "is unaffected by Dr. Beecher's infidelity? As I recall, God doesn't care for adultery. Was it the Seventh Commandment, Grandfather?"

Samuel couldn't stop. "Tilton lied to bring a good man down."

After long silence, Pauline said, "Well . . ." and collected the coffee cups, though Mr. McNeil still had coffee in his. "The clock strikes ten," she announced.

"Ah." Curry stood and stretched. "Just when matters were getting interesting."

A vein throbbed in Pauline's forehead. "Tell me, Mr. Curry," she said. "If Ireland does get Home Rule, will Irishwomen vote?"

LATER THAT NIGHT, lying in bed, Samuel said, "I'm worried about Pauline, dear. She is far too forward. It was an error, I now believe, letting her . . . 'agnosticism' go unchecked."

Molly sat at the dressing table combing her long thick gray hair. She cocked her head at Samuel's word.

"Molly, is our Pauline becoming a free thinker?"

Molly snuffed the gaslight and slipped under the bedclothes beside him. "I don't know why men are afraid of women, dear. We will always love you, you know."

CHAPTER 53

—

OFFICIAL CORRESPONDENCE

To: E.P.Smith, Commissioner of Indian Affairs
November 9 1875

*SIR: I have the honor to address you in relation to the attitude and
condition of certain wild and hostile bands of Sioux indians in
Dakota and Montana, that came under my observation during my
recent tour through their country, and what I think should be the
policy of the government toward them.*

*I refer to Sitting Bull's band and other bands of the Sioux
Nation, under chiefs or 'headmen' of less note but no less tamable
and hostile. These indians occupy the center, so to speak, and roam
over Western Dakota and Eastern Montana, including the rich
valleys of the Yellowstone and Powder Rivers, and make war on the
Ariska, Rees, Mandans, Assinaboines, Crows and other friendly
tribes on the circumference.*

*Their country is probably the best hunting ground in the United
States a "paradise" for Indians, affording game in such variety and
abundance that the need of Government supplies is not felt. Perhaps
for this reason they have never accepted aid or been brought under
control. They openly set at defiance all law and authority, and boast
that the United States authorities are not strong enough to conquer*

them. The United States troops are held in contempt and, surrounded by their native mountains, relying on their knowledge of the country and powers of endurance, they laugh at the futile efforts made thus far to subjugate them, and scorn the idea of white civilization.

They are lofty and independent in their attitude and language to Government officials, as well as the whites generally, and claim to be the sovereign rulers of the land. They say that they own the wood, the water, the ground and the air and that white men live in or pass through their country but by their sufferance.

They are rich in horses and robes, and are thoroughly armed. Nearly every warrior carries a breech-loading gun, a revolver, a bow and quiver of arrows. From their central position they strike to the east, north and west, steal horses and plunder from all the surrounding tribes as well as frontier settlers, and luckless white hunters, or emigrants who are not in sufficient force to resist them, and fortunate indeed, is the man who thus meets them, if, after losing all his worldly possessions, he escapes with his scalp.

And yet these indians number, all told, but a few hundred warriors and these are never all together or under the control of one chief.

In my judgement, one thousand men, under the command of an experienced officer, sent into their country in the winter, when the indians are nearly always in camp, and at which season of the year they are the most helpless, would be sufficient for their capture or punishment. They richly merit the punishment for their incessant warfare on friendly tribes, their continuous thieving, and their numerous murders of white settler and their families, or white men whenever found unarmed.

The government owes it too, to those friendly tribes, in fulfillment of treaty stipulations. It owes it to the agents and employees, whom it has sent to labor among the indians at remote and almost inaccessible places, beyond the reach of aid, in time, to save. It owes it to the frontier settlers, who have, with their families, braved the

*dangers and hardships incident to pioneer life. It owes it to civiliza-
tion and the common cause of humanity.*

*Very respectfully, your obedient servant,
E.C. Watkins, United States Indian Inspector*

*To the Hon Secretary of the Interior
November 27, 1875*

*SIR; I have the honor to transmit herewith, enclosed, a special
report from E.C. Watkins, United States Indian Inspector, dated
the 9th instant, in relation to the status and condition of certain
wild and lawless bands of Sioux indians, giving an expression of his
views in reference to the future action of the Government toward
them . . .
I respectfully recommend that this communication be referred to the
War Department for consideration and such action as may be
deemed best by Lieutenant General Sheridan, who is personally
conversant with the situation on the Upper Missouri, and with the
relations of Sitting Bull's band to the other Sioux tribes.*

*Very Respectfully yours, your obedient servant
Edw P. Smith, Commissioner*

*To The Commissioner of Indian Affairs
December 3, 1875*

*Sir: Referring to your communication of the 27th ultimo, relative to
the status of certain Sioux indians residing without the bounds of
their reservation and their continued hostile attitude toward the
whites, I have to request that you direct the indian Agents at all the
Sioux agencies in Dakota and at Fort Peck Montana, to notify said*

indians that unless they remove within the bounds of their reserva-
tion (and remain there) before the 31st of January next, they shall
be deemed hostile, and treated accordingly by the military force.

Very respectfully, your obedient servant
Z. Chandler Secretary of the Interior

To J.S. Hastings, United States Indian agent, Red Cloud agency
CC: Agents Howard, Bingham, Burke, Beckwith, Alderson, Reily
and Livingstone
December 6, 1875

SIR: I am instructed by the Honorable Secretary of the Interior,
under date of the 3d instant, to direct you to notify Sitting Bull's
band, and other wild and lawless bands of Sioux indians residing
without the bounds of their reservation, who roam over Western
Dakota and Eastern Montana, including the rich valley of the
Yellowstone and Powder Rivers, and make war on Ariska, Rees,
Mandans, Assinaboines, Crows and other friendly tribes that unless
they shall remove within the bounds of their reservation (and
remain there) they shall be deemed hostile and treated accordingly by
the military force.

Very respectfully yours, your obedient servant,
EDW. P. Smith, Commissioner

CHAPTER 54

THE BONE GAME

RATCLIFF CAUGHT SHILLABER IN THE STABLES SCOOPING CORN into panniers. It was so cold the air snapped. "So," Ratcliff said. "You're goin' with Yellow Hair."

"Maybe I'll scout for Terry or Crook. That's up to the army. Hold my reins while I check the pack."

Streaks of pine pitch had frozen hard as white amber on fresh-cut log walls. This Red Cloud Agency had opened for business in November, three months ago. Shillaber hefted one side of the packsaddle, then the other. He took three boxes of ammunition from the left saddlebag and pushed them into the right one. He slung panniers of grain over the horse's withers.

"They won't come in," Ratcliff said. "Can you picture Sitting Bull, Crazy Horse, Gall as blanket indians?"

"I reckon they won't."

"Ben—"

"We talked about this until I'm plumb sick of it. This ain't gonna be no cakewalk."

Ratcliff growled, "You sayin' I'm 'feared?"

Shillaber snorted.

"I don't get 'feared. I get mad. On New Market Heights, I recall lookin' around for the white officers, but they was dead and a couple colored sergeants was kneelin' beside the corpse of this dumb boy lieutenant. They was weepin'. I'd never seen anything stupider. Like a couple chickens, they were, and it made me mad. So I took command. Led them through the abatis and through the Reb's guns and, hell, Ben . . . I didn't know till afterwards I might of got kilt."

Shillaber put a boot against his horse's belly and cinched the surcingle. After the horse let out its breath he took up another notch.

"You sayin' you don't want my company?" Ratcliff chuckled. "Maybe I ain't white enough for you?'"

The horses' breath rose from them as if they were steam locomotives.

"I'm a good interpreter."

"Top, your wife almost went back to her brother after the Yellowstone Expedition, and that one was relatively peacable. This time is different. The army's unleashed Yellow Hair."

"Hell, Ben. She Goes Before, she don't care for me no more. She all the time prayin'. Prayin' to Low Dog and Jesus like they was one and the same. We don't ever . . . Ah, the hell with it. Tells Him's supposed to have a bone game this mornin'. Maybe I'll go watch."

"You don't play, do you?"

"Naw. After you done what you and me done, betting on which man's hand has a bone? The bone game passes the time." He started for the stable door.

"Wait."

He spun around angrily. "I ain't gonna beg you, Ben. When old Master laid the bullwhip on my back, I never begged. When White Bull was goin' to cut my damn throat, I never begged. I ain't beggin' now."

"Oh, God Damn it to hell." Ben Shillaber reached in his saddlebag for a flask, took a drink, rubbed it with the heel of his hand, and passed it to Ratcliff. "It'll cost you. You know it will. If you ride with Yellow Hair you'll never be a Lakota again. She Goes Before . . . Baby Tazoo . . . she'll have to choose you or her own people."

Ratcliff barked a laugh. "Which you think she'll choose? The Lakota . . . are finished. They ain't enough buffalo left to keep 'em from starving.

They gonna be locked up on these reservations for God knows how many generations with nothin' but the bone game."

"You could go back East."

"Back East, out West. Ben, It ain't no different. This ain't my world. It's General Custer's world. It's President Grant's world. Hell, even flat busted it's still Jay Cooke's world. Got no room in this world for me nor She Goes Before, nor any other nigger be he red or black."

"Jesus, Top. Hang on to that flask. You need it more than I do."

"No, Ben. What I need is the army."

Ben Shillaber eyed his friend for a long time. "Go tell She Goes Before," he said. "Get your horse. I'll be waitin' at the sutler's."

PLENTY CUTS TOLD his wife he was leaving with Shillaber. He said he would interpret, he would not fight the Lakota. They needed money. On the Yellowstone Expedition he'd been paid fifty dollars a month.

Their lodge was outside the new stockade. It was less ragged than the blanket indians' lodges. They spoke outside it, as if it weren't his home anymore. She Goes Before told Plenty Cuts she would not be here when he came back.

Smoke rose straight into the air from fifty lodges.

Plenty Cuts tried to think of reasons why she should be his wife but could not think of any.

She raised a hand in farewell. "Ki ya mani yo, Top. Ki ya mani yo."

CHAPTER 55

IN THE MOON OF
RIPENING BLACKBERRIES

*F*at white flakes batted my cheeks like moths. Snow blurred flowering primroses, fattened and bowed the sagebrush.

My visible world was those few yards in front of my pony's ears. Snow thickened his rough black mane and muffled his hoof-falls on the Dakota prairie.

"Oh," I murmured. "Oh, oh, oh!"

My face was wet.

"Tazoo will not be Washitu": my vow had separated me from my husband like a sword in our bed.

Again and again Low Dog repeated my father Red Leaf's dream. Night after weary night I'd fly over the Shadowland whose lush green meadows have never been blackened by Washitu plows. The fish in the sparkling streams have never been offended by Washitu steamboats. As my father had before me, I saw the Santee who loved JesuChrist and were forbidden the Lakota Shadowland, just as they were unwelcome in the Christian heaven. Some of these unfortunates were known to me. When I was a child at the mission I had prayed with Two Magpies and Blackberry Woman.

Where can you go if you are not one person, nor another?

I had loved Plenty Cuts. I had opened myself to him. I thought our twoness was stronger than our onenesses. I thought we could protect us.

Bundled in Real Dog skins our second child nestled against my back. My Tazoo's breath fluttered the hairs on my neck.

Plenty Cuts no longer knew if he was Washitu or Lakota, black man or red. When he put on his blue uniform coat, his walk stiffened and he walked like a Seizer walks. The lyrical Lakota cadences I loved gave way to guttural talk.

Sometimes I wanted to burn that coat. Sometimes I thought if he didn't have the coat, he wouldn't be the man who wore it.

Shillaber called him "Top."

Who was "Top"? The stranger who had been my husband walked like "Top" and talked like "Top." But if Plenty Cuts was "Top," who was I? Just another blanket squaw? Who was Tazoo? One more worthless papoose?

The man who had been my husband didn't need a wife; Top needed a woman. He who had hunted blackhorns for us didn't need meat, he needed rations. My beloved Plenty Cuts didn't need the Lakota. Top had his regiment.

Oh, and this was my heartbreak, that sometimes my beloved Plenty Cuts was who he was, the warrior who had fooled Chasing Crane, the husband who embraced me before the Lakota as my brother's wives giggled behind their hands. It hurt when something he did or said recalled the husband who had stood naked beside me while we gave away everything to own our dead baby's ghost.

Sometimes Plenty Cuts was Plenty Cuts.

But when he dressed himself in his blue coat, he was "Top."

My pony shook his mane free of snow.

"Ah, Tazoo," I murmured to my child. "Poor fatherless Tazoo."

As we rode west across the Dakotas toward White Bull's village the snow moths melted on my cheek like tears.

—

CHAPTER 56

HOKA HEY

"AND WHEN HIS FATHER ASKED, 'WHO CHOPPED DOWN MY CHERRY tree?' what did young Washington reply?"

Catesby Gatewood's grandfather Samuel had known men who fought with George Washington. Samuel'd never said anything about any darn cherry tree.

Joe Lindquist, who was sixteen and in his last year of school, snickered. "Prolly told Pop the redskins felled her."

The freckled teacher with the high forehead touched the switch on his desk but hesitated: Joe Lindquist was big for his age.

As if Lindquist hadn't said anything, Mr. MacMillan smiled at the younger pupils and answered the question himself. "Young George Washington said, 'Father, I confess I did it. I cannot tell a lie.'"

Catesby couldn't stand this anymore. "If it was a cherry tree, why'd he hack it down? Heck, every darn fool knows what a cherry tree looks like. If it was winter, even, and the leaves were off, he'd know a cherry tree by the bark."

Which brought Mr. MacMillan's switch down on the back of Catesby's hand.

Catesby said, "Ow."

Slow spring flies buzzed the windows of the log schoolhouse on Olive

Street; windows that had been freighted, their previous teacher Professor Vernon had informed them, "At considerable expense," all the way from Salt Lake City.

When J. L. Vernon taught, school had been interesting. Vernon knew Latin and French and he spoke so knowingly about Paris and Vienna and London, you'd swear he'd lived there. "Learning, boy," he'd told Catesby, "is the gentleman's finest ornament."

In December, after Vernon ran off with the two hundred forty-four dollars the Masons had raised for a school library, MacMillan took over. He'd been a preacher before he failed as a homesteader. The back of Catesby's hand burned.

"Washington confessed, boy." Catesby recoiled from the teacher's breath. "George Washington could not tell a lie."

Last month the Centennial Exposition—one hundred years of American progress—had opened in Philadelphia. Catesby had read about it in his mother's magazines. They had a machine that talked and the biggest guns ever forged and the biggest blast furnace and all sorts of amazing machines. Catesby would have loved to hear about them, but when this schoolteacher mentioned the Centennial, "One hundred years, boys and girls. One hundred years!" he'd talk about the "Founding Fathers" who never made a mistake and apparently never farted.

Catesby's grandfather was a fading memory: a big ruddy face and disheveled white hair. Catesby's actual memories of Stratford Plantation had been overpainted with the postwar myth of a verdant Southland tended by contented darkies under benevolent masters.

One evening in the parlor as his mama was reading one of Molly's letters, Catesby'd interrupted, "Ma, who is Jack the Driver?"

His Mama put her hand to her mouth. "Oh, dear . . ."

Mr. MacMillan paced in front of the room, prattling about Lewis and Clark. How Meriwether Lewis had "found" Montana.

Catesby bit his tongue where the words "Who lost it?" quivered. There'd been indians here before the white explorers: Joe Lame Deer told Catesby all about them. French trappers too. What was all the fuss about?

Some Virginians had traveled up the Missouri until the Great Falls and they followed the Yellowstone to the Missouri on their way home. They hadn't run into any Lakota war parties, which was lucky for them.

Pain! His ear! MacMillan was dragging Catesby out of his seat. "You *will* pay attention, boy . . ."

Instinctively, Catesby kicked the teacher in the shins. The man paled and emitted a soundless "Ohhh." He released the boy's throbbing ear. When the teacher bent to rub his ankle, Catesby punched him, aiming for the man's ear. Instead, he knocked the teacher's glasses across the room. Catesby heard a lens break.

After their first shock, the other pupils started laughing and huzzahing while Mr. MacMillan hopped on one leg like a whooping crane.

Fists clenched, appalled at what he'd done, in a room of hooting children, Catesby Gatewood was in the biggest trouble of his life. Catesby's mama was dead set on "education." Despite the postage and three-month delay, Sallie Gatewood subscribed to the *Century* and the *Nation*. Sallie read these purveyors of history, education, and ideas from "back East," before they nested three days on the parlor table while his father didn't read them before Catesby and Abby took their turn. Abby couldn't scribble in the magazines because after the Gatewoods finished they were passed on to "less fortunate families." Catesby's father had put up ten dollars of the library fund J. L. Vernon stole. When his father remarked, "Too bad the vigilantes stopped hanging whites," Sallie'd snapped, "Mr. Vernon is an educated man, Duncan. Isn't that worth something?"

"Two hundred forty-four dollars, I reckon."

Sallie Gatewood was so angry with her husband—or maybe at J. L. Vernon—that for three days dinner table conversation had been restricted to "Pass the peas."

Catesby couldn't believe what he'd done.

MacMillan hobbled to a bench his students hastily evacuated and rolled up his trouser leg. "Young Gatewood . . ." he began as if he had something profound to say.

Joe Lindquist jeered. "You're in the johnnyhouse, now, Catesby. Damned if you ain't."

Catesby's sister Abby ran to him, and he looked down into her tiny frowning face.

Nothing was going to get better here. That much was plain. Things had to cool down first. "Come on, Abby," he said. "We're going home."

It had been a hard winter and the dirty remains of last week's snowfall glistened under the boardwalks. Catesby's Gitalong was tied beside the teacher's shabby rig and pony.

He had made a failed man fail again. Despite his pounding heart and burning ear, Catesby Gatewood was ashamed.

"Catesby," Abby asked, as he boosted his sister onto the horse's rump, "what's Mama going to say?"

Mama's father had been a schoolteacher. Sometimes Mama talked as if her school days had been the best time of her entire life.

"Things are different out here!" Catesby mounted the horse.

His sister put her arms around his waist. "What's different, Catesby?"

Didn't he wish he knew.

It was Friday, so maybe he could hang around town until three o'clock or so and ride home like nothing had happened. He'd come back to school Monday and take whatever licking old MacMillan gave him and that'd be the end of it. Maybe if he worked extra hard Saturday and cleaned up extra good for church on Sunday, maybe his parents . . .

Nope. They'd find out. Some blabbermouth would ride all the way out to SunRise Ranch just to spill the beans. Grown-ups just can't wait to tell on somebody else's kid.

"What's different, Catesby?" His sister hissed in his ear, "Slow down!"

Without meaning to, he'd been galloping his mare. How many times had Joe Lame Deer told him, "Don't take your troubles out on your horse"?

Gitalong was a three-year-old. His father hadn't let Catesby ride the powerful young horse until Joe Lame Deer assured him, "That mare would step on a timber rattler before she'd hurt that boy."

Catesby fed her, watered her, curried her, trimmed her mane, held her while Joe shoed her, and rode her all over the valley. One night when he came home after dark, his mama had been half worried, half mad until his father said, "Remember Gypsy, Sallie?" For some reason, his mama burst into tears.

"Where are we going?" his sister now asked.

"To Meadowbrook. Joe's helping with their branding."

"Aren't we going home?"

"I got to talk to Joe first."

Instead of crossing at the SunRise ford, they continued downstream toward the Anceneys' bridge. Meadowbrook was a big spread and when they needed help with branding or roundups, sometimes his father sent Joe and sometimes his father helped too.

Must he tell his parents? "Father, I cannot tell a lie." Darn it, hadn't *that* come back to haunt him. Maybe Joe would have a better idea. Joe knew things.

Catesby dismounted and led Gitalong through the timber to a creek trickling through a cottonwood grove. On the bank above the meandering stream, lightning had struck a tree. Big and little limbs were scattered around the blackened trunk as if the injured cottonwood had shrugged them off. Gitalong lowered her head to drink. Little Abby muttered and swatted at mosquitoes. Catesby hunkered upstream of the horse and scooped water into his cupped hands. The snowmelt was so cold it numbed his fingers.

"Catesby!" Abby's strangled cry jerked him to his feet.

"What?"

Abby was turned around in the saddle, staring behind her. "Catesby!" she whimpered.

The boy bounded up the bank into a party of Lakota warriors. The two nearest ones—chiefs, he supposed—were smiling. Not good smiles.

"It's all right, Abby," Catesby managed. "They won't hurt us."

The younger chief said something to the older one who slapped his knee and laughed.

They weren't the indians he'd seen in the shantytown outside Bozeman. They weren't the drunk indians weaving and shouting down Main Street Sunday morning when the Gatewoods came into town for church.

Wolves aren't dogs.

Their clothing had seen hard use. Fox pelts in the young chief's head-dress had been taken years before and his moccasins were patched.

Bows and quivers were strapped to their backs. Some had pistols. The chiefs carried repeating rifles.

The older chief was shirtless and his chest was quartered in red and blue paint.

Catesby swallowed. "I am Catesby Gatewood. This is my sister, Abigail Gatewood. A hundred men will come at my shout."

The younger chief said something in Lakota and the older chief explained, "White Bull says, 'If a hundred men will come, perhaps we should kill you before you can shout.' "

White Bull thought that was funny.

"Who are you?"

"I am Inkpaduta. Scourge of the Washitu. This is White Bull, the Santee who took a Seizer's knife from his hand and made the Seizer cry."

"You're not from Bozeman," Catesby said, knowing it was stupid as soon as he spoke.

" 'Bozeman'? What is 'Bozeman'? We have come from the Grand-mother's land to join the Lakota on the Rosebud. That will be something to remember."

The other indians brushed by Catesby and spread out along the creek to water their horses.

Inkpaduta turned to White Bull. "Young Man Afraid of His Horses took a white beaver in this creek. The Washitu have killed all the beaver. I cannot remember when I took a good beaver pelt."

Horses lapped cold water. Some of the indian riders stretched. One turned to another and said something. The other shrugged.

Catesby's throat was so dry he was afraid he'd squeak. "The army is coming. They will make you go to the agencies."

Inkpaduta raised his eyebrows. "Make us?" He laughed as if that were the funniest thing he'd ever heard. "There will be good hunting on the Yellowstone. Perhaps the Seizers will come. Perhaps we will hunt together."

White Bull started his horse down the bank. The horse's tail swished and the manurey tip slapped Catesby's shirt.

He would have no better chance. As if annoyed at the swipe, he pivoted, bent for a cottonwood limb, and jabbed the ragged bat into Inkpaduta's pony's testicles. Squealing, the pony reared onto its hind legs as Catesby jerked Gitalong's head around, tossed her reins to Abby, and cried, "Meadowbrook! Ride like the devil!"

Gitalong lunged into a gallop and Inkpaduta's rearing, dancing horse blocked pursuit. The indians laughed while Inkpaduta subdued his snorting beast. White Bull said something mocking. Cursing. Inkpaduta dropped to the ground and drew his scalping knife. "I am Inkpaduta," he said. "I have counted many coups."

Catesby was too scared to be scared. "My coup on your horse—does that count?"

White Bull snorted. An indian laughed: a high-pitched whinny. Catesby had that length of lightning-hardened cottonwood and maybe he could get in a lick before Inkpaduta killed him. Catesby set the limb on his shoulder like a baseball bat and he remembered something Joe Lame Deer had told him. "Hoka hey," young Catesby Byrd said.

An arm, strong as an iron band, snaked around his chest. He was jerked off his feet. "Wait," a voice commanded.

Inkpaduta crouched for his lunge.

"One step closer, and by God, I'll knock your head to Virginia City," Catesby yelled.

The man holding him said, "Inkpaduta, wouldn't you be proud to have a son like this? Hoka hey! Hoka hey! He has saved his sister and his horse and he has counted coup on a great warrior. Inkpaduta, killing this boy will bring no honor."

Sweat beaded Inkpaduta's forehead. After indecision, he sheathed his knife, wordlessly mounted his pony, and kicked it. Hard. He galloped east toward the rivers: the Yellowstone, the Missouri, the Rosebud, the Tongue, and the Little Bighorn.

White Bull dropped Catesby onto his feet. When White Bull said, "Put away your stick," Catesby dropped it. It was just a stick.

The other indians lost interest, finished watering, and rode after Inkpaduta.

White Bull would have been a handsome man except for his jagged, frightening scar. He jabbed his finger at Catesby. "Tell your father what has happened here. Tell him a Santee Lakota warrior, White Bull, spared his son's life. 'Hoka Hey,' eh, Washitu? That is truth. Today is a good day to die. But there will be better days ahead of you." Swiftly, he was gone.

Catesby felt a sudden chill, as if a cloud had covered the sun. The hairs stood up on his goose-pimpled arms.

He watched the warriors until they disappeared over a ridge below the snowcapped mountains that once belonged to them. He half hoped they'd turn and wave, at least that White Bull would wave, but they didn't.

CHAPTER 57

LETTER FROM RANDOLPH HOWLAND
TO MRS. EBEN BARNWELL

NEW BEDFORD, MASSACHUSETTS
JUNE 24, 1876

Dear Pauline,

Thank you for your letter. The letters accompanying your repayments of my little loan have been more welcome interest than I could earn at any savings bank! How I'd like to serve you again at table six. How I miss your enlightening conversations!

In my years at Del's, I've never looked for a face so much as I looked for yours.

I am glad little Augie is doing better in Richmond than he did at your family plantation. Augustus Barnwell is a city boy like me!

I have sad news to report. Mother passed away quietly in her sleep Friday last. She had accepted her fate and was glad to join her husband in the realm of peace and joy. Mrs. Jacob Howland was buried this morning in the family plot amidst grand tombs and headstones incised with sea captains' names and depictions of their vessels. Though the occasion was solemn, I was reunited with kinfolk I had not seen in years. All the grandest Howlands know Delmonico's!

Mr. Barnwell has not returned to the city. Rumors persist that he is in Pittsburgh. Without mentioning you or Mr. Barnwell by

name, I have taken the liberty of inquiring about your circumstances with acquaintances in the New York legal profession. They
are unanimous in their opinion that Mr. Barnwell's desertion is
adequate grounds for divorce.

Dear Pauline, "divorce" is an ugly word, but in a case like yours . . .
Perhaps I say too much.

Last fall, Temperance advocates persuaded the city to make a
law that "spiritous liquors cannot be sold on the Sabbath." These
sincere people have confused morality with the wine our Savior
took—without ill effect—on the night he was betrayed. The law was
widely disregarded until, following Temperance complaints, one
memorable Sabbath the city police pounced on five hundred establishments, small and great. They dared to arrest Mr. Charles
Delmonico.

Mr. Delmonico's outraged employees elected me to deliver our
message of support. I believe our unqualified devotion helped Mr.
Delmonico through some difficult days.

Nothing came of it. Mr. Delmonico was released on one hundred
dollars' bond and every Manhattan establishment resumed serving
wine and liquor as before. But my employer was more shaken by the
experience than he publicly allowed and last Thursday he summoned me into his office.

Mr. Delmonico asked if I knew Richmond, Virginia.

I confessed I did not, but I did have friends there.

Mr. Delmonico was gratified I had connections in a city he has
always associated with Southern grace and charm. He is considering opening a restaurant in Richmond.

Consequently, two weeks hence I will travel to Richmond to
determine whether Delmonico's could succeed there.

I will be in your city at least a fortnight and would like it so
much, dear Pauline, if I might call on you.

> I will always be your friend,
> Randolph Howland

CHAPTER 58

—

ORDERS TO GENERAL GEORGE CUSTER, JUNE 22, 1876

The Brigadier General commanding directs that as soon as your regiment can be made ready for the march, you proceed up the Rosebud in pursuit of the indians whose trail was discovered by Major Reno a few days ago. It is, of course, impossible to give you any definite instructions in regard to this movement, and were it not impossible to do so, the Department commander places too much confidence in your zeal, energy and ability to wish to impose upon you precise orders which might hamper your action when nearly in contact with the enemy. He will, however, indicate to you his own views of what your action should be, and he desires that you should conform to them unless you shall see sufficient reason for departing from them. He thinks that you should proceed up the Rosebud until you ascertain definitely the direction in which the trail above spoken of leads. Should it be found, as it appears to be almost certain that it will be found, to turn toward the Little Big Horn he thinks that you should still proceed southward, perhaps as far as the headwaters of the Tongue, and then turn toward the Little Big Horn, feeling constantly however, to your left so as to preclude the possibility of the escape of the indians to the south or southeast by passing around your left flank.

(Signed) Gen. Alfred Terry, Commanding

CHAPTER 59

—

KILL SONGS

WAVING A TELEGRAM, MARK KELLOGG PUSHED INTO THE
sutler's tent. "At last! The man of the hour is coming! Our purgatory
is ended."

"Hurrah for Yellow Hair," Bill Shillaber wiped beer foam from his
upper lip. "Bloody Knife told me last night."

"How the dickens . . . ?"

Shillaber shrugged. "Indians know things. Bloody Knife's already sent
his wife and young'uns back to the Agency."

The unusual bustle outside the tent confirmed Kellogg's news. After
months of inaction, this army was stirring into life.

"Well . . ." Kellogg eyed Shillaber's beer. "I say thank God. Thank God
for the man of the hour!"

The man of the hour's chief of scouts pointed to a stool and yelled for
the sutler, who was somewhere in the back of his double tent opening
whiskey cases. If Custer was returning to the regiment, maybe he'd bring a
paymaster. The men hadn't been paid in months. When the red-faced,
huffing sutler put his hands on the bar, Shillaber ordered beers for the
reporter and Top.

Outside, a sergeant was berating a hapless trooper. Shillaber grinned
at the imaginative ritualized profanity. "Army never changes, does it,
Top?"

Top cracked his knuckles. A circle of condensation leached onto the counter from his untouched beer glass.

The three men were alone in the tent outside Fort Abraham Lincoln, Bismarck, Dakota Territory, which, three years after the Yellowstone survey, was still the Northern Pacific end of track.

"Top?" Kellogg knitted his brow. He cleared his throat. "When I lost my dear wife, I think I . . . I died a little too . . . I was a . . . a different . . ." He coughed apologetically. "A *better* man before Martha passed away."

Top's dress cavalry uniform bore no insignia. His pants were pressed into knife creases, his boots were polished to a mirror finish, and his jacket was buttoned at the throat. "I'm not the man you are," he replied.

Kellogg looked away and drained half his beer. He set his lips like he was going to whistle. He belched. "'Scuse," he said. "Shillaber, will I go with the expedition?"

"Don't fret, son. Yellow Hair needs a reporter who thinks he's, what did you call him: 'The Man of the Hour'?" Shillaber drained his beer. Top didn't look up when Shillaber appropriated his glass. "For Christ's sake, Top," Shillaber said.

When Top raised his red-rimmed eyes, Shillaber winced. "Okay, Top," he said. "Have it your way."

The expedition—the Seventh Cavalry, two companies of the Second Cavalry, and the Sixth, Seventh, Seventeenth and Twentieth infantry—was supposed to march against the Lakota in April, but its commander had made an error in judgment; maybe several errors. George and Mrs. Custer had enjoyed their lengthy leave in Manhattan, where they'd been feted by prominent men who were no cleverer or more perspicacious than George Custer. They had made fortunes; why shouldn't he? General Custer lent his name to a noxious financial scheme, and after it failed, George Armstrong Custer was forced to sign a note for eighty-five hundred dollars, which was a large lien against his army pay. Consequently, he was overjoyed when the Redpath Agency asked him to deliver a lecture series. Five nights a week for four or five months at two hundred dollars a night.

But Secretary of War Belknap said Custer'd already had five months' leave and refused to extend it.

So Custer headed to Dakota Territory to ready his expedition. When a blizzard blocked the track, the Northern Pacific laid on a special train for him: three engines, two snowplows, and forty men to buck the drifts.

Not three weeks after Belknap refused Custer's perfectly reasonable (and, to Custer's mind, necessary) request, the Secretary of War was arrested for taking bribes.

Whoopee. George Custer wrote the congressional committee offering to testify against Belknap.

Okay, they said. Come now.

I didn't mean right now, Custer said. I'm going to lead a campaign against the Sioux. Maybe later.

Now, they said.

So George Armstrong Custer returned to Washington.

The national hero—the *Democratic* national hero—testified before a Democratic committee and probably Custer expected it would be all right to repeat old rumors, make baseless allegations, and implicate President Grant's brother in Belknap's misdeeds.

Sheridan and Sherman were quick to disown their favorite. President Grant removed Custer from command and refused to see him or hear his increasingly abject apologies.

So Custer talked to a sympathetic New York reporter. The headline was: "Grant's Revenge."

Naturally, Grant was livid.

Custer begged General Terry to intercede for him and that kindly officer, the only Union Civil War general who hadn't attended West Point, begged Grant to let Custer come on the expedition, if not in overall command, then in command of his own regiment.

Grudgingly, Grant agreed. Sherman warned his subordinate: no more reporters.

The whirlwind himself descended on Fort Abraham Lincoln. Officers yelled orders to grunting privates loading tons of stores into a hundred fifty wagons. Although the army had been waiting for months, much hadn't been done that now couldn't be. They hadn't time for rifle practice, nor to reshoe the horses, and they couldn't spare time to teach the troopers how to pack the mules. Some officers didn't think they'd need the mules anyway.

Their Commander electrified his officers, his troopers, even his indian scouts. The Commander's youngest brother, Boston, had come west for his health and begged to join the expedition. Seventeen-year-old Autie Reed, the Commander's sister's son, wanted to go too. Why should the boys miss the fun? Although his wife couldn't accompany them, General Custer promised she could come out on the supply steamer after he'd captured Sitting Bull and Crazy Horse.

General Crook would attack the Lakota from the south, General Gibbon from the north, and the Crows, the Lakota's traditional enemies, blocked their escape to the west. Together, they were the anvil. Custer, coming from the east, was the hammer.

A scant one hundred years after the United States of America declared its independence from Great Britain, the last of its free indigenous peoples were to be rounded up so their lands could be crossed by railroads and parceled out among God-fearing whites.

Shillaber warned Custer that the indians wouldn't run; this time they'd fight. Um-hmm, he said.

A rare meteorological phenomenon attended the Seventh's departure that chilly May morning, and afterward some believed it had been an omen. The image of the horsemen, gun limbers, and supply wagons appeared, mirrored on the clouds high above the earthbound column.

It would be years before the Washitu learned about Sitting Bull's dream and could compare the two portents.

ALTHOUGH THE COLUMN followed General Stanley's route, it was delayed by an unseasonable blizzard and didn't reach the Yellowstone River until June seventh, where the *Far West* was waiting to take General Terry upriver for a confab with General Gibbon.

Gibbon told Terry his Crow scouts had located a tremendous Lakota village—as many as fifteen hundred lodges—on upper Rosebud Creek.

AT THEIR CAMPFIRE that night, Shillaber passed Kellogg his flask and yawned. "Custer's famous luck! He's lucky Grant didn't ask for his resignation."

Top sat in the shadows, his face a mask.

Kellogg said, "Grant hates him because Custer's a Democrat."

Shillaber snorted. "Son, here's a rule for you: serving officers don't call the President's brother a thief."

Kellogg's mind was on a higher plane. "Wouldn't Custer make a fine candidate? For President, I mean."

"'Spect he's considered it." Shillaber yawned.

"You think we'll surprise 'em? The indians, I mean."

Shillaber scratched his nose. "Hell, yes! Oh, hell, yes! This expedition's been in every newspaper for months, but, son, you know: indians can't read." He shook his head. "If Custer doesn't pull this off, he's washed up. You got to think how he's thinkin', son. The Centennial Exposition is going great guns, the Democrats are choosing their presidential candidate, and the Boy General is on the Yellowstone with a crack regiment looking for Sitting Bull. What do you think he'll do, Top? Use that nigger juju. What do you *prognosticate*?"

Top stared through the dancing flames. "Somebody's gonna get killed."

"You got that right," the chief of scouts agreed.

At the Tongue River, I fell in with Laughing Bear, a Cheyenne I'd known at Fort Smith, and Laughing Bear's silly wife Grasshopper. That night in Laughing Bear's lodge Tazoo tended Grasshopper's baby as if it were her own.

We crossed more lodge trails and Laughing Bear said many Cheyenne and Sioux had quit the Agency, that all the young warriors had left.

Some Hunkpapas caught up with us and when we said we were going to Sitting Bull's village they joked that they would ride along to "protect us from the Crows."

With so many Lakota and Cheyenne on the move, there was no danger from Crows.

The young Hunkpapa boasted of the coups they would count and the brave deeds they would do and sometimes one would look at another, just a glance, and, yelling as young men will, they'd race their ponies pell-mell despite the prairie dog holes and the gullies that opened suddenly under their pounding hooves.

On Rosebud Creek we turned south, climbing toward the divide. At a bend where the creek was shallow and wide, we entered a broad meadow whose grass had been grazed to the roots by thousands of ponies. One old man was sitting beneath the Sun Dance. I knew him, although I hadn't seen him in many years. When I lived with the Santee in Minnesota, Inkpaduta had led the uprising for which my father, Red Leaf, had been hung.

Inkpaduta was rail-thin and only his smile was young. "It is good to see my Santee sister."

"I am—"

"You are She Goes Before. Yes. Your father Red Leaf killed trader Myrick and stuffed grass in his mouth. What a fine joke!"

After all these years Red Leaf's lie had become the truth because he had died for it.

The Sun Dance pole stood in a circle of buffalo skulls whose hollow eye sockets faced the sunrise. A tangle of leather lines dropped from the crown. Hardened and darkened by dried blood, the leather tips rattled when the wind shook them.

"I hope the Seizers come." Inkpaduta's eyes glittered. "I have been waiting a long time."

This dusty meadow beside a shallow creek was sacred to the Lakota. The bravest warriors had cut this tall pine and borne it here while young women who had never lain with a man sang its passage.

The next morning, before the sun was a hot sliver on the horizon, the dancers inserted its thongs under the flesh of their arms or legs and danced as the sun rose higher in the sky; pulling against the lines until they ripped the thongs through their flesh.

Older or weaker men inserted a single thong under thin skin which would tear easily.

Sitting Bull had asked Inkpaduta to insert two thongs under the thick muscles of his back.

"It is too much," Inkpaduta told him. "You will faint before you pull them out."

"The sun is rising," Sitting Bull had said. He bent so Inkpaduta could slit his back and push thongs underneath the muscles.

Inkpaduta closed his eyes now, remembering. "He danced all morning. The sun wasn't so hot at first but became hot later. Everyone was sweating and chanting with the dancers. Unseen, our medicine animals circled the pole. The sun was nearly gone when Sitting Bull pulled a thong out. Hearing the awful sound it made, we groaned with him. He reeled and would have fallen, but the second thong held him upright. He shouted a great shout and lunged and we saw the tent raised on the muscles of his bloody back and the white wooden thong as it emerged. He fainted then and we carried him to his lodge, where his wives washed his wounds."

Inkpaduta's face reminded me of vultures descending onto a carcass: that same rapt concentration.

Why had I come here? What had I hoped to find? Did I wish that one day my beloved Tazoo would see her husband agonize below the Sun Dance pole? Would I wish to see Plenty Cuts hanging from these lines?

"That night, Sitting Bull dreamed for the Lakota," Inkpaduta continued.

Dizzy and ill, I sat on a buffalo skull. The sun scorched this dusty meadow. The grumbling drums, the chanting, the shuffle of dancers' feet, the shrill eagle-bone whistles. That liquid thuck as a thong ripped free. "What was it . . . ?" I licked my lips. "What was Sitting Bull's dream?"

"Seizers, hundreds of blue-coated Seizers, falling out of the sky into our village."

I was too weary to go on. Inkpaduta and the Hunkpapa left, but Laughing Bear and his family stayed with me. That evening, when Grasshopper brought food, she reminded me I had bought her aunt's lodge at Fort C. F. Smith many winters ago.

"Your husband, Plenty Cuts?" she asked.

"Plenty Cuts is dead," I told her.

That night I slept under a buffalo robe with Tazoo snoring and blowing wet bubbles against my cheek. The stars arced from here to there. They were beautiful as icicles are beautiful.

The next morning on the divide, we rode past the ancient lookout everyone called the "Crows Nest" and descended into the broad valley of the Greasy Grass.

ALTHOUGH HE WOKE before reveille, Top kept his eyes shut, clinging to his dream. In his dream, he'd been running away. It was the first time he'd run from Master, a boy of fourteen running down the road in the early morning, heading he had no notion where. Away; he was running away. To some promised land. Or where a promised land would arise. He ran so fast no man could catch him, a fleet negro boy running down a country road through the dewy Virginia morning; taking his life in his hands.

When he crested the rise, he saw the patrollers but didn't believe in them. He ran straight at the mounted white men as if they weren't there, and they were astonished and he passed between them and down the road with nothing in front of him but air and freedom and the rattle of galloping hooves behind. In his dream the patrollers never caught him.

"Damn hincty nigger," Top grunted as he rolled out of his blankets.

Campfires were kicked into life. That thud, thud, thud was a trooper crushing beans with the butt of his revolver. A trooper cried, "Christ, Goldin, look where you're pissing. That's my damn haversack!"

Dark shapes interrupted the firelight when the horse guards came in.

A single star hung in the western sky. The half moon had set hours ago. They'd be in the saddle by sunrise.

Top had folded his pants and coat beneath his ground cloth. When he pulled them on, his pants were clammy but pressed. His boots had been his pillow. He rubbed them with his coat sleeve before he put his feet in them. He stood and stretched.

Some officers wore buckskins and civilian blue shirts, some soldiers preferred brown shirts to the issue gray pullover. Slouch hats were popular. Top smacked his forage cap against his pant leg before setting it at a proper military angle.

Top hadn't made friends. Some muttered he was a "garrison soldier." Top didn't care what they said so long as they didn't say it to his face.

Shillaber and Kellogg had stayed with General Terry and the main force while Top went as Major Reno's scout. "Where is the big village?" That was all Reno wanted to know.

Reno scouted from the Yellowstone to the Tongue but hadn't found any Lakota—just three burial lodges, which the soldiers looted before the Ariska scouts burned them.

Wordless soldiers made room for Top at the cookfire. Top dropped his chunk of salt pork into the communal pot and while it changed from gray to furry gray with dark stripes, he continued the interior monologue that cluttered his waking mind. His remonstrance to She Goes Before reused the same words, over and over until he was sick of his mind: "What can I do? What *else* can I do?" (He'd emphasized "else" when he'd explained his decision to go with Yellow Hair again, and that "else" was fixed in place, as if "else," the word, had forced his choice.) "Me? Live at the Agency? A God Damned blanket indian? Maybe I should have let you and Tazoo starve? Can you eat buffalo bones? What *else* could I do? In my entire misbegotten life the only home I ever had was the army. Course I'll miss you and Tazoo. I'll ache missing you. I won't fight the Lakota. I promised I wouldn't. What *else* can I do? I been a damned slave. I been bought and sold. Bein' a slave was better than this godforsaken Agency . . ."

"'Scuse," Top said, reaching past a corporal to spear his breakfast with knifepoint.

The eastern sky turned gray. Sunrise came early this time of the year.

When the bugle sounded "Officers' Call," Top buttoned his collar and joined others at Major Reno's tent. There was something *odd* about the plump, vague Reno, and his junior officers were just this side of openly contemptuous.

Major Reno announced today's line of march: to the Rosebud, then back to the Yellowstone to rendezvous with General Terry.

Captain Keogh asked for more detail—as he always did—and irritation flared behind Reno's eyes. "Are you *slow* this morning, Captain? Are you stupid?"

Keogh grinned at his superior. "Yes, sir. Us Irish boyos ain't noted for intellect."

"Just follow orders."

Officers looked away. Someone cleared his throat.

"Strike my tent. Bugler, sound 'Boots and Saddles.' "

Major Reno, his staff, interpreter, and scouts rode silently at the head of the column.

The same land Plenty Cuts had once hunted, that Eden teeming with game and sparkling rivers, was altered. Its ridges were too bare or too wooded, too rocky or too steep; its creeks were muddy or alkaline and the gullies interrupting the landscape might conceal hundreds of hostile warriors.

When they struck the Rosebud, a little after eleven, they found what they were looking for. A disbelieving Top got off his horse.

It was June in the shadow of the Bighorns and the prairie was blooming. Bunchgrass, wheatgrass, and false oats waved feathery seed heads, wildflowers colonized every gap between them.

They'd struck a dark, broad scar—a gouge in the earth. In a three-hundred-yard swath, the earth was as bare as if teams had harrowed it.

The back of Top's neck prickled. Eyes shaded, Major Reno stood in his stirrups, peering around. "Top?"

"'Spect this is the village," Top said, more easily than he felt. He walked onto the tremendous lodge trail, stepping around pony and dog droppings, trying to estimate from the scars how many lodgepoles had scored this riverbank.

The lodge trail proceeded upstream and disappeared around a bend. Reno asked, "Top?"

He stooped for a discarded child's bow. "Blackfoot," he sang out. He turned over a worn-out moccasin with his foot. "Sans Arc."

Captain Keogh asked, "We goin' after 'em, Major?"

Major Reno shook his head as if it had come unbolted. "We are on a scout, Captain. A scout. Those are my orders."

Top knelt beside a broken papoose board, tracing decorative paint with his fingertip.

Captain Keogh picked his way through the pony droppings to the interpreter's side. "Sans Arc?"

Top shook his head. "Santee. We used to have one like it . . ."

Straightening, he kicked the discarded papoose board.

"I don't believe I've ever seen anything like this," Captain Keogh said. "Must be a couple thousand lodges."

"That's what I'd guess," Top said.

"Do Blackfeet, Sans Arc, and Santee travel together?"

"Nope." Top rubbed his hands. He stuck them into his armpits as if they were cold. He glanced upstream where the trail vanished. He said, "Christ."

Major Reno was already turning his horse's head toward the Yellowstone. He said, "The pack mules are worn out." He said, "We're only a scout."

MAJOR MARCUS RENO was the Seventh's second in command. Next in line was Captain Frederick Benteen, a hearty, angry officer who thought Custer was a fraud—and said so. Captain Keogh had served in the Papal Guard before immigrating to America. Some of Custer's officers, like Captain Yates of the Gray Horse Troop, were martinets; Smith and Keogh were liked by their men. Tom Custer and Lieutenant Calhoun, the

Commander's brother-in-law, were the worst poker players. Lieutenant John Crittenden was an infantry officer detailed to the Seventh Cavalry at his own request. All but the youngest, Lieutenant Jack Sturgis, had seen action in the War.

West Point had trained these officers for Napoleonic conflicts: eighty, a hundred thousand men fighting standup at musket range. The Lakota hadn't studied the same texts. They didn't like casualties and if they lost the element of surprise or lacked overwhelming superiority, they melted away. Indians were notoriously hard to catch. Their ponies could outlast cavalry horses and a fleeing village would divide and subdivide until the pursuing cavalry regiment was chasing one family's lodge.

General Sherman, who'd perfected civilian warfare in Georgia and South Carolina, brought his expertise into play: hit the indians in their winter camps when they couldn't maneuver. Warriors and whoever got in the way could be killed and their food, clothing, goods, and homes destroyed. At the Washita fight that made Custer's reputation as an indian fighter, after the warriors had been driven off, troopers wagered who could kill the most indian ponies. When ammunition ran low, the troopers cut the ponys' throats.

Sherman's strategy guided the thinking aboard the *Far West* that evening of June 21, 1876, when General Terry, General Custer, and General Gibbon made final plans. Although Shillaber had warned that the indians were numerous, confident, and angry, these officers intended to attack their village, shoot every man, woman, and child who resisted or tried to escape, destroy their means of survival on the plains, and escort the survivors across the Dakotas to the agencies.

They hadn't heard a word from General Crook, coming up from the south, and wanted to beat Crook to the punch.

Late that same evening, Major Brisbin of the Second Cavalry came aboard for a private word with General Terry. Brisbin believed four companies of the Second Cavalry should accompany the Seventh, with General Terry in command. Terry asked if Brisbin had confidence in Custer. "None at all," the major replied. "I have no use for him."

General Terry wanted to give Custer a chance to redeem himself with

President Grant, but if Brisbin could convince Custer to accept the extra troopers, why, yes, Terry would command.

When Brisbin made his offer, Custer replied tersely, "The Seventh can handle anything it meets."

At dawn on the twenty-second of June, Myles Keogh and Tom Custer stumbled off the *Far West*, hungover and broke from a night of the worst poker hands either could remember.

THAT MORNING, Kellogg wrote:

> *And now a word for the Most Peculiar Genius in the Army, a man of strong impulses, of great-hearted friendships and bitter enmities, of quick nervous temperament, undaunted courage, will, and determination; a man possessing electric mental capacity and of iron constitution; a brave, faithful, gallant soldier, who has warm friends and bitter enemies; the hardest rider, the greatest pusher, with the most untiring vigilance, overcoming seeming impossibilities and with an ambition to succeed in all things he undertakes; a man to do right, as he construes the right in every case; one respected and beloved by his followers, who would freely follow him into the "jaws of hell." Of General G. A. Custer I am now writing. . . .*

WITH THE REPORTER nattering in his ear, Ben Shillaber watched Custer's troopers loading pack mules. These troopers hadn't been taught mule skinner's skills and the mules were outraged at this fresh test of their patience. Overloaded packs obeyed inexorable laws of gravity and slid underneath braying animals' bellies. A poorly balanced pack clung to a mule's side like a giant carbuncle while one cursing trooper tried to heave it upright and another clung to the animal's halter and kicked at its head. Kellogg said, "Isn't this truly grand, sir? Isn't this the grandest sight you've ever seen?"

"No," Shillaber said

"Isn't this a splendid time to be alive? Do you hope to visit the Centennial? They say half the country will see it. After we defeat the Sioux . . . This is my big chance, you know. The *New York World* is taking my articles. After we're back in civilization, I'm going to take my daughters to the Centennial. I'm afraid I . . .well, I haven't been the father I might have been."

Shillaber said, "Did I hear right? Custer's letting Autie and Boston ride with us?"

"You know what Autie Reed told Major Brisbin? 'Major,' the boy said, 'you're just jealous you can't go.' Wouldn't it be splendid to be seventeen years old commencing this adventure?"

After a while the reporter went away.

Top had promised She Goes Before he wouldn't fight the Lakota. What was he doing at the sutler's buying cartridges for his Winchester?

"Get you a army carbine, Top," Ben said. "Quartermaster'll give you a hundred rounds free."

"They shoot too slow."

"Thought you weren't going to shoot at all."

"Uh." Though most troopers wore comfortable homemade canvas cartridge belts, Top stuffed his cartridges into the clumsy regulation leather box.

"You get your rations?"

"Six days' corn for my horse, all the Cincinnati Chicken [salt pork] I can carry."

"Thank God the army's feeding Kellogg. That boy's got a hollow leg."

Top shut his cartridge box. "You want somethin', Ben? Or you just jawin'?"

"You don't have to go. Stay with Terry. He'll need an interpreter more than Yellow Hair will."

"Ben . . ."

Shillaber sighed. After a while he said, "I was with Johnson's army when he finally surrendered. My horse was so poorly I abandoned him and walked three weeks and two days to the Low Country. My house was burned to the ground. They'd killed every animal on the place, even my hunting dogs. My dikes were breached and my rice fields filled with salt water. My wife, she—"

"Ben," Top said softly, "knowin' about your troubles won't cure mine."

Ben Shillaber set his lips in a soundless whistle. After a moment he said, "Okay, Top. Can't say I like tellin' them anyway."

Three hours later the inexperienced mule skinners finally had their mules more or less packed. Everybody else mounted and fell in behind their company guidons.

Shoved by a cold wind, dark clouds scudded across the sky.

General Terry, General Gibbon, and their officers waited atop a cutbank for the Seventh to pass in review. Ignored by the officers, Mark Kellogg was scribbling furiously.

In white buckskins and new slouch hat, George Armstrong Custer galloped up and threw his commanding general an extravagant salute. His battle horse Vic had been brushed until Vic's sorrel coat gleamed. As Custer was shaking hands with the reviewing party, the Seventh's buglers were sounding "Boots and Saddles."

Led by indian scouts, the regiment passed in a column of fours behind their guidons: Keogh's I Company, Yates's F, and Calhoun's E dipped their banners. Protesting pack mules hee-hawed.

Kellogg's pencil raced down a page which almost got away from him when he turned it sideways to write across. He was whispering to himself. He had tears in his eyes.

After his regiment was out of sight, George Custer shook hands and saluted Terry again. Custer's grin split his face from ear to ear.

As the Commander galloped after his regiment, General Terry called, "Now, George. Don't be greedy. Wait for us."

Was it some trick of the wind, or did Custer cry, "No! I won't!"?

I had not dreamed there were so many Lakota in the world. Grasshopper ceased chattering as we rode down that wide valley past uncountable pony herds. The sun was low, and blue shadows fingered from the bluffs to dim the sparkling river. The Little Bighorn looped through the valley like a discarded lace. I sneezed from the campfire smoke. Some lodges were tucked into the timber beside the river, but six great villages stood in the open valley between the river and the pony herds. I sneezed again.

We rode through Sitting Bull's Hunkpapa: hundreds of lodges guarded the east entrance of the village. One of the young men we'd traveled with called that we should come to his lodge and eat, but I was eager to find my brother. We rode through Blackfeet and Sans Arc before splashing across a small creek into the Minnecon-jou camp. Smoke, pony droppings, dogs yapping, children's shouts, so much singing and drumming. It might have been a Washitu city, it was so noisy and smelled so bad. After passing through the Brulés, I was among familiar Oglala lodges greeting old friends as my sorrows lifted off my shoulders.

As befitted a Shirt Wearer, White Bull's lodge was at the mouth of the village where the Oglala joined the Cheyenne.

His lodge was familiar and comforting. Smoke trickled from the smoke flap. Painted buffalo skins glowed from the firelight within. As I said goodbye to my Cheyenne friends, Tazoo couldn't keep still. Her sharp eyes flashed. I whispered a prayer to Low Dog and JesuChrist that Tazoo would grow up Santee.

I hobbled my horse behind the lodge but hesitated at the entrance because my husband was with Yellow Hair. Those words choked me as if someone had me by the throat. "White Bull," I called, "it is I, your sister."

Rattling Blanket Woman jerked the flap aside and rushed out to embrace me. She stroked my hair as if I were a lost child. "Tazoo, Tazoo! Sister, she is so beautiful. I had forgotten how dark she is!" When she pinched Tazoo's cheek, my daughter did not flinch.

"I have come because—"

"Oh, I am so glad our family is together! Your brother and I missed you so."

Rattling Blanket Woman was dressed like a bride. Blue and black beads swirled across her bodice and her braids were fastened with a trader's amber comb. "But come in, come in. White Bull is preparing for the dance."

Before a mirror dangling from a lodgepole my brother was paint-ing his cheeks with horizontal red and green stripes. Like Rattling Blanket Woman, he wore his finest clothing: his fringed leggings, shell necklaces, and foxskin cap. Without pausing his application or look-ing at me, he said, "I welcome you, Sister. Please sit and have some-thing to eat."

A pot was steaming on the back of the fire. Tazoo lifted the lid.

I hissed at her bad manners.

"She is Santee." Rattling Blanket Woman approved of my child's boldness. "The young men will be drawn to her like bees to spilled honey."

Hesitantly, I asked if White Bull was preparing for war.

"Oh, no, no. My husband has been to war." Proudly she pointed to the fresh scalp on a hoop. "Shoshone."

That scalp would add another brave warrior's strength to my brother's own.

"White Bull took a Seizer scalp too, but the Seizer was running away." She sniffed. "There is no honor in Seizer hair. I threw it to the dogs."

Rattling Blanket Woman had crimsoned her cheeks. Her dark eyes glittered.

As my brother made ready, the drums grew more insistent and women began chanting.

Sitting Bull had dreamed of Seizers falling into the camp. He said the Seizers would be killed but the people were not to loot their bodies. Two days later, scouts found General Crook approaching the camp. Crazy Horse and my brother drove General Crook away. Many Lakota had died in that fight, but many had won honors. The people had mourned for three days, but the mourning was over and grum-bling drums anounced the victory dance.

My brother turned from his mirror and embraced me carefully so I wouldn't smear his paint. "Ah, Sister. Tazoo, you have grown so big. Soon you will be as tall as my war pony."

Tazoo hid her face in her hands.

White Bull met my eyes directly. "Plenty Cuts was a brave Lakota warrior. I mourn my friend." That was what White Bull said about the man who had been my husband.

A burst of drumming pulled us outside. Many people were hurrying to a great bonfire roaring in the meadow. Already, young warriors were dancing around the fire. Since they had not taken wives yet, their fathers waved their scalp sticks and boasted of their sons' coups. Young women watched excitedly and from time to time a young warrior and a young woman would slip away together. When an older warrior danced, his wife shook her husband's scalp stick and sang his kill song. One after another, each warrior was honored, not just for defeating General Crook but for every one of his brave deeds.

A few renowned warriors watched without dancing. Crazy Horse's medicine paint was white hail spots on his chest and a lightning streak down his face. He wore a pebble behind his ear and a red-tailed hawk on his head. Though he had killed more Seizers than anyone, Crazy Horse let others take their scalps. All the young men wanted to follow him because he brought them honors. While we celebrated, Sitting Bull and Crazy Horse talked together.

My brother had many honors and I was proud when Rattling Blanket Woman recited them. I am White Bull's sister. My honor comes from the Shirt Wearer White Bull and my father Red Leaf, who killed the trader Myrick and stuffed grass into his mouth.

THEY MADE TWELVE MILES that first afternoon. Whenever a mule pack slipped, that mule was left behind with two troopers: one to repack it, the other to stand nervous guard. The regiment straggled into bivouac beside the Rosebud: a shallow alkaline stream the horses didn't like to drink.

As campfires flickered into life and soldiers scooped bitter water into their cook pots, the officers, chief of scouts, and interpreter waited outside the Commander's tent waving away smoke from a fire his orderly had built from green wood. Firelight, shadows, and smoke illuminated and obscured their faces.

The Commander had spewed energy like a lightning storm, sucking ordinary mortals into the rush of his passage. He had never, not in anyone's memory, consulted his officers.

Tonight an ordinary, slight, balding, sunburned man sat on a camp stool staring into the fire. He said, "I've always been fortunate with my officers. You've always done more than my bidding, more than I ever dared to hope. No one has ever had braver companions. Gentlemen, I am counting on you."

Captain Keogh shifted from one foot to the other. Captain Benteen may have sighed.

Henceforth the pack mules would travel at the rear. There'd be no more bugle calls. "I expect to meet fifteen hundred indians. If the Seventh can't whip them"—this slight man shrugged—"who can?"

He was silent for so long, Lieutenant Sturgis knelt and poked the fire into a sturdier blaze.

"Brisbin wanted to give me four more companies." The Commander chuckled. "Can you imagine the jealousies . . . ?"

"Jealousies": that word whirled away in the smoke.

He shrugged. "Four more companies wouldn't have made any difference anyway."

An officer coughed. Captain Benteen took a cigar from his case and inspected it thoughtfully.

When the Commander rose, he peered around brightly as a curious swallow. "We'll follow them wherever they go. All the way to Nebraska, if need be. By God, gentlemen, we may be eating horseflesh before this is over!"

When the wind shifted, he turned his back to the smoke. So softly they strained to hear, he said, "I'd appreciate any suggestions you gentlemen might have. Any suggestions at all."

After some time the officers understood he was finished and they dispersed. Captain Keogh crossed himself.

At three A.M., pickets shook sleepers awake and by daybreak the long column of men, horses, and mules were toiling up the Rosebud.

Just past noon, the lead scouts struck the tremendous lodge trail Reno had discovered.

The Commander told Shillaber Major Reno had missed his chance. Reno could have hit the Lakota village six days ago.

Shillaber said, "We're soldiers, sir. They're warriors. Let a warrior get close enough to grab hold of you, and he'll tear your arms off and beat you to death with them."

The Commander smiled distantly. "Like you rebels did?"

Tiny wild roses blossomed beside the sparkling bitter river.

The column halted three times to let the mule train catch up while the restless Commander rode ahead with Shillaber and the scouts. The regiment traveled more than thirty rough country miles that day and the last bands of a spectacular western sunset were fading when they called it quits. Their bivouac had been grazed bare by the indian ponies they were following. Some troopers gave their horses handfuls of dried corn, others jerked their saddles off and lay down to sleep. No fires. The night was lit by the brilliant arc of the Milky Way.

Kellogg whispered, "You asleep, Top?"

"Yes."

"You ever wonder if anyone lives up there, if there's other earths? Maybe they're lookin' down at us wonderin' like I'm wonderin'."

"This is Dakota, Kellogg. Dakota'll answer all your damn questions."

"I'll be so happy to see my daughters again."

"Shut up."

THE NEXT DAY they rode twenty-five miles. Fresher trails merged with and swelled the trail they were following. When they bivouacked that night the troopers didn't unpack the mules and most didn't feed or unsaddle their horses.

The tireless Shillaber and his indian scouts went on ahead.

Just before midnight Shillaber returned to wake the Commander. The indian trail crossed the divide into the valley of the Little Bighorn. The trail was fresh.

The Commander looked at Shillaber blank-eyed for a moment. "Very well," he said. "Wake my officers."

Officers rubbed their eyes and yawned as they got their orders. The regiment would be at the divide before dawn and attack the village in the morning. "Mr. Shillaber, you will ride ahead and find them. Questions, gentlemen?"

"How the hell . . ." Benteen shook his head and shut his mouth.

A thin slice of moon rose while troopers collected their horses and brand-new mule skinners untied hobbles. It was an hour before the column was moving again.

The trail climbed sharply, zigzagging across a narrow creek that tumbled from ledge to ledge. The troopers walked single file, leading their horses and mules. The lead horses' dust obliterated the scant moon and the trail under their feet. Troopers clung to the tail of the horse ahead. Others followed the *tink, tink tink* of noncoms banging tin cups against their saddle brass. When a trooper misstepped, he and his mount slid off the bank into the creek. Mules brayed. Men said, "God Damn it to hell!" and "Holy Mary, Mother of God."

Riding well ahead of the dust, the Commander asked Top, "You lived with them, didn't you?"

"Yes, sir."

"For God's sake, why?"

"My wife, she was a—"

The Commander's hand abruptly dismissed the subject. "No matter. That's your affair. You have seen lodge trails before. What is their strength?"

"Twenty, twenty-five hundred warriors. Maybe more."

When the Commander stopped, behind him Martino stopped too, as did the next man and the next, and curses rose from the dust cloud. "Two thousand? That's impossible. We haven't been following that many lodges."

"So. You reckon this is their only trail?"

The Commander grunted and spurred Vic up a stretch of gravelly scree. On the level again, he waited for Top to catch up "You have a soldier's bearing."

Top ran his tongue over his cracked lips. "Just another hincty nigger."

The Commander waited for more. Absent satisfaction, he resumed the climb. A sweat stripe divided the back of his buckskin shirt.

Daybreak found the regiment, after ten miles of stumbling progress, on a dusty plateau short of the summit. When the halt was finally called, nobody unsaddled and some didn't bother to loosen their girth straps. Those horses and mules led to the creek wouldn't drink from it.

Waiting with his scouts in an indian lookout on the summit, Shillaber watched the smoke rise from the regiment's cookfires. "Yellow Hair must think the Lakota are blind."

Bloody Knife grunted. "Deaf too."

The vista at their feet was partly timbered rocky slopes descending into a broad valley, perhaps thirty miles long. At the far end of the valley they could see something. Was it fog? Smoke?

At the base of the fog/smoke they thought they saw a faint shimmer, a shimmer like ten thousand maggots on a four-day-old corpse, a shimmer like maybe the biggest pony herd on earth.

Unlike the grown-ups, Tazoo hadn't danced half the night, so she was up early the next morning. She pulled on her dress and went outside, barefoot. Behind the lodge, she squatted to pee.

An old Big Belly hobbled down the street. When he felt Tazoo's eyes on him, he straightened and pretended he was still young. Tazoo giggled as she wiped herself with a handful of grass.

Ever since she could remember she'd lived at the Agency among indian children whose parents were scouts or interpreters for the Washitu. Yesterday evening, when Tazoo and her mother passed through the villages, Tazoo saw some indians she knew from the Agency, but they looked different here: as if they'd been sick but now they were well.

Tazoo did not make friends easily but thought that here, where there were so many girls her age, she might make friends.

Fires were smoldering outside the sweat lodges and glistening, naked men emerged from the low wickiups to dive into the chilly river.

Tazoo's mother was so sad. Tazoo did everything her mother asked and was as cheerful as a girl could be, but her mother's sorrow never lifted.

Others were stirring. Thick smoke exited smoke flaps and settled to the ground. Tazoo's eyes watered and she wiped her nose on her sleeve. She shaded her eyes against the rising sun. Joking hunters started for the pony herd to catch their mounts. Three women were stretching a blackhorn hide on a fletching frame. The youngest was big with child. She said, "Little girl, where is your lodge? Who is your mother?"

Tazoo pointed. The woman groaned and put her hand in the small of her back and bent backward and gave no more thought to Tazoo.

Two boys were playing a game with a basket hoop and rabbit arrows. One would roll the hoop while the other shot through it. An older boy addressed Tazoo. He said he was Bird in the Ground and Tazoo told him her name. Bird in the Ground was a Sans Arc. He told her the Sans Arc got their name many years ago when a powerful wican dreamed they could conquer the Rees if they left their bows behind. The Rees slaughtered them and that was how they got their name. Tazoo said she had never known a Sans Arc before. Bird in the Ground had known many Oglala.

"I am Santee," she corrected him sharply. "White Bull is my uncle."

When Tazoo's belly growled, she pretended she hadn't heard. When Bird in the Ground patted her stomach where it had growled, both children giggled.

When Tazoo returned to White Bull's lodge, he and Rattling Blanket Woman were still asleep, but her mother reached out to her and took her into her arms.

THE COMMANDER SAID, "I've got as good eyes as anyone and I don't see any village, indians, or anything else."

"Well, General," Shillaber said, "if you don't find more indians in that village than you ever saw together, you can hang me."

Snapping his spyglass closed, the Commander said, "It would do a damned sight of good to hang you, wouldn't it?"

By ten-thirty when Captain Benteen's lead company crossed the divide, the sun was well up. It was going to be a scorcher.

The scouts thought the Lakota must have spotted their smoke. A trooper who'd lost his coat backtracked their trail and found indians digging through a discarded pack.

The Commander said they would press on lest the main body escape.

Autie Reed and Boston Custer trotted past Top. Young Autie was wondering if the Commander might take them on his triumphal tour after he whipped the redskins.

"You bet, " the older youth assured him. "Who's gonna guard his prisoners? Sitting Bull and Crazy Horse are slicker'n grease. They'll want plenty of watching."

Top's gut was hollow as a drum. Why should he warn these boys? Who were they to him?

Unexpected relief, cool and blissful, washed over him and he straightened in his saddle. Maybe from here on out, old Top wouldn't give a good God Damn.

The Commander made swift depositions. Major Reno would command three companies, Captain MacDougall and one company would stay with the pack train. Captain Benteen would lead three companies to investigate the bluffs across the valley.

Five companies and most of the scouts would accompany the Commander. When Keogh asked Benteen where he was going, the burly captain shrugged. "I'm going to drive everything before me."

The sun was just past midway in the sky when our scouts galloped into the village. Village criers ran down the streets shouting, "Many Seizers are coming. They are not coming to talk. They are not carrying white flags. They are coming to attack us."

Tazoo and Rattling Blanket Woman were on the riverbank digging camas root.

When Rattling Blanket Woman heard the criers, she dropped her digging stick and the roots she had dug. Tazoo bent for them, but her hand was jerked and then she was running faster than she ever had in her life, her feet only sometimes touching the ground.

Some warriors ran for their war ponies, others for the council lodge. Warriors galloped down the street dismounting on the fly, tossing their reins to anyone while they armed themselves.

All was confusion. Nobody seemed to know where to go or what to do. Tazoo felt as if her arm were being pulled out of its socket. "Auntie, Auntie!" she sobbed.

Nobody was at White Bull's lodge. Rattling Blanket Woman let go of Tazoo's hand. As if sharing a secret, Rattling Blanket Woman whispered, "The Seizers are coming to kill us."

IT MIGHT HAVE been any hot, dirty afternoon. As they came off the divide, dust whitened their horses' manes and blackened the sweat streaks on the horses' necks, pasterns, and rumps. Weary men thought stupid thoughts.

Beside his chief of scouts and interpreter, the Commander led the straggling column. The mule train was miles behind.

They trotted down jack-pine lined slopes into a green valley beside a clear creek, but they didn't stop to water their horses. Thirsty troopers jerked their horses' bits savagely when they tried to drink.

Twelve miles on, they found a Lakota burial lodge, all buttoned up. When a trooper opened the flap, he backed out, gagging. "Jesus. Oh, Jesus!"

Holding his nose, Autie Reed darted inside for the dead man's beaded moccasins, but outside again he hurled the stinking things as far as he could. Tom Custer grinned at the red-faced youth. "Bet you thought indian fighting was glorious?"

The scouts were setting the lodge afire.

"Cooked his goose." Tom Custer laughed.

Just ahead, Shillaber was standing in his stirrups and waving his hat. He pointed at a retreating dust cloud: thirty indians, forty maybe.

"Decoys?" Top suggested.

"They'll warn the village," the Commander said.

The Seventh Cavalry broke into a gallop, Reno and his companies on one side of the brook, the Commander, his companies, and his family on the other.

Top's sweat-sticky leather saddle clung to his pants on the rise and slammed his spine on the fall.

Horses foundered. A corporal rode his collapsing steed to the ground, rolled free, and crawled around the animal, screaming at it.

The Commander's courier splashed across to Major Reno. "The indians are two and a half miles ahead. Follow them and we will support you."

While Reno's command charged down the valley, his indian scouts rode far ahead, hoping to steal a few ponies before the fighting began.

The Commander's detachment turned to the right and climbed the steep bluffs which overlooked the valley. It was a little after two in the afternoon, June the twenty-fifth, eighteen hundred and seventy-six.

I looked everywhere for Tazoo. Warriors, women, and children appeared and disappeared in the choking dust. Crying, "Hoka hey," warriors flung themselves onto their horses. I ran toward the firing. When wind dispersed the dust cloud, I saw three Ariskas—Seizer scouts—shooting into Chief Gall's lodge. Chief Gall's enraged roar was louder than their gunshots.

In a line Seizers rode down the valley toward our village. Their buttons flashed. Dust billowed from their horses' hooves. They were shooting as they rode.

Warriors came forth to meet them. All at once the Seizers stopped and dismounted, except two who couldn't hold their horses and galloped into the Hunkpapas. One passed by me. He had voided himself

in his fear and his stench lingered after hands pulled him from his
horse and ended his fear.

A boy ran from the pony herd toward us and bullets pocked all
around him as the Seizers tried to bring him down.

Eagle-bone war whistles trilled.

Where was my Tazoo? Where was Rattling Blanket Woman?

Chief Gall was so big his feet almost touched the ground under
his pony. The Seizers' scouts had killed his wife and two children
and his heart was bad. Gall led warriors around the dismounted
Seizers' flank.

In the Oglala village, Crazy Horse was painting a blood-purple
hand on his horse's left hip. After he prepared himself, Crazy Horse
would be ready to die.

The Seizers jumped back on their horses and fled into the timber.
Whipping his warriors with his quirt, Chief Gall tried to overtake
them. The Seizers stayed in the timber only a little while before they
fled again. The riverbank was high, but the Seizers jumped down the
bank anyway. Gall and his warriors pulled many Seizers off their
horses and killed them. The Seizers who escaped Gall scurried up the
bluffs on the far bank like frightened mice.

A Seizer's blue cap floated down the river and hung up on a snag.
A Brulé boy called Brown Leggings waded out for it.

A few minutes later, Brown Leggings's uncle brought a pony and
rifle for the boy. When the boy got on the pony, his mother grabbed his
arm and dragged him off. "You are too young to be a warrior," she
sobbed. "It is not your day to die."

THE COMMANDER'S STAFF paused on a rise behind the bluffs which
dropped away steeply to the river. The troopers dismounted. The horses
hung their heads, too weary to graze.

The Commander waved his hat and cried, "Courage, boys. We will
get them."

But nobody was looking at him.

Kellogg whispered, "Jesus Christ. Will you get a look at that."

The indian village stretched for miles. It was bigger than Duluth, bigger than Bismarck, bigger than any white city in the Dakotas. "Mercy," Top said.

Tom Custer sent a courier to fetch Benteen.

Below them, indian women and children were scattering like alarmed prairie hens.

Bright bugle calls announced Major Reno's attack as cavalrymen charged down the valley. Up here, their gunfire sounded like firecrackers.

A dust cloud rose from the village, obscuring lodges, horses, and indians.

"Reno's kicked up a hornet's nest." Top's observation earned Tom Custer's frown.

Young Autie Reed stood agape, transfixed by the terrible beauty of war.

Reno's tiny soldiers drew up and dismounted to form a skirmish line. Two horses bolted with their riders into the heart of the indian village. Autie Reed clamped his eyes shut as the troopers were swallowed.

Pop. Pop. Pop. The Commander rubbed his jaw. Troopers slumped in the heat. Horses shuffled their hooves. Pop. Pop.

The indians divided, threatening to envelop Reno's line. More whistles, more pops.

Toy soldiers. Toy indians.

Shillaber, Hairy Moccasin, and White Man Runs Him had found a way down from the bluffs into the village. The Commander asked, "Did you attend West Point, Major Shillaber?"

"Didn't have the honor."

"There were thirty-four cadets in my West Point class," the Commander confided affably. "Thirty-three graduated above me."

Pointing at Reno's beleaguered skirmishers, Hairy Moccasin asked, "Why don't you cross the river and help?"

"Oh," the Commander said, "there's plenty of time. Let them fight for a while. Our turn will come."

Reno's troopers broke and scattered into the timber with the indians right behind blowing their eagle-bone whistles.

The Commander's adjutant scribbled a note and gave it to bugler Martino. "Bring Benteen!" Martino kicked his horse into a stumbling gallop. White Man Runs Him unbuttoned his blue jacket and dropped it on the ground. Other scouts took their jackets off. Hairy Moccasin shook out his braids, found a metal mirror in his parfleche, and began daubing his cheeks with paint.

"Shillaber," Tom Custer called. "What the hell are they doing?"

"They want to die as warriors. They don't want to die as white men."

Tom Custer snapped, "Christ! Get those damn cowards out of here."

Shillaber clasped each scout's hands. He told them they had done their duty and now should save their lives. Shillaber turned to the reporter. "Kellogg? You can go out with them."

The reporter's Adam's apple bobbed when he swallowed. "Bu . . . bu . . . Ben? Man like me—how . . . how often does opportunity knock for a man like me?" He clamped his trembling right wrist with his left hand to take a note.

Then the chief of scouts turned to his friend. "Top? Top, listen to me! You didn't sign on to fight. You aren't in the army now, you're just a civilian interpreter." He paused. "Top, the palaverin' is done. Didn't you promise She Goes Before you wouldn't fight her people? Didn't you?"

Grinning, Tom Custer stepped between the black man in the neat uniform and the chief of scouts. "How 'bout it, Top? Want to die like a white man?"

It was hot. Top was thirsty. His mind was blank. His strong fingers unbuttoned the top button of his jacket and fished inside for a tarnished five-pointed star. He let the medal lie in full view.

Mock-solemnly, Captain Custer saluted.

Top sneezed. "God bless," Shillaber said.

The indian scouts fled.

Unseen marksmen's bullets cracked over the troopers' heads. An arrow arced into the dirt. Another arrow thumped into a sergeant's saddle. "Son of a bitch!" He jerked it out and snapped it over his knee.

Troopers watched the angry noncom through weary, indifferent eyes.

Captain Keogh stretched.

Another bullet cracked by.

Shillaber picked up the broken arrow. "Brulé," he said.

C Company formed a skirmish line and volleyed into the sagebrush. Four or five hundred yards behind the concealed sharpshooters, a Cheyenne in a feathered headdress emerged from a coulee and trotted his pony across their front: bold as brass. The Commander yanked his Creedmore sporting rifle from its scabbard, ran up its leaf sight, took careful aim, and squeezed off a round. A half second later the indian flattened on his pony's neck and disappeared into another coulee.

"Gave him something to chew on." The Commander smiled. "Mount up."

With the Commander's Vic in the lead, they proceeded along the bluffs at a trot. At the head of the coulee Shillaber had found, they split into two wings: Companies E and F and the Commander's staff would go down the coulee, while Captain Keogh's companies stayed here to protect the rear.

A tiny creek meandered through the broad downsloping coulee. They crossed and recrossed it until its water ran brown.

Top's mind was blessedly empty of excuses and sorrows. He had lived as well as many men and longer than some better men. Maybe the Commander would live up to his legend. Maybe he wouldn't. Top's daughter and wife were at the Agency. They'd be fine. They were better off without him.

The sagebrush along the coulee's rim seemed to glow. That skeleton pine had died hard, twisted in anguish. Top's mojo felt smaller outside his tunic where everyone could see it. His horse lurched but caught itself. It wouldn't last much longer. In its boot, his rifle chafed his thigh.

When the cavalrymen emerged from the coulee on the banks of the Little Bighorn, terrified indian women scooped up their children and fled into the village. Empty sweat lodges smoked on the riverbank. A few warriors collected fleeing women and escorted them away. Top heard the patter of gunshots somewhere upriver. That'd be Reno's fight. Three boys and one old-timer came to defend the crossing. When the old man triggered his antique musket, he vanished in a tremendous puff of gray-black smoke. C Company dismounted to form a skirmish line, while F Company trotted downstream to a ford at the mouth of another, narrower coulee.

The Commander asked his brother, "Captain Benteen doesn't like me does he?"

"What?"

"Yet Benteen is popular with his men, is he not?"

Shillaber turned to Top, "I guess we'll hit 'em here."

"Ain't much to stop us."

A boy who couldn't have been twelve years old drew his rabbit bow to its utmost and lofted an arrow at the Seizers.

Behind the boy, the village was in turmoil. Scattering indians, shouts and yelps.

"They're . . . ?" Shillaber asked.

"Sans Arc lodges," Top said.

"You got no business here," Shillaber said.

"Got no business anywhere."

Tom Custer urged his brother to attack. "We'll cut through them like a knife through jack cheese."

"Some may escape, Tom. We haven't the force to capture them all."

"So? We'll round them up later."

"Tom, Tom . . . you've always been impatient. We'll wait for Benteen. Maybe I'll show Benteen a thing or two."

Shillaber clucked to his horse, rode to the river, dismounted, and waded into the water to check the ford's bottom. He waved his approval.

Instead of crossing, the Commander led his companies back up the bluffs through the narrow coulee. Some indians followed. After one trooper was hit in the arm with an arrow, E Company dismounted and fired two volleys into their pursuers. They shot the indian boy with the rabbit bow. He flopped in the dirt like a fish out of water.

As soon as they emerged on the bluff tops, Captain Keogh's companies cantered toward them, pausing three times to volley from the saddle at sharpshooters they couldn't see.

Two Lakota riders appeared in the coulee they'd just vacated and Tom Custer fired at them. An indian pony went down, and its rider rolled into the brush.

"Damn, Tom." The Commander laughed. "You never could shoot straight."

The village streets were noisy, dusty, and confused. The Seizers who had attacked us had been driven away, but there were more Seizers on the bluffs above the river trying to come down and kill us. No one knew what to do. Some warriors quit fighting to help women, old men, and children flee. Some who had started fighting without preparations came back to make their medicine and dress for war. Young warriors who wanted to follow Crazy Horse waited impatiently as he chanted and prayed to his medicine animals.

I searched for Tazoo.

A young Cheyenne beat his drum and sang a suicide song. When other warriors heard his song, they sang too. The warrior who sings the suicide song vows to fight until the fight is won or he is killed.

Someone had seen Rattling Blanket Woman and Tazoo digging camas, so I went there. When the Seizers came to the river, a few old men and boys hurried to defend us.

I saw him there. I could not be mistaken. In his blue coat. He was with Seizers watching the village from a flat place above the river. It was too far for me to make out his face, but I knew he was Plenty Cuts. "Oh," I said. "Oh."

Our old men and boys fired at them. A man in buckskins walked into the ford a little ways but did not cross the river.

Then they all rode into another coulee and climbed back up the bluffs. The men and boys who'd stopped them at the river followed.

The warriors had made their medicine and were ready. Crazy Horse and hundreds of Lakota and Cheyenne warriors splashed across the ford and up the coulee after Plenty Cuts's Seizers. I followed behind.

ALTHOUGH HIS OFFICERS couldn't understand why he was waiting and his brother Tom was nearly mutinous, the Commander smiled and said they had plenty of time, that anyone who wanted to pot a redskin should try for one of the sharpshooters. "If you can't see them," he counseled, "aim for the stink."

Captain Keogh dismounted a company as skirmishers above the narrow coulee. His horse holders and two reserve companies moved behind the low ridge at their rear.

"Keep them off our backs, Myles," the Commander admonished. "Benteen will be here any minute and between us and Reno we'll round up every mother's son." He smiled at his brother. "I'll bet you'd like another go at Rain in the Face."

The Commander's red-and-blue personal guidon fluttered bravely as he led three companies a half mile or so farther along the bluffs until they found another coulee to descend to the river, to a second ford well below the indian village.

This ford was as good as the first. A few mounted Cheyenne shot arrows from the far bank. The Commander tugged his chin.

Tom Custer stood in his stirrups. "Now will you attack? In God's name, what are you waiting for?"

"Sir, are you waiting for General Terry?" Mark Kellogg asked. For an answer an arrow thumped into his throat. He clutched at the arrow. Shillaber snatched at him but missed and the reporter slid off his mule. On the ground, Mark Kellogg hunched and writhed like a dog crushed by a wagon wheel. He wanted to pull the arrow out of his throat, but pulling hurt too much. That's how he died.

WHEN AUTIE REED vomited, Captain Yates made a face. "Be a soldier, son."

Tom Custer said, "Now, by God, will you attack?"

"Remember when I said you were a better general than I was?" The Commander turned Vic back up the coulee. "Tom, I'm afraid I lied."

Although the indian sharpshooters were busier than they'd been, firing was still light and the indians pulled back as the Commander's men returned to the bluffs. On a hogback ridge, E Company deployed as skirmishers, with F in reserve.

"Where the hell's Benteen?" Tom Custer demanded.

"Do you think I'd make a good President, Tom?" his brother asked. "You don't have to answer immediately. Think about it."

Keogh's skirmishers were volleying steadily. "I think we should join Keogh," Tom Custer said. He turned to Top. "What do you think, Top?"

At a cry and a grunt, Top spun around. A Cheyenne had gotten among their horses and stolen one. Knocked back on his heels, trying to control the three animals he still had, the horse holder fired his carbine but missed. Other troopers were too startled to fire and the Cheyenne galloped away with his prize. "I think they want our horses," Shillaber answered for Top.

"It's time to sing our death song," Top answered for himself.

The Commander shifted them to a new position a thousand yards above where Keogh's skirmishers were firing at blurs and briefly seen feathers and skin.

Tom Custer said, "For Christ's sake! Where's that God Damned Benteen?"

Shillaber said, "Reno's behind us somewhere. Maybe Benteen linked up with Reno. Maybe Benteen couldn't get through."

"Get through who?" Tom Custer demanded.

"Ever fight a Lakota warrior, Captain?" Top asked. "Man to man?"

Tom Custer's eyes flickered.

Shillaber breathed, "Look at that son of a bitch!"

A lone warrior popped up beside Captain Keogh's position and walked his pony between Keogh's skirmishers and his reserve company. He rode sedately for a long time before he whooped, wheeled his horse, and rode back as slowly as he'd come.

"Hands painted on the pony's hips: that's Crazy Horse," Top said.

"Hell, Tom," the Commander joked. "Keogh's boys can't shoot any straighter than you can."

A horse escaped from Keogh's horse holders. The horse had a Cheyenne on his back. Another horse followed, carrying another Cheyenne.

"Watch now," the Commander said. "Myles will put a stop to that nonsense."

With some boys who were too young to fight, I had climbed the coulee behind Crazy Horse and his warriors. We found the Seizers on the bluff. They were fighting with their medicine flag planted at the end of their line. Other Seizers were behind the hill with their horses. The warriors wanted to steal their horses, but Crazy Horse said no, not yet. More and more Lakota and Cheyenne came along. They stood to fire and lay down again. Then they crawled to a new place to fire again.

Crazy Horse's caution was proved when a second band of Seizers appeared on a ridgetop a little north of the first. We had not known they were here. They put out their fighting line and started shooting too.

Then Crazy Horse told us that the Seizers could not kill us today. He dug into a prairie dog hill and rubbed dirt all over himself. He rubbed dirt over his pony and sang his kill song. Then he rode between the Seizer firing line and the Seizer horse holders. The firing line could not shoot because Crazy Horse was between them and their horses, and the horse holders could not because they would shoot into their own people. When Crazy Horse came back unharmed, he told the young men, "You see? They cannot kill us today."

The Seizers' horses were in a shallow ravine behind the ridge, behind their firing line, and Cheyennes got into this ravine and stole two Seizer horses.

This angered the Seizers and thirty or forty rushed down the coulee after the horse thieves. They dismounted there and formed their line to fire.

But in that coulee were hundreds and hundreds of Lakota and Cheyenne warriors. At first the warriors ran away when the Seizers attacked, but soon they came back. So much smoke and dust rose from that coulee I could not see what was happening there. Then the Seizers who had ridden into the coulee reappeared with many warriors among them. Behind them, still more warriors came. More horse thieves got among the Seizers' horses. Frightened, wounded horses bolted out of the ravine onto the ridge and trampled Seizers on the firing line. Arrows hissed down on the Seizers and I wondered why the second band of Seizers did not come to help. Could they not see? Were they afraid? A warrior snatched their medicine flag and rode off with it. When the Seizers who had ridden into the coulee got to their firing line, our warriors were among them. Then all the warriors who had been creeping toward the Seizers rose up and rushed to count coup with hatchets and war clubs. The Seizers quit firing and were quickly killed. On horses and on foot those who still lived ran to join Seizers who had not come to help but the suicide riders cut them off and killed them.

WHEN KEOGH'S C COMPANY galloped down the coulee after the indians who'd stolen their horses, Tom Custer yelled, "Give 'em hell."

Firing wasn't heavy, Benteen would be up soon, and the Commander was taking potshots at sharpshooters. It was three o'clock. The sun burned their heads, arms, and shoulders. The village below was quiet. Dust on the far side of the valley showed where the indian women and children were fleeing.

Shillaber turned to Top. "Maybe we'll get out of this with our hair."

Top's grin glistened in his dark, wind-roughened face. "Hoka hey," he said.

Two volleys roared from the coulee into which Keogh's company had charged. Then no more volleys. Then shots were drowned out by eagle-bone whistles. Something that was more like a clot than a company of disciplined soldiers reemerged at the head of that coulee with indians clinging to it like leeches.

Two breaths after the clot rolled into Captain Keogh's position, the position disintegrated. Keogh's force was like an unlucky grasshopper fallen into a red ants' nest. They were overcome, swarmed over, disappeared. Lakota and Cheyenne whooped joyfully as they galloped off with their horses.

Keogh's survivors fled toward the Commander, but hard-riding young warriors pulled them down, clubbed them, shot them, stabbed them, trampled them, hacked them, and rolled with them in the dirt.

That's how they died.

A handful reached the Commander's position.

"In God's name, what?" Tom Custer cried.

"Christ, they cut Findley's head off!" one survivor screamed.

There was no time to understand what had happened to Keogh and less time to prepare as on every side thousands of warriors rose up within touching distance. Arrows rained down. Pierced troopers fell.

That's how they died.

George Armstrong Custer was slack-jawed when Tom shot beautiful Vic in the head and guided the crumpling horse into a makeshift barricade. Yates and Smith cried, "Fire at will!" but most troopers were too stunned and terrified to fight. Troopers raised their hands in surrender. When Autie Reed begged a warrior not to kill him he was scalped alive.

That's how they died.

Dust from charging warriors and horses made thick fog. Top tasted death in the dust on his tongue.

Shillaber went down under two burly Cheyenne. The indians were killing close and the last thing most troopers saw was an indian's painted visage.

When a warrior jerked a dead trooper's pants off, paper money skittered across the ground.

When a bullet took the Commander in the chest, he sat down. Disbelieving, he touched the wound. His unlined face contorted into a baffled, protesting moan.

This was where Top had been running to. All those other places had been waypoints to here. No more running. He felt sorry for the Commander, whose face betrayed no understanding that this place, this dust, these screaming hurt horses, those shrill whistles were where he'd always been bound. The Commander had thought he was meant to come to some other place, to be general of the army, perhaps, or perhaps he'd live in the White House. He'd thought he'd always be loved. Sergeant Major Edward Ratcliff felt a twinge of sympathy for the Boy General who'd go to hell not knowing how he got there.

Sergeant Major Ratcliff put a bullet into a warrior who leaped over Vic. The man—a Cheyenne, by his paint—collapsed on the carcass. Soldiers raised their hands in surrender to indians who killed them anyway. Rain in the Face cut Tom Custer's throat and as the captain backpedaled clutching the gash, Rain in the Face gutted him from belly to sternum, reached in, and dragged the man's pulsing heart into the light. Gleefully, he held the thing before the dying captain's eyes. As Tom Custer slumped to his knees, the indian bit into the gory meat and spat into the dirt.

Sergeant Major Edward Ratcliff, United States Colored Troops, free as he'd ever be, charged three thousand warriors, swinging his rifle over his head like a war club, yelling his kill song, "Hincty Nigger! Hincty Nigger! Hincty Nigger!" into their whistles and cries.

What a Santee Plenty Cuts would have made!

It was soon over. Afterward the Washitu said Yellow Hair and his Seizers had fought to the end, but most did not fight at all. The warriors killed them like sheep. There was no honor in it. One Seizer walked through the fighting as if charmed until a Cheyenne brained him. Others ran down the narrow coulee to escape, but it was a death trap lined with warriors on the rim firing down at them.

At the end my husband was a true warrior. I was proud of him.

I tried to catch Plenty Cuts's eye, just once, to summon him to my heart one last time before his soul departed for the Shadowland, but it was not to be.

CHAPTER 60

AMERICA'S TEMPERANCE DRINK

*Add the contents of one package of Mr. Charles Hires's medicinal
extract to each gallon of water and boil twenty minutes. When still
warm, add 3 tbsp. yeast and 1/2 pound white sugar. Cover your
container with a cloth and let stand for two hours before bottling.*

THE LITTLE GIRL DROPPED HER MOTHER'S HAND AND SLIPPED
forward to touch the statue's cold bronze toe.

A broken manacle dangled from the slave's left wrist. In his right hand
he brandished the Emancipation Proclamation. Naked save for a rumpled
sarong, he strode into the future, powerful and exultant.

The child's father's dark suit was more respectable than new. He put
on spectacles to read the statue's name aloud: "*The Abolition of Slavery in
the United States.*"

The mother said, "He 'most naked, Jesse. In Richmond that boy be
locked up."

"It's an allegory, Sudie," Jesse Burns said.

"What's a 'leg-ory'?" his daughter asked.

Sudie snorted. "That leg-ory best put his pants on."

The child lifted her eyes. "Mama, I want some soda water. I'm right
thirsty."

"You're *very* thirsty, Soj," her father corrected.

"Well, I is!" Sojourner Burns took refuge with her mother.

Hands clasped behind him, Jesse Burns leaned closer to examine the statue. "Reminds me of a boy I used to know." He removed his spectacles and rubbed the bridge of his nose. "Rufus meant to become a farrier. Rufus's hands . . . shaking his hand was like grasping a boot sole." Jesse cased his spectacles. "Haven't thought 'bout Rufus in years. He was shot dead not long after Lincoln signed that." He nodded at the bronze proclamation. "I buried Rufus." Softly, he added, "Buried Rufus's ambitions with him."

"Like Jimson," Sudie said.

"Yes." Jesse didn't know what to say about Jimson so he rarely spoke about him. Jimson's mother mentioned him often.

The family withdrew when two young white men approached. In striped blazers and straw hats, they might have been college boys. The pair eyed the statue solemnly until one opined gravely, "If this 'un's freed, I say, stuff him back into slavery."

His friend snorted. The speaker tipped his hat to Sudie. "Hot, ain't it?" he observed.

Sudie hid behind her fluttering fan.

The Memorial Hall at the Centennial Exposition was America's first art museum, and visitors touched anything they felt like touching and were more curious than awed.

That July third, 1876, the summer's long heat wave had shrunk the exposition crowd to thirty thousand. Here and there in the manicured park grounds, a footsore visitor could find shade.

As Mr. and Mrs. Burns proceeded down the crowded aisles, eight-year-old Sojourner darted into the next gallery, popped back out, and recaptured her mother's hand. "Soda water, Mama?"

"Soon, honey. I thirsty too."

They'd arrived in Philadelphia yesterday and taken a room at the United States Hotel, built specially for the exposition. Jesse had made their reservation on Virginia Assembly stationery. The desk clerk had welcomed him and called him "Mr. Burns" as if Jesse were white.

The hotel overlooked the exposition's main entrance, but their small room overlooked railroad tracks in back. They'd supped in the hotel that evening and after Sojourner was asleep in a cot beside their bed, Sudie had loved Jesse with an eagerness that surprised him.

The next morning, they'd toured Machinery Hall, where Sojourner asked the man adjusting "The Telephonic Instrument," "What that do?"

The man looked up and smiled. "It's supposed to talk."

Hands on hips. "How it gonna do that?"

"Well, you see," its inventor explained, "it's supposed to change sound into electrical impulses and re-create them over there." He pointed across the hall where an assistant knelt with his ear pressed to a similar instrument.

"That man can hear what you saying?" Sojourner didn't believe it. "Way 'cross the room?"

"That's the idea." The man bent to what looked like a black megaphone stopped with a brass layer cake. He waved his hand and enunciated, "To be or not to be."

When his assistant stood and shrugged elaborately, Sudie said, "I guess it ain't to be."

Jesse was fascinated by the Corliss, the two-thousand-horsepower steam engine whose hissing overhead belts, clattering pulleys, whirring gears and shafts powered the hall's exhibits. Sojourner clamped her hands over her ears.

They took an early supper at the Scandinavian Pavilion, where a smiling blond waitress fetched tinned herring on thick dark bread and mugs of effervescent golden beer.

Sudie said they should go back to their room so Sojourner could nap. Her daughter protested, "Mama, I'm not *little* anymore."

Jesse said, "Dear, she'll remember this day the rest of her life."

"Why this day, Jesse? How you know what day Soj gon' 'member? Other day I ask my child 'bout her brother and only thing Soj remembered was how Jimson lift her up and spin her until she sick. Didn't 'member what he look like nor anything he said; just that spinnin' foolishness."

"If Jimson had seen this, he might have understood . . ."

"Understood what, Jesse: that white men know how to make things work? Jimson knowed that. Everybody knows that. Was white men made the boats brung us to 'Merica wasn't it?" She discarded the strong-flavored bread and got up. "Come along, Soj. Your daddy wants to see more white men's marvels."

"Don't you see, Sudie? They're our marvels too."

"Don't you get pouty with me, Mr. Assemblyman Burns. You got no call get pouty!"

Jesse grinned despite himself.

In Memorial Hall they went directly to *The Abolition of Slavery in the United States*, the single Centennial artwork every negro in Jesse's ward had heard about. The only other works which interested Jesse's constituents—particularly Jesse's Baptist constituents—were in the French exhibit. That outpost of Gomorrah was wall to wall with intensely curious (apparently blasé) adult Americans whose small sons furtively caressed the nude sculptures' cold marble breasts.

Sudie hissed, "This ain't decent, Jesse."

He leaned to her ear. "They aren't near as good-lookin' as you, Sudie."

She smacked his hand.

The Burns family escaped into the American galleries, where too many paintings crowded the walls of too-small rooms.

Jesse paused at the moody sunset, darkening clouds, and frightening sheer cliffs of Bierstadt's *Yosemite Valley*.

Sudie pinched her husband. "Don't you get to dreamin', Jesse. It's just a picture. Painter man paints whatever comes to mind. Yose-mite might be no pretty place. Might be a desert or a darn mud hole or filled with savage indians."

"I wonder how Duncan and Sallie are faring," Jesse mused. "Edward Ratcliff is in the West too. I had the strangest dream the other night. We were both back in uniform. It wasn't a parade ground or a battle—nothing like that. With hundreds of other soldiers, Edward and I were falling through the air."

"Why you thinkin' 'bout that man, Jesse? You ain't thinkin' 'bout uprootin' and draggin' us out West?"

He kissed her forehead. "For better or worse, dear, our future's in Virginia. Sojourner's too."

"Mama, I'm wearied of pictures 'n' statues. I'm thirsty!"

Outside Memorial Hall heat struck them like a blow. The huge winged stone horses looming over Republic Avenue were so white they hurt the eyes. Sudie's fan fluttered like a panting butterfly.

"I came to this city for the Republican convention after the war. I met Thaddeus Stevens and your husband shook Frederick Douglass's hand."

"So you told me 'bout a thousand times."

Sojourner cried, "Mama, Mama! Look over there, Mama!"

Sojourner found her soda water at a vaguely moorish kiosk whose minarets flags advertised: "The Greatest Health-Giving Beverage in the World!!" and "Hires Root Beer Stands for Health, Temperance, and Home!"

Six soda jerks were busy serving the crowd. Jessie laid down his nickels on the zinc counter and iced glasses were produced.

Sudie dipped her tongue into the foam. "Jesse, this is sassafras tea!"

The chief soda jerk materialized before heresy could spread. "No, madam, it is not sassafras. Mr. Hires is a licensed pharmacist. Mr. Hires used his vast understanding of medicinal herbs to select the rare, costly ingredients in Hires Root Beer. I assure you"—he said with a condescending chuckle—"There is more—far more—to Hires Root Beer than sassafras."

Jesse called a truce. "It deserves a great future."

But when Sojourner's empty glass clattered on the counter, the little girl announced, "Tastes like sassafras to me."

Jesse had marked his Centennial catalog with the exhibits and pavilions he particularly wanted to see. Froebel's kindergarten was a one-story wood schoolhouse with a red tile roof.

The model schoolhouse had a spectator's gallery facing the schoolroom. The Burnses took seats near the front.

"Why, they ain't nothin' but babies," Sudie said wonderingly.

The children, age three to five years, were orphans from the Home for Friendless Children. Seated before their workbench, these industrious waifs assembled wooden blocks: squares, triangles, and circles. A teacher tutored a small dark-haired girl. "Elaine," she asked, "what does this remind you of?"

"It's my house," the child named the block construction.

"This one?" The teacher turned a rectangle on its side

"I don't know."

"Imagine, child. Imagine."

The child knocked it over. "That's the wall 'round the home," she added happily. "All fall down!"

"What they doing, Mama?" Sojourner spoke through her yawn. Lacking a response, she slumped against her mother and closed her eyes.

The attentive children, the click of their blocks, the whisper of brightly colored paper shapes becoming lions and tigers and steamships, the mild tones of the yankee teachers' voices: all this unlocked Jesse's memory. When not much older than these children, he'd been Uther Botkin's slave: cleaning the milk cow's stall, feeding the hogs, splitting and carrying the old schoolteacher's firewood. Jesse made excuses to be near the porch where the old schoolmaster instructed the Gatewood children and his beloved daughter Sallie in the mysteries of reading, spelling, and arithmetic. One morning, the schoolmaster caught Jesse puzzling over Sallie's *McGuffy's Reader*.

It was illegal to teach slaves to read. The notorious Nat Turner had been literate and his slave rebellion had slaughtered a hundred innocent whites.

When Jesse dropped the reader, it landed on its open pages. He remembered as if yesterday how frightened he'd been.

But gentle Uther Botkin picked it up and said, "I guess I'll have to get you a book of your own."

A book of his own!

The hushed schoolroom was stuffy. Jesse heard a tiny snore. Eyes closed, her mouth slightly open, Sudie leaned into him.

"Education is the negro's best hope!" Jesse'd argued in the assembly, where negroes mostly agreed with him and white assemblymen were reluctant to pay for white public schools, much less the separate black schools Virginia's constitution required.

Most of Jesse's constituents couldn't read, and since the Freedmen's Bureau schools had closed, many would never learn to read. Watching Sudie work so hard to extract meaning from an ordinary newspaper was painful to him. Eight-year-old Sojourner read better than her mother.

Once, in an ill humor, Sudie had snapped, "You only married me to uplift me, Mr. Assemblyman Burns."

Nothing she'd ever said in anger hurt him worse, because there was a kernel of truth in her accusation. Jesse almost snapped back, "There aren't many literate negro women to pick among," but he was wise enough, that once, to embrace his angry wife and whisper, "I married you because I never saw a finer, prettier woman. First time I saw you at the First Baptist social, you were pouring iced tea and I thought to myself, That girl bound to melt every piece of ice she touches . . ."

She wept then, bitterly, and said, "Jesse, I know I disappoint you. I try not to. You should be married to some high-toned gal, not no ignorant pickaninny like me."

A child scholar laughed, and a teacher shushed the child. Some spectators got up and left. Sudie's head was heavy on Jesse's shoulder.

Jesse'd seen Samuel Gatewood in Richmond outside the Gatewoods' rooming house. The planter who'd once held absolute power over his life hadn't recognized Jesse, and Jesse hadn't introduced himself. To the old man, Jesse was just another black face in a city of black faces.

When Jesse heard Stratford had been sold, he didn't care. Unlike Uther Botkin's schoolroom porch, Stratford held no memories the former slave wished to revisit.

Sudie woke and took Jesse's handerchief from his pocket to blow her nose. A child was noisily clattering blocks together. Sudie said, "At that girl's age, I was brushing Mistress's hair, two hundred strokes morning and night."

"Things are different now. Our Sojourner will attend Hampton Institute one day."

Sudie's eyes pleaded. "Jesse, if Soj go—she be ashamed of her old ma. She get 'elevated' and she never come home no more."

Jesse took a moment to think. "Wouldn't you want her, dear Sudie, to have a better life than you've had?"

"Oh, Jesse—mostly I do. But sometimes I don't want my little child to get above her rearin'."

"Mama?" Their daughter rubbed her eyes. "What you sayin' 'bout me?"

"We sayin', honey, that you're gonna be grown up one day."

"I always love you, Mama. You know I will!"

Just inside the cavernous iron-and-glass Machinery Hall, three enormous Krupp cannons loomed over the aisle.

"What they for?" Sojourner stared at the huge guns.

"They our marvels too, Jesse?" Sudie whispered.

"Oh, yes," he said. "I'm afraid they are."

THE CATARACT—an exhibit of industrial pumps—was at the far end of Machinery Hall. Water cannons shot silver arcs from all sides of a hundred-yard pool, whose centerpiece was a four-sided waterfall without a river.

Jesse led his wife and child to the rail, where cool mist drifted over them.

"This my kind of marvel," Sudie said.

A red-faced white man was running through the crowd. He was waving his arms and yelling something. His words were nearly lost in the cataract's rumble. They heard "Little Bighorn." They heard "Every last man." They heard "General Custer."

"Papa," Sojourner Burns asked her father, "what's a 'massa cure'?"

EPILOGUE

———

In the Moon of the Falling Leaves in the year when Plenty Cuts was killed, Tazoo and I and several hundred others followed Sitting Bull across the Medicine Line into the Grandmother's land. Fearing the Seizers' revenge, most Lakota surrendered their guns and went to the agencies. The Seizers killed everyone who didn't come in or run.

I rode a mule I found on the Greasy Grass. I found papers in its saddlebags: words about the Seizers and Yellow Hair. I knew more about them than I wanted to know and threw the papers into the fire.

My Tazoo was not as dark as Plenty Cuts and she had no scars across her back. I never told my husband I was afraid of his scars. Sometimes when he was asleep the thick ridges in his flesh seemed like snakes writhing their way into his heart. In the end, Plenty Cuts became his scars.

The country on both sides of the Medicine Line was flat and windy, bordered in the far distance by the mountains the Blackfeet call the Backbone of the World.

We didn't see much game—few deer, no antelope or buffalo. We lived on jackrabbits, prairie dogs, and camas root.

The Dakotas are an empty land. They will be emptier when we are gone.

Perhaps men will be different in the Grandmother's land.

Perhaps they won't abandon what they know to seek paradise.

Perhaps they will make paradise where they are.

ACKNOWLEDGMENTS

ISTORICAL NOVELS BLOOM IN THE BRIAR PATCHES OF HISTORY.
Ground plowed every spring by eager PhD candidates is too exhausted for
Story to germinate. We can know too much to dream.

So while this novelist can—with a twinge—alter the signatories of the
"Address from the Colored Citizens of *Virginia*" (was *"Norfolk"*), bringing
imagined characters to the valley of the Little Bighorn in June 1876 takes
more guts than brains. Lucky for me, new archaeological data and our
latter-day willingness to credit survivors' (indians') accounts has revised
our understanding of the final hours and movements of the five troops of
the Seventh Cavalry. Scholars are fairly well agreed on what Custer did and
why he was overwhelmed. What that officer was thinking—why didn't he
attack? why didn't he support Reno? why didn't he anticipate and prepare
for the indian assault?—will be debated for years.

Little Bighorn students will complain rightly that Ben Shillaber is a
composite of several historical figures and that I have oversimplified
Custer's indian scouts. Though Isaiah Dorman, a black interpreter, married a Sioux woman and died at the battle, he certainly wasn't Edward
Ratcliff. I admit these sacrifices to Story without apology.

The recipe for Terrapin Soup is Charles Ranhofer's.

The menu for Charles Dickens's dinner at Delmonico's is reprinted with permission from *Delmonico's: A Century of Splendor*, by Lately Thomas (Boston: Houghton Mifflin, 1967).

The recipes for Rainy Day and Son-of-a-Bitch Stew were adapted from Dan Cushman's *Cow Country Cookbook*, reprinted with permission of Clear Light Publishing, Santa Fe, New Mexico, www.clearlightbooks.com.

It takes more than one cook to make a book. My grateful thanks to:

Knox Burger
Chris Calkins
Dr. Lucious Edwards
Dr. Susan Doyle
Dr. Doug Christian
Dr. Douglas Gordon
Bud Griffin
Christian Higgins
Professor Ervin Jordan
Starling Lawrence
Jeri Lynn Tingley
Evelyn Timberlake

And thanks to the helpful staffs at the Leyburn Library of Washington and Lee University, the Library of Virginia in Richmond, the Library of Congress, the Montana Historical Society, the Gilliford Baptist Church, the Gallatin Valley Historical Society, the Virginia Historical Society, Fort Laramie, Fort Phil Kearny, the McFarland Curatorial Center in Virginia City, the Little Bighorn Battlefield National Monument, the New York City Historical Society, the University of North Carolina, the University of Virginia Alderman Libary, Swem Library of the College of William and Mary, and Special Collections at Virginia State University.